Praise for TEMPTATION RISI 11/2012

"Deliciously edgy, sexy, ...
A.C. Arthur knows how t...
—Lora Leigh, #1 ...

"The shifter universe ju...
to Arthur's sizzling new ...
launch book introduces an intriguing cast of characters
functioning in the human world, yet keeping their true
natures a secret. The sparks between this hero and heroine
are plentiful, b... ...lationship is tougher.
Looking forwar... ...next installment."
—RT Book Reviews

"*Temptation Rising* has everything a good book should:
action, adventure, suspense, mystery, and fiery-hot
passion."
—Romance Junkies

"This book has depth and an interesting storyline, complete
with unique characters that will keep you entranced,
starting at page one."
—Night Owl Reviews

"A.C. Arthur begins a new series with a bang."
—Sensual Reads

Also by
A.C. Arthur

Temptation Rising

SEDUCTION'S SHIFT

A.C. ARTHUR

St. Martin's Paperbacks

This is a work of fiction. All of the characters, organizations, and events portrayed in this novel are either products of the author's imagination or are used fictitiously.

SEDUCTION'S SHIFT

For information address St. Martin's Press, 175 Fifth Avenue, New York, NY 10010.

ISBN: 978-0-312-54911-4

Printed in the United States of America

St. Martin's Paperbacks edition / October 2012

St. Martin's Paperbacks are published by St. Martin's Press, 175 Fifth Avenue, New York, NY 10010.

10 9 8 7 6 5 4 3 2 1

Glossary of Terms

Shadow Shifter Tribes

Topètenia—The jaguars

Croesteriia—The cheetahs

Acordado—The awakening, the Shadow Shifter's first shift

Amizade—Annex to the Elder's Grounds used as a fellowship hall

The Assembly—Three elders from each tribe that make up the governing council of shifters in the Gungi

Companheiro—Mate

Companheiro calor—The scent shared between mates

Curandero—The medicinal and spiritual healer of the tribes

Elders—Senior members of the tribes

Ètica—The Shadow Shifter Code of Ethics

Joining—The union of mated shifters

Pessoal—The secondary building of the Elders' Grounds that houses the personal rooms of each Elder

Rogue—A Shadow Shifter who has turned from the tribes, refusing to follow the *Ètica*, in an effort to become their own distinct species

Santa Casa—The main building of the Elders' Grounds that is the holy house of the Elders

SEDUCTION'S SHIFT

Chapter 1

The Gungi rain forest
Brazil

Rage was like a nightcap to Sabar, violence the prelude to a blissful dream. This feeling he was now experiencing, this loss of control and defeat, was unfamiliar and not at all pleasing. His dick hurt it was so hard. His incisors elongated painfully, pricking into his lip and drawing blood. To say he was angry was a bold understatement.

The East Coast Faction Leader was still alive, and so was his bitch of a mate. They'd both escaped the fate he'd planned for them. As for Rome Reynolds, he still wanted the shifter dead—and his mate . . . well, since she'd chosen so unwisely she might as well die, too. Sabar wanted all those fake leaders dead so the shifters would have no choice but to look to him for guidance—stupid animals that they were.

And dammit, it was hot like an inferno in this place. The air was thick and stifling, the sounds of nightlife in the Gungi rain forest raking against every one of his human nerves. Sabar wanted to be out of this godforsaken place as soon as he possibly could. He wanted to get back to his business in the States. But there was business here in the forest, too. Old business that he'd never forgotten.

He was a busy shifter with plans the shadows would never imagine he could dream. He was resourceful and tenacious, determined to have what he most desired, by any means necessary. That's what tonight was about, showing the shadows who was in control. Always the most powerful, controlling everything no matter where it was.

Stepping into the small hut with its trampled-mud floors and damp stale aroma, he looked every bit the ruler he claimed to be. On his feet were shit-kicking steel-toed boots. Black jeans clad his muscled legs, while a black T-shirt covered his tattooed chest and Ray-Bans cloaked his eyes. His hair, which grew faster than the average human's, was now thick tresses, pulled back by a black band. He came to a stop and looked directly to the corner where she was tied and gagged.

His mouth watered, heart rate picking up instantly at the sight of her. She was not only powerful but damn pretty as well. She wore the thin suede dress that was the usual attire for female shadows living in the forest. Her sun-kissed skin glowed in the firelit corner of the hut. On her feet were leather boots, rising just past her ankles. These weren't a normal fashion must-have for female shifters, but this wasn't just any female shifter. Long strands of dark hair hung past her shoulders. Her ankles and wrists were bound, a gag stuffed into her mouth. Whether she heard or scented his approach, Sabar didn't know, but she turned, looking up at him with glittering amber-colored eyes.

The outrage rolling off her in thick rivulets poured into Sabar, rubbing against his already dark nature, coaxing his insides into a state of perpetual arousal.

"Beautiful *curandero*," he said in a voice thick with lust, his dick aching with the same. "You are finally mine."

She made an attempt to get up, to charge at him, he supposed, but her bindings held her in the corner. His blood pumped quickly at the display of violence in her, the strength he scented pulsing through her veins. She was a strong one, this designated *curandero* as the tribes referred to her, a healer to their kind. Wise for her young age and courageous in her endeavors. He wanted her, to touch, to taste, to feast upon, and to show the shifters his ultimate power over them.

Not that she was his mate. No, those thoughts had died the night Roman came in and took Kalina away from him. He'd decided that Kalina would be his mate. Unlike the shadows, who believed the *Ètica* preordained who their mate would be, Sabar made his own decisions. He'd watched Kalina fight his men and choose the shadow over him. She had defiled herself by sleeping with another, by committing herself to the shadow and his kind. For that, the bitch would die with the rest of them. Sabar refused to think any other way about the situation.

But this one, this spirited little shifter, could be his, too. She could join the other playthings he'd acquired to do his bidding, to quench his every desire. Oh, yes, he thought, feeling the length of his arousal pressing painfully against his jeans, she could provide so much pleasure as well as the medicinal knowledge he required.

"Aren't you a tempting little morsel," he said, bending down so he could get a closer look at her. "And powerful, I hear."

Reaching out a hand, he pushed back thick patches of matted dark hair. She didn't move a muscle, and he smelled not fear but rage emanating from her delectable body. Her cheek was bruised and swollen, her legs pulled up close to her chest with her arms wrapped around them. Her body trembled with anger and the need to lash out at him or anyone who came near. When her eyes glared at him, sending a rush of heat through his body, Sabar wanted nothing at that moment but to hear her voice, so he pulled out the ugly rag that had been stuffed into her mouth.

"Say something!" he yelled.

But there was silence. She didn't speak, only licked her dry lips and kept glaring at him.

"We can do this the hard way or the easy way. I'm not one for giving a lot of choices, so you'd better take advantage while you can."

"Go to hell," she said in a raspy tone and squared her shoulders.

So she had spunk. Well, he liked when they fought him. It made the taking much more exhilarating.

"Stand her up," he said to the two shifters standing guard at the door. They were rogue jaguars with heavy builds who spoke few, if any, words but took orders like they'd sworn allegiance to only him. Just the kind of shifters Sabar liked to employ.

They came to the female, lifting her without any kindness until she stood, her back against the wall. She let her head fall forward so that her long hair draped her face. Sabar stepped closer, grasped her chin roughly, and pushed her head back. Eyes a strange reddish brown combination stared back at him hauntingly. Pert lips were drawn into a tight line. Her hair gave her a wild untamed look, but he knew that was a lie. She was tame, and she was one of the most intelligent shifters in this forest. That's why he wanted her. She would serve his purpose well.

"Clean her up and get her ready to travel," he said, still staring into her hypnotic eyes.

His gaze was still held by hers when those pert lips moved and she spat in his face. A muscle ticked in his jaw, and for a few seconds he saw nothing but rage. With the back of his hand, he wiped the moisture from his cheek. Then he stepped closer to her, taking her bound hands and moving them to the hard bulge of his arousal. She balled up her fists to resist but he uncurled her fingers, pushing them until they almost broke and she gasped in pain. Sabar rubbed her opened hands over his length, loving the warmth spreading through him at her touch.

"You'll learn quickly to be nicer to me." Leaning forward, he licked the cheek that wasn't bruised and moved back to whisper into her ear. "That's the only way you'll stay alive. I've slit throats of shifters and drunk their blood for breakfast. Don't think I won't do the same with you."

She tried to pull her hands away, but Sabar simply laughed. Taking a step back, he pushed her until her back slammed against the wall. He didn't want her like this, all dirty and acting like a mute. When he fucked her, which he decided he would definitely do once she was cleaned up, he wanted her completely coherent and participating— whether by force or by choice, he didn't actually care.

"Nobody touches her again. I don't want any more marks on her," he ordered, then turned away. "And get her out of this filthy-ass place. Then burn it to the ground. It stinks like rotten shadows in here."

The shifters nodded, one reaching for her while the other moved alongside Sabar. "I want to be out of here in a couple of days. Get her to the lab, now!"

"Yes sir." The other shifter nodded.

Sabar stepped out into the night air, inhaling deeply. He'd been born here, in the Gungi rain forest, and here the lowly shifter that had been abused and disregarded had died. He hated everything about this place now, from the thick cover of trees just a few feet away to the range of different animal sounds that tickled his ears. He didn't like the smell, the rain, the forest, the animals and evidence of their living off the land. He hated it all and wanted to get back to the civility of the States as soon as he possibly could. He had what he'd come here for—the *curandero* whose talent for mixing medicines would help grow his drug empire to proportions that would make him the richest shifter in all the world.

Chapter 2

It was dark, but at least it was clean. The last hut reeked of filth, body odor, and other, less appealing things. When they'd stuffed that gag into her mouth Ary wanted to vomit, and when she'd seen him she'd wanted to kill.

Sabar Tavares, adopted son of Elder Julio and Maria Sabien Tavares, kidnapped when he was ten by Boden, a sadistic shifter who used his strength to rape and kill humans in nearby villages. As a result, the Topètenia shifter—who should have walked in his parents' footsteps, striving to maintain peace and equality among their kind—was instead a poster child for what the humans called Stockholm syndrome, repeating his abductor's crimes over and over.

And this time she was his target.

Ary had heard of him before; she'd seen him in the village through the years before he left for good sixteen years ago. After that she'd only heard about what he was doing, and even that was just whispers. Nobody wanted to be caught talking of the shadow who'd gone rogue.

Now he was back, and he was holding her captive. Why, Ary had no idea, but she knew it couldn't be anything good.

This new location was an old building. She'd seen a

little through the blindfold she'd managed to loosen by rubbing her head against the cab of the truck they transported her in. It was a dilapidated shack once used to mix the drugs that were eventually shipped out of the forest and sold. They were beyond the Gungi now, on the other side of the river and through thick brush that was good for hiding drug houses such as this one. The boards around her creaked, and slats were missing from the walls. But it was covered with a huge dark-colored tarp that kept the elements out—and whatever unlawfulness was going on inside in.

They'd dragged her through one large room, her legs slapping against table legs that wobbled and fell. The racket they'd created was deafening, but they were so far out that there was no one to hear. They could do whatever they wanted to do to her out here; she could scream until her lungs dried of air, but nobody would hear her. Nobody would come to her rescue.

Ary inhaled deeply, exhaled slowly. Her chest hurt with the action because to capture her they'd had to fight her. She'd been trained in what the humans called self-defense using martial arts techniques. Coming from behind and grabbing her wasn't exactly a good idea. When she'd finally fallen to the ground in hopes of rolling out of their reach, one grabbed her up, throwing her over his massive shoulder. The other had tied her ankles and hands, and when she'd screamed a string of obscenities at them they'd gagged her. She suspected the bruise to her face came when they dropped her to the floor and she'd landed painfully on her cheek. After Sabar's directive, they'd moved her a little more carefully this time around.

This time only her hands were tied—she figured because they were tired of carrying her. Still, escape wasn't going to be easy. The disgusting gag was thankfully gone, left on the floor in the first hut where Sabar had thrown it. And they'd taken the blindfold off, probably figuring she couldn't see much. But her cat could see everything. If she could just get outside, she could figure out her exact location, shift, and go home. Or she could just shift.

The idea had come to her many times since they'd taken her. Shift into a jaguar, kill her assailants, and call it a day. Then what? The bodies would be found; autopsies would prove a vicious predator had taken their lives. Humans would be outraged and pour into the forest looking to shoot anything on four legs. It would be like leading a lamb to slaughter, and it was something she would never do to her people.

But she would escape. There was no way in hell Sabar Tavares would have the satisfaction of killing her. That's what she assumed this was all about; after all, killing was what Sabar was best known for.

Closing her eyes to that thought, Ary let her head fall back against the rickety wall. She felt spears of loose wood sticking into her scalp but didn't care. She needed to think, needed to figure out what to do.

Only when her eyes closed, the one thing Ary saw— the single person appearing in her mind—wasn't Sabar or her other two captors. It was Nick. The only man to hold her and her heart captive and live to tell.

She didn't want to think about him, didn't want to remember the contours of his face, the shape of his eyes, the feel of his lips. All she wanted to do was forget. But that wasn't going to happen. She'd figured that out years ago. What had happened that night between them wasn't going to go away, especially since she'd never allowed another male to touch her intimately, ever. Dominick Delgado had been her first and only.

And it was times like these when that realization sent a

piercing ache through her heart that rivaled only death itself.

Speaking of which, the dank stench of Rogues in the vicinity pierced her nostrils. She sat up straighter, ready to do whatever was necessary to stay alive.

They came inside with loud, clumsy movements. Ary knew instantly they weren't trained soldiers, probably just some outcasts Sabar had picked up when he arrived in the forest. One of them held a bowl and nodded to the other, who came closer to her.

The taller one—whose name she heard shouted by his companion—was Jose. He didn't speak a lot of English, and he looked at her with hungry eyes. Even hungrier hands had groped her until she'd bitten him in defense. The other one—Franco—stank of liquor and moved with a lazy tangle of limbs. He preferred kicking to fondling her. She despised them both and could probably kill them without too much trouble. Once more, she axed that idea. If she didn't act with caution, the repercussions to the tribe would be too deadly. Besides, there had already been reports of suspicious deaths in the forest, and Ary didn't want to add to them.

It took monumental effort to calm the wild beating of her heart, but Ary was determined to handle this. Jose came closer, grabbing her by the hair and lifting her off the floor. She kicked out, catching him at the knees and thighs until he wised up and backed away, still holding her hair with his outstretched arm. Her hands were tied behind her back or she would have simply punched him.

"*Mal-humorada* bitch!" Jose yelled, spittle flying into her face as he jerked her hair hard.

Ary kicked again, catching him in the lower stomach. "I'll show you a feisty bitch!" she yelled right back at him.

"Should have kept her ass gagged," Franco said, moving

closer with the bowl. "Hold her still so we can get this over with."

"Ainda! Ainda!"

"You keep still!" was her retort, which was answered by another yank of her hair and a quick reversal of his limbs that had her midsection clasped between his legs and her head pulled back so that her neck was bared. If they were vampires, she would have been deathly afraid. As it stood she was wondering what would happen next.

She didn't have to wonder for long.

Franco approached, standing over her with a sick grin on his dirty face. "Now, open up like a good little girl."

Ary instinctively clamped her mouth shut, only to have her jaw jerked open and squeezed so tight she thought it would break.

He laughed as he poured the warm liquid into her mouth. She spit and shook her head, spilling more than she swallowed. Still, her throat constricted, pulling some of the liquid down into her stomach. She had no idea what it would do to her.

"Drink it all," he said, turning the bowl until it was upside down. "Then you'll see who is boss."

They both laughed. Jose let her fall to the floor once more where she coughed and tried to spit out any of the remaining liquid. Chuckling wildly, they left. Alone again, Ary gasped for breath, her mind scrambling as her nose recognized a scent. It was in that bowl, what they'd poured down her throat. It was familiar. Something she had smelled before, possibly handled in her work as a *curandero*. It was something . . . something . . . that could be deadly, she thought with another wrenching cough that unfortunately didn't bring up enough of the liquid to save her life.

Chapter 3

The cat roared as it stood with its front paws propped up on a huge rock, while its back paws were rooted in the damp soil. Its head rocked back, mouth opening wide, teeth baring to the wild, and it roared again and again. Rage and pain warring inside, edging it to the point of total despair.

When its flanks heaved with the effort of its ruthless howls, the cat stepped down, its paws moving wearily. Night had already fallen over the forest, like a dark cloak that made everything beneath the canopy even darker for those that did not possess night vision as the jaguar did. Mist floated in the distance as the waterfall roared and cascaded over the cliffs. The cat had been to this spot before, had remembered the comfort and serenity of this location. It had been long ago, but the cat knew, it remembered, and it hungered.

Moving closer to the water, it rested its head right beside the bank so that the sprinkle from the waterfall would rain onto it, tickling along its head and back: a soothing cool against the raging heat that threatened to consume it. Lying there its eyes closed and lifted, closed and lifted slower and slower until they finally stayed closed. Its breathing was slowing, more normal as it lay, paws pulled under its flanks, flat on the forest floor.

Where is she? Nick's human mind thought. His cat had covered miles and miles of the forest in an unsuccessful attempt to track her. But she was here, he knew that, felt it deep within. She was still in the Gungi, being held somewhere against her will for a reason he could not fathom. At the moment the why did not matter. To him it was only about getting her back and keeping her safe. He would settle for nothing less.

His temples throbbed as the shift rattled through his human body. He stood, his bare feet padding over the damp floor of the forest. Kneeling once more, he dipped his hands into the creek, scooping water up and splashing it onto his face. Around him verdant mosses and vines hung like beards surrounding the stream that bled into the larger body of water known as the Amazon basin.

"They haven't gone far."

Nick didn't turn toward the voice. He didn't need to. It was Roman Reynolds, his best friend. The black jaguar had shifted, and now the six-foot-two-and-a-half-inch man stood head held high as he continued to scent the area. Behind him and to his left was Xavier Santos-Markland, Nick's other best friend. X was still in cat form coming up on his haunches, his claws raking down a tree as he tried to pull the scent of a Rogue from its bark.

They were with him, always. Nick was comforted in that fact, even though he wasn't certain this time their companionship would be enough.

"They'd have to stick close to the river. Only the water can mask their scent," Nick was saying, his gaze scanning the terrain.

It had been years since he'd been in the forest—sixteen

to be exact. And none of them were used to running free in cat form. They'd almost forgotten to leave their clothes buried beneath some rather large buttress roots just outside the village. A light drizzle tickled Nick's naked body, and he inhaled its fresh dewy scent with just a touch of homesickness he hadn't anticipated. The Gungi never had a dry season, only a wet one and an even wetter one, so the rain was as natural as breathing here. And it felt different, Nick admitted. In the States he'd grown accustomed to putting up an umbrella and running to get out of the rain. Here in the wild where he'd been born, he tilted his head back and let the cool dampness welcome him.

X roared from beside him then shifted and waded into the water. Jaguars were not fans of swimming, but X had always been the best tracker of the threesome. If a scent was dimmed by water, X could still find it. Nick watched his longtime friend dip his bald head beneath the surface of the river and come back up seconds later, dark eyes blinking.

"They've been here," he said, turning his head and looking toward the west.

"There's nothing that way but more land, no shelter," Rome offered.

"No tribal shelter," Nick said, trying to peer through the thick brush of trees in that direction. The air was heavy with moisture, and the drone of cicadas and crickets filtered through the area.

"Outsiders," X replied with a nod.

"We should head back to the village and ask more questions. I don't like that her father hasn't been seen, either."

That was Rome, ever the cautious one of the group.

"I want her found now," Nick said through clenched teeth. He was already walking toward the west end of the forest regardless of whether his friends followed. Frustration dogged him daily. He wondered where she was—if she was even still alive.

"We all want her found," Rome said, clasping a hand on Nick's shoulder.

Nick pulled away. "You don't understand."

Rome shook his head. "I do."

That's right. Rome was mated now. Kalina Harper was his *companheiro*. Their joining ceremony had taken place just two nights ago. Out of respect, Nick had held off ripping through the forest to find Ary until now. But he refused to wait another moment.

"When Sabar had Kalina, I wanted to tear down every building in DC to find her and kill anyone who dared to touch her. I understand more than you know. But you need to be smart about this. Think before acting."

"She's been missing for days!" Nick roared. "She could be dead!"

Saying it aloud was like a knife in his chest. Nick staggered back at the mere thought that he'd never see Ary again. It had been so long—sixteen years—since he'd seen or heard from her. The latter he could blame himself for, because he'd never tried to contact her once he was gone. That had been a part of the deal he'd made with his parents and Ary's. It had been the biggest mistake of his life.

"Search yourself," Rome said, still speaking in that calm tone that drove Nick crazy half the time. "Close your eyes and focus on her. You would feel if she were dead."

Nick didn't want to close his eyes, didn't want to admit that Rome was probably right. Of the threesome, Nick was known as the impulsive one, the one who acted first and asked questions later. X was more reserved, but moved with lethal precision. Rome, the Faction Leader, was just that: a leader at all times. He acted in the best interests of the entire Topètenia tribe and the Shadow Shifters as a whole. He considered everything, all possibilities, before he acted. Nick didn't possess that type of calm, unfortunately, and never claimed to be anything other than what he was.

"She's alive," he said finally. A fraction of the stress he'd been enduring slipped away with thought. He wasn't just saying what he knew Rome wanted to hear. He believed it, in his mind and in his soul; he believed she was still alive.

Rome nodded as X came around to stand beside them. "Then let's head back to the village for the night and get a fresh start in the morning. If shifters have her, they'll be expecting a night attack. They won't anticipate our city mentality of getting up early."

"He's right. Their defenses will likely be down at that time," X said in agreement.

At his sides Nick clenched his fists. If he shifted and charged into the forest in search of Ary, Rome and X would no doubt follow him. They'd protect him to the end whether or not they agreed with his actions. They would also die for him. Nick knew that for a fact and admitted he wasn't ready to risk his friends that way. Coming up with a plan could also keep Ary safe. The way he was feeling right now, he'd go in ready to rip throats out. If there were other jaguars holding her, they'd defend themselves and their catch. Ary could be hurt. That was not an option.

"Fine," he said reluctantly.

He didn't like it, but he would do what was necessary without putting anyone else in danger. With long strides he passed Rome, heading toward the village. Within a few steps the human reached for the solace of the cat, shifting and blending into the forest atmosphere seamlessly. Behind him his friends followed suit, and the big cats ran through the forest they'd once called home.

Only home was a lot more dangerous than it had been years ago.

Life in the Gungi was centered on community and ritual. That community was grounded in the leadership of the Elders, and they led steadfastly from their location called the Elders' Grounds. The Grounds consisted of two main huts connected by an annex called the *amizade,* which was used as a place for the tribesmen to fellowship with the Elders. The *santa casa* or holy house was the larger of the circular huts made of vine and leaf thatch located in the center of the village. Each of the Elders lived in rooms in the second hut, called the *pessoal.* Throughout the day when the Elders were not in special meetings, tribesmen were allowed inside the *amizade* to speak to the Elders or simply to pray among the pioneers of the tribe.

Tonight Nick, Rome, X, and Kalina were meeting in the *amizade* with Elder Alamar and Sheena Serino to discuss Ary's disappearance.

"Rogues have been spotted outside the village, near the border," Elder Alamar said.

Nick listened to the older shifter's voice, noting the air of authority coupled with the slightest bit of compassion. He figured that's what was called for in a leader. Right now, Nick was having a hard time coming up with any compassion for the woman who sat cross-legged on the floor across from them. They were all in a semicircle with Elder Alamar at the head.

The Elder was in his midfifties with a formidable muscular frame. His complexion wore the weathered burnt orange look of the Topètenia who stayed in the Gungi, but his eyes were clear, his speech impeccable.

Sheena Serino, wife of Davi Serino, a family of *curanderos* within the Topètenia shifters, was a thin woman, her curved back complementing the downward hang of her head. Long, dark hair reached past her shoulders in glossless strands. Everything about the woman screamed defeat, and Nick wanted to scream alongside her to help her only daughter. He remembered Sheena from before, when he'd been only nineteen years old and had fallen helplessly in love with her daughter. The woman had looked at him that night with watery eyes imploring him—as did his own parents—to leave the Gungi and never bother Ary again. He'd let her hopeless look sway him then. That ploy wasn't going to work now.

"When was the last time you saw Ary?" Nick asked.

Rome gave him a stern look, but Nick ignored it. He'd spoken out of turn, but he didn't give a damn. The hierarchy of the Topètenia was strictly upheld in the Gungi, whereas at home, even at a meeting with the Faction Leaders, Nick, as a commanding officer, held enough authority to talk whenever he wanted to. Here he was supposed to yield to the Elder and to Rome as the Faction Leader.

Sheena lifted her head slowly, her mud-brown eyes already blurry with tears. Her face looked ashen and sunken in, as if she were suffering from malnutrition even though the Serinos were responsible for receiving and disbursing food and supplies in the village.

"She is gone," Sheena mumbled.

It looked as if her lips barely moved, the sound almost inaudible.

"We know that!" Nick roared, only to have Rome reach out a hand and touch his shoulder.

"When did you see her last?" Rome asked.

Sheena didn't answer immediately, and Kalina scooted closer to the older woman. Kalina Harper was a cop back in DC. She was a beautiful officer of the law with a quick trigger finger and dangerously accurate aim. She was also a Topétenia shifter who had mated with a Faction Leader. This made her as close to royalty within the world of the Shadow Shifters as Queen Elizabeth in the human world.

"Do you recall what she was doing when you saw her last?" Kalina asked in a much friendlier voice than either of the males had been able to achieve.

In turn Sheena's response was a little less fretful, but still not very informative.

"She is a talented *curandero*" was the woman's reply. "Her skill is more than I or her father possess."

Kalina nodded. "That makes her very important to the tribe. We want to find her as soon as possible."

"Did she go off with someone?" Rome asked. "A male or female? Human or shifter?"

Sheena shook her head adamantly, and Nick swore. This was getting them nowhere. When X came beside him, nodding that he go outside, he obliged. Not because he was used to following X's directives, but because his body was tight with restless energy. He needed to move, to walk, to do something that would help find her. This being still and waiting was definitely not working for him.

"Man, you've got to calm down," X said the moment they were beyond the opening of the *santa casa*.

"I need to run," Nick said pacing back and forth. "I just need to go and run."

"You need to get some rest for tomorrow. We're going to find her," X insisted.

Nick paused. "And what if we don't?" he asked. The possibility was there, ripe in the air like the scent of fresh-fallen rain. Whoever had her could kill her. Then what? Nick would go on a killing spree that would make Charles Manson look like a saint.

"Nick, I know this is personal for you. It's sort of personal for all of us, because she's a shadow."

"Her father's involved," Nick said, ignoring X's attempt at calming him down. X didn't possess the same steadfast cool that Rome did. And the shifter was edgy himself. Nick could scent the tension rolling off his friend in thick waves. He wanted to believe it was because of the situation at hand, but wasn't sure. X had a lot of things brewing in his mind, within his own issues. Nick respected those boundaries and didn't pry. But he'd be there to back X up whatever he needed. He wanted his friend to have that same undying support.

"The mother's not talking much. That's a problem," X admitted.

Nick rotated his neck, letting the cracking sound soothe him momentarily. "She's scared of Davi. Always has been."

"Does he abuse her?" X asked with a frown.

He steadied his breathing, focusing his energy. "Not physically. I think it's more of a mental intimidation. I sensed it the last time I was here. He sort of controls his whole family like that."

"So it's strange that he would go missing as well. He was the one who reported Ary missing, right?"

Nick nodded. "He went directly to Elder Marras, telling him that she didn't return home."

"She didn't return from where?"

"That's what we were hoping Sheena could tell us. But she's not being real helpful. If I'd been raised by anyone

other than Sofia Delgado, I'd shake the truth out of her."
His hands mimicked the motion of shaking someone.

X shook his head. "Not only would your mother roll in
her grave, she'd get up and kick your ass for that type of
disrespect toward a female. But there's hope. Kalina may
be able to get some answers out of her."

"Yeah, you're definitely right about that," Nick replied,
then sighed. "I hope Kalina can get through to her."

The minute Nick spoke those words, Rome and Kalina
came out to stand beneath the cover of darkness provided
by both the night sky and the thick canopy above.

"She was picking up supplies from the drop-off on the
mainland then heading to see someone called Yuri,"
Kalina reported.

"Yuri is the shaman," Rome added. "Sheena says that
Ary often helps Yuri in creating new medicines designed
specifically for the shifters."

"So Yuri has her?" Nick asked. "I don't buy that."

Rome shook his head. "No. Neither do I."

"Who is this Yuri? Is he a shifter, too?" Kalina asked.

"Yuri is a different type of medicine man than the
tribe's *curandero*. His healing is more spiritual," Rome
told her.

Nick smirked. "Like a voodoo witch doctor."

"Not voodoo, just blending spiritual beliefs with medicinal." Rome frowned at Nick then turned back to Kalina. "Yuri's been around the forest forever. He's not a
shifter, but a tribal man who knows his way around. He's
powerful in his own right and would really have no reason
to kidnap Ary if they were already working together."

"Then somebody knew where she was going and caught
her then. Yuri still lives beyond the Gungi borders, right?"
X asked.

"Right," Rome said.

"So somebody knew where she was going and tipped the kidnapper off." Nick's temples throbbed incessantly. In his gut, he had a good idea who this person was. But for now he'd remain quiet. He was trying to go about this the smart way, as Rome had advised. Accusing people, especially other shifters, wasn't going to go over real well with the Elders. But if his hunch turned out to be true, the bastard better pray the Elders' wrath was all he'd have to deal with.

"We've got about three hours left before dawn. We can get an early start and head out to Yuri's place. If Ary made her scheduled stop with him, we'll work our way back from there. Hopefully we'll pick something up from that trail."

Kalina touched a hand to Rome's bicep. "That sounds like a good idea."

Nick watched as Rome stepped closer, wrapping his arm around his mate's waist and kissing her forehead. "Let's get some rest," he said in a hushed tone that was probably meant just for Kalina.

X cleared his throat. "I'll camp out here to keep watch," he said.

Rome nodded. "You. Go to the north side and rest. You're no good tomorrow if you're tired and cranky and ready to kick ass instead of think."

"I'm not a toddler," Nick said with a scowl, then wished he'd simply kept his mouth shut because that response sounded like he was exactly that.

"Just do it and stop bitching." Rome was already turning away with Kalina, fully prepared to ignore any more of Nick's protests.

But Nick wasn't going to protest.

His parents, Henrique and Sofia Delgado, a Topètenian and the missionary born in Panama he'd fallen in love with, had built a home in a section of the Gungi called North Side. Even though Nick did not live in the Gungi, his father had worked closely with the Elders before his death, and Nick was a commanding officer with the state-side shifters. This meant their home was of royal status and was kept for use by descendants of the Delgado clan only. The dwelling sat with its back against vines and fig lattice covered trees. It was a peaceful locale—which worked out for Nick, who intended to get some rest.

Because come hell or high water he was finding Ary tomorrow. If he didn't there was going to be hell to pay.

Chapter 4

Nick never dreamed. He never spent time wondering about the "what ifs" or "has beens." That was useless and a waste of time. He was a busy man and didn't take kindly to wasting his time for any reason.

So as he lay beneath the netting that covered a clean mattress on evergreen logs, he welcomed sleep but cursed the vivid images that tagged along under the pretense of slumber . . .

She was close, her scent undeniable.

Soft, innocent, elusive, enticing.

Nick sat straight up, his eyes instantly focused past the thin layer of mesh surrounding his large platform bed. It was late night in the forest, sounds of its inhabitants echoing through the air. Crickets, leafhoppers, and cicadas were singing an evening lullaby.

His bed was in the center of the second room of the bungalow owned by his parents. After years living in the States they'd returned here, to the forest, to their home. Nick was nineteen now and had left the forest when he was four. His younger sister, Caprise, was with them, experiencing her first time in the Gungi. Henrique and Sofia Delgado understood the importance of knowing where one came from and embracing that heritage. They also knew that in the coming years Caprise's body would change; the *acordado* would begin, and she needed to learn as much as she could early on from the other females in the village. Caprise was anything but happy about the trip, but Nick attributed that more to the fact that she'd left some young boy back in Washington, DC, pining for her than her actual distaste for the shifters and the forest. Caprise was a pretty girl, with a cheerful personality and a body that would most likely have Nick fighting off every male within feet of her. She was a Topètenia Shadow Shifter, just like Nick and his parents. And they had come back here to usher her into her destiny. But there was another destiny to be fulfilled on this night.

Outside, the female moved slowly, stalking him as she would her prey. When he'd lain down in the bed, he knew she was approaching from the patch of trees that separated the Topètenia from the Gungi border. She lived there in a series of huts connected to form their main house and the tribe's healing center. The center skirted the perimeter of the Gungi. She lived there with her parents. Nick knew because he'd seen her with them at the *santa casa* and followed her home. Their hut was a distance away from the other tribe members because her father, Davi Serino, was a *curandero*. He and his wife, Sheena, provided all the medical care in the village. Aryiola was their only child.

With stealthy movements, Nick pushed back the netting and let his feet soundlessly hit the floor. She was nearing the door now, the scent of her growing need sifting through the windows as a tailwind to the evening breeze. Naked and fully aroused himself, Nick made his way across the room and into the large opening toward the back of their bungalow. His parents and Caprise were asleep, their rooms facing the front of the unit. The interior was dark but he didn't need light to guide him. He came to a stop at the back door, where he stood perfectly still, his body tense and waiting, knowing that she was just on the other side.

Her cat appeared seconds after he eased the door open; entrancing eyes, the color of fading sunlight, appeared luminescent against the dark forest backdrop. She'd awakened early, her body assuming the graceful curves of a young female jaguar sooner than most female shifters, which was most likely due to her healing abilities.

"You shouldn't be here," he whispered.

She grunted, tossing her head around and to the side. Stepping from the cover of trees, her tail swished as she turned and walked slowly away.

It was an invitation, one Nick knew he should ignore. Not ignore, but decline, respectfully. *Curanderos* were like a quiet royalty to the Topètenia. They were needed like water and supplies to keep the race alive. For that reason it was forbidden for them to marry outside their race—meaning they were not to mate with any shifter other than a *curandero*. Their life was dedicated to the tribes' welfare and nothing else.

Yet Nick had felt drawn to Ary since the moment he'd set foot in the forest. She was three years younger than him. A more beautiful shifter he'd never seen. They flirted with each other every time she came into the village and whenever he happened to be near the medical center—which was frequently since he knew she was there. He wanted her, there was no doubt about that. But he knew better. Or he should have.

Still, here he was, now shifted into his cat and following her into the forest. She was leading him away from the village, along the river's edge. When she stopped it was close to a waterfall, a scene that made the forest look like an exotic vacation destination instead of the dangerous lair that it was. Her cat moved close to a rock, backed up, and stood still, shifting until it was her five-foot-five-inch, honey-toned naked body he saw.

Inside his cat grunted, its heart rate picking up the moment a breeze caught her *calor*. It was a different scent, sort of a signature that only her *companheiro* would recognize. Other males might scent that she was in heat, needy, vulnerable. His cat scented her need, her desire, to mate only with him.

As he shifted Nick recognized the implications, knew what each inhale and exhale they both took meant. Stepping toward her, his human heart thumped as the next steps would bind them inextricably. She would be his and he would be hers, for all time. And though she was only sixteen, though his lineage put him closer to the Elders and the Assembly and hers made her a permanent fixture in the Gungi community, though there would no doubt be others surely against what they were about to do, Nick could barely find the strength to care.

"Do you know what you're doing, Aryiola?" he asked, his voice a low rumble against the crashing sound of the water.

She took a step closer to him, her long brown hair ruffling only slightly in the wind. When she looked up at him, her eyes grew brighter, hungrier, and his body hummed with desire.

"I am making the first move, as the Americans would say."

Her voice was refreshing compared with the Americans he'd been used to over the years. She had the accent of their native Portuguese language even though all Shadows were required to learn proper English. It was soft and husky with need, still a bit young, but definitely coming of age. He wanted to hear her speak again and again so that the sound would never be forgotten.

"If we do this, we can never go back to what we were. It's dangerous," he warned, but his hands were already moving. His arm reached out until his fingers cupped her face.

Ary leaned into his touch, turned slightly so that her lips brushed his palms, and whispered, "Then tell me to go."

Those words would not form on his lips. He could not send her away, could not deny what he'd been feeling for weeks now, what was obviously destined between them.

Nick grabbed her hand, pulling her behind him as they moved. If anyone happened near this bank they would be seen, their interlude over well before it had a chance to begin. They entered the water, its coolness sluicing over Nick's heated body. Ary was right behind him when he turned, tugging her even closer. Instantly her legs wrapped around his waist and Nick groaned, lowering his head to claim her lips.

She was so ready for him, her lips already parted, her mouth opened and eager to receive him. His tongue delved deep, seeking, searching until it scraped alongside hers, finally finding heaven. Her arms wrapped around his neck, matching the hunger of his kiss precisely. His fingers tangled in her hair until his blunt nails scrapped along her scalp. Water lapped around them but it was all Ary, everything about her, that consumed Nick.

Moving farther out into the water, their mouths remained connected even when the heavy fall of water rained down on them. Ary clung to him and Nick held her tightly, not wanting to let her go for even a second. His legs continued to carry them both until they'd passed right under the glorious waterfall and now stood on its other side, sheathed by its damp curtain.

There were rocks on this side, some rugged, some flat, jutting in and out of the cliff behind. Then there was a small opening in the wall, an alcove that would perfectly hold two bodies. Reluctantly dragging his mouth away from hers, Nick maneuvered them slowly over the rocks until they were out of the water, bare feet slapping against stone lightly covered with vegetation. When they came to the alcove, Nick turned to Ary wondering if now would be the moment she begged him to stop. But when he looked into her eyes, he only saw what was most likely mirrored in his own—desire, plain and simple.

"You are the one for me," she said, moving closer and coming up on her tiptoes to cup his face with her hands. "Now and forever."

Nick didn't know what to say, didn't know how to respond to such a declaration. Never before had he felt what he was feeling for her, not with the numerous young women he'd had in the States, not with anyone. The moment he'd set foot in the Gungi again, Nick had known this would be different. This time the forest would take a part of him he wasn't sure he was ready to give up. What he hadn't known was that it would be this tiny bit of a woman, this amazingly talented shifter. He had no idea before he came and now he couldn't think beyond her, beyond the softness of her hands, the slick coolness of her wet naked body pressing against his hard and aroused one.

He kissed her again, because all he could do was act. Words were not easily coming to him, but his body knew exactly what to do. This kiss was even hungrier, laced with a definitely wicked edge as her teeth scraped along his jawline, her hands moving down his muscled arms, over his rock-hard abs, around to grab his tight buttocks.

Nick's hands had a journey of their own to travel, coasting down the long line of her neck, over the handful-size breasts with hardened nipples. She gasped as he squeezed each breast then lowered his head until he could take the small globes into his mouth one at a time. Her body arched for him as his tongue drew sensuous circles beneath her breasts, over her stomach, delving deep into her navel.

When he thought she might break in two from bending back so far, Nick grasped her waist, wanting desperately to see all of her. Taking a step back, he gazed his fill: from the breasts he'd just tasted to the small curve of her hips, the muscle of her thighs, and the juncture covered with what he knew would be soft brown curls. He slipped a finger there, right between the plumped folds of her vagina. She hissed through her teeth, braced her hands on his shoulders, and opened her legs wider.

Nick moaned at the feel of her slick heat. Back and forth he slid his finger, touching the tightened bud of her clitoris at the front, then sliding back farther to awaken the opening that would soon take him deeply. She was tight there, virginal, he knew, and his blood pumped even faster. He should go slow, make this a memorable first experience for her. But it didn't seem like the time for romance. The way Ary was bucking beneath his touch, calling out his name, her fingernails scraping along his skin, said she wasn't really in the mood to wait much longer, either. He wouldn't hurt her; that was not an option for Nick.

His cat was struggling to break free, pacing hungrily, wanting, needing. Standing straight again, Nick grasped Ary's hips, turning her so that her back faced his front. He grunted and licked his lips, loving the view from behind just as much as the front. Her back was straight, good posture, strong bone structure, leading to slender hips and a bottom so round and so plump he wanted to weep with joy.

"Why did you come?" he asked, trying desperately to keep all the reasons why he shouldn't be doing this at bay.

With his palms splayed on both her generous globes he spread her cheeks apart, marveling in the beauty he saw there. She'd flattened her palms on the smoothest edge of the rocks, bending forward to offer him more. Now she was in a perfect stance, her legs spread, her ass and pussy open to him.

"I came for you," she said with conviction.

Moving his thumbs closer to scrape along the opening slit in her buttocks, Nick fought like hell to keep control—if only for a moment longer. "What do you want from me?" he asked just before a ragged moan escaped.

Lifting one hand, Ary reached between her legs to grasp his thick erection. "This," she answered simply.

With a growl he pulled out of her grasp, cursing as his erection continued to jut forward, aiming for the opening that now made him salivate.

This would change everything, he knew without a doubt. Neither of them would be the same if he continued to touch her, if he took her. Their lives would be altered; the lives of those around them would be shifted. They'd be breaking the Code of *Ètica,* going against everything their tribe believed in. He could not mate with her, his mind roared. But Nick's body was taking full charge. The cat inside that did not follow any code of ethics or rule book provided by anyone or anything was pressing for this joining, strangling the human half until it obeyed.

Gazing down again, Nick looked at the folds, damp not from the waterfall but from arousal, from her own needs and wants. She said she'd come for him, she wanted him. He couldn't ignore that. She was almost a woman; wouldn't she know what she wanted? The war raged on between Nick's mind and his body until suddenly he could no longer take the struggle.

With two fingers he pressed into her entrance, spreading his fingers to make her passage ready for acceptance. Ary bucked wildly against him, thrusting her buttocks back against his hand. Nick wrapped his other hand around her hair and pulled gently, loving the strangled sound that erupted from her as he did.

"Yes," she whispered. "Take me, Dominick. Please."

More welcome words he'd never heard.

Nick discovered early how much he enjoyed sex, how his beast needed more to be satiated than normal humans. At an early age he was introduced to a variety of sexual acts, some that gave him great pleasure, others that made him feel a bit darker and more out of control than he liked. But here, right now, he simply wanted to feel Ary wrapped tightly around him. He wanted to breach her entrance for the first time, to claim this part of her that no man or beast ever would again. He wanted to own her in this way. Why? he wondered briefly. So that no other man or beast would have her heart.

That thought startled him. Instead of thinking on it any further, Nick slid his fingers out of her, slowly slipping his thick erection into its place. She sucked at him, pulling him deeper. His release threatened to rip prematurely through him at the sight of his thick length being sucked into her so slowly and surely. He pulled back, watched as his dick now coated with her arousal slid out of her, then clenched his teeth as he pushed back inside her, watching inches of his arousal disappear into the pleasurable abyss.

Removing his hand from her hair, Nick grasped both her cheeks, pulling them apart for an unfettered view. His body was taut with arousal, his mind wrapping slowly around everything that was Aryiola. She bucked and mewled like the big cat she was. The sound echoing through the rumble of the waterfall, pounded in his head like a litany. With another thrust he pushed farther inside her, until his balls pressed firmly against her wetness. Nick sighed, even as his cat's growl rumbled in his chest.

"You shouldn't be here," he groaned. She felt so good and tight around him. Sweat dripped from his forehead, falling in big slashes onto her buttocks. "You should have stayed away."

Her movements became more frantic, her thighs shaking beneath him. "I could not. Not a moment longer."

Nick clenched his teeth as, thanks to her movement, more of his length slid into her canal. "It's not right. It's against our laws."

"It feels right," she countered and sucked in a breath. "It feels fantastic."

"We will be punished," he said then without preamble pulled almost completely out of her, only to thrust back inside with fierce strength.

She screamed, a feral sound surely traveling beyond their cavernous seclusion.

"Yelling won't save you," Nick said, pulling out then thrusting deeply inside her once more.

Ary was most definitely small and tight. His big hands almost completely covered her ass cheeks. As he continued to thrust, he closed his eyes, loving the feel of her inner muscles gripping him. She was taking everything he gave her, all his length and most of his lust he'd been holding at bay for the weeks he'd watched her from afar.

Yes, he'd seen Ary at the monthly meetings, watched the sinful sway of her ass as she moved through the courtyard. She knew the males ogled her, males of all tribes, no matter the rules against it. She was a temptress, but a still-untutored one. Nick desperately wanted to be the one to teach her the full art of her bounty. But it wasn't right. He knew it wasn't and that there could be no second time for them. Which was probably the reason he tried to hold back even more, to draw out this one moment in time they had.

"This cannot happen again!" he yelled, his groin slapping loudly against her ass.

"I . . . I cannot . . . help . . . it," she hissed.

"It cannot!" He pounded into her mercilessly. "Never . . . again!"

Ary spread her legs even farther, anchoring herself then meeting him thrust for thrust with a push of her own hips. The mere thought that she was enjoying his roughness, taking his punishment as some sort of reward, was driving Nick mad.

"Say it! Say it will not happen again!" he insisted, needing to know that this would soon be over. This blinding lust that had his spine stiffening, on the brink of shifting from its intensity, would end soon and the world as he knew it would resume. Nick had to have that reassurance, had to know that this one instance would not be repeated because there simply were no other options.

"No!"

Shocked and equally pissed off at her disobedience, Nick pulled his dick almost completely out of her.

"Please . . . ," she whimpered, a quick change from the assertiveness he'd just heard in her voice. "Don't stop."

Knowing that was impossible, Nick leaned over her, pushing two fingers softly against her anus. He'd wanted her there, had seen the virginal entrance and craved like never before. But he hadn't dared, hadn't wanted to hurt her with the intensity of his desire for anal play. Clenching his teeth, Nick closed his eyes. "I won't stop. This time," he said through a throat clogged with some emotion he didn't want to claim, then proceeded to push his fingers farther inside her tight rear entrance. His dick slid back into her pussy like a welcomed guest and she moaned.

Nick kept his hips perfectly still, his thickness pulsating inside her. She squirmed against him and he moved his fingers gingerly around the rim of her rear, loving the simultaneous feeling of pleasure.

Her head thrashed wildly, her hair swinging in the air. He wished he could see her breasts, feel their weight in his hands. But this wasn't about that type of pleasure. It was about slaking an immediate need. One they both obviously shared. Once this was done, however, it would be it. This would not happen again, regardless of what she said. It could not happen again.

And it hadn't. After he returned Ary to her home that night, things had changed. And Nick wasn't just thinking of the ultimatum given to him by his father and Ary's father, but the things that he'd seen when he'd returned to the riverbank. From that moment on Nick had never been the same. And as he'd left the Gungi early the next morning, he swore he'd never feel the same for another female again.

Chapter 5

"You think she good? She is weak, *não*?" Jose asked, trying to speak what little English he knew clearly.

"Are you a *curandero*?"

Jose shook his head so hard, long, oily strands of black hair scraped his forehead. *"Não."*

"Are you a shaman?

"Não."

"Then shut the hell up!" Sabar roared, pushing Jose out of the way and moving to the table where he pulled out a chair.

"Sit down," he said to the *curandero,* whose curvaceous body called to him even as her zombie-like state pissed him the hell off.

She did not move.

Jose had carried her into this room from where she'd slept and propped her against the wall. When Sabar spoke, he expected those around him automatically to move to do his bidding. She did not.

"I said sit!" he said louder.

Her head lolled forward, all that long hair draping around her, covering her face. After yesterday's trek through this god-awful jungle, Sabar had wisely chosen his long reaper-style boots with the reinforced steel toe and ankle straps. His black cargo pants and T-shirt fit perfectly, giving him the soldier look he was aiming for. He didn't want any trouble from the natives but wouldn't hesitate to kill whoever was looking for some in the meanwhile. There was a clunking sound from the boots as he walked closer to the *curandero*.

Clasping a handful of her hair, he pushed her head back. Her eyes rolled in her head, but she didn't look at him.

"Fuck! How much did you give her?" he yelled at Jose.

"Franco poured. I just hold her," the man said, his eyes wild with fear. Clearly he wasn't about to take the blame for his partner.

"Then find out how much Franco gave her. She can't help me if she's too drugged to think straight."

Sabar dragged Ary over to the table and sat her in the chair himself. Her limbs were completely limp, her arms hanging down at her sides, her head falling forward again. Cursing, he pushed the chair up to the table so that he didn't have to hold her upright; the table would do the trick. Her hair fell onto the dirty surface, and he could see nothing else of her face.

Jose had left the room, no doubt scrambling outside to where Franco stood watch over Sabar's Hummer and to make sure nobody came near the dwelling unannounced. Seconds later both shifters entered the room, Franco looking a little less afraid than Jose.

"How much did you fucking give her?" Sabar roared the minute he looked up. "She's a goddamn zombie! How's that going to help me?"

Franco shrugged with a casualness that didn't quite meet his eyes. He looked from the *curandero*'s head lying on the table to Sabar, who looked like he was surely about to shift and break their necks.

"I gave her what you gave to me. But she spit most of it out" was his defense.

"True. It run all down her face," Jose put in but clapped his mouth shut when Sabar spun around to glare at him.

"She's not moving at all. That's not what's supposed to happen," Sabar spat.

Jose and Franco shrugged because they had no clue about drugs or the herbs Sabar had lifted from the forest to dissolve in the mixture the *curandero* was given. But this, he swore again looking at her, was definitely not the desired effect.

Actually, he had no idea what the effect of the damiana mixture was, and that was the real reason he'd given it to her. If the information he'd paid for was true, it was in essence his golden egg. The plant that was generally found in the Amazon rain forest could add astronomical value to the product he was already moving on the streets in the United States. So he needed this to work. Problem was, she—the *curandero* who was presently passed out—was the only one who could make it work.

"Wake up, dammit!" he yelled, smacking the side of her head.

What came next was a roar that shook the walls of the ratty old dwelling and sent Jose and Franco backing into the corner. The impact of Sabar's slap pushed the *curandero*'s limp body off the chair, but instead of her falling to the floor there was a blur of motion as she shifted midair, landing on all fours, the big cat roaring and baring its lethal teeth.

As Jose and Franco cowered in the corner, Sabar stood level across the small room. His heart pounded, adrenaline soaring through his wicked veins.

"Such a pretty beast," he said, admiring the perfect female jaguar that stood across from him. "Come to me."

Her tan-colored coat was gorgeous. She was at least five feet long with eye-popping black rosettes in a picture-perfect pattern and hypnotic golden eyes. Poachers would die for the opportunity to be this close to such a magnificent specimen.

With all its beauty, the cat lunged, toppling the table and knocking Sabar to the floor in a matter of seconds. He rolled quickly to the side before it could hold him to that spot on the floor, knowing instinctively that this would mean instant death. Inside his own cat roared, threatening to rip free at any moment. It took everything in Sabar to hold back, to push his instinctive nature to the side. It wasn't a battle he wanted; it was more power.

The cat swiped a huge paw into the air, growling its discontent once more. Coming up on his knees, Sabar made a motion behind his back and heard the clicking of the rifle in Franco's hand. Finally the stupid bastard had found some sense.

"It's going to be okay," he said, still staring into the cat's golden eyes.

It roared again and pounced in the other direction, this time knocking Jose down and swiping its paws down the man's back. Jose yowled in pain, then shifted, his own cat turning to take a bite out of the female in defense.

The fight was short-lived. Sabar figured it would be and signaled for Franco to hold his fire. She was even more beautiful in cat form, he thought, watching her hind legs balance her weight as she stood swiping at the male with vicious force. The male, who in human form was sloppy and stupid as hell, was even worse in cat form. His charging was weak, his combat skills almost nonexistent. So when the female took a bite out of the male's left flank, it fell to the dirty floor with a sickening thud. The female, a trained huntress, went in for the kill, taking the male's neck between her strong jaws and clamping down until the cat could no longer move.

The howl that came from the female when it finally backed off the dead carcass was deafening. Franco dropped the rifle to cover his ears, and Sabar winced inwardly as the sound pierced something deep inside him. Then the cat turned and lunged right through one of the cloth-covered windows.

"We'll go in slow and quiet," Rome said after they'd had breakfast and left the village about forty-five minutes behind them.

Lucas, a teenage Topètenia, was their designated guide. He walked in front of them, his bare feet cushioned by the soggy forest floor. The boy didn't speak English, which was strange since he looked to be about fifteen. Most shadows knew both languages by now. Elder Marras, who had greeted them this morning, had not given much information about Lucas. All he'd said was that the boy could help with the search. Rome had readily agreed, since it had been years since any of them had traipsed around the forest. Lucas simply walked in front and expected them to follow, which they did.

"If he's a true shaman, he'll know we're there, regardless," Kalina said from beside Rome. This was her first trip to the forest, yet her appearance was that of an experienced Shadow Shifter.

"Elisa said his power is beyond anything they could explain. She said most of the Elders are even afraid of Yuri," she continued.

Elisa was the shifter who'd been helping Kalina since the joining. Nick assumed she'd also been giving Kalina a crash course in Topètenia history—which normally would have been okay. But the more Kalina talked, the more irritated Rome looked.

It was only from years of knowing him that Nick recognized that look. Rome hated the fact that his mate was with them on this expedition. The last place he wanted Kalina was in danger. Hunting the Rogue who'd kidnapped a *curandero* was beyond dangerous.

Kalina most likely knew this, too, and that's why she kept right on talking and walking beside Rome, no matter how angry he looked. She had a stubborn streak about her that sort of amused Nick. "He'll sense our spirits approaching and prepare himself," she told them finally.

"He'd be a fool to try to fight us," X said stepping over a particularly large buttress root that snaked out at least seven feet across the forest floor from the tree it belonged to.

"No. We'd be fools to walk in there thinking we have some kind of control. He has a power we know nothing about," Kalina insisted.

"He's just an old man living in the forest," Rome said with irritation.

"You cannot believe that" was Kalina's response. "He's well respected throughout the forest. Sheena said so last night, and the other Elders agree. Apparently Ary had a lot of respect for this Yuri and his work."

"She would respect anything that had to do with healing," Nick finally put in. "All she's ever wanted to do is heal and help others. If he was teaching her that, she would have been forever indebted to him."

"Enough so that she'd run away with him?"

The entire forest seemed to still at X's question. Nobody moved; everyone stood perfectly still as rage rippled through Nick's body in heavy waves. It was a feeling Nick was familiar with, as it seemed he'd been in a perpetual state of anger since he was nineteen. During that year he'd found and lost love and discovered his father was a liar and possibly a traitor to their species. Nick figured with all that he had a right to be as mad as he wanted, for as long as it took.

Thinking of Ary missing only exacerbated the emotion.

"She did not run away with the shaman," he said finally through clenched teeth.

X clapped him on his back. "Just trying to break this sour-ass mood we're all in. We're going to find her and she's going to be all right," he told Nick seriously.

"Not funny," Nick snapped. A quick glance at the others said they didn't agree, since they all seemed to be smiling.

Turning his back to all of them, Nick took the lead, using quick strides to get to the edge of the Gungi as soon as possible.

Another hour later when the group stood at a small embankment, Nick's shoulders bunched. His head lifted to the air as a breeze blew. Inside his cat howled, his gaze roaming all around.

"Rogues," Rome said. "I picked it up, too."

"From that direction," X said, pointing south from where they stood.

"Only he will know the way to go. The one that is a part of two," said a small gravelly voice.

The group turned to the voice, all of them silent. A man who couldn't have been more than five feet tall and a hundred pounds stood on a moss-covered hill.

"You will know where she is." With an arm that looked no wider than one of the thick vines stretching from one tree to another, the man pointed at Nick.

Not that the man asked, because he certainly didn't. Still, Nick felt like the pointing thing sort of singled him out. He took a step forward. "Yuri?"

"It is you she seeks." His voice was like a whisper, yet it echoed over other forest sounds as if it had some sort of power.

"Where is she?" Rome asked from behind Nick.

Yuri did not look away from Nick. "She has been calling to you for a long time. Now you will need to reach out to her. Call her and she will answer."

"Is this guy serious?" was X's whispered question.

Yuri's skin looked like old leather, hanging off his bones as if it were ready to touch the ground at any moment. From a distance Nick could see the bone that went through his lower lip, adding to the wispy sound of his voice and signifying his high spiritual status among the forest tribes. His hair was long and thin, hanging like pieces of thread from his scalp. He wore a thatch of material around his waist and what might have been some sort of vest to cover part of his torso. His arm was still extended toward Nick.

"There's only one way to find out," Nick said with a shrug, making his way up to where Yuri stood.

It was Lucas who stopped the procession.

"Você deve oferecer-lhe um presente."

Nick sighed. This was taking too much time. He just wanted to question the guy, find out what he knew about Ary's disappearance then move on to finding her. With a curse he rubbed a hand down the back of his head.

"I have to give him something for him to help us," Nick said, translating Lucas's statement.

"You're an attorney. You should know you don't get something for nothing," X joked again.

"Here." Kalina removed a gold necklace from her neck. "Give him this. He can sell it to one of the humans for cash or food or something."

With a shrug, Nick took the necklace from her. "Thanks. I'll replace it as soon as we get home."

"Don't worry about it," she told him.

Lucas took the necklace Nick held out to him and led them up the path toward the rise where the shaman stood expectantly. Nick was right behind him; X, Rome, and Kalina followed closely. He was tense all over, ready and waiting to find Ary so he could . . . could what? He'd spent most of the night—after the vivid dream of his last time with her—thinking of what would happen after this.

Ary was the one woman who'd made him feel something, the only woman to ever accomplish that feat. And she'd done so unassumingly. Would he be able to walk away from her a second time?

Lucas dropped to one knee, his head bowed low enough to touch the other knee. His arm was extended, the gold chain dangling on his fingers. Yuri moved slowly, as if his bones refused to go any faster. He stood in front of Lucas, tilting his head back and whispering something to someone they couldn't see. Then he inhaled deeply and took the necklace from Lucas's hand. A touch to Lucas's shoulder from the shaman signaled him to stand. He did so with an arm extended toward Nick.

Nick stepped forward, but before he could speak the shaman came to him, put his flat palm on his forehead, and began to mumble again. It wasn't Portuguese he spoke. Nick knew the language of the Gungi well. This language was different. He had no idea what the man had said.

"Come" was the English directive he gave to Nick.

He followed without hesitation, hoping this didn't take

long. Every minute Ary was missing was like a thousand needles being driven into his temple.

"Sit," he said when they'd come to what looked like a hole in the side of a huge boulder.

For Nick, Rome, and X, it wasn't easy getting their bodies through the small space. Especially X, who of the three of them had the bulkiest build due to his obsession with the gym. Once inside, the opening grew wide enough for them to step onto a mud-packed floor and stand at least partially upright. A pitted fire was already burning in the center of the floor while all types of roots and ritual tools hung around the space on nails drummed into the walls.

"All sit," Yuri indicated to them when they stood staring around the fire pit.

Lucas motioned for them all to sit in a circle around the pit, then sat behind Rome, his head bowed in allegiance to the Faction Leader.

When Yuri returned to them again, he had a handful of some type of plants. As he crossed his thin legs and sat in front of the fire, he dropped the plants in the fire. Seconds later a thick smoke rose in thin rivulets, polluting the air around them.

"Hmmmm, sage," Kalina said inhaling deeply. "He's burning sage."

Behind Rome, Lucas tapped him on the shoulder. *"É para a limpeza de energia."*

"It's for cleansing energy," Rome translated.

"Purification," Kalina whispered. "Magdalena, the elder female shifter, performed a similar ritual with me the night before our joining."

Yuri made some sound and wacked his arm over the fire. Everyone assumed that meant for them to be quiet.

After a few moments of moaning and whispering, Yuri

reached for Nick's hand. Not too keen on having a man—a strange man at that—pulling his palm into his own, Nick cleared his throat and reminded himself that this was for Ary.

"Her spirit fights," Yuri said in a whisper meant only for Nick to hear.

"Fights who? When was the last time you saw her?" Nick was running out of patience.

Yuri continued to hold Nick's hand, tracing the lines in his palm and moving up the veins in his arm. "You were connected once and will be again. It is imperative for you both to be whole."

Snatching his arm away, Nick rose to his feet. "Where is she?" he yelled.

Yuri went back to his smoke, leaning forward and inhaling, sitting back on his heels and closing his eyes as if he was praying. What he wasn't doing was talking anymore, which the group figured out after about five minutes.

"This is wasting time," Nick said, heading for the small-ass hole in the wall he needed to climb through once more to get back to the forest, where Ary could be dead somewhere.

The others were moving to follow him when Yuri began to whistle. "Follow your heart," he said finally. "Your soul recognizes hers."

With a curse Nick crawled through the opening. Falling out onto the moist forest floor had him swearing fluently by the time the others made their way out.

"Well, that was a waste of time," Nick was saying. "He didn't tell us anything we didn't already know."

The others remained quiet. Nick didn't know if that was because they agreed with him or if they were just letting him work off some steam. Lucas also did not speak. He did not assume the lead, either. Nick looked at him for a moment and was about to ask him where to go—then he figured fuck it, he'd find Ary on his own.

He began moving south, where the scent of the Rogues had come from. The farther he walked, the stronger the scent. Something else also grew stronger as he moved through the dimly lit forest. Desire boiled in the pit of his stomach; a raw hunger like he'd never before experienced was pressing him farther and farther. Now there were two scents guiding him—the stench of the Rogues and a stronger, sweeter scent that filtered through his body like a tonic.

Nick didn't know what the new scent was or why he was picking it up so strongly. And he really didn't care. All he knew for certain was that it would lead him to Ary.

Chapter 6

"She's terrified. Her heart rate is out of control. What did you do to her?"

"You," Sabar said, sweat beading his forehead, his fingers clamping around the other shifter's neck, "do not get to question me!"

The man gulped, the movement of his Adam's apple rippling against Sabar's thumb. He jerked his hand back.

"I never wanted her hurt," Davi Serino sobbed.

Walking across the room, stopping at the closed door, Sabar slammed his palm so hard the door almost broke free of the frame. "She's no good to me hurt, either! Dammit! She killed him without a second thought."

"My daughter is no killer," Davi Serino said adamantly. "She would not willingly hurt another shifter. Something is wrong with her."

"You bet your ass something is wrong with her. You told me the damiana would enhance my drug. That it would make my product worth even more on the street based on its potent sexual high. I'm supposed to be creating a new-age drug here, not watching after some crazed shifter."

"I don't know what's going on. I just don't know. Ary

knows about the medicines of today. I don't know." Dropping his head in his hands, Davi sobbed louder.

"Bring her out here and if she shifts again shoot her ass," Sabar ordered.

It had been hours since she'd killed Jose. Franco had dug a shallow grave, burying the remains. Not that Sabar gave a rat's ass what happened to the remains of the pitiful shifter. He wasn't going to amount to anything anyway. Hell, she'd actually saved Sabar the trouble of snapping the idiot's neck. Then she'd run off into the forest roaring and circling back and forth like a confused house cat. Not until her father had gone out to talk to her did the feline calm down, allowing her to shift once more even though the human still appeared delirious.

She'd slept and been fed. Now Sabar wanted to know what the hell had happened.

Franco came through the door with Ary, her hands tied behind her back and her ankles shackled. Her hair had also been pulled back with a dirty band because Sabar wanted to see her face at all times. That had more to do with the stir in his dick when he looked into her sultry eyes than any of this drug business.

"Aryiola," Davi whimpered, moving closer to his daughter as she was dragged into the room.

As the table had been destroyed, Franco just propped her against one of the walls and let her limp body slide down onto the floor. Davi fell to the floor with her, cupping her face in his hands.

"Answer me, my dear. Tell me what you are feeling," he implored.

Ary's head lolled back, her eyes open but not really focused. Through cracked lips she tried to speak. "Father, you are here?"

"Yes. Yes, baby. I am here. How are you?"

"My head hurts" was her reply.

From across the room Sabar stood with his legs slightly parted, arms folded over his chest.

"How did you feel when you killed Jose?" he asked.

It was a quick motion compared with her otherwise sluggish movements. Ary's gaze shot past her father to Sabar and instantly paled. Her pupils seemed huge, dancing around as if she were overly excited even though she was sitting perfectly still.

"What? Why? Where am I?" she finally managed to ask. "How did you know where to find me?" This question was aimed at her father.

Davi paused, not sure what his response should be.

"He knew where you were because I told him where I was going to take you," Sabar provided. "And I really don't have the patience for the domestic issues. I have some questions about the damiana that I need you to answer, and I don't have a lot of time."

This fucking forest was driving him crazy. The incessant rain was making him cranky as hell and he needed some pussy and some real food, fast. Staying out here in the depths of trees and rivers and dirt didn't afford him the lifestyle he was growing accustomed to back in the States. He drove an Audi R8, owned several Hummers, lived in a converted brownstone that he'd decked out in class A style, and had a staff that cooked and cleaned for him on command. These basic elements out here were killing his mojo.

"What's he talking about?" she asked Davi. "Father, do you know what he's talking about?"

"Of course he knows. It was his idea. Tell her, *Father*," Sabar said with his signature sadistic laugh.

An eerie sort of glee slipped down Sabar's spine as he watched her heated gaze land on her father. There was tension there, a situation clearly about to blow. Too bad he didn't really care.

"Tell me about damiana, *curandero*. What are the effects?"

"I wouldn't tell you the time of day," she spat in his direction. "Father, why am I here? Did you know he was coming for me?"

Sabar growled. "Tell her, Father. And while you're at it, teach your little bitch some manners. She's staying alive only because I allow it. Make sure she knows that!"

"Leave us alone?" Davi asked Sabar, his voice just short of frantic. "Please. A few minutes?"

Sabar spit on the floor then laced his fingers together and cracked his knuckles. "Yeah, whatever. Five minutes then I'm coming back and she better start talking or Franco here's gonna start shooting."

He walked out of the room with the satisfaction of knowing he'd scared the shit out of them. The heavy scent of fear permeated his nostrils, giving him a hard-on that kind of annoyed, but was good nonetheless.

Ary swallowed hard, the effort hurting her throat, which felt raw. There was a bitter taste in her mouth, like medicine, and as she closed her eyes she remembered those idiot shifters pouring something into her mouth.

Damiana.

The salty taste and smell she remembered. But something else had been in that mixture. Another herb, possibly; whatever it was, she couldn't figure it out at the moment. The fact that they'd drugged her was fuel enough to push her cat to the brink.

Her eyes snapped open. "They gave me damiana. Why?"

"Aryiola," Davi began in a hushed voice. "You have to do this for us. For our people. He will kill us all if you do not."

"Do what? I don't understand," she told her father.

A dreadful feeling was creeping its way around her stomach as she watched him.

He looked nervous. Sweat poured from his temple; tendrils of his hair were soaked and stuck flat to his forehead. The shirt he wore was dirty and likewise damp, probably with sweat as well. He wreaked of fear, pure and putrid.

"He will kill us, daughter. You must understand that."

"Tell me what you did," she said slowly, because there was no doubt in her mind that her father was involved in whatever this was. Her chest clenched at the thought, but her mind would not let go of the notion. "What did you promise him and why?"

"He gave us money and supplies and everything we needed to survive out here. All he wants in return is your help."

Behind her back the rope cut into her wrists. She was already trying to break free, her cat prowling close to the surface once more. But Ary was afraid to let her loose again. The last time she had been uncontrollable, and that was something new for her.

"What help does he want from me?"

"He wants you to create something for him. To mix some sort of drug. I do not know everything, but he will tell you. Then he will go and we will have our lives back."

"Are you crazy?" Ary asked her father. Or should she say the man who sat in front of her, because what he was saying made him feel like a foreigner to her.

Davi shook his head vehemently. "He has helped us all along. The money, the supplies."

"You mean the money and the supplies that have been

dwindling? If he told you they're from him, he's a filthy liar!"

Davi looked away from her, then back again. There were tears in his eyes. Ary opened her mouth to say something else then clapped her lips shut. She'd never seen her father cry. Ever. But it looked like he was about to, which meant this wasn't a good situation. As if she needed proof of that.

"I won't help him," she told her father. "He's a murderer and a lunatic. I will not do what he wants. He'll have to kill me."

One tear rolled down her father's cheek, streaking his dirty face and dropping onto his shirt. "He will."

Ary didn't know how much time passed, how long she and her father sat in silence. She didn't know what to say to him. Or who he was, for that matter. How could the man who had taught her how to save the lives of their fellow shifters be working with a Rogue who wanted them all dead? It just didn't make sense. And yet, on some disappointing level, it did.

Finally, she whispered, "Untie me."

"Ary," Davi begged.

"Untie me," she said again. When he continued to hesitate, she looked him directly in the eye. "You put me in this position. You gave me to this murderer. The least you can do is allow me to fight for my life. After all, what will you tell my mother when you return to her?"

Her words hit the exact spot she wanted them to. Ary loved her mother, had stayed in the forest and done the job they were born to do because of her. She'd tried valiantly to respect her father as well as love him, but that had never been easy. Davi was an opinionated and sometimes cruel man. He could say the harshest things one moment, then sit at a table and eat a meal with them the next. There were times when Ary thought he might be two people instead of one. Today he just looked like one stranger.

"All you have to do is help him," Davi said, reaching behind Ary's back to work the ropes.

She sat up, scooting around so he'd have a better grip. All her thoughts were on escape now. She wasn't listening to what her father was saying because there was no way she'd ever help Sabar do anything. She would definitely die first. But really, she didn't feel like dying. She felt like finding a nice soft bed and lying down until the throbbing in her temples ceased. Since she couldn't do that, she opted to fight.

When she was completely untied, Ary stood. A second later Sabar walked into the room—or what was serving as a room but was actually four walls that hadn't fallen down yet and a patchy ceiling that dipped with the weight of the rain. She took a step back, not to run, but to get her legs in a better stance to lash out at him if necessary. Admittedly she wasn't feeling 100 percent, but she would have to think about that part later.

"I already told my father I will never help you," she told him.

He tossed his head back and laughed, his white teeth shining in the midst of his dark skin. For all intents and purposes Sabar looked normal, clean, almost sociable. But it was all a mask, she knew. She'd heard the stories and in some cases tried to heal the bodies of those attacked by this shifter or others trained by him. So Ary was on guard. There was no other option, no other way to be.

"You can help me or you can die," he replied simply.

Okay, those were simple enough options. "Then you might as well kill me now."

He took a step close to her, lifted a hand to touch

her face. Ary smacked his hand away. "I said kill me, not touch me."

"Aryiola!" her father yelled.

She ignored Davi and glared at Sabar. "Do not make threats you don't plan to carry out," she taunted.

When he pulled back his hand Ary knew he would strike her. Catching his palm with her cheek stung. Her cat roared. She tried to breathe through the pain and turned back to him.

"Is that all you've got?"

Nick began running.

He didn't know why exactly, and he figured the others didn't, either. But his feet chewed up the ground as he moved faster and faster, his heart pumping wildly. The need was urgent, pushing him, making his human legs move as fast as they possibly could. The cat wasn't far beneath the surface, pacing, watching, waiting.

He spotted something dark green, a green that didn't quite fit the decor of the forest, and headed there. Rain had begun falling in rapid sheets, trickling through the canopy and casting a silvery haze over the dark region.

As he moved closer, pain seared through his chest and he roared, loud and long. Coming closer to the dwelling he saw the truck and kept right on going. In a flash a cat pounced in front of him, baring its sharp teeth as a warning.

Nick didn't have to react: A darker cat landed on all fours, baring its bigger, sharper teeth. Nick recognized X and kept moving toward the dwelling, making note to thank his friend later.

The minute he kicked in the door Nick knew she was here. His cat knew. It latched on to the rogue scent and roared loudly to announce his arrival.

So much for Rome's suggestion to go in quietly.

Chapter 7

When Nick entered the room, all human morals fled from his mind. His gaze zoned in on the male slapping his female, and rage rippled through his body like a disease. Before another thought could register in his mind his hands were tangled in the male's clothes, pulling him off Ary and throwing him to the floor.

In that instant, the room was filling with roaring and crashing sounds. But all Nick could see was the one who'd dared to put his filthy hands on Ary. He pounced, pounding fists into the man's face and torso until something struck him in the back, knocking him off kilter for a moment. The male, whom Nick vaguely registered as Sabar—the head Rogue they'd been chasing back in the States—took advantage of that moment and rolled to his feet, baring his sharp canines.

Nick had canines of his own, bared them and let his claws elongate from his fingers. If he wanted to fight like animals, then so be it. Nick was happy to oblige. Instead the head Rogue took a step back, nodding his head, his glowing eyes moving about frantically.

The roof, or what was supposed to be a roof, picked that moment to collapse under the weight of the rain pelting onto it. Pieces of tarp landed on top of them as wind and water tore through the open space. Nick heard his name being called but ignored it. Instead his nostrils flared, and he followed the scent. Searching for her, the one he'd come for, the one responsible for the interminable heat weaving throughout his system. He was inexplicably drawn to her, his jaguar senses reaching out to her. Inside the cat roared and stretched, knowing its female was near.

It was dark and chaotic, but Nick kept moving, finally extending his arms toward the body in front of him. Clapping his arms around her waist, he pulled her close and launched them both through an opening in the flapping tarp. A familiar whistle had him turning in a northerly direction and running as fast as he could.

Ary struggled against the strong grip around her waist. Her feet didn't touch the ground as he moved through the pelting rain and warm wind. There were others—shifters, she could tell. Frantically she'd looked for her father, but she hadn't seen him since the roof collapsed on the dwelling where she'd been held. Her heart hammered in her chest, her cat hissing wildly just beneath the surface. And she still had that damn headache that threatened to split her skull in half.

Whoever carried her didn't seem like the type to ask if she was okay. Hell, he hadn't said a word, just scooped her up and took off. There was no foul stench, so she felt safe in assuming it wasn't a Rogue. Still, she wanted to be put down, to escape on her own. As they tore through the trees in the dismal and rain-drenched forest, she realized that probably wasn't going to happen.

When they finally stopped, Ary thought she'd be re-

lieved. Instead, when she was unceremoniously dropped
onto a slightly drier hard-packed surface, her back slamming against rock so sharp it almost dug right into her
skin, her anger won over her relief.

"Could you be any more careless?" she snapped, coming up on her knees and gathering her strength before
trying to stand. Her throbbing head hurt like a bitch and
caused her entire body to shake.

"Excuse me, I'll keep my carelessness in mind the next
time I come rescue your ass."

Every muscle in her body—all the ones that already tingled with pain—tensed. She knew that voice. Only momentarily did she wonder why she hadn't known his touch
instinctively or why said touch had caused her discomfort.
It was him. After all this time, he'd come back to the Gungi.

Her personality wasn't that of a simpering female, falling at the feet of any shifter who ventured out to save her.
She hadn't asked to be saved and would have managed to
get herself free, at some point. So despite her past with
him—more *because* of that past with him—she stood and
glared at the man who had once been everything to her.
"I didn't ask you to save me," she told him, knowing that
really wasn't what she'd wanted to say.

"Aryiola, you are okay? Thank the spirits," Davi said,
running into what looked like a small cave and stopping in
front of Ary.

He took her hands as he blocked her view of Nick
slightly. Ary pulled her hands back. "I am fine, Father."

That was a lie. A huge one. She was anything but fine.

"You're welcome," Nick said tightly, his voice louder
than it had been before.

Ary suspected it was an attempt to bring their attention
back to him. That would be just like the selfish, arrogant
shifter that she remembered him to be.

"Again, I didn't ask you to come," she said looking around her father.

Davi spun around to look at Nick. "But we are grateful. Very grateful," he said.

Another man stepped up, a darker man with eyes that probed deep even though he didn't readily speak whatever assessments they made. He was from the States as well—Ary could tell because he wore long pants and boots, a T-shirt that displayed really great abs, and arms that made her a little leery about eyeing him so suspiciously. Still, she didn't get any resentful or negative sense from this one.

"We were happy to help, Mr. Serino. Your family is a great value to the tribe."

He spoke in a smooth, dominating voice that brooked no argument from Ary. Still, she tingled with a need-to-know vibe. "Who are you?" she asked, her own voice lower and less agitated because for some reason she sensed this shifter deserved that courtesy.

Coming closer, the shifter extended a hand to her. "I am Rome, East Coast Faction Leader of the United States."

Obligingly, Ary took his hand for a brief shake and nodded. "A pleasure, sir. And thank you for your kindness," she said out of respect for his title and all that he worked for in their tribe. She'd heard of him. He was the one who sent money and medical supplies. Yes, he deserved her respect and her gratitude. As for Nick, she didn't even look his way.

"This," Rome continued when he released Ary's hand, "is my mate, Kalina." He extended his arm and a female with lovely honey-toned skin and light brown eyes stepped to him, looking at Ary with a genuine smile.

"Hello, Aryiola," she said, her teeth perfectly white. High cheekbones lifted as she smiled.

"Hello and thank you as well," Ary said. They were a striking couple, this dark shifter leader and his lighter, only slightly less imposing female.

"Miss Serino." The biggest of the three men came forward with a nod of his bald head. "Glad to see you're safe. My name is X, commanding officer of the East Coast Faction."

Wow didn't quite describe this one. Bulging muscles, a fierce but extremely good-looking face, and eyes that just about devoured on impact had Ary swallowing hard. He looked like a warrior who never lost a battle, the epitome of a commanding officer. She could only imagine what type of cat he was. If there was fear somewhere within her personality, this shifter would certainly incite it.

"Hello" was all she could manage to say to this one.

Behind him she saw the skinny boy and nodded. "Lucas, I see you were kind enough to help the men through the forest," Ary said in Portuguese. The young shifter was known throughout the village as the only jaguar to have been captured by humans then rescued by fellow shifters. No one knew what Lucas had experienced under human captivity, because he rarely spoke of it—or anything else that wasn't absolutely necessary. Also unknown was whether the humans knew Lucas was a shifter or just considered him a lofty jungle prize. Unfortunately, the humans were not allowed to live to tell the tale.

"Do I need to introduce myself?"

She'd hoped if she ignored him he would somehow vanish. That hope was short-lived. Everyone cleared a path, and at the end of the cave stood Dominick Delgado. His face seemed fixed in a frown, golden-complexioned, thick eyebrows in a furrowed line across his forehead, medium-size lips clasped together in consternation, and eyes that were fiery and alluring at the same time. He hadn't changed one bit.

"I know who you are," she replied.

He nodded. "Good. Introductions are officially over. Now you can tell me what the leader of the Rogues wanted with you."

Her fists clenched at her sides. Less as a show of resentment toward him than as a way for her to keep her hands to herself. Just because her mind screamed for her to stay far away from this man didn't mean her body had to listen. "I don't answer to you."

He moved as fast as a flickering of light and was standing right in front of her before Ary could say another word.

"I'm not really in the mood for games. Just tell me what he wanted so I can have another reason for killing the bastard."

"Nick," Rome said in a mediating voice, "give her a minute to get herself together before you interrogate her."

Kalina stepped forward, pushing past Nick to get to Ary. "Rome's right. Let's you and I go out to the creek and clean up a bit before we start traveling again."

"We should stay here for the night," X interrupted. "If those Rogues are still out there, they may be following us. We don't want to lead them back to the village."

Rome nodded. "X is right. We'll stay put for the night. Get a fresh start in the morning. Hopefully the rain will subside a bit by then. Lucas has some supplies for us so we should be fine for the night."

Davi was already nodding his agreement. "That is good. Good to stay here for the night."

"I want to know what happened," Nick insisted.

"Then why don't you go find that Rogue and ask him?"

Ary spat before pushing past him and heading out of the cave with Kalina.

Later, as the fire Lucas had built began to die down and they'd eaten the energy bars that they'd brought, the shifters all found a spot in the cave that suited them and settled in. Ary knew instinctively what would happen next.

"Did Sabar tell you why he kidnapped you?" Rome asked.

Throughout the time she'd been with them, Ary had noticed how in love with his mate the Faction Leader was, and vice versa. They would die for each other—there was no doubt about that. The knowledge stuck in Ary's chest like a lump of coal. There was also loyalty here, and dedication. The stateside shifters were a unit, one that would be hard to break apart if anyone dared to try. They had joint causes and similar ways of dealing with those causes. Then there was Nick.

She'd avoided eye contact with him as much as she could, but that didn't mean he wasn't there. No, quite the contrary, the more she ignored him, the more intense his presence became, pushing quickly against her personal limits.

"My father knows what Sabar wanted," she said to Rome with a glance to where her father had found a spot in a corner by himself. She still hadn't found the words to say to him. There seemed to be none. He'd betrayed her. She knew that now and was afraid to ask just how far his betrayal had gone.

All eyes turned to Davi, who cowered closer to the wall where he sat. "It is over. All over," he mumbled.

"What is over, Mr. Serino?" Rome asked him.

Davi shook his head, his watery eyes finding Ary. She refused to feel anything. He was her father, yes, but he could be a cruel and evil man. Her mother usually took the brunt of his negative energy, which made Ary hate it all the more. For years she'd begged her mother to stand up for herself, to tell Davi to go to hell or something of that nature. But Sheena Serino was not that type of woman. She said it was her duty to honor her mate; that's what a female did when she was mated. That statement alone had convinced Ary: She'd never mate with anyone if she was expected to act like a simpering idiot.

"You knew he was going to take me all along," she said, not necessarily to Davi, but to the group at large. "You know what he wants." Then she licked her lips, which had suddenly gone dry. "You know what he wanted with the damiana."

"Damiana?" Nick asked. He was the first to get up and stand near Davi. "What's that?"

"Veneno," Lucas whispered.

Davi sobbed, his head falling down to his chest. Nick grabbed him by the back of his shirt and pulled him up off the ground. "Who was he poisoning?"

Ary stood, because the sight of Nick being so rough with Davi didn't make her feel as good as it should have. "Sabar's men gave me some sort of mixture. I recognized the taste, but it was too late. Sabar seemed to be upset with my reaction to the mixture, but I don't know why."

"And you think your father knows?" Kalina asked.

Ary could only nod; saying it aloud sounded pathetic.

"Talk, Serino!" Nick ordered.

"You will let him speak to me this way? You are the leader here. He should show me some respect," Davi said to Rome, who simply shrugged.

"I get the feeling you know more than you're telling us. If his tactics get you to talk, then so be it."

With that Nick slammed the man's back to the wall

and stared down at him. "You can talk on your own or I'll beat it out of you. The choice is yours."

"It was to help us. You . . . you," Davi stuttered, his eyes moving quickly from Nick to Rome then to X and back to Nick. "You stay in the city with the humanfolk and forget about us here. We cannot live on the peanuts you send."

Rome looked shocked—then as quickly as that emotion registered, it turned to rage.

"I send thousands a month in cash. Medical and household supplies are sent as well. What are you talking about?"

Davi shook his head adamantly. "It's not enough."

"Not when we don't get everything he sends," Ary added quietly. It had only been a hunch, one she'd been considering for a few months now. She'd mentioned it before, and Davi had not responded. Now she knew why.

Her father led the healing center, which meant that all of the medical supplies and a good deal of the cash sent through the U.S. accounts came to him to manage and filter throughout the village appropriately. As an only child, Ary worked by his side. She knew how things in the healing center should flow, what supplies they used most and how much was spent on the village necessities each month. But in the last five or six months, those amounts had dwindled significantly.

"You weren't giving out everything that came in. Or you were sending it elsewhere," she said, taking a step toward Davi.

"You know not what you speak," he spat at her. "Your mind is clouded by that poison."

That solicited a growl from Nick, and he tossed Davi onto the floor. "You had her poisoned, you bastard!"

This was a side of Nick she had never seen. His anger

was so real, so raw, and yet she wondered if it were all truly centered on her kidnapping. Just as he took another predatory step toward Davi, she grabbed his arm.

The contact sent bolts of electricity straight through her fingers and up her arm. She jerked back in surprise and glared up into his dark eyes. His cat was awake—wide awake as evidenced by the shift in eye color, from dark brown to an eerie green. Pushing her arms behind her back, she tore her gaze from Nick and looked down at Davi.

"What did you do with the rest of the money and the supplies?" she asked him.

"You will get us killed! Do you not understand? He will kill us all!" Davi whined.

X leaned closer, put his face right in Davi's, and pointed at Nick. "I don't know who you're talking about. But this one here, he's going to rip your fuckin' head off if you don't start talking soon. You might want to consider that the most immediate threat."

Suddenly the room was filled with so much tension, so much . . . testosterone, Ary thought she'd choke. Cats lurked ready to strike, while unanswered questions served as fuel to the simmering fire.

"I pay him to leave us alone. Is that such a bad thing?" Davi asked, rolling to his side and coming up on his knees. He coughed and coughed and for a split second Ary thought of going to him. Then she changed her mind.

"You are paying Sabar?"

Davi shook his head. "Every month I bring money to the place where he held you. I leave it there in bags he provides. I do not know how he gets it but he does and it keeps him away."

"Then why would he suddenly need Ary?" Kalina asked. She'd been quiet, mostly watching what was going on as if she were an outsider. Ary wished she, too, could pull herself out of this situation, sitting on the side as if she'd just tuned in. She hated that her father was a traitor and that he'd resorted to trading her.

"I will tell you all," Davi said finally and stood staring at them. "He works with medicines, some kind that he sells in the United States. A while ago he asked if we had something to help him. I said I did not know, that my daughter knew of all the medicines and such. I know because she learned from Yuri. He wants to know what you know, Ary. That is all. You should just tell him."

"I would never tell him anything!" she raged. "And you are lower than bile for giving your own flesh and blood to a creature such as Sabar!"

X looked at Davi with a sick kind of pity, while Rome shook his head, his contempt bubbling just beneath the surface. Nick's face showed nothing but rage. It was controlled, as witnessed by the way his fists clenched at his sides and the throb of his temples, but just barely.

Tears stung her eyes and Ary cursed. "Go back to where you came from, Dominick Delgado! We can take care of ourselves here." She said the words and meant them as grand bravado. Instead they were her breaking point. Ary felt like everything was falling down around her. She turned quickly and ran out of the cave, wishing like hell none of this had ever happened. Especially the part about her touching Nick, and liking it way too much.

Chapter 8

Nick told himself he wouldn't go after her. He swore he wouldn't rescue her when she so obviously didn't want to be rescued again. But she'd been gone more than twenty minutes. Her alone time was up.

He didn't have to track her, didn't have to scent the air to know which direction she'd gone. All he did was close his eyes, and the visual of her appeared—just as she had been all those years ago, but better. Nick had seen beautiful women back in the States. He'd had quite a number of them for himself. But none of them compared to Ary.

She had a decidedly sultry look, with pouty lips and a stubborn chin. Thick eyebrows and long eyelashes only made her look more exotic. Wine-colored eyes that shifted to a deep gold when her cat lurked added a touch of mystery. As for her body, Nick shivered remembering the moment when his arm had clasped around her waist. Ary had never been model-thin; she was full of lush curves, heavy breasts and alluring hips. His dick hardened and his pace increased.

He knew where she was—or should he say his cat knew, and he followed accordingly.

The rain had stopped, the forest growing even darker in the twilight hours. Just ahead he heard the rustle of water and breathed a little easier. With his nocturnal vision Nick proceeded until he stood across from a small fall of water. He had to struggle to catch his breath.

She was there, just visible through the thin curtain of water trickling down into the creek. In the same place he'd taken her sixteen years ago.

She was beautiful. The cat was, that is. With seemingly perfect symmetrical rosettes across its golden body, the animal stretched and dipped beneath the streaming water. Its mouth opened wide, tongue licking over viciously sharp teeth. Then it stretched again, this time shifting in a blur of motion and rivulets, until now the woman stood in all her naked glory.

Licking his lips, Nick felt an insane jealousy toward the water that sluiced over every inch of that glorious body without censor. Her back arched, her head held back as the thick mane of hair drank freely of the waterfall. Curved hips flared to voluptuous buttocks. When she turned slightly, the clean-shaven V of her mound appeared and Nick wanted to roar. The craving inside him beat a steady rhythm that finally had him taking a step toward the creek. He removed his clothes slowly, using her movements as a guide.

When she lifted her arms, her breasts rose higher, and her nipples puckered against the cool spray of the water. Nick pulled off his shirt and let his palms run down his torso, over his abs, to the waistband of his pants. She leaned forward, lifting a leg and pushing it sinuously through the curtain of water, rubbing her hands up and down the length. Nick pushed his pants over his muscled thighs and stepped out of them, his palm moving quickly to cup his heated erection, applying some much-needed stroking.

She stood straight again, her arms lifted, and pulled

her hair around one shoulder. Nick walked slowly, his feet entering the creek silently. In seconds he was at the waterfall, standing just on the other side, only inches away from Ary.

Her body stiffened and she turned to face him. Through the water she looked like a goddess, droplets resting seductively on her lashes, her lips damp and swollen. He stepped through the spray, feeling the chill of the water against his heated skin but not letting it dissuade him. With one arm he reached out, clasped her at the waist, and pulled her to him. Her head instantly tilted, her mouth opening slightly. And that was all Nick needed.

His lips found hers in a heated touch. His tongue traced those lips and suckled the bottom one as if it were a piece of candy. When she gasped he delved deeper, letting his tongue mingle wildly with hers. She reached up, wrapping her arms around his neck, pulling him closer. Nick backed them farther into the cavern, letting his hands run up and down the slickness of her skin. Cupping her buttocks, he sucked in a breath and pressed his erection into her abdomen. She came up on tiptoe until his dick slid sinuously between the folds of her pussy and he wanted to roar.

As he lifted her into his arms, she wrapped her legs around him. He stood there kissing her, his fingers moving between the slit of her buttocks to the heated moisture between. She felt delicious, and he licked at her lips the way he wanted to lick at her pussy. Tossing her head back, Ary arched into the motion of his fingers, riding him with quick strokes. She looked heavenly and Nick dipped his head to run his tongue over one puckered nipple.

Drawing a hand down, she cupped her own breast, squeezing and pushing it farther into his mouth. He gorged on her, sucking and licking until they were both breathless. With his teeth he snagged her nipple, tugging until

she whimpered then licking lavishly while his dick
rubbed along her heated cove. He wanted in, desperately.
His spine tingled with the very thought of slipping inside
her, being clamped by her walls, his dick being milked
until he sobbed. It was an enticing thought, an arousing
thought, and damn if he would allow it to remain only a
"thought."

When they were as far into the cavern as they could
get, he laid her down on the wet stone floor. She reached
for him, her eyes glazed with arousal. "The last time I
came to you because I wanted you," she said, her chest
heaving, lips swollen from his kiss.

He stood over her, his dick jutting forward in invitation, or begging; it didn't really matter at this point.

"Now I'm here because I want you," was his reply.

She touched her breasts again and Nick wrapped his
fingers around his aching length. Apparently she was no
stranger to touching herself, probably pleasuring herself.
Fuck, he was going to come right at this moment if he
didn't get a grip on himself. A mental grip this time . . .

"Show me how much" was her sultry reply.

Propped up on her elbows, she let her knees fall open,
baring herself to him totally. She looked like a porn star,
all wet and aroused and ready and willing. He felt like the
luckiest bastard alive as he took another step toward her
and fell to his knees. His face was buried between her legs
in record time, his mouth closing hungrily over her pussy,
sucking and kissing, loving the smooth texture and sweet
taste of her. When she draped one long sleek leg over his
shoulder, Nick grabbed hold of her thigh and sank in
deeper. His tongue stroked her from her clit to the base of
her weeping center, stayed there and speared deep inside
her entrance. She bucked and rocked against his mouth
and Nick stroked her deeper. In his arms she was alive and

as fiery as the look in her eyes when she was angry. Her cat was wanton and reached out to his as if it had been waiting for this precise moment.

With a start Nick realized his cat had been waiting, too, in a predatory stance since the second they'd stepped into the forest. It had known she was here, known that they would reunite like this, and dared Nick to stop it. He had no qualms there: He would never stop wanting her, especially after tasting her this way. Her scent permeated his senses, and he thought he'd die right here between her legs with her dripping her essence into his mouth.

Pulling out of her he focused on her clit, circled the tightened bud with his tongue, then sucked it completely into his mouth. She shivered, convulsed, then purred her pleasure, his name a whisper on her lips.

His dick ached, almost screamed with need, and Nick reluctantly pulled his mouth away from her. He was about to replace his mouth with his length and pound into her mercilessly, but she stared up at him. He caught the wicked gleam in her now golden eyes and chuckled. "You want some?" he asked, his fingers stroking his length again.

"I want some," she said propping herself up once more. "Now."

"Your wish is my command" was Nick's ready reply.

He shifted above her, holding his dick and directing its tip at her mouth. The temptress had the audacity to lick her lips, wetting them generously and soliciting a bead of excitement at the tip of his dick. She laughed, throaty and confident, then extended her tongue, swiping that clouded bead of moisture into her mouth.

Nick was not in the mood to be teased. If she wanted him she was going to get him, all of him. With a thrust he touched his tip to her lips. She pouted and he pressed further.

"Open up, you tease," he taunted her, loving this jaunting little game of need they played. He hadn't played with a woman in years.

She pursed her lips into a sucking position and let only the tip of him inside. There she worked him, sucking the engorged head with enthusiasm. He tasted like heaven, like ten times heaven. Ary's entire body shivered with need. Extending her tongue, she licked the underside of his length. He gasped, cupping the back of her head and pushing her farther.

With tremendous strength Ary resisted sucking him in completely, instead licking at the tightened sack, pulling him into her mouth and releasing him when his body tensed over her. Only when he was trembling did she open her mouth to take him inside and when she did, she came.

It was an explosion, a long-held explosion of need and desire and hunger that racked through her body like an earthquake. Her mouth quivered with him inside, and it took her a moment to gain her bearings before she could start to suck him deep. He pumped into her mouth and Ary took each stroke with care and eroticism. Her hands cupped his taut buttocks and pulled him in deeper.

"Fuck!" he bellowed, and she sucked harder and harder.

When he throbbed in her mouth and she thought he would come, Ary pulled back, letting his ready length flop between her lips. She'd waited what seemed like forever. Nick always kept her waiting and she despised him for that. Hated that she still wanted him this way but wasn't inclined to deny herself or her cat this delectable pleasure.

"Take me, now," she gasped, falling to lie on her back, opening herself to him once more.

"Definitely" was his deep moaning reply.

He speared into her center and thrust deep. She gasped, lifted her hips, and accepted him completely. Thick and hot and long, he filled her until she thought she would burst. Her legs were lifted and propped on his shoulders as he went deeper, pulling out and pushing in. Her nails stung as they scraped against the damp rock beneath her; sharp teeth bit into her lips when she struggled not to scream.

"Sweet. Sweet," he murmured over and over, rotating his hips, stroking her lovingly.

But it wasn't love.

Like a neon light in the dark, lust-filled recess of her mind, the realization blinked on and off. A vivid reminder of her biggest heartbreak.

"Only you," he whispered as he leaned forward, finding her ear.

Ary tried to hold on to those words, to let them douse the flame of that neon reminder. It felt so good, so real. His motions pushed her to a glorious precipice, one she'd never been able to reach on her own. She wanted to go there, to fall over that cliff of pleasure one more time. And so everything else was pushed from her mind. She moved her hips, matching his strokes, wrapping her arms around his neck and holding him close so that the connection wouldn't be broken too soon.

He pulled out of her then and she gasped, wanting to tell him to stay but being too out of breath to come up with the words. It didn't matter because before she could speak he'd lifted her and turned her so that she was on her stomach. With a strong pull he had her on her knees and was spreading her buttocks, slipping his length into her from behind. Then she screamed with the force of his thrust, the depth and the intense pleasure rushing through her body coming out in the high-pitched sound.

"Please," she begged. Yes, pathetically, she was begging him to make her come, to bring her glorious relief. "Please."

No matter how degrading it was she said it again and again.

He pumped her mercilessly, holding her hips to keep her in place. She bucked back against him, loving the sound of their joining echoing throughout the cave. It lasted forever, and then not long enough. They screamed together . . . no, it was more like a symphony of roaring, two cats joined, forever intertwined. Whatever, it was amazing.

And when their breathing had returned to normal it was over. Again.

Chapter 9

"Where are you going?" Nick asked when she'd stood and walked across the stone floor.

"You were famous for your exit last time. I'll take the lead this go-round," she snapped, then dove through the curtain of water, splashing into the creek below.

Cursing, Nick followed, reaching the shore just in time to grab his clothes, cuff them under his arm, then stop her just as she was stepping into her dress. "You don't go anywhere alone," he gritted. Taking advantage of the seconds he had while she dressed, he hurriedly stepped into his own pants and shoes.

"I don't need a babysitter. I live here, remember?"

She was angry, her amber eyes flaring at him. Her scent, while still intoxicating, was lighter, like a crisp winter's breeze.

"While I'm here, I'm your shadow. Deal with it," he told her.

"Go to hell!" Drops of water dampened his shirt as she spun around, her hair flailing behind her.

Her strides were surprisingly long for a woman nearly a foot shorter than him, but Nick kept up. She knew the forest much better than he did, stepping over poisonous snakes before he'd even seen them, ducking beneath roped vines, pushing them so they'd sway right in his face. At that he'd cursed, but let her keep her mad on for a while longer. She'd been through a lot; she was definitely entitled to unwind the way she saw fit. He'd hoped their little tryst at the waterfall would have been enough. Obviously not.

"Sabar's not going to stop looking for you if you have something he wants," he said when they were walking through a clearing with owl monkeys conversing above.

"I don't have anything that parasite wants." She didn't turn to him, just kept on walking.

"What's this damiana drug he gave you? What does it do?"

"It gives you a big-ass headache" was her tart reply.

"Is that what it's supposed to do?"

She jumped down a small incline, twigs cracking beneath her. "Damiana is from the turnera leaf. It's mainly used to treat high blood pressure."

"And?" Because what she said didn't sound all that appealing. He wondered what Sabar would want with the drug if all it did was regulate blood pressure. "Lucas said it was poison."

She sighed. "If it's not purified before use, it can be toxic. It's also an aphrodisiac. It can induce euphoria."

Now it was starting to make sense. "He can sell that in the States and make a shitload of money with it." Even though the effects sounded a lot like ecstasy, which was already a huge part of the drug market, Nick knew there was always room for something newer and better where drugs were concerned.

"I don't know what he can do in the States. I don't live there, remember?"

The way she said "remember" gave the impression she was holding some type of grudge. Nick didn't know what to say or do about that.

"Can he get the leaf readily here without you?"

"Of course he can, that's why he gave it to me." She stopped walking suddenly. "Yuri taught me the purification process. It takes the poison from the leaf so it doesn't enter the bloodstream. I have the poison in me but I'm fine, except for the headache. That's strange."

She gasped.

Nick came right up behind her, grabbing her by the arm. "What is it?"

"He gave me damiana, boiled like a tea," she said, not looking at him. "But I didn't get sexually aroused or feel remotely euphoric."

The sound of him gritting his teeth was extremely loud. "What did you feel?"

She looked up at him, hating the words in her head. "Anger, that's what I felt. A raw, fierce anger that made me uncontrollable." She gasped then sank to her knees fighting to gulp air.

Nick went down with her, wrapping his arms around her. "It's okay. It's finished. He won't touch you again. Understand? I won't let him touch you again."

She shook her head as he rubbed her back. The forest seemed smaller all of a sudden, as if its walls were closing in on her. Panic speared through her as she remembered Sabar striking her, the feel of something snapping deep inside her as he did. It was like he'd flipped a switch and she'd immediately reacted. Jose had been in her line of sight and she'd attacked without further thought or provocation.

Opening her mouth, she flexed her jaw, remembering. "I killed a shifter."

The words lingered in the evening noise of the forest.

"I'm a healer. I'm not a killer. And he was one of us."

To her own ears, her voice sounded utterly defeated.

She was a disgrace to her kind, no better than her father on some deranged level.

Nick grasped her chin, tilting her head until she was looking into his eyes.

"It wasn't you. It was the drug," he told her. "You are not a killer."

It sounded good—just like being in his arms felt good, having him here felt good and sharing his kisses was the icing on the cake. But Ary didn't believe him. She'd wanted Jose dead and she'd killed him. Sure, the unpurified damiana in her system had incited the rage, but she'd done the deed. That was the fact that sickened her.

As the group made their way back to the Gungi, Kalina walked alongside Ary while the guys stayed ahead of them. Every couple of steps either Rome or Nick would look back, as if either one or both of them thought she or Kalina would vanish into the forest. Ary could scent the *calor* between Rome and Kalina, not to mention the closeness the couple seemed to share on a human level. A part of her longed for that same type of connection—but another part acknowledged she might never have it.

"He wants to protect you," Kalina said after they'd taken their time to cross a silent river that happened to be the home of more than one anaconda.

"I don't need his protection," she said defiantly. "I don't want it."

Kalina nodded as if she knew precisely what Ary meant. She was a very pretty woman with a decidedly city look to her. Maybe it was the short sassy cut of her hair, or the way she carried herself—as if she had inside knowledge of everything and everyone around her. Ary should hate her for that, but actually found it hard to since Kalina had been the nicest of the entire group to her since the rescue.

"You probably know them a lot better than I do," Kalina continued. She had a calm voice, like she was constantly negotiating with whoever it was she was talking to. "But it seems they need to protect their women even if the women don't necessarily need it."

"I don't know those three well, specifically. If you mean Shadow Shifters, yes, I guess you're right. But it's only the mated males that have that sort of streak," Ary said.

Kalina was shaking her head, keeping up with Ary's pace without problem. "Nick and X are pretty protective, and they aren't mated. And for the record, I think it's *all* females they aim to protect, with a special emphasis on the ones they mate."

It sounded right to her, but Ary really didn't want to talk about this. "I guess. I just don't need it. I've been in the forest all my life. I know my way around here better than they do."

"But they know Sabar better than you," Kalina said with a sort of finality.

"That's over. He won't get anything from me and he knows it," she responded. Still, Ary wasn't so sure of that statement.

"It's not over for him. Believe me, I know what it's like to be on his radar. He stalked and kidnapped me, too."

That was a surprise, and Ary couldn't hide her shock. "Really? Is he a professional kidnapper?"

Kalina laughed. "He's a killer, a sadistic, evil killer."

Ary believed that statement undoubtingly. "I'm not going to help him create something that might hurt people. I'm a healer; it's against everything I've been taught."

"He won't care. He doesn't care about anyone or anything but himself."

"I don't understand that," Ary said honestly. "Since I was a child I was taught how to save people, to take care of them. I can't imagine not doing that." Even after she'd killed a man.

"You would make a great doctor in the States," Kalina said with a chuckle. "You'd be one of the few who actually cared about the patients versus the payments."

Ary didn't really know what she meant by that statement. *Curanderos* were not paid for their services; they were born to serve their tribe. Yet she'd secretly longed to study medicine formally and had thought about going to the States more than once. "He wouldn't let me go."

"Who wouldn't let you go where?"

Kalina was asking the question before Ary realized she'd spoken aloud. Her father was just a short distance in front of them, and it wasn't really her intention to talk about him.

Each time she thought about the respect she'd given Davi Serino and how he'd repaid her for said respect, Ary cringed. She wanted to strike out at something or someone because a father wasn't supposed to betray his child or his people.

"Him," she replied quickly nodding in Davi's direction. "He said I was born to help the tribe, it was my responsibility to stay here with them forever. Even after Nick—" She let the rest of that thought go in silence. Kalina didn't need to know how young and foolish she'd once been. And had been fairly recently, she thought with a shake of her head.

"Where did you want to go? If you don't mind my asking."

Ary didn't really mind. In fact, since she'd already

started, it was sort of a relief to get this off her chest. It was even better that Kalina was from the States. Someone who was born and raised in the Gungi who would tell Ary she was being foolish for wanting anything beyond the canopy of trees.

With a deep inhale and slow exhale she said, "To the States to study medicine."

Now it was Kalina's turn to look shocked. "Why wouldn't he want you to get an education? You could learn so much more about medicine in college, then you could use that knowledge to continue to help the tribe."

"That's what I said. But he didn't agree."

"What about your mother?"

Ary shook her head. "She believes whatever he says. Like every word that comes from his mouth is straight from some higher being."

"That might change when she hears what he's done. What do you think will happen to him when we return? I mean, will the Elders invoke some type of punishment?" Kalina asked.

Ary shrugged. "I do not know about the Elders. But as for my mother, she will not care what anyone says. It is always what Davi says. And it makes me sick."

"Can't say I blame you. I'm not letting any man think for me. No matter how much I love Rome, we're partners, each with thoughts and reasoning that can contribute to the tribes and our lives. It's not all about the mighty male."

Ary had to laugh at the way Kalina said that last part. Her voice had deepened like a male's and she'd puffed up, banging her fists lightly on her chest. "I know what you mean. I hate that way of thinking."

"It's barbaric," Kalina offered with a chuckle of her own. "Me man. You woman. You fetch."

Ary nodded. "You heal and cook and clean. I lead, you follow."

They both laughed, and for the first time in all her life Ary felt like she had a friend, or at the very least someone who saw things the way she did. That made her feel good, even if it was only momentary.

"What's so funny?" Nick asked.

He'd obviously fallen back from the group to catch up with them. Or eavesdrop, which sounded better to Ary.

"None of your business," she snapped back. It sounded catty. No, juvenile. But she didn't care. She was pissed at herself for falling into his arms so easily again. Yet she was also proud of the way she'd walked away from him, as if it meant absolutely nothing.

She was sure that's how he saw it—sex with the poor little forest shifter one more time. Then he'd be on his way back to his home, where he undoubtedly had other females to have sex with. The bastard.

Kalina stifled a laugh and skipped ahead of them so that Nick now walked right beside Ary.

"You don't have to bite my head off every time I say something to you," he said tersely.

"Really? Tell me, what should I do when the great Dominick Delgado decides to speak to me?"

"You could try being civil. We are adults, you know."

"You're right. We are adults. So what Kalina and I were discussing was private. Is that better?" Ary didn't feel better, that was for sure.

Last night had been wonderful on a purely physical level. In the light of day—or the dim sunlight that managed to creep through the canopy of the forest—she thought it was a mistake. Yet another one she'd made where he was concerned. In the last few hours she'd steeled her resolve to not let him get to her, on any level. And yet, now that he was beside her, warning bells were going off in her head. Her body—that traitorous shell—was responding in its own way. The way it always had where this man was concerned.

"It would be better if we weren't in this situation."

How did he do that? How did simple words spoken from him cut her so deep?

"I've said this before and I'll say it again." She paused and took a deep breath. "And I'll try to say it with as much civility as possible. I didn't ask you to come."

"You didn't have to. As soon as I heard you were missing, there was no other option for me." He spoke quietly, as if the words were meant only for her.

No. That's not the type of man he was.

"Then I thank you," she said reluctantly. It was the right thing to do. Besides, she couldn't blame Nick for being who and what he was. It was mostly her fault for fantasizing where there were no possibilities.

"When we get back to the Gungi, I want you to stay with me."

It was her turn to stop walking. "What?"

"I want you to stay with me. That way I'll know you're all right."

He looked at her as if his words should have been self-explanatory, as if she should fall into his arms or onto her knees and kiss his feet with gratitude.

Her insides churned with irritation. "I'll be all right in my own home. I'm the one who lives here."

Nick shifted the backpack that Lucas had been carrying earlier on his back. Ary had seen him take the bag from the young shifter, hefting it onto his back as if it weighed no more than a feather. Lucas's small frame had been hunched over while he carried supplies for the little group.

"I'll feel better if you're with me."

"I won't." Which wasn't a lie. Already, the thought of being in close proximity with Nick longer than it would take to get them back to the Gungi was causing her heart to pound.

"Why are you being so difficult?" he asked, his voice rising.

"Not doing what you want makes me difficult?" she fired back.

"I came here to help. You're acting like I was the one who kidnapped and betrayed you."

"No, Nick. You're the one who left me."

They were the hardest words that had ever escaped her lips. Her throat felt dry and tears threatened to spring from her eyes. With fingers clenched into fists, Ary walked away before she could say or do anything else she'd regret.

Chapter 10

The walls shook with the vibrations from his roaring. Rome and X shared a knowing glance and walked inside the dwelling owned by Nick's parents anyway. Nick hadn't come to the *santa casa* where they'd gathered for dinner and the discussion of what would happen to the Serinos. Neither had the Serinos, for that matter.

It wasn't that Rome and X didn't have an idea of what was going on with Nick, but there seemed to be something else that he wasn't telling them. And while Rome was all for giving his friend the space and time to share what was going on in his personal life, if there were something that could add to the situation they were presently going through, he wanted to know now.

"You tryin' to redecorate?" X asked as they walked to the back of the dwelling, where wicker furniture was tossed to the side and there were scratches on the mud-packed walls.

Nick turned, not in the least surprised to see them.

"I'm trying not to go out and kill somebody. Per your orders," he said, nodding in Rome's direction.

Rome picked up a chair, turned it right-side up, and sat down. X opted to stand, folding his arms across his massive chest and glaring at Nick. He looked calm enough;

Rome had to assume he'd made this mess prior to finding Ary.

"You didn't come to the *santa casa*," Rome said.

"Didn't want to" was Nick's nonchalant reply.

Rome continued, "The Elders are trying to figure out what to do about Davi."

"Kill the bastard and burn his remains. How's that sound?"

X chuckled. "I actually agree with that."

Rome shook his head. "No. We won't kill one of our own. I've given them some ideas that will hold Davi accountable and warn against any other types of treason against the tribe."

"Always the diplomat," Nick retorted.

"If you have something to say, Nick, just say it." This wasn't the Nick he knew; it wasn't the Nick he'd grown up with, worked with. There was definitely something else eating at his friend.

"I said what I had to say. Kill Davi. Find Sabar and kill his sorry ass."

Rome nodded, holding back his own discontent around the situation. "Then what? Who do you want to kill next? And are you going to be in a better mood once they're all dead?"

"Damn right," Nick replied, running a hand down his face.

He understood Rome's concern. His longtime friend probably thought he was overreacting when he should be in some sort of celebratory mood. Sure, Nick was relieved that Ary was safe—more than relieved if he was totally honest with himself. There was no way to describe how holding her in his arms and running out of that burning house made him feel. She was still a very strong part of him. That wasn't going to change.

But without Sabar's head on a platter, he was still a danger to Ary. In Nick's mind, that meant he still had a right to be more than cautious.

"What do you want me to say, Rome? He sold his only child out for what? For some extra cash in his pocket? Davi's always been sneaky and conniving. That's why he wasn't here when we arrived. He knew where she was all along. He's always kept secrets, always tried to control the situation."

"Is that why you left all those years ago and never came back? Because Davi was trying to control the situation?" Rome felt they now might finally be getting to the root of the problem. He watched Nick carefully.

Nick grew quiet, turning away from Rome. It wasn't what he wanted to talk about, even though he'd been unable to think of anything else. Especially not since Ary had reminded him yet again of that night so long ago. Nick knew coming back to the forest was going to trigger memories. He knew seeing her again wouldn't be easy. And he'd touched her, tasted her. No, this wasn't fucking easy for him. It was probably the hardest thing he'd ever had to do—besides the night he'd walked away from her.

"Davi and my father thought it was best that I go and not come back. They thought—" Nick stopped, took a deep breath.

Just how much did he want to tell them? Everything, he decided. He'd held it in for too long. Whatever had gone down that night, what Nick had seen in the forest, all of it circled back to Davi Serino. And that was no coincidence.

"After we moved away from the forest, my parents were obsessed with creating a better life for the shifters. Caprise was about to experience her *acordado*. My father took advantage of that and planned a return trip for all of us, said it would be good for Caprise to see where she'd come from since she'd been born in the States. I just thought of it as a vacation.

"Long story short, I met Ary. We hit it off. The next day her father got all territorial and demanded an apology from my parents because I'd deflowered his daughter and *curanderos* weren't supposed to mate with regular shifters. It was such bullshit," Nick said through gritted teeth. The thought of that conversation years ago still rubbed him the wrong way.

"They're the true slaves to the tribe," X said with disgust. "We need new laws around here."

Rome nodded. "That's what we're working on."

"But that's just in the States. I'm talking about in the forest, too. Why should she have to stay in that house with a father who dictates to her then serves her on a platter to the highest bidder?"

X had a point, and Nick was glad somebody else was talking about drastic change instead of him.

"So Davi wanted you gone because you slept with Ary?" Rome asked.

Nick shook his head. "I don't think that was the only reason."

"What else?"

"Before the showdown with Davi, my parents and I went for a run. I picked up the scent of Rogues and followed it."

"Always the hunter," X said with a nod of approval to Nick.

"When I found them, it looked like strangers, not shifters. They were making some sort of exchange. There were crates marked with black symbols—like a shield of some sort—and they loaded them into a jeep. My guess is they were paying with cash in those brown bags. Later, when I asked my father about it, he told me I'd caused enough trouble and that I should forget what I'd seen."

Rome shrugged. "I guess you did, since this is the first time I've heard this story."

"I don't like talking about the past." Which was true: Nick's philosophy had always been to live for the moment, to do what could be done in the here and now. The past was already done.

"What was that, sixteen years ago? Right about the time Sabar was kidnapped by Boden. So what was with that little transaction?" Rome asked, rubbing a hand over his goatee as he contemplated the new information.

X had begun pacing, something he did a lot when he was in deep thought. "We know Sabar's dealing drugs now, since that's what he wanted Ary to help him with. Boden had already left the forest, but he probably got started with drugs here and carried it over to the States. He would have taught Sabar everything he knew, which isn't good. Question now is, how long was Serino helping Sabar, and was there anyone else involved?"

"I think Davi and my father knew," Nick answered, recalling that night now with more clarity since he had no other choice. "When I told my father he seemed really nervous, wanted to know everything I'd seen and if I'd recognized anyone. The Serinos came in on the tail end of the conversation but could have easily heard what we were talking about."

"I don't see your father as a drug dealer," Rome said.

Nick shrugged. "You know our parents weren't what we originally thought they were. Dad had secrets even from the Assembly."

Rome had discovered his father, Loren Reynolds, had also broken one of the *Ètica* rules—he'd told a human about the shadows. So far it looked like the human Loren decided to confide in was Julio Cortez, previous head of the Cortez Cartel. The current leader of the cartel was Julio's son, Raul. How convenient would it have been if Boden thought Loren and Nick's dad were working against an opposing drug cartel and decided to retaliate on all the shifters? But Boden hadn't been heard from or seen in a few years. Sabar was the new Rogue leader as far as they knew.

"If Serino was involved in giving away the tribe's supplies even back then, and he thought you'd seen something you weren't supposed to, that would be a big reason for him to want you gone," X said.

"The fact that you'd slept with his daughter was like icing on the cake," Rome offered.

"And I did exactly what they wanted me to do. I left and never looked back." Nick cursed, feeling as used and betrayed as he supposed Ary had.

A heavy hand clapped onto his shoulder, but Nick didn't turn around.

"You did what you thought was best at the time. Don't beat yourself up about it."

"I hurt her," he admitted on a whisper.

"That's something you need to fix," Rome said. "Especially since she's obviously your *companheiro*."

"I am glad you are well," Sheena Serino told her daughter in her hushed tone.

Ary didn't turn to her mother's voice. She was sitting on the edge of her bed, looking out the window. This was where she'd been since her return. Elisa, one of the female shifters, had come to tell them of the Elders and their meeting with the stateside shifters about the kidnapping. Her father had cursed and refused to go. Ary just didn't want to be bothered.

Really, she didn't want to see Nick again.

"We will go back to our lives now," Sheena continued. "Father thinks we should have a bigger medical center and maybe closer to the border so we can receive shipments with more ease. We may have to get some of the other females to help us find a location and get started with the building."

"I'm not a builder," Ary snapped.

Behind her Sheena moved about, most likely picking up the things that had fallen onto the floor when Ary had swiped a hand over her desk. The moment she'd returned it had been her first act of rage—on the only thing she could lash out against, unfortunately.

"We do what we must, Aryiola."

That mildly spoken statement had Ary whipping around. "No we do not! We do what he says. And I'm sick of it!"

Sheena looked startled. "Do not raise your voice."

"Why? Because he's sleeping?" Ary had raised her voice even louder as she stood. "Because he does not want to be bothered right now?"

"Father has been very worried. He has been troubled in these last days."

"That's because he's been lying and stealing! Did he tell you that, Mother? Did he tell you that he's been taking the money that the stateside shifters sent to us and some of the supplies?"

Sheena smoothed down her long, thinning hair and resumed picking up the ink pads and sheets of paper from the floor. "I do not ask questions. You should not speak of such things. You are but a *curandero*."

"I am a person, Mother! Just like you. We don't have to live like this," she said.

Her mother paused. Kneeling on the floor, she looked

up at Ary. "What way do you wish to live? This is our life."

Ary shook her head adamantly. "It's *your* life. I want more."

Now Sheena shook her head so hard her hair fell around her frail shoulders. "You do not."

"I do."

Sheena's entire body was shaking as she stood, dropping the paper onto Ary's desk. "I will not speak of it."

"You never do," Ary replied. "But that doesn't change how I feel. It doesn't change what I want."

"You should want to be a *curandero,* to help your tribe." She was wringing her hands now, looking down nervously.

Ary felt sick to her stomach. This is how she would forever remember her mother: head bowed, soft-spoken, no will.

"I want to heal and help all people, not just shifters. And you should support that," she told her honestly. That's what parents were supposed to do, right?

"You will stay here where you belong."

Her gaze shifted to Davi, who stood in the doorway, warm candlelight bathing the background behind him as if he were the devil coming from the fiery pit of hell. There was so much she wanted to say to him, and then there was nothing. Words just could not explain how she felt about this man that called himself her father.

"I will not stay here and continue to help that animal," she told him defiantly.

He stepped fully into the room. "You will do as I say."

"She will stay here. She will be a *curandero* just like us," Sheena said, stepping between Ary and Davi.

"No. I will not!"

Davi reached for her but Sheena blocked him. "She is tired and does not know what she says."

"She is a grown woman and will speak when she is spoken to. You don't have to protect me from him," Ary told her mother.

Davi shook his head. "You have no idea what you say. He will get what he wants without us, and we will be dead."

Ary didn't care. She simply did not care what Davi said. There was no way she would stay here and willingly work for Sabar. Of course, she had no real idea where she would go. She had no money of her own, so traveling to the States was out of the question. The humans had a village outside the forest; maybe she could work there.

There was no time to really think that through, however, because Davi grabbed Sheena by the shoulders and tossed her to the side.

"You will not endanger us! You will do as I say!"

He yelled as he reached for Ary, but she stepped to the side out of his way. "Do not run from me!"

As her father yelled once more, Ary stopped in her tracks. She was not her mother and she was not going to run from him. Standing still, she squared her shoulders and looked right into Davi's almost black eyes.

"You cannot control me," she told him.

"Then I will put an end to you."

Ary thought she saw tears sheen his eyes as he said those words, but anger pushed past that thought and she lunged for him. Pushing him back, she began swinging, her flattened palms landing against his face and chest. Because he was substantially taller than her, with a much more powerful body, he only had to slap her once and Ary stumbled backward. There was something in one of his hands as he approached her, but Ary didn't have the chance to see what it was.

In a blur of motion there was yelling and crashing as

her desk was broken; the contents her mother had just picked up from the floor scattered once more. Sheena began to scream and cry, a gut-wrenching sound that hurt Ary's ears. But her eyes were focused on the two men slamming against the wall in her room.

Nick was there with his hands wrapped around Davi's neck.

"You sonofabitch. I warned you never to put your hands on her again!" Nick yelled in his face.

"She is my child. You are an outsider," Davi said in chokes and gasps.

"Let him go," Ary screamed when it looked like Nick was going to kill Davi right this minute.

"Get your stuff, Aryiola. We're leaving," Nick told her, still holding on to Davi.

"I mean it, Nick. Let him go!" she repeated.

"Get your stuff so we can leave!"

Two men telling her what to do. Two men yelling at her as if she had no brain of her own. Ary was so tired of this nonsense.

"Fine! Kill each other. See if I care."

She left the room and the entire bunch of crazies behind her—but as she approached the front door of their home she was rendered speechless.

Through the door came the shifter named Franco—the one who had been with Sabar. Ary gasped and took a step back. Franco looked crazed. His cat's eyes were an eerie orange tint and glazed as if a layer of glass was covering them. He walked with a staggered gait and couldn't seem to talk as his mouth opened and closed and repeated the action.

"Kill . . ." was the word that finally escaped his throat. Ary knew what she needed to do next. She ran.

But he caught her, moving surprisingly fast given how bad he actually looked.

"Kill . . . ," he said again.

He'd grabbed her by her legs and they both tumbled to the floor. Ary kicked and kicked, her feet landing in his face, on his shoulders, on the back of his head. She scrambled away from him then tossed a chair in his direction. He stood just in time and caught the chair with one hand, breaking it with the other. He lifted the table and did the same, his strength seemingly endless.

He was coming for her again when gunshots echoed around her. Ary covered her head and ducked, not knowing where the shots were coming from. Through half-closed eyes she watched as bullets riddled Franco's body. He jerked and jolted but did not fall. He looked like someone was doing target practice with his body as the shots simply kept coming. Finally they stopped, and the bullet-riddled shifter's body fell face-first to the floor.

Cats came through the front door and from the bedroom until there were at least seven shifters fighting in the living area of what Ary knew as her home.

"Come on, we have to get out of here," she heard a female voice say as she stared mutely at the scene before her.

It took another shake of her arm and someone screaming her name to snap Ary out of her shock. It was Kalina.

"Let's go. Rome wants us out of here now!"

With a nod Ary followed behind Kalina. They both hunched down and made their way to the back of the house where they fell through the door, crawling on the wet ground until they were covered by a small thatch of bushes.

"We have to go back and help them," Ary said.

"No!" Kalina grabbed her by the arm. "Rome said to

stay here and wait for them. They'll take care of it, then we're leaving."

"What? No. That's my home. My mother's in there. I'm going."

Ary tried to make a run for it, but Kalina pushed her down by the shoulders and held her to the ground.

"Your parents are in cahoots with Sabar. That rogue that walked through the front door was one of Sabar's men. He and four others were sent to the Gungi to deliver the message that Sabar has left the forest but will return to kill all shifters who do not follow his orders. You were first on the list. That's why Nick came looking for you."

Judging by the edgy look in Kalina's golden cat eyes, Ary knew she was speaking the truth. "No" was all she finally managed to whisper. "My mother."

"I'm sorry. It's too late for her," Kalina said in a softer voice. She moved off Ary, let her get to a sitting position, and shook her head. "Your mother knew what they were doing, Ary. She knew all along."

Tears freely fell from Ary's eyes, without her consent. She hated crying as much as she hated weakness. But at this moment she didn't know how to conquer either. It was all so overwhelming. Everything that had happened in the last few days was more than she'd ever imagined, more than any one shifter should have to endure.

Her chest felt constricted but the sobs broke free, and when she was cradled Ary let herself go. She welcomed the comfort from someone who seemed to understand. Because in the distance, that house she'd grown up in and learned how to be a *curandero* in was being destroyed. Everything that her life had been was gone.

Chapter 11

The bed was comfortable. As Ary lay her head down, that was all she'd allow herself to think about.

She was in Nick's house, where he'd wanted her all along. But she'd had no other choice. The Elders would take her in, but then Nick would sleep on the floor right outside her door. He'd sworn to do just that. Ary was tired of all the attention and didn't want to upset the tribe or the Gungi any more than she already had.

So she'd agreed to come here.

Her parents were dead. Both of them killed by the Rogue shifters who came for them. It was what Sabar had threatened. Only she still lived. Rome, X, and Nick had made sure no other Rogue had that privilege. Maybe Sabar would never know she was still alive.

She shook her head, trying to clear the thoughts and memories from her mind. It wasn't working.

"I made you some tea."

Ary didn't turn over, didn't even move as she heard Nick's voice and listened as his footsteps came closer to the bed.

On the small table beside the bed he set a mug with rising steam and looked down on her. She'd pulled down the netting since a good portion of one wall in this room was a window with adjustable flaps to either keep out the elements or let them in. The majority of the time the Gungi was hot and sticky. Tonight was no different, so the flap was opened wide.

In came the night sounds and a breeze cooled only by the light drizzle now falling. The constant pitter-pat sound was lulling, but unfortunately not enough. And now that he was close by, she knew sleep would take even longer to come.

"Thank you," she whispered finally.

He squatted so that his face was level with hers. She wanted to turn over, to close her eyes. Anything not to look at him. Why? Because he was so handsome it was painful. Because his eyes pierced deep into her heart and he could surely see how helplessly in love with him she still was.

Nick cleared his throat. "I'm sorry," he said.

Then his brow furrowed and he had that frustrated look about him. A second later he pushed the netting back so fast and hard it almost ripped.

"What are you apologizing for?" Ary asked when her heart threatened to hammer right out of her chest.

He was close enough she could reach out a hand to touch his cheek, to trace the hard indentation that lined his lips. She could kiss him, if she thought that's what he wanted. As it was, she kept her hands lodged beneath the pillow that cradled her head.

"For leaving you. I should have stayed."

And she shouldn't be so touched by the apology. But she was. "Maybe I should have followed you," she said, feeling emboldened by his admission.

Nick shook his head. "I could have handled things differently. I should have."

Because I'm the man. He didn't say that, but the words sort of lingered between them.

"So what now?" she asked with a sigh. She was too tired to do anything more.

"You come back to the States with me in the morning," he said simply.

So simply and so matter-of-factly, fatigue was quickly forgotten. His bossiness was getting on her nerves. "My plans are to head to the human village and find work there."

"Work? What type of work? You don't even know any of them."

"I know they're on the brink of a forest filled with animals and disease they could never really understand. I know that some of those missionaries head out with good intentions and come back dead or fatally ill. I know that I can help them."

"The same way you were intent on helping the Topè-tenia," he said flatly.

"It's my job," she defended. "You know what, Delgado, I don't have to explain anything to you. I don't care if you understand what I want to do with my life or the type of person I am. That's your problem, not mine."

Now he was defensive, staring at her as if she'd had the audacity to strike him. "I don't have a problem."

"Oh, that's right, you are perfect. Raised in the big city, with money and cars and luxury. I'm just the poor little forest cat with no family and nowhere to go." By then she'd sat up in the center of the bed, her arms at her sides, fists bunched and resting on the mattress.

"I didn't say that!"

"You didn't have to. I know what you think of me. I know how you feel about me."

She was flipping her legs off the other side of the bed, getting tangled in the netting on that side, when he reached for her. He had a habit of doing that, grabbing her around her waist and pulling her to him like she was some frail object. An object that belonged to him.

Ary shook her head and struggled to break free of his hold. "Let me go, you idiot!"

"You don't know me, Aryiola! You have no idea about the man I've become."

He held tight to her as he now sat on the bed, her back pulled up against his front. She felt him breathing, the up-and-down movement of his chest, and the thumping of his heart. He held her tightly, his lips right next to her ear as he talked. The warmth of his breath sent warm waves washing down her spine.

"I don't care," she yelled defiantly. "I didn't ask you to come here and I don't want you here! You can just go back to your big house and big money and . . ."

"And what, Aryiola?" he still whispered into her ear, his arms loosening only slightly around her. "What else do you think I have in the States? Tell me, what type of life you think I've led since I left you?"

Ary closed her eyes, hating the sound of his voice, the feeling of complete safety in his arms, and just about everything about Nick Delgado. Except she reluctantly accepted that he was right. She knew about as much about him as he did about her.

"I don't know what type of life you've had. I tried not to think about it," she answered honestly.

One of his arms shifted until his fingers traced lazy circles over her cheek. "Last night I saw the bruise from when you were with Sabar. Tonight I watched your father strike you. Whether I had stayed in the Gungi all those years ago or not, I'd still be ready to kill for you."

Ary didn't know what to say to that, didn't know if a response was even required. And Nick didn't give her a chance to decide, either.

"Lie down and sleep tonight. We'll deal with the rest tomorrow."

When she didn't move on her own, he pulled back slightly, straightening his body on the bed then pulling her down with him. His long strong arms enfolded her, keeping her close. Ary wanted to pull away, but a bigger part of her wanted to stay right there. His breathing was slow and steady and after a while matched her own.

As sleep finally reached for her, Ary had a fleeting thought. What if there were a future for her and Nick? What if she did go to the States with him? What if . . . what if she never got over loving a man who couldn't love her in return?

"This is unheard of. A *curandero* cannot leave the Gungi," Elder Marras said in an even tone. Only the rise of his thick, bushy eyebrows gave away the fact that he was angry.

"I'm not asking for permission," Nick said, stepping forward so that Ary was partially behind him.

Rome and Kalina stood a short distance to his right. X, with his legs slightly parted, arms folded over his chest, stood to Nick's left with a dour look aimed at the six Elders who sat in a straight row before them.

They stood in the center of the *santa casa*. Sheer white material hung from the ceiling to the floor, covering all four walls around them. A long table sat to one side with stools for each presiding Elder on one side, pots full of lit candles on the other.

The walls of the *santa casa* were a muddy brown, thick and resilient against the elements of the rain forest. The entire dwelling was meant to serve as a pillar of strength in this village, the one place all Topétenia could come and be heard. Today it felt like a sentencing.

"It is not your place to demand such a thing," Elder

Ragata, the tallest and slimmest of the Elders, said. "We have laws here in the Gungi that you may not be familiar with."

Nick was about to speak, but Rome put up a hand to stop him. Nick's lips clapped shut. There was so much he wanted to say to the Elders. They were such hypocrites, spouting unification in one breath then keeping the shadows under a code of ethics that totally segregated them.

"We know of the laws of Ètica and we respect them," Rome began. "Up to a certain point."

None of the elders looked happy. Only Elder Alamar, who had just been in the States at a meeting with Rome and his Faction, looked as if he might understand their plight.

"Aryiola has dedicated her life to the Topètenia. She has given everything she has to this tribe. In return, her father betrayed her—and the tribe, for that matter. She has been kidnapped, her parents killed, and she is now virtually homeless."

"Her home is here," Elder Marras interrupted.

Rome stood tall, his voice just as firm and authoritative as the Elders. "Her home should be where she chooses. She is an adult Shadow Shifter, not a slave to your whims."

Elder Marras jumped from his seated position, his long white robe unfolding like a cloud around him. "You will not speak to us this way! You may lead in the States, but here it is we who decide."

Alamar stood slowly, his warrior's body still in shape. Intelligent but weary eyes looked to Marras and the other Elders. Then Alamar stepped out of their line, moving to stand near Rome.

"As we have given the Faction Leaders leave to create a government for our kind in the States, we should also open our minds to changes within our ancient laws here.

The Gungi is not what it once was. Violence has marred our serenity lately, and we must put a stop to it before it is too late. The environment and the humans surrounding us are ever changing as well. We must be willing to embrace new ideas and suggestions."

A part of Nick exhaled at the Elder's support. The bigger part of him didn't give a damn what any of these old geezers thought. It was their stupid-ass rules that made it a problem for him to be involved with Ary in the first place. If they thought for a second he was going to walk away from her again because of some bogus laws, they were all smoking some of whatever Sabar was trying to sell.

Ary spoke up: "I won't stay here another day." She moved from behind Nick and stood with her shoulders squared, her voice strong. "No matter what you say, I will not stay in the Gungi."

The sound of her voice had become as familiar to Nick as his own. Sleeping with her wrapped in his arms last night had given his already possessive streak where she was concerned an even bigger boost. His need for her was mighty, her scent reaching out to him, scraping along his nerves each second they were near, and most of the ones they weren't. If he could, he'd stay buried inside her for hours and hours. But he needed to go home, to get back to his life and his business there. And she needed to go, too. Ary needed to be with him in case Sabar decided to come for her again.

"The tribe will have no *curandero* if she leaves," Marras said, still frowning. "What will happen then?"

"There are other *curanderos* in the tribe. They can take over. If she does not want to help here, maybe she can elsewhere," Alamar said, turning to Ary. "You are a great talent and will be missed. I understand your desire to go. And even though you will no longer be in the forest, you are still bound by our laws. The laws of the Shadow Shifters."

Ary nodded. "And I will honor those laws. Except for the one that would hold me here."

Alamar shook his head. "That rule will be changed. It is not our goal to hold our people captive, but to promote growth and loyalty."

"I agree," Rome added. "Loyalty and prosperity need to be the foundation for the Shadow Shifters worldwide. We will all work together to see that our new direction is fully embraced."

Nick reached for Ary's hand, but she pulled away.

"I'm returning to the healing center to get my things," she said softly.

"I'll help you," Kalina volunteered.

Nick took a step toward Ary but was held back by X. "Let her go. Kalina will be with her. She'll be fine. There's something I need to show you and Rome."

Squelching his discontent, Nick followed as X and Rome left the *santa casa,* moving toward the far corner of the *amizade.* Alamar also followed the threesome.

"Sebastian sent me an email last night," X said, pulling out his iPhone. "It was long and very informative."

Rome slipped his hands into his pockets. "What'd he have to say?"

"One of his guards witnessed a boat coming in the night before last. He reported crates with black symbols on the outside being unloaded from the boat and put into two Hummers. They broke off, so the guard could only follow one of the vehicles. He followed it all the way to Albuquerque to a gated property there. The guard snapped a picture of the symbols." X had been pushing buttons on his phone while he talked. Now he turned the phone to face Nick and waited. "Look familiar?"

Nick looked at the screen and cursed. "Shit, it's the same symbol I saw on those crates leaving here all those years ago." The same shield, but closer up he could see it had four smaller shields inside.

This time Rome cursed, too, which got the attention of all three shifters since he normally held his emotions in solid check.

"Sabar needs capital. There are rumors that he is no longer Boden's liege. Yet he craves the power his former captor had. He needs to establish himself in our world and in the human world," Alamar said.

Boden had been a sadistic killing machine, ravishing and killing female shifters and humans without remorse. He'd been the first to go rogue from the tribes, taking Sabar with him.

"So he's selling drugs to get money. Using the money to set up safe houses across the country and recruiting new Rogues," X went on.

Rome sighed. "All of this is the calm before the storm. Whatever he has planned for the shifters is going to be big. We have to be ready for it when he comes."

"Or we can diffuse the problem now."

Everyone looked to Nick, not with surprise on their faces, because really, what did they expect him to say. "Stop him now before he has the chance to kill anyone else. He killed those prostitutes back in DC just like I believe he killed that senator and his daughter. Hell, his Rogues were probably responsible for the deaths you saw here in the forest. He's making his moves right in front of us. And we're not doing anything but talking."

Rome shook his head, still not convinced. "We don't know that for sure. I agree he might be responsible for some of what's going on, but not everything."

Nick frowned. "The cops don't know for sure, Rome.

But we do. We know exactly what Sabar is capable of. And if he's been in the forest messing with poisonous herbs and wanting Ary to help him break them down into a drug, then he's about to launch an all-out attack against the humans. Either way, he's a threat that needs to be neutralized. And the sooner, the better."

To everyone's shock, Alamar nodded in agreement. "He is right."

X switched his phone off. "I'm going to set up a meeting with Bas. I'll probably have to fly out there to see what's really going down. But if he's shipping his stash through New Mexico, he's gonna need runners to bring it to him in DC."

"You think he's headquartered there?" Nick asked.

X nodded. "Almost positive. There's something in DC that he's connected to or he wouldn't have been there before tracking Kalina and Rome. He could have focused on any Faction Leader, but he picked you and our city. I'll bet everything I own he's there right now."

"You're probably right," Rome agreed. "We need to get back to the States and inform all the FLs of what's going on so they'll be on the lookout. Then we'll get a smaller group together to focus on tracking Sabar."

"We should track the drug he's selling as well. Get a lock on that symbol and trace it wherever it's seen throughout the country," X said.

"True," Nick agreed. "Ary refuses to help him enhance his drug but that's not going to stop him."

"It's going to make him more desperate to find her," Rome added solemnly.

"So he's going to come for her," Nick said. "And when he does, I'll be waiting for the sonofabitch."

Chapter 12

Washington, DC

Regrouping. It seemed like he was always regrouping. Sabar was more than a little tired of this and swore the next time he came face-to-face with those shifters—the East Coast Faction Leader and his crew—he was killing every one of them. Whether it was by using the heat he was now packing or by shifting and ripping their fucking throats out, he was going to be rid of them once and for all.

He'd wanted to do that in the Gungi, but when they surprised him at the dope house he'd been unprepared. It was four of them against his one—Franco wasn't one of his trained Rogues, and he would never have been able to kill them. Kalina had also been fighting right beside them, the traitorous bitch. He wanted her to die an especially gruesome death. And he'd hated leaving the *curandero*. She was the sole purpose for him being back in the Gungi. His shipments could come to the States without him overseeing them.

But he swore he wouldn't leave the Faction Leader and his groupies breathing another time. And he'd make sure they wouldn't catch him off guard again.

Walking down the steps of the brownstone he'd had renovated, Sabar let his manicured fingers run over the silky soft wallpaper that lined every room on the first floor. It was blood red with silver swirls and matched the thick cranberry-colored carpet perfectly. Most of the furniture still needed to be delivered, but this was a good start.

Sabar moved through the rooms surveying the progress, noting everything the cocksucking designer—who liked looking at Sabar a whole lot more than looking at females—hadn't done. His name was Freid and Darel had found him, so Sabar had agreed to give the guy a shot. But the first time he made an out-of-line comment about Sabar or his sexuality, the bastard was fired!

Darel had been with Sabar the longest and was his most loyal Rogue. Sabar relied heavily on him, which was big since Sabar didn't trust anyone. That's why he'd left Darel in charge while he'd traveled to the forest. Now Darel was on his way to New Mexico to take possession of the shipment that had been sent. Sabar figured it worked best if he and his product were in different places. That's why he'd also bought that run-down old warehouse near the Virginia border. While he and Darel had sleeping quarters there as well, he didn't want them to be taken down if his drugs were ever traced.

Speaking of which, his cell phone rang. Sabar slid it from the holder at his waist.

"Talk," he commanded, and the voice on the other end obeyed.

"Pickup successful. On my way back now."

That was precisely what Sabar wanted to hear. "Good. What about the females?"

"They're at the warehouse."

See, that's why he'd known he could leave Darel in

charge. The Rogue knew automatically Sabar would not want any dirty-ass strippers in his new house, so he'd left them in the warehouse. Fucking fantastic.

"They'll bring the *curandero* here. But I don't want to wait. Is Hanson ready to get started?"

"He's a bit jittery. Maybe you should talk to him again," Darel said drily. "He's a punk with a big ego and an even bigger mouth. I've got Gabriel sitting on him now."

Gabriel was a new shifter. He'd come to Sabar after escaping Boden's clutches. The sonofabitch that had taken Sabar from the Gungi liked young boys. He just never counted on those young boys eventually growing into strong shape-shifting men.

Sabar nodded, rubbing his fingers through his thick locks. He did that when he was thinking, usually when he was thinking about his money. And Hanson, the chemistry student they'd plucked from Georgetown a couple of weeks ago, might be messing with his profits. The kid thought he was the shit. He thought all his scholarships and the pharmaceutical companies and research labs dogging his heels for him to work for them once he graduated made him a step away from God. Then he'd met Sabar. Funny how, as smart as the kid appeared, he didn't seem to get how huge a mistake he was making if he didn't do what Sabar wanted.

"Yeah, I'll check on him. Make sure he knows the plan and his place in it." Either alongside Sabar as an employee or in a body bag in bits and pieces. "You just get the product here safely and we'll go from there."

"No problem," Darel said.

Disconnecting, Sabar smiled. That's the shit he liked to hear—immediate agreement. Darel was his second for a reason. He wasn't his partner. Sabar would never have any equal on any level. But Darel was a good second Rogue. He'd have to repay the shifter, maybe give him one of the strippers they were using when they finished. That was the least he could do.

Law office of Reynolds & Delgado
Washington, DC

Working was futile.

Nick dropped his pen and let his head fall in his hands. Then he thought about tomorrow's nine AM deposition and figured he'd better move on. He reopened the manila folder he'd previously closed and started reading.

The case was of a female who had been forced to abort her twenty-eight-week-old fetus because of an erroneous amniocentesis that misdiagnosed multiple sclerosis. Nick represented the doctor's firm and felt sick to his stomach each time he read the deposition testimony of the female who had been orphaned at birth herself, then in an abusive marriage, and lastly losing the one thing she'd wanted most in this world—a child—because of a doctor's mistake.

Normally, this was open and shut for Nick. Defend his client's actions and obtain a favorable verdict, or at the very least minimal payment to the plaintiff. But on this morning, with the beautiful woman lying in a bed in the guest room of his apartment, he couldn't focus.

They'd arrived at the shifters' private airstrip just outside DC close to three o'clock this morning. Eli and Ezra, the top guards for the East Coast Faction, were there with vehicles to pick them up. Rome and Kalina were driven to their house by Eli. Nick had instantly ushered Ary to Ezra's SUV, with X climbing in with them as well since his condo wasn't that far from Nick's in the city.

"I will get my own residence soon," Ary remarked as she settled in the backseat.

Nick had been either too tired to argue, or too distracted. Probably a little of both. But he'd remained quiet for the duration of the ride home.

When they'd arrived at his place, Ary had taken her duffel bag and entered the guest room without speaking another word to him. Waking only hours later to come into the office, Nick decided it was better not to disturb her.

In actuality, he was keeping his distance. Every time he was around her, he either said or did the wrong thing. Or what she considered the wrong thing. And damn if he knew what the right thing was. He'd saved her life. She should be a little more grateful instead of so spiteful. And he'd admitted to the part he'd had in whatever pain she'd harbored in her life. Wasn't that enough?

On his now cluttered desk Nick's phone buzzed.

"Yes?" he answered with about as much irritation as he was feeling. Or possibly more.

"Mr. Scher's office called to cancel tomorrow morning's deposition. They'll be sending more dates shortly."

Nick sighed. That meant he didn't have to sit here and review all the medical records in this case right at this very moment. "Fine, Kerry. Thank you."

"Ah, and there's someone here to see you, sir," his assistant added just as Nick was about to push the button that would disconnect their call.

"I didn't have anything scheduled" was his reply.

He never had anyone come in the day before a deposition unless it was the client; there was no need for him to talk to the doctor who was facing multiple medical malpractice charges about this specific case. Nick knew all he needed to know and was just trying to figure out how he was going to defend the idiot.

"It's, um"—Kerry cleared her throat and continued in a whisper. "She says she's your sister, sir."

Nick frowned. He only had one sister and she'd been gone for about five years now, traipsing along the globe—doing what, Nick had no idea.

"Send her in," he said wondering if it wasn't Ary visiting and afraid to use her real identity.

Of course that made no sense to him. Still, Nick stood from his chair and adjusted his tie. He was walking around his desk when the door to his corner office opened. In that instant it seemed as if all the air had been sucked out of the room.

Another blast from the not-so-distant past hit him and Nick had to catch his breath. Her hair was straight and dark as sin, hanging down her back in layered sheets. Even her eyes were dark, or smoky he figured would be a better description of the long lashes and thick arched eyebrows. She was his sister, so looking at her body was weird, but he'd be blind if he didn't recognize how she'd matured since the last time he'd seen her. Dressed in a short black skirt, netted stockings, and a white shirt that looked as if breathing wasn't a priority for her, she came closer and put her hands on her hips.

"Dominick." She spoke his name with just a hint of an accent, and Nick couldn't figure out where she would have picked it up. Her lips twisted into a smile and her eyes lit up as he opened his arms to her.

"It's about damn time," he said, wrapping his arms around her and holding tightly. "Damn, Caprise, it's been a really long time."

She hugged him back, laughing as he swayed her from side to side the way he remembered their father used to do when she was younger.

"You're choking me," she said, smiling.

Nick released his hold only slightly. "You've been killing me staying away all this time. Where the hell have you been?"

She pulled out of his arms and waved a hand at him dismissively. "Doesn't matter. I'm back now."

"So I see. What are you doing? You working? Going to school?"

Caprise was four years younger than Nick; she'd just celebrated her thirty-first birthday a month ago. Nick grimaced at the fact that she may have been alone on that special day.

Dropping her lithe body into one of his guest chairs, she crossed her legs and let her arms fall in her lap. Bangles dangled at her wrists, and he noted a large sterling silver ring in some weird shape that encompassed almost three of her fingers.

"I'm looking for a place to stay. And no, not with you. There are a few apartment buildings I'm going to check out this afternoon. So I figured now was better than any other time to stop by."

He partially agreed with what she'd just said. "Now *is* a good time since I just got back in town earlier this morning."

"Really? Where were you this time? In Hawaii with the flavor of the month? Or was it Turks and Caicos? You still love it down there?"

Nick smiled and went back to sit in his chair. "You know it. The best tropical getaway ever. But that's not where I was. I went to the Gungi."

Nick knew the minute he said it that she'd grow quiet, possibly irritated. He was surprised to see her shrug.

"So we should get together for dinner or something. I don't really know what siblings do anymore."

"You don't know what siblings like us do anymore," Nick corrected her and was rewarded with her frown.

"Don't start, Nick. I'm trying to make some progress here. To move forward with my life."

"I'm still trying to figure out what caused the progress to stop five years ago. You just left and you never called or tried to contact me."

"You didn't try to contact me, either," she rebutted as if she were the litigator.

Nick drummed his fingers on his desk. "You can thank Rome for that. I wanted to tear up the nation trying to find you but he suggested I give you some space. I obliged, but I didn't like it."

Caprise smiled, and Nick's heart melted instantly. He couldn't be mad at her, not when he was so damn happy to see her.

"That sounds like something Rome would say. Is he still fine as ever?"

Nick shrugged. "I'm not answering that. But I will tell you he's mated."

"What? Get out! Roman Reynolds settled down with one woman?"

Nick chuckled because it was still a little hard for him to believe. "Kalina's cool. She's a shadow like us."

Again with the blasé look. Caprise had never embraced her heritage, even after her time in the Gungi. And it seemed she wasn't about to start now.

"Hooray," she said with a roll of her eyes. "How's work?"

And that was all his little sister planned to say about being a Shadow Shifter or being in the Gungi. After the trip Nick had just taken, he wasn't so sure he could blame her.

"The firm's doing well. How about you? What are you doing with yourself?" Sitting back in his chair, Nick really looked at his sister.

On the outside she was a lovely young woman, with stunning features that any man would look at twice. On the inside, however, Nick suspected there was something totally different going on. At one time he and Caprise were as close as twins, but that was before her *acrodado* and before the death of their parents.

"I'm trying to get my life together," she said simply and cocked her head as if she didn't expect any further questions.

She should have known better.

"And how do you plan to do that? What have you been doing for these past five years?"

Her head was shaking before he could finish the question.

"I don't want to talk about that. I just want to come home and get myself together. Is that all right with you?"

Nick contemplated his answer. Saying too much, holding too tight, would certainly send her running again. He definitely did not want that. With the same definitiveness he wanted to know where she'd been and what she'd been doing. The litigator in him decided to proceed with caution, giving her just enough space to let her circle for a bit before he clamped down and got the facts he wanted.

"Cool. Where are you going to live?"

She smiled again. "You know, I was wondering why you didn't immediately demand I stay at your place. But now, sitting here, I'm getting the sense—" She stopped and inhaled deeply. "Yeah, I'm getting the sense that you don't have room for me."

Deny being a shifter in one breath, but fall back on her innate feline senses the next. Nick had to smile: She was still the girl he'd known.

"I told you we just returned from the Gungi. Rome, X, and myself. We were there rescuing a *curandero*. We brought her back with us." *We,* he repeated to himself. Not *I* brought Aryiola back with *me.* Strange.

"Big time," she said. "You're rescuing people and all that. Mom and Dad would be proud of how you're interacting with them."

"With the shifters in the Gungi," he corrected. "You know Rome's the East Coast Faction Leader and I'm his commanding officer. We're working for *all* the shifters. Including you."

She shook her head again. "I take care of me."

Nick's cell phone rang, and he peeped at the screen to see who it was. "I have to take this."

"That's fine. I just wanted to stop by and let you know I'm back. I'll get in touch and let you know where I'm staying."

Nick held a finger up to keep her standing there and pressed the button to answer his phone. "Delgado."

"FLs are conferencing tonight at Rome's," X said in his usual gruff voice.

"Cool. I'll be there. Later," Nick replied quickly.

"You okay?" X asked before letting Nick go.

"Yeah. Caprise is back," he said, then hung up because X would most likely have just as many questions about her whereabouts as Nick did. That was something he'd deal with later.

"Who was that?" she asked the moment he dropped the phone on his desk.

"X. Look, I've gotta tell them you're back. They've all been going just as crazy as me worrying about you."

"Just tell them to keep their distance" was her curt reply. "The same way I'm telling you. I'm not a little girl anymore. I can handle myself and my life."

Nick walked around the desk, stopping when he was

only a few steps away from her. "You're still my little sister."

"That," she said, the right edge of her mouth tilting in a slight smile, "is not something I can change. But I'm good, Nick. I'm finally good. So let it stay that way."

She looked sincere, like she really wanted him to believe her words. Problem was, Nick had known her a hell of a long time. And he was no ordinary man who might just fall for those big dark eyes batting at him and those full lips almost pouting. No, he knew much better. Just as he was sure she'd scented the *calor* a shifter carried for his mate, Nick scented her anxiety and the carefully masked fear she didn't want to show.

"No more disappearing or this time I will tear some shit up looking for you," he said.

"I'm here to stay," she said with certainty.

"Then I'll see you soon."

This time when Nick held her, he paid much more attention to how she felt in his arms, how she smelled, what his senses picked up from her. And his heart felt heavy with what he found.

"Take care of yourself," he whispered into her ear.

She nodded, and when she pulled back he was only slightly satisfied to see the sheen of tears in her eyes.

"I will. And you do the same since you're out here playing warrior."

Nick let her walk out of his office without another word, because he wasn't sure if the next thing out of his mouth wouldn't be to ask her to stay with him. He had a large condo with three bedrooms. She could stay.

But Ary was there.

Chapter 13

The sounds were different.

That was one of the first things Ary discovered about being in the United States. Last night when she'd gotten off the plane it had been dark, much like in the Gungi. The air had smelled different, and then there were the sounds. There were no owl monkeys, tamarins, no hissing reptiles or harpy eagles. Sleep didn't come easy and she wasn't sure if that was because she was in Nick's house—his American house—or that she was in America, period.

All her life she'd dreamed of coming here, of becoming a real medical doctor, as they called them. And now she was here, penniless, jobless, and for all intents and purposes homeless. Pitiful was what she really was. No, she didn't like that word. She was making a change, finally taking steps to live the life she wanted. All she needed to help her was a job, money, a place to live. At that she had to chuckle because crying again was not an option.

Getting out of the bed after she'd heard Nick moving around was easy because she knew she wouldn't have to face him again just yet. Ary had no idea what was going on between them. Sure, they'd had sex in the Gungi, but it was the forest and it was hot and she was a shifter and he was a shifter, and cats did what they knew.

Now, here, on his turf, she was uncertain once more. He was a man and she was a woman. What the hell that meant, she had no clue. Except she probably shouldn't be living with him if they weren't involved in some type of relationship. And they probably needed to get that situation defined sooner, rather than later.

Food was actually what she figured she needed on the soonest end of the clock.

With bare feet she padded out of the room, on floors that looked like wood but were entirely too smooth to be the real thing. She kept going until the floor stopped and spiral steps took over. On the lower level the floor was more of the same; to her left was the kitchen. Sparkling silver fixtures greeted her, and she moved in for a closer look. Dragging her hand over a cool marble surface, she pulled an extended handle and grinned at the water that came splashing out into the silver sink.

Ary opened cabinets, saw supplies. She opened the refrigerator and saw even more food. Her stomach grumbled and she took out a pitcher of orange juice. There was a bowl half filled with oranges and she took one of those. Across from the sink and refrigerator was a tall table and stools. She took a seat and began peeling her orange.

A shrill ringing sound scared her so badly she dropped the orange and almost slid off the stool. It was the phone, she told herself when her heart threatened to jump right out of her chest. "Crazy girl," she chastised, walking around trying to find the contraption with the intent of making it stop that exasperating noise.

Bingo!

She found it on a glass table in another room filled with furniture.

"Hello?"

"Hi, Ary!" The voice on the other end was very cheerful, almost too much so. But Ary recognized and appreciated it.

"Hi, Kalina. How are you?" she asked, taking this opportunity to look around the room.

It was bigger with more furniture—their homes in the Gungi had the necessary furnishings like chairs and tables, beds and tables, so this seemed more than luxurious to her—and glass doors that looked outside to where the sun was bright. The phone did not have a cord or anything to keep her still so Ary moved instantly to the light. She wanted to feel the warmth from the sunlight on her skin, not just the humidity that she was used to.

"I'm a little tired from the travel but glad to be home. Hey, I was going to come over so we could go out and have lunch. Probably do some shopping since I know you don't have nearly enough clothes."

Ary looked down at the bra and panties she wore. Nope, she definitely did not have enough clothes.

"Ah, sure. I would love to go out."

The door had some kind of latch on it, and Ary was trying to work it free.

"Great. I'll be there in about an hour to pick you up."

"That is fine," Ary said. "Just fine."

She pushed the OFF button on the phone and dropped it to the floor, much more concerned with getting the damn door open. With a crack that didn't sound good but didn't bother Ary too much, the latch flipped, a small piece falling to the floor. But the door opened, and for that she would be forever grateful.

The air wasn't damp; instead it was warm, like a cloth from the boiling water she used to put on swollen limbs. There was more wood on the floor out here, but it was coarser than inside. A chair that looked more like a bucket had the softest leather covering it.

Ary sat in the chair and crossed her bare legs. For endless seconds she simply sat there, inhaling and exhaling, letting the different scent in and out of her lungs. It was quiet out here, or what seemed like quiet to her in comparison with all the forest sounds she was used to.

There were voices. Turning her head, she could see there were other balconies across from her and below her. All the way down on the ground was a fountain with water rushing over smooth stones. Her chest clenched at the slight memory of home, but then she focused on the people moving about. She had no idea where they were going but figured wherever it was, it was their choice.

That's what Ary wanted above all else, the right to make her own choices and live her own life. She buried her face in her palms and let emotions roll inside. She'd taken a big step, one she was more than ready for, if only she could pull herself together and get out there.

"My neighbors are going to call the cops with reports of indecent exposure."

His voice interrupted her thoughts, sending spikes of desire through her body instantaneously.

"I thought you were gone."

He stood between the glass doors, dressed in a suit and tie. He looked professional and dour and sexy as hell. Why couldn't she stop her body from wanting this man?

"I came back to check on you."

"You shouldn't have. I'm fine."

He nodded, folding his arms over his chest. "That you definitely are."

She didn't like the way he was looking at her. Or rather her body liked it way too much. Ary stood, intending to move back inside the house. Of course Nick didn't move, so she ended up facing him.

"I'm going to ask you not to come out on the balcony or leave the house in only your underwear again."

"Why?" It sounded stupid, but that seemed to be protocol for most of the things she said to Nick.

He frowned, thick eyebrows drawing close together, two lines forming on his forehead.

"I like living here, but I'll kill any bastard that looks at you. Is that clear?"

"That's barbaric. Aren't you supposed to be working with Rome to make the shifters more appealing to humans?"

"No. That's not my job. I'm the enforcer, didn't they tell you? What I'm good at is combat." He stood up straight and took a step toward her. Wrapping his arm around her waist, he pulled her close then turned so that she was inside the house and his back was facing the balcony.

"And other physical endeavors," he finished with a smile that felt like a hand on her breasts.

Ary gulped. "Anybody can have sex."

She knew she shouldn't have said it but damn, he was one cocky shifter. All she wanted was to knock him down a peg or two, put him in his place once and for all.

It simply wasn't meant to be.

Nick had come home on impulse to check on her. The fact that he hadn't spoken to her since last night was gnawing at him. Besides that, he just wanted to see her again. Caprise's arrival had reminded him of how long it'd been since he'd seen the two women he cared most about in this world, and Nick vowed never to waste the time he had with them again. So he'd packed his briefcase with the baby file and told Kerry he'd be working from home.

If somebody had told him he'd walk in to see a just-about-naked woman standing on his balcony, Nick probably would have stopped for some champagne and strawberries. On second thought, he wouldn't have. Romance wasn't his strong point. Women were attracted to him, enough so that all he had to do was talk to them for a few minutes and they'd end up in his bed shortly thereafter. That was the extent of any effort he'd ever had to make for female companionship.

Just looking at Ary in her bra and panties made him want to do more. His body ached for her, his heart slamming wildly against his chest, ripples of the beast within tickling along his skin. She smelled like rain, fresh and damp.

She squirmed in his arms, rubbing her body against him, and Nick grit his teeth.

"Careful, baby. One more move like that and we're going to end up on this floor."

The glow in her eyes meant she didn't like what he'd said. The way her body went pliant in his arms said she liked what he was doing. So he did more, moving his hips so that his thick arousal rubbed against her stomach.

"You think you're irresistible to all females, don't you?" she asked.

"Not at all." Moving his hands down her back, he slipped his fingers beneath the band of her panties. "I know *you* cannot resist me."

Parting the softest cheeks he'd ever had the pleasure of feeling, Nick lowered his head to hers.

"I do not want this," she told him.

The fact that her hands came up to clasp his shoulders meant something totally different. But Nick wasn't a rapist, so he said, "If you don't want it, all you have to do is tell me to stop."

She didn't speak immediately, so his fingers continued to explore. He touched the rim of her rear entrance and felt the prick of his sharp teeth against his lips. His chest heaved now, his breath coming in quick pants.

Her forehead rested on his chest. Nick pulled once, not using all his strength but enough to rip her panties off and toss them across the room. He lifted one of her legs, locking it around his waist. She was shaking her head, her fingers digging into his biceps. Then her small hands slid beneath the lapels of his jacket and pushed it off his shoulders.

Nick didn't want to move his fingers from her, but he did to let his jacket fall to the floor. She tore at his tie, popped the buttons to his shirt, and hissed as her teeth raked over his bared chest.

"There she is," he murmured in a low voice. "My little cat."

"You have on too many clothes," she said.

Quick fingers undid his belt and pants as Nick stepped out of his shoes. They were standing in the middle of his living room, with the balcony window uncovered behind them. But he didn't care. His focus was only on Ary, who was growing wilder with each passing moment.

When he was naked and he'd yanked on the snap of her bra to release the binding, they both stood staring at each other.

With a tilt of her head, she rubbed along his pectorals, down to the sculpted ribbings of his abs. "I've always wanted you," she whispered. "Even when you were gone I used to dream of touching you, lying with you again."

He pushed her hair back and clasped the back of her head, pulling her mouth to his. "You don't have to dream about it anymore. Touch me all you want. Lie with me whenever you want. I'm all yours," he whispered seconds before his lips ravaged hers.

She grabbed on to his wrists, coming up on tiptoe to deepen the kiss. Teeth and tongues scraped and dueled as their kiss quickly turned from passionate to downright lustful. When he had enough of the playing, Nick lifted her into his arms and headed for the couch. He was about to sit when she shifted out of his arms and pushed him so that he fell back on the chair.

Straddling him, her glowing gold eyes stared down at him and she arched her back, a mewling sound escaping her throat.

"Gorgeous," he whispered, rubbing his palms over her heavy breasts, fingering her taut nipples.

"You make me wild," she answered, bringing her head forward, her hair falling around her shoulders and covering her face.

Nick wanted to see her eyes, her lips, every inch of her. So he pushed her hair back, holding it tight in his fist as he kissed her once more. "Wild and wanton, that's what you are, Miss Serino."

"Yeah," she cooed, lifting her hips until her moist center touched the tip of his dick.

"You want it baby, take it," he told her, letting her settle over him and slide down slowly on his length.

A keening ache moved up Nick's spine at the precise time her pussy sucked him in completely. In her hair his fingers began to shake. And when her fingers splayed over his chest, he sucked in a breath. She began moving, lifting her hips then dropping them down, pulling up off his length then settling down to take it all inside again.

It was the kind of pleasure that made a man's vision blurry, his tongue too thick to speak. All Nick could do was sit back and enjoy as she rode him as if it was what she'd been born to do. Her movements were wild and stemmed from her own pleasure and arousal. He could see it in the deep flush over her skin. When her release was near her bright eyes fastened on his, sharp teeth bared. He bared his own teeth in response and felt their cats reaching out in this time of ecstasy.

She screamed his name and fell forward, her teeth sinking into the bare skin of his shoulder. Nick held her hips still, pumping into her feverishly as her release rippled through her body. When he thought she'd caught her breath he flipped her over, staring down at her perfect ass until his mouth watered.

Falling to his knees, Nick kissed each rounded globe of her buttocks, loving the feel of the soft, warm flesh against his tongue.

Even through her climax-hazed mind Ary knew what he wanted, what he possibly needed. She couldn't explain their attraction and didn't want to fight it. He was her *companheiro,* she knew that without a doubt, had known years ago. The fact that she was here with him right now was fate. What would happen tomorrow, she had no clue. All she could do was bask in the here and now.

So she climbed up onto the couch, planting her knees firmly on the pillows and spreading her legs wide. With her palms on the back of the couch she bent forward.

"Take me," she whispered.

He kissed her, his tongue tracing long heated lines along her flesh. His strong hands held her buttocks parted open, and she shivered with the eroticism of his warm breath over her skin.

"So long. So long," he was mumbling.

She knew exactly what he meant and how he felt. Her thighs trembled with need.

"Please, Dominick," she begged and didn't care how it sounded. She wanted him to take her, right there where he was; she wanted his thick length planted deeply inside her.

When he stood over her, he licked up and down her spine. She felt his fingers probing her anus and clenched her teeth. "More," she was finally able to say.

He went farther, stretching her slowly. She clasped the material of the couch and moaned. With his other hand he slid between her legs, touching the hood of her pussy, rubbing slowly, milking her center.

Her body began to shake, a keening sound coming from deep within. Ary arched her back, the cat inside hungry for more.

He wanted her, there was no doubt. The feel of him tapping the tight head of his dick against her anus was like heaven, and she whimpered.

"Yes."

"Slow, baby. I want you slow and deep."

She bit her bottom lip, pushing her hips back because his slow was just too damn slow for her. With a quick stinging sensation the head of him was buried inside her.

"Dammit!" he yelled through gritted teeth. "I said slow."

"Now!" was her reply as she pushed back again.

Nick was thick and long and stretched her farther the deeper he went. The pleasure/pain sensation was bordering much more on the pleasure side and Ary cried out again. She rotated her hips, needing him deeper, faster.

He slipped two fingers into her opening and thrust quickly in and out. "There you go, little cat. There you go."

Ary worked those fingers, pushing herself closer to another release. "More!" she demanded.

"Bossy," he quipped and slapped his free hand on her buttocks.

With his dick moving inside her anus and his fingers thrusting faster and faster inside her center, Ary was out of control. Every nerve in her body seemed heightened, sensitive. Her blood rushed through her veins so hard she could swear she heard it. And her cat scratched and mewled and chuffed. This was her mate, she wanted to make sure he knew it.

When Nick began moving faster simultaneously she thought she would lose her mind, the pleasure was so intense. Her head jerked with Nick's motions, her breasts slapping against themselves, the sound of her sweaty flesh even more arousing.

"Gonna come, little cat. We're gonna come together," he growled, leaning low to her ear.

"Yes!" Ary yelled the moment everything inside her exploded.

Nick stiffened behind her, his sharpened canines finding a spot at the nape of her neck and biting down.

The combined roar that came from them was probably enough to ensure that the neighbors would be calling the police on them very soon.

Chapter 14

The second Kalina entered the condo she knew what they'd been doing. Their *calor* was spicy and lit the air like incense. Nick had answered the door wearing basketball shorts and a T-shirt that still clung to the dampness of his back. She followed him inside and watched with interest as he seemed to be fixing his patio door.

"So where's Ary?" she asked, taking a seat in one of the chairs that faced the balcony.

"She's getting dressed," he answered in a clipped tone.

"I called her over an hour ago, figured she'd be ready by now." Kalina tapped her fingernails on the edge of an end table that sat beside the chair. She found it interesting that Nick wouldn't face her. Very interesting.

"You know it takes females a long time to get ready."

"Maybe an ordinary female, but Ary's not ordinary, is she?"

"No, she's not."

"She's a very special shifter. One with a special future, I'd imagine."

"I guess" was his noncommittal reply.

Kalina almost laughed. He would not look at her and would not answer her questions with any sort of commitment. This was not the Nick Delgado she knew. It wasn't the cocky attorney or the kick-ass shifter she'd met a couple months ago. No, something had definitely changed within this shifter, and Kalina was willing to bet the ten-carat William Goldberg Ashoka ring Rome had purchased for her that that something was the female shifter in the next room.

"Why did you really leave her?" she asked him seriously and waited for his answer.

His back stiffened as he stood straight. "I told you it was an agreement between our parents."

Kalina remembered the story Nick had told them back in the Gungi, and she didn't doubt that was the way things happened. But something told her there was more. In all her years of interrogating suspects, she'd learned how to read people. And Nick's tight posture and stiff responses definitely said he was lying, or at least holding back.

"The Nick I know would never let somebody tell him what to do, especially someone like Davi Serino. The guy was a slimy piece of crap. I could see that and I'd only known him for a day."

Nick turned to her then, the scowl he'd been wearing a lot lately etching his face. It was funny how she clearly remembered their first meeting. Nick Delgado was charming as he'd smiled at her that day in Rome's office. He was just an average man to her at the time; he'd surveyed her assets and made a half-assed play for her to anger Rome. The first thought Kalina had was that he matched his profile: rich, good-looking, terribly arrogant, immensely enticing.

He was still all that, but now that she'd seen him in action, she knew there was so much more to him. More that included Ary.

"What are you trying to say, Kalina?"

"I just want to know why you walked away from a female you knew was your *companheiro*?"

"Because I don't give a shit about that crap!" he snapped. "She was a female like any other."

"That's a piss-poor lie, counselor." She kept her eyes on him and he kept his on her. No more hiding from the interrogation, she thought. Okay, that was fine with her.

"You were in love with her then and it scared you. One of the most eligible and sought-after bachelors in DC was afraid of a young healer in the forest."

"First," he said folding his arms across his chest, "I wasn't one of the most eligible bachelors when I was nineteen. And second, it was more than that. You have no idea how hard it was."

"How hard what was?" Ary asked, coming into the room.

Something told her they'd been talking about her, or about something they didn't want her to know about. Guilt had a crisp scent that opened the airways and made Ary take notice.

"Well, don't you look cute," Kalina said, rising to her feet and looking at Ary.

For a minute she felt self-conscious. Nick was also looking at her, and the little dress she had on was nothing spectacular. She didn't own many regular clothes, but she did have some outfits for those occasions when she went to the human village. This was one of the dresses she wore there. It was a dark orange color with capped sleeves and was tight around her breasts because she'd had it for years. The length stopped midthigh, and the only shoes she had were her ankle-high boots. Not a gorgeous picture, she knew.

"I look confused" was her reply to Kalina. Then her gaze found Nick's.

"Kalina's right, the dress is cute," he said in a dry tone.

Yeah right. Even the smile that followed his sentence didn't convince her.

"Well, if you could make me a loan, I'll be able to get some more appropriate clothing today. I don't know when I'll be able to pay you back, but—"

She had been talking to Kalina when Nick interrupted. "Here, use this. If they ask any questions just have them call me."

Because Ary stood speechless, staring at the card he extended to her, Kalina snapped it out of Nick's hand.

"Never turn down a man's credit card," she told Ary and slipped the plastic into her purse.

"You need a purse, too. We're going to have a good time," she said, smiling at Nick.

"I will repay you," she told him seriously.

He shook his head. "Don't worry about it."

"No. I want to repay you."

"Ary," he started, then stopped. "Fine. You can pay me back."

With a nod Ary felt uncomfortable all over again. How was she supposed to leave the room? Were they supposed to kiss or say good-bye or what?

"I'll have her home by dinner," Kalina said.

"Dinner?" Ary asked.

Kalina nodded. "Yes. Nick's taking you to dinner."

Nick looked as surprised as Ary felt. Then he cleared his throat and gave her that partial smile again. The one that made her heart skip a beat even though she suspected that wasn't his intention.

"Our reservations are for seven," he told her. "Buy something sexy to wear tonight," he added. Ary's cheeks warmed.

"I will buy what I need."

"She'll buy *everything* she needs," Kalina said, looping her arm in Ary's and leading her to the door. "See ya later," she called to Nick.

* * *

Almost six hours later Ary wanted to scream. Walking wasn't foreign to her, and she wore her boots all the time. Still, her feet hurt like hell from walking on all this concrete.

"There was a time when I would have rather walked on fire than walk around a mall. Or two in our case," Kalina said with a chuckle.

They'd just come from the car where they'd dumped off bags that were too heavy and too many to be carried around with them. Ary had three bags with shoe boxes in them on her arm, and Kalina had a huge bag with two purses she'd just purchased.

"I mean, I hated shopping," she finished.

"What changed?" Ary couldn't help but ask because, wow, they'd been shopping all day long.

Kalina shrugged. "I don't know really. I just got up this morning and figured we'd head to the mall. It's been sort of fun, I guess."

Ary had to chuckle. Kalina really looked as if she were trying to figure out if all this walking and trying on clothes and shoes and hats and other stuff she'd probably never wear could be construed as fun.

"I don't know if its fun. I guess it was necessary, however." Ary figured all she could do was be honest.

"You don't sound very pleased. Was there something you wanted to get that we missed?"

She shook her head. "Oh, no. I have no clue what I'm supposed to buy anyway. So it was really great of you to make this offer. I just wish Nick weren't paying for everything."

Kalina waved a hand at her. "He can afford it."

"But I don't want to owe him—or anyone else for that matter. I want to be independent."

Kalina had just steered them into another store. Ary followed her just as she had been all day long.

"My foster mother used to tell me that you have to crawl before you can walk. You just crawled out of the forest, out from your father's clutches. Independence isn't going to come overnight."

"I know," Ary admitted. "It's just with Nick . . ." She trailed off. With mechanical motions she pushed hangers on the rack from side to side, mimicking Kalina and the other women in the store.

"What about Nick?" Kalina asked.

When Ary looked back at her she saw that Kalina was no longer going through the clothes but rather paying close attention to her. The glare she was giving her was quizzical or knowing; Ary couldn't quite tell which. Either way it was a little annoying and made her feel very uncomfortable.

"That's just it. I don't know about Nick. Or about Nick and me."

Kalina nodded, her lips tilting slightly into a smile.

"What's so amusing about that?"

"It's just amazing to me that you two can't see what everyone else does."

"And what's that?"

"That you're meant for each other."

Ary was only slightly surprised by that answer. "I knew he was my *companheiro* the first time we met. That doesn't mean anything to him."

Kalina made a face that confused Ary even more.

"I don't think any of them like to hear that word or even consider that they have a mate that needs to be claimed."

"I don't want to be claimed," Ary replied quickly. "I mean, I do. But I don't. Do you understand?"

Kalina was quiet. "I think so," she replied. "Here's what

I suggest. You need to buy something so sexy and so enticing that Nick won't be able to keep his hands off you."

She was leafing through the dresses on the rack again. Ary didn't even look at the clothes. "We don't have any problem in that department."

Kalina nodded. "I know. Rome and I didn't, either. It was all the specifics that tangled us up."

"Specifics," Ary repeated. She wondered if that's what was plaguing her about Nick. Was it the specifics that they didn't speak about? Or was it the arrogance with which he just assumed what they were?

"So like I said—" Kalina held up a black dress that looked like nothing more than straps and swatches of material. "—you need to knock him off his feet. Keep him so flustered he won't want to do anything but mate with you."

Ary was already shaking her head. "I don't know. Shouldn't he want to do that already? I mean, shouldn't he just know that this is what we're supposed to be?"

"Look, Ary. I don't claim to have a lot of experience with men. Actually, I have very little. I just go with my gut instinct. And now my gut's telling me that you and Nick simply need a little push in the right direction."

"This dress is going to be a big push in a direction we've already mastered," Ary said to Kalina. But she took the dress and dutifully went into the dressing room to try it on.

They were in Rome's home conference room again, Nick and X on either side of Rome, who sat at the head of the long mahogany table. Eli and Ezra sat beside them. There were no other guards or officers at the meeting; they needed all hands on deck to cover the streets in search of Sabar. Both of the speakerphones in the center of the table were activated as Sebastian Perry, the Mountain Faction

Leader, Jace Maybon, the Pacific Faction Leader, and Cole Linden, the Central Faction Leader, joined in from their respective locations.

"Bas, why don't you start us off with your update," Rome began once Baxter, Rome's butler, had set pitchers of water and carafes of coffee on the table with all the accompaniments and left.

"Sure," Bas said.

His voice sounded a little low so Nick motioned for Eli to adjust the speaker. The guard moved one of the speakers closer to the end of the table where they were sitting.

"I informed X of the shipment that came in two days ago. As I stated, one of my guards followed one of the drivers to a location in Albuquerque. We've had guards rotating watch on that house ever since. For the first day and a half it was quiet. Then earlier today an SUV approached. It was a rental, which instantly alerted the guards that they might be moving whatever was in that shipment. We were right. About an hour later the SUV left the house, boxes loaded in the back."

"Fuck! They're making deliveries now," X said with a frown.

"We still don't know what's in those boxes," Rome stated.

"My money's on drugs," Nick added.

"I have to agree," Bas put in next. "We've had a rise in the movement from the Cortez Cartel as well. Border Patrol has their hands full with those guys."

"Competition," Cole said. "They're seeing who can move more product."

"At this rate we're going to be looking at an all-out drug war soon," Jace added. "We've been monitoring the police blotters: three ecstasy ODs in the last week."

"I don't think he's moving ecstasy," Nick said.

Rome looked at him. "What do you think it is?"

"He wanted Ary to help him mix something new. The herb he gave her, the damiana, has the same aphrodisiac effect that ecstasy does. So why try to duplicate a product you're already selling?"

"True," X said with a nod.

"What do you think it is?" Bas asked. "I mean, you know the *curandero,* has she given you any thoughts on what Sabar could be trying to create?"

Ary was the one person Nick did not want to talk about at this meeting. Coming in, he'd known that wasn't going to be possible with all that was going on. Still, he didn't like that on some level she might be considered an accomplice to Sabar.

"She just said the damiana induces relaxation and awakens the sex drive. He's not going to re-create the wheel. He's going to look at whatever brings him more money, faster. If that's a new synthetic drug, then that's what he's going to aim for."

"I agree," X said. "Bas, were you able to keep a tail on the SUV?"

"They stopped at a private landing strip. We're still working on getting the manifests to see where the plane was going," Bas told him.

"Bet a million dollars its here in DC," Nick said, slapping his hand on the table.

Rome nodded his agreement.

"What are the odds of Sabar getting this new drug made without Ary's help?" Rome asked Nick.

Nick didn't know the answer. "He wanted her specifically, so I've got to believe there's something she knows that another chemist doesn't."

"Find out what that is," Rome told Nick. "X, you use your FBI intel to figure out where new drugs are being sold. Get one of the guards to go undercover if you need to, but I've got a feeling that if we follow the drugs, we'll find Sabar."

"You're probably right," Jace agreed.

"Where do we stand with the Assembly? Did you get a chance to meet with them while you were in the Gungi?" Cole asked Rome.

"I did. Neutralizing Sabar is a priority. But we're still going to start the process of appointing leaders of the Stateside Assembly. I figured it would be good to start with finding a central location for us to use. In the Gungi the Elders have their Grounds. I'd like for us to have something like that here."

"I think you should head up the Stateside Assembly, Rome," Jace suggested.

Jace was the wild card in the group of FLs. His reputation among humans was of a brash and opinionated talent agent in Los Angeles who was the go-to man for all the A-list actors. With the shifters, he was one hell of a fine specimen that could kill with the same cutthroat viciousness he used to negotiate a contract for his clients.

Still, it didn't take long for everyone to agree with him on this point. Rome was a born leader. He was an excellent warrior, and he was the only one of the Faction Leaders that had mated. That gave him a look of stability and commitment to the tribes that was undeniable. So he was the obvious choice.

With mild reluctance Rome accepted the duty.

"In that case, I'll have Kalina start to look into establishing a headquarters for us."

"She probably has some street contacts we can also use to track the drug," X added.

Rome looked at X. It wasn't a pleasant look. "I don't want her on another undercover operation."

X shook his head. "I'm just talking about her calling a few people, putting her ear to the street to see what she comes up with. She's probably going to pull more info locally than I will going through the federal database. Hell, Rome, she's your mate. I'm not going to let anything happen to her."

Nick wanted to agree with X, but a huge part of him was siding with Rome. Putting Kalina back into the drug investigation game was dangerous. Nick didn't even want to think about Ary being in that type of danger.

"We'll talk about it later" was Rome's terse reply.

"So the *curandero* is with you?" Cole asked.

Even though the question hadn't been specifically aimed at anyone in particular, all eyes in the room fell on Nick.

He cleared his throat. "Yes. She's staying with me."

Silence.

Ezra was the first to speak up. "We should put a guard on her. Sabar doesn't give up easily."

"I agree. She's with Kalina now, and Jax is permanently assigned to Kalina, so they're safe for the moment. Ezra, let me know who you assign to Ary. I want that done within the hour," Rome said.

"I'll be with her tonight so there's no need to rush," Nick said. He regretted it the moment he did.

"Then she'll definitely be in good hands."

This and the first line of chuckles came from Bas. The Faction Leader had started his own hotel and resort chain and was now working at his newest resort in Sedona. He ran a tight ship of shifters in the Mountain Faction, focusing most of their efforts on training new shifters for service. He was also heavily against the mating ritual. Most likely because his parents' union hadn't ended well. Still, Nick wasn't in the mood for his wisecracks.

X tried to cover his grin, but Eli and Ezra openly guf-
fawed at the remark.

"Very funny," Nick said snidely. "She'll be safe is what
I'm saying."

"Who's going to protect her from you, Delgado?" Cole
joked.

Cole was an investment broker living in Dallas, sur-
rounded by his matchmaking sisters. Nick felt this might
make him more amenable to finding a mate, but the brother
didn't seem in any hurry. His focus was on making sure
the stateside shifters were financially stable.

"I'm betting the same person who's protecting you
from the ass kicking I've got reserved for you," Nick
retorted.

Nick eventually broke into a grin. These guys were his
family. They knew a lot about him. Not everything, but
a lot. And for the most part Nick trusted them all. Just not
with what was going on between him and Ary.

Because truth be told, Nick didn't have a definitive
answer on that topic himself.

Chapter 15

Slipping his phone back into its case, Nick verified the reservation he'd hurriedly made earlier at Fogo de Chao. He wasn't sure if Ary would like the Brazilian restaurant, but was hoping so.

Nick hadn't seen her since she'd left the condo earlier today with Kalina, but not a minute had gone by that he hadn't thought of her. If he was being perfectly honest, he'd say that was nothing new. Ary had occupied the majority of his thoughts since he'd left her. He'd always wondered what had happened to her, if she thought of him, if she'd even cared that he'd left. Of course, Caprise would say he was too damn stubborn or proud, or some sickly combination of the two, to ever find out. That assessment would have been true. He'd never tried to contact her, never tried to find out if she was even still in the Gungi. He'd simply walked away and never looked back.

Through some great divine intervention he'd been granted a second chance, and he didn't want to mess it up. Stepping out of his gray metallic Porsche 911 Carrera 4S, he grabbed the bouquet of flowers from his passenger scat, tucking them under his arm as he closed the door and activated the alarm. His footsteps echoed through the parking garage as he crossed the concrete toward the elevators.

A few minutes later when the elevator doors opened Nick stepped in, thinking more about tonight and spending time with Ary. Of course, that meant his thoughts circled back to the morning tryst they'd had. Nick's body hardened. He wanted her again and he wasn't surprised by that fact. There was a hunger there that he feared would never be sated. Ary, thankfully, seemed up to the challenge. More than. Closing his eyes to that thought, he was vaguely aware of the elevator stopping on another floor. It was a female, he knew, because he heard her shoes on the floor and smelled her perfume. Even though he'd opened his eyes Nick didn't pay too much attention to her. She moved to the very back of the elevator car. He just waited to finally get to his floor.

In his wildest dreams, or in any of the escapades he'd ever had with a female, Nick could have never predicted what happened next.

"Remember me?" a definitely female voice cooed.

A hand reached around him and long red nails ran along the line of his zipper, pulling downward immediately.

Nick had about ten seconds to turn around, register the voice and the face, and flip through his mental Rolodex to see who the hell this chick was. By that time she had his pants unzipped and was pulling his hard length through the slit of his boxers until cool air hit the tip. Her fingers wrapped around him and his dick hardened even more, because yeah, what the hell else was it going to do?

"Whoa," he warned. He had to place his hand on her shoulders as she'd already began lowering herself to her knees. "Stand up," he told her and took a step back, bumping right into the door of the elevator.

She gripped his dick and held on tight. Nick wasn't taking another step.

"You're all ready for me, baby. I want to taste you so

bad," she told him. Her voice was sultry, her breath hot as she breathed over him, prepared to do much more.

"No!" Nick yelled and tripped, moving backward as the elevator dinged and the door opened.

"Yes." She followed him off, crawling on her knees, her tongue flicking out just in time to lick the tip of his dick.

The flowers he had for Ary dropped from under his arm and he grabbed the woman by her shoulders roughly then and lifted her upward, until he knew her feet weren't even touching the floor. "I said no!"

"You didn't say that before," she frowned, her bottom lip poking out much farther than the top so she looked like a BBJ—Bad Botox Job.

Nick didn't know who this woman was, even though she was talking to him as if he should. A minute wave of guilt and disgust flowed through him when he realized he didn't remember half the women he'd slept with. But this one looked older, or more weathered, than the women he usually went for.

"Look, I don't know who you are or what you want. But I'm not interested," he told her adamantly. Nick had a feeling that wasn't going to do the trick.

She shook her head. "You don't remember me? Well, let me show you." She touched his arms, rubbing along them. "I remember every hot delicious inch of you."

Nick lowered the woman to her feet and took two steps back. He bent down and picked up his flowers, then held another hand out to keep her away. "I don't remember and I don't want any reminders. So you can just leave now." Of course she didn't; that would have been too easy.

She licked her overinflated, very red glossed lips. There was nothing sultry about that movement. Not only because Nick had absolutely no interest in this woman, but because it just looked weird, like it wasn't normal. She took another step toward him, and he noticed she sort of limped.

Now, that was a sight. A woman who might be in her late forties, with hair she'd obviously purchased from a store flowing down her back in blond waves. She wore a skirt so short he knew instinctively she had no underwear on beneath because what would be the point. Her breasts were huge, too big for her slim frame. And she didn't look right at all.

"This is a private building. I suggest you leave before security catches up with you." Nick turned away from her after speaking because he didn't really like looking at her. Besides that, he didn't want to believe he'd actually slept with a woman who looked the way she did. He couldn't believe it.

"You don't want this, baby?"

He heard her talking, her voice a little more slurred now than it had been before. Nick knew he should have kept walking, knew with every gut instinct of the lawyer in him as well as the jaguar, that he should just get away from her as fast as possible.

But he turned to face her again.

She'd ditched the skirt so that her bushy vagina was visible. Her shirt was unbuttoned, those huge breasts hanging from her like overfilled balloons.

"What the fu—" Nick started but didn't have the chance to finish the sentence.

The woman suddenly collapsed to the ground. Her entire body just went limp. He dropped the flowers again and knelt down beside her. Nick reached out, brushing the fake hair aside so he could check her neck for a pulse. But the second he touched her sweaty skin the woman's head jerked and she snapped long, sharp teeth at him.

Nick jumped back, staring into a face that had shifted

to something grotesque, half female, half creature. She snapped again and slid her body along the concrete like a slug. He stood then, looking down at her wondering what the hell was going on.

Reaching into his pocket he hurriedly pulled out his phone to snap a picture. Then he pressed a speed dial number.

"You and Ezra get to my place right now. I'm on the tenth-floor parking garage. And call Rome to tell him we've got some serious shit going on down here."

Fifteen minutes later six shifters were lined up in the parking garage of the Allegro Apartments. Nick had just finished explaining what had happened to X, who was looking at him like he'd lost his everlasting mind.

"Are you serious?" X asked.

Nick rubbed a hand down his face. "Man, I couldn't make shit like this up. She just came at me, pulling at my pants, coming out of her clothes. I didn't know what the hell to think."

"And you're sure you don't know her?"

"Does that look like something I'd sleep with, X?" he asked, extending an arm to the body one of the shifters had rolled into a garbage bag and was now lifting into the back of Ezra's SUV.

X could only shake his head. "This is weird."

"Tell me about it."

"Rome's going to freak when he hears about this," X told him.

"I told Eli to call him," Nick said.

"He's out with Kalina tonight."

At X's words Nick cursed.

"What now?"

"I was supposed to take Ary out to dinner." Turning

his wrist he looked at his watch. "Shit! We missed our reservation."

It was almost seven thirty. Nick couldn't believe he'd been in this garage for two hours.

"Calm down, I'm sure she'll understand. You know, once you go up and give her your winning smile, slap some of that Delgado charm on her. She'll be putty in your hands."

All Nick could think of when X said "putty" was the way that woman had crumpled to the ground. "Shut up and take care of this. I've gotta go."

X nodded. "Go ahead. I've got this."

Nick had turned to walk back toward the elevators even though he wasn't sure he wanted to go back into that enclosed space again. Flashbacks of the creature-woman were sure to come to mind. Then he had a thought and looked back. "Where are you taking her?"

X shrugged. "I guess this is why we need a headquarters. I need to find a shifter doctor who can look at her and figure out what the hell happened. Hey, you think Ary might know?"

Nick shook his head. "I'm taking her to dinner, not asking her to look at Miss Gruesome in that truck. Find somebody else."

"You and Rome and these *companheiros* you have to protect. This shit is getting contagious."

"Don't worry, I'm sure you've been vaccinated. No *companheiros* for the big bad FBI shifter," Nick quipped then moved on to the elevator.

X stood there a minute longer watching his friend go, then walked to his F-150 SVT Raptor and opened the door. Stepping up into the driver's seat, he tried not to let what Nick had said get to him.

He didn't have a mate.

He wouldn't have a mate.

Ever.

Why?

Because he was a deranged sonofabitch that no woman in her right mind was going to want.

That was a good answer, he figured, sticking the key into the ignition and starting the truck. The engine had a vicious roar that X loved because it rubbed along the skin of his inner beast, made the rugged animal in him feel like he wasn't really as alone as he appeared.

As he maneuvered his way around the garage, X leaned forward and pulled his laptop from beneath the passenger seat. With one hand on the wheel, he slid the other fluidly over the keys, booting up the computer until he came to the database he'd started keeping on East Coast shifters. The way he figured it, they were only as strong as the shifters who stood with them. So they'd better have a damn good idea which shifters were walking around in their backyard, and what side in this impending war they were on. The fiasco with the shifter who had been working for Rome and Nick without either of them knowing was a mistake X did not want to confront again.

So far he had about six hundred shifters listed in his database. He knew where they lived, if they were mated and to whom, kids, jobs, salaries, hobbies; everything the FBI had on them as humans, X had on them as shifters. They were all jaguars, which was another concern of X's. There were other species of shifters in this world, but so far they didn't know where any of them were. The cheetah that had shown up a couple months back with Sabar's crew was an anomaly to them all. Cheetahs did not normally run with jaguars.

Still, there were new developments every day. Like whatever it was that Ezra was carrying in his truck. They needed to find out what it was and where it came from, and heaven forbid if there were any more. Driving through DC streets wasn't easy on a good day. At almost eight o'clock in the evening, while his attention was divided between his laptop and the traffic, it was damn hectic. But X wasn't intimidated. He was the one who did the intimidating. Always.

When he found a name he thought was a good match, he picked up his cell and dialed the number. Frank Papplin was an internist at George Washington Hospital. He was mated and had two children whom X had already tagged as up-and-coming shifters to watch.

"Dr. Papplin," he said when the man answered his cell phone. "This is Xavier Santos-Markland. We need your help."

Dr. Papplin's response to the situation was exactly what X had expected. He was a jaguar shifter with a history of returning to the Gungi to help the family he still had there.

"Bring her to the morgue. I'll come down and sign the body in myself," he'd told X.

In the next few minutes, X emailed the info to Ezra, and they headed to the hospital.

He didn't give another thought to not having a mate—or the urge to fuck the first woman he saw, either.

Chapter 16

"If you didn't want to take me out that's all you had to say" were the words that greeted Nick the second he walked into his home.

His temples throbbed from the scene he'd just left, and guilt pressed heavily against his chest. "Something happened," he said, immediately moving into the living room where he could fix himself a drink.

"What happened?" Ary asked, following behind him. "Is it Sabar again?"

Nick stopped, glass in one hand, bottle of Hennessy in the other. "Why would you think it concerned Sabar?"

He hadn't really looked at her when he came in; his mind was already screaming that it needed a drink with every step he took from the garage. Now he could see that her hair was pulled up high in twirly curls that draped down to brush lightly over her neck. The dress she wore had his dick twitching without a doubt. It was black and had straps that wrapped in an intriguing maze all around her, leaving as much skin bare as it did covered. She looked fine as hell. But she'd asked about Sabar as if she knew something was going to happen with him. Nick was curious about that.

"I just figured that's what held you up" was her cool reply.

Nick fixed his drink, lifted the glass to his lips, and let the powerful liquid run down his throat to move in a quick trickle through his body. One sip wasn't enough; he took another and another. All the while his gaze continued to pierce hers. She was uncomfortable, her fingers twitching at her sides. Then she folded her arms over her chest and let them drop again.

"Is there something you want to tell me about your time with Sabar, Ary?"

Jerking her head back, she looked a little startled at his question. But Nick sensed she was hiding something. He only prayed that something wasn't going to help Sabar build his army of Rogues.

"Why would you ask that?"

Finishing off his first glass, Nick shrugged. "Don't know. Just find it strange that he was the first person to come to your mind the minute I walked in."

"The first thing to come to my mind when you walked in was that you're too arrogant to even call me and say you would not be taking me out. I could have saved the time getting dressed and primped and all this if I was going to simply stay in this house tonight." She took a step toward him when she finished, then thought better of it and stopped, just about a foot from where Nick stood at the wet bar.

"My next thought when you said something happened was immediately about Sabar because that's all I know. Or did you forget you just brought me to your big city last night? If there is something besides Sabar happening, how would I know that when you'd rather fuck than talk to me!"

That was said in a voice much higher than the one she was previously speaking in. So much so that Nick fixed himself another drink and swallowed half of it before putting his glass down. Wiping both hands down his face, he took a deep, steadying breath.

"I'd rather fuck you? Where did that come from?" he asked in the calmest voice he could muster. Even though the last thing he'd say he was feeling right now was calm.

Inside his cat paced and scratched and wanted to break free. It wanted to fight, to find Sabar and kill. The rage inside him was at a bare simmer, only because Rome and X kept telling him that to kill now and ask questions later wasn't going to work in the States. There was also this infernal heat that cloaked him every second he was away from Ary. It covered him in need, had his dick in a state of perpetual arousal, his nuts bursting to let free his essence.

And here she was, standing in front of him in fuck-me heels with straps that wound their way up her bare legs and a dress that screamed *I'm ready!* and she could wonder why he wanted to fuck her all the time. Man, he needed another drink.

"It comes from your actions that speak louder than words. Although I don't get a lot of words from you anyway."

Nick could only shake his head. He had no idea how this conversation had changed or why it had changed so drastically. And maybe that was the point.

"I asked you about Sabar."

"No. I asked you about Sabar, Dominick."

She said his name succinctly, with a click of her tongue and a heated flash in her eyes.

Nick closed his eyes and tried again to take a deep breath because any minute now he was either going to rip that dress off her and fuck her senseless or he was going out to find somebody to pummel. Those were his only options.

"I'm going to shower. We'll leave in fifteen minutes."

He walked away before she could say anything and prayed she didn't have anything else to say.

Okay, in his defense he did look like he'd had a bad day. Even though for Nick, that meant he still looked damn good. Still, Ary had seen the worry in his dark eyes. The neatly trimmed goatee had masked the tight line of his lips only slightly. He was upset about something. And she'd instantly thought it was Sabar. Considering his reaction, maybe that wasn't the right guess.

She didn't want to go to dinner now. Ever since she'd come back from the mall with Kalina, she'd been thinking this was a mistake. She and Nick did not talk, they did not do what Ary supposed was civilized dating. They had hot and passionate sex. That was it.

Companheiro or not, there was nothing else between them but the physical. And, unfortunately, they could not deny the physical if either one of them wanted to function at least semi-rationally. It just wasn't a choice for shifters.

The simple truth was, Ary wanted more. She wanted so much more than her parents had ever had. The Serinos had a partnership, where Davi gave the orders and Sheena acted them out. Ary knew she shouldn't be thinking such harsh thoughts about her parents who had just died in a bloody battle of shifters, but she couldn't help it. She didn't want to be like them, ever. Alone was a much better option, to her way of thinking.

Sitting on the couch, she tried to think of a way to get out of this dinner, to get out of this dress. While they were out Kalina had also shown her two local colleges where Ary could enroll in something Kalina called pre-med courses. She wanted to be a doctor, and this was the way to go about it: She'd have to become a student. She could do that. Actually, she'd been a student for most of her life, learning from first her parents then from Yuri.

A pang in her chest at the mere thought of the old shaman reminded her that she wouldn't have her weekly visits with him anymore. He would no longer teach her the art of spiritual healing. She'd miss that terribly.

Ary sat up straight on the couch, her eyes blinking as if something were in front of her and she couldn't help staring at it. But nothing was there. She was staring blankly because she'd just figured something out, something that might help them discover what Sabar wanted.

Without a second thought she was up and running up the stairs to get to Nick. Entering the bedroom where he slept, she was bombarded with his scent. Strong, masculine, divine. Pushing those thoughts aside, she headed straight to the bathroom, where she could hear the shower running. She stopped only momentarily to catch her breath as his beautifully naked body faced her from the back. Nick had a buttery complexion that ran the entire length of his magnificent form. Strong legs held him as tight buttocks made her mouth water. A slim waist moved upward to splay into perfectly broad shoulders and muscled arms at his sides.

She backtracked to his shoulders and gasped. On his left shoulder was a tattoo. The Topètenia tribal insignia—a paw print with claws that dripped into a swirling circular collage. With shaking fingers she lifted her hand to the glass and touched where the tattoo was in her vision. Water trickled over his downturned head, over his shoulders, and down his back.

In an instant Ary knew they'd never make it to dinner.

Her cat paced and roared, struggling to be set free. The insignia brought home more memories of the Gungi, the scents, the calls of other animals when they needed to mate. Ary's sharp teeth bared as she pressed closer to the glass. Her breasts imprinted on the cool surface of the door and she let loose a low chuffing sound.

Even through the roar of the water Nick heard her. His cat heard its mate calling to him. He turned slowly, saw her through the steam rising from the marbled floor of the shower. His dick jutted forward, leading him to where it needed to be. She took a step back as he pushed open the shower door.

When he reached for her hand she willingly put hers in his and entered the stall. Her hands moved to his shoulders and turned him so that his back faced her. She licked over his tattoo, her tongue swiping over the symbol that marked the man and beast that he was. It encompassed his entire shoulder, and her tongue touched every nuance of it.

His body tightened all over, his fists clenching at his sides until he thought he would burst. Instead he reached a hand back, cupped her buttocks, and pulled her closer, so that she was pressed against his back. Running his hand down her thigh, he lifted one leg, bringing it around his waist. The four-and-a-half-inch heel of her shoe scraped along the length of his dick and Nick threw his head back and roared, erotic tingles moving through his body like an outbreak.

Her nails had extended, sharp claws prickling over his skin as she moved her hands around to his pectorals, pressing her center into his back.

"Nick." Her voice was a raspy whisper that unlocked parts of Nick he thought were cemented closed.

He turned, keeping her leg around his waist, finding her lips like a thirsty man to water. And when their lips collided, Nick proceeded to drink his fill. Her sharpened teeth clashed against his, their lips swiping longingly, then moving as their tongues dueled. One hand cupped her ass while the other yanked at her hair, vaguely realizing he was pulling it down from its style and not caring in the least. Their breathing came in heavy pants that echoed in the acoustics of the shower stall. Warm water ran over their bodies, but they barely noticed.

Desperate need punched at Nick and he pushed that small-ass, tight-ass, sexy fucking dress up over her hips, ripping the small thatch of material that served as a thong, and plunged his dick deep inside her pussy.

Ary gasped then purred, rotating her hips over his length. Nick pounded into her, turning her so that her back was to the wall just beneath the showerhead. He lifted her other leg, locked her ankles behind his back, and fucked her with all the desire and anger and confusion that flooded his mind, his body, his soul.

When she came, she shivered around him, her pussy tightening until he almost couldn't breathe. Nick pulled out, then sank his dick back inside the drenched depths of her center. She cried out his name and something else in Portuguese. His mind couldn't translate; nothing existed, no words, no sounds, nothing but his dick inside her pussy. That's all he could wrap his mind around. The perfect slip and slide of their union. The sound of her voice was there, the feel of her arms tightly wound around him, the clenching of her thighs at his waist, the rub of her water-slicked breasts, and the rasp of the dress material against his chest—all of this barely registered, but was there somewhere in the blurred background.

And as Nick's hips continued to pump back and forth inside her, there was something else. Home. The word resonated in his mind. Home. Home. He was home.

He buried his face in her neck, felt the wet tendrils of her hair against his face, wrapped his arms around her even tighter as his essence ripped free, bursting inside her, filling her completely with everything he had.

Her name was barely a whisper as his teeth scraped along her collarbone. He didn't bite down; he licked the spot he'd pricked over and over, not wanting to let her go. Not wanting his dick to leave the warm sheath of her pussy. Never wanting to be without Ary again.

Forty-five minutes later dinner was delivered to Nick's condo. The delivery guys moved swiftly to set the table in the dining area with a white linen tablecloth, tall white candles that illuminated the room with a golden glow, crystal and china, and one long-stemmed rose.

When Nick guided her into the small room, he nodded a good-bye to the four guys who'd come in black suits with boxes and bags of food that smelled heavenly.

Ary now wore a lovely hot-pink silk robe that rubbed against her skin like sunshine, with slippers to match. Nick wore boxers beneath his own black robe that to some would look plain, but made Nick look like a god.

He helped her into her chair, pushing her up to the table before moving around to the other side to take his own seat.

"Forgive me for having to eat in tonight. Tomorrow I'll take you anyplace you want to go," he said, opening a napkin and handing it to her.

Ary watched Nick open his napkin and place it in his lap. She did the same with the one he'd handed her.

"What are we having? It smells delicious," she said, clearing her throat. For some reason it was harder to look at Nick now, harder to just sit here with him without feeling . . . something.

"A little of everything since I don't really know your

likes and dislikes yet. Top sirloin steak, stuffed chicken breasts, roasted potatoes, macaroni and cheese, broccoli and cheese, steamed green beans. And there's a tossed salad with a variety of dressings in that dish," he said, pointing at covered platters and bowls on the cart-like table the guys had brought in with them.

"And for dessert—" he continued after taking a deep breath.

Ary laughed.

He glanced at her and smiled, then moved on. "—we have cheesecake, strawberry shortcake, and chocolate decadence cake."

"Just for the two of us?"

It was Nick's turn to laugh. Ary found she liked the sound very much. He didn't laugh enough, she thought, didn't relax enough. She wondered why.

"We'll put whatever we don't eat in the refrigerator. I don't cook often. Do you know how to cook?"

Ary was already helping herself to one of the rolls that smelled so heavenly. "I can do soups and bake bread. That's really all I know."

"Yeah, we're going to need to keep leftovers from dinners like this. It's a good thing I have a lot of take-out menus."

"I think I'd like to learn to cook," she said.

Then she decided to go with the stuffed chicken because it looked like something tasty was oozing out of its inside. She scooped up green beans—they were easily recognizable to her—and decided to try the macaroni and cheese.

"Really? You don't strike me as an apron-strings type of woman."

Nick had steak and chicken on his plate, along with a

heap of potatoes and two rolls. She assumed he wasn't big on vegetables and thought, finally, she knew something about him.

"I'm just discovering the type of woman I want to be," she said with clarity. "I'm also going to enroll in college as a pre-med student."

Nick watched her as he chewed then replied, "Now, *that,* I can definitely see. You'll make a wonderful doctor."

"Really?" Ary warmed all over. And it wasn't the sexual type of warmth that buzzed throughout her body whenever she thought about Nick. It was something comfortable and soothing. She liked it. "You think so?"

He nodded. "Of course. You're a natural. Besides, formal training, combined with what you already know from being the tribe's *curandero,* will give you an advantage over human doctors."

"They won't accept my tribal healing in this world."

"Probably not, but we're putting the Stateside Assembly together, forming a headquarters for the shifters. I think it would be logical to have our own medical center as well. Humans won't know how to heal shifters all the time."

"I guess you're right. Our genetics are different from theirs."

"And you could run the medical center," he told her after filling another plate.

"I don't know about running it," she started, then paused. "But I could train other shifters in the tribal and spiritual healings."

"Like Yuri trained you?" Nick asked.

His question circled back to what Ary had originally gone into the bathroom to tell him. That seemed so long and so many orgasms ago.

She dropped her fork and hurriedly chewed the mouthful of macaroni and cheese she'd eaten—and really enjoyed. "I was coming to tell you what I remembered."

"What?" Nick asked.

She wiped her mouth with the napkin then continued. "The first thing Yuri taught me about using the leaves and vines of herbs found in the Gungi was that they needed to be cleansed. See, using them in their natural state could sometimes cause side effects that would prevent the healing desired. If they were cleansed beforehand, you could ask the spirits to bless the herbs, make them potent in the area you need them to be, and wash away all the other negative energy."

Nick sat back, watching her with what Ary could only describe as intent interest. "Go on."

"Sabar wants to use damiana, I guess for its relaxation and sexual enhancement purposes. But he wants to mix it with some other drug. I heard him talking to Franco about this. That's what they made me drink."

"But you said you didn't feel aroused once you'd taken it?"

One of Nick's thick eyebrows raised in question. "No," she answered quickly, adamantly. "Not at all. But I was angry and ready to fight. To kill. That was the negative energy."

"Because Sabar didn't know to cleanse the herb before mixing it," Nick finished for her.

Ary nodded. "Correct. He cannot know the ceremony that needs to take place to cleanse."

Nick rubbed the neatly shaved hair at his chin. Ary loved that hair on him, loved the precise way it circled his tempting lips and gave him a more masculine look. No male in the Gungi wore facial hair. Ary hoped Nick would never shave his off.

"We went to see Yuri, and he did something with smoke

and sage. Lucas said he was cleansing the air, ridding it of negative energy."

"Right. There are many cleansing rituals, depending on what you want to achieve. Positive energy is crucial to positive healing."

Nick looked like he wanted to say something, then shook his head and continued to think about what she'd said.

"If he brought damiana here and is planning to keep mixing it, he will not be successful. It will continue to produce the same negative results."

Nick's eyes focused on her and he leaned forward. His brow immediately furrowed, and Ary resisted the urge to reach across the table and smooth out the lines. She wanted his smile back, his laughter. This, the way he looked now, said the rage had returned full force.

"Get dressed. We have to go see Rome," he said, standing from the table. "I'll put this stuff away."

"It is bad, isn't it? What I just told you means it's really bad," she asked him.

"It's damn sure not good," he replied.

Then he shocked her by coming around the table and touching a hand to her chin, his other hand wrapping around her waist. "But you did good. You figured out what Sabar's trying to do. Now we can stop him."

That warmth was back. Ary smiled slightly up at Nick. "Hopefully, we can stop him."

"We'll stop him or we'll kill him. That's the bottom line," he stated seriously.

"Death is always the bottom line with you, isn't it, Nick? Your answer is always to kill."

He shook his head. "No, Ary. My answer is always to survive."

Chapter 17

Norbert Hanson III came from a long line of chemists hailing from the northern regions of the United States. He was a short, pudgy man who after his last birthday—which marked his twenty-ninth year on earth—had accepted that his receding hairline would continue to recede and gone completely bald. That allowed him to purchase custommade hairpieces that he thought made him look younger.

He'd tried out the first hairpiece at Athena's—one of DC's premier adult entertainment clubs. Yes, Norbert loved chemistry, but he loved strippers even more. It didn't really matter what sex the strippers were, either, but Athena's featured a majority of female performers, with a couple of transsexuals thrown in for flavor.

That night Norbert received two lap dances and dropped more cash in the place than a high roller in Atlantic City. But his ego had been boosted, and that was all that mattered. He needed to buy more hairpieces since he was convinced that's why he received all the extra attention that night. It never dawned on him that the ladies were seeing the wad of green in his hands much more clearly than that jet-black rug on his head—which had begun to slip, since his sweating dome had weakened the glue.

Custom-made hairpieces weren't cheap, and while he

made a good salary as a researcher at George Washington University, he needed more. As if his wish had been spoken directly into the ear of a god, a man had approached him about making some extra cash. Norbert had immediately jumped at the idea. Until he realized it was illegal.

To date, he hadn't been to Athena's in two weeks, his constant hard-on proof that all the personal hand action in the world wasn't enough for any man. The man, or person, who'd approached him had a funny gleam in his eye when he'd spoken to Norbert—and when he'd smiled, Norbert saw sharp teeth. Not human teeth, either. So Norbert, being the spineless creature that he was, had taken a leave of absence from work and took refuge in his brownstone in Park Potomac.

He was craving sex like a drug-addicted teenager but he was more afraid for his life. So porn flicks, lots of lotion, and twenty-four endless hours every day would have to suffice.

Until today.

The knock on his door came early one morning. Norbert thought it was his grocery delivery and happily padded down the foyer to the vestibule where he opened first the inside door, then the split-window outside one. That was the last conscious memory Norbert had of that day.

He had no idea how much time had passed when his eyes rolled back into his head, his eyelids peeling back like skin off a dead fish. Light hurt his pupils so he dropped his lids down again. His fingers moved at his sides; his chest felt as heavy as if bricks were planted there when he tried to breathe.

"Wakey uppy, little doc," an unfamiliar voice said before breaking into a cackling laugh.

Norbert rolled over with the help of a heavy foot on the pit of his stomach. He coughed and spat on the floor, his eyes opening again, this time out of self-preservation. Maybe if he saw the foot coming next time he could avoid it before it made contact, causing his insides to ripple like an earthquake had hit him.

"Get your ass up!" a deeper voice yelled. "I don't have all day to sit and babysit you."

He'd decided he was definitely going to try to stand. Putting his palms to the floor and pushing himself up ward wasn't that successful: It appeared his knees did not want to cooperate.

"Time's up!" another man yelled.

And Norbert was yanked by the collar of his shirt and pulled up off the floor. He stumbled and collapsed into a chair. Then he gazed up into the faces of three of the deadliest-looking guys he'd ever seen. One, he knew.

"I . . . I . . . can't help-p-p you," Norbert stuttered. "I c-c-can't."

The biggest guy, the one who stood in the middle— dreadlocked hair hung past his shoulders, and thick tendrils fell into his face as he took a step toward Norbert—smiled. His dark lips spread over white teeth . . . sharp white teeth that hung too low to be human.

"You will do whatever I tell you," he said in a low whisper.

Then he lifted his hand. Norbert didn't know if he should chance taking his eyes off the guy's killer chops to see what he was doing or not. It didn't matter; both actions were deadly. Norbert hissed in pain when the guy's fingernail pierced the skin at his temple, then traced an equally painful path down the side of his face.

"If you don't, Dr. Hanson, I'm gonna slice you up into little pieces and stuff you into those slim vials you like to work with in your lab."

The smile never wavered and seemed only to highlight

the evil gleam in his eyes. Tears rolled down Norbert's cheeks and no doubt blended with the blood from his wound. He didn't know what to say or do. Rather, he knew exactly what not to say and do—if he wanted to keep breathing.

He shook his head because the action came long before words finally dropped from his lips. "I can't use the university lab. I'll . . . um . . . I'll need my own sp-space."

Sabar stepped back, letting his claws retract. "No problem. Darel, see that he gets what he needs. I want something ready to be tested by tomorrow."

"That's too f-f-fast," Norbert said, using his shoulder to wipe at the blood and tears dripping from his chin.

Sabar had turned to walk out of the room, but looked back at Norbert over his shoulder. "Then you better get to work."

"We're waiting for the results from the autopsy," Rome told Nick as they sat in his living room.

Kalina and Ary were both seated on the couch, glasses of lemonade in hand, thanks to Baxter. Ary had watched the tall, thin man move in absolute silence throughout the room. He'd brought in a silver tray with a crystal container of lemonade and four glasses. He left and came back with another tray full of cookies, which nobody touched but were very aware they were there. When he came back the last time, he pulled the drapes over the floor-to-ceiling windows tight, then went off to stand in a corner as if his body were needed to hold that particular wall in place. He didn't look at her, but Ary got the feeling he knew she was watching him.

"I'll bet her blood and tox screens come back with traces of damiana," Nick said grimly.

Rome nodded, his hands slipping into his pockets. This was a familiar stance for him. Ary realized she'd seen him do this many times before when he was in deep thought.

"You think Sabar's got the drug on the streets already?" Kalina asked after sipping from her glass. "That's not smart."

Nick shook his head. "He's going to test it out on people first, before it goes on sale, Sabar's no fool."

"No. He's just a sadistic killer," Ary surmised. She got no argument from the others in the room.

"I don't get why he's so into death and suffering," Kalina said, shaking her head.

"Sabar was born to good parents," Ary stated. "But when he was taken by Boden, he was lost. There's no telling what kind of evil Boden inflicted on him all the years they were together. And the split was rumored to have happened as recently as two or three years ago. He's totally messed up now."

Nick nodded. "True, he is. But I believe that kind of evil has to live in you already for it to manifest as thoroughly as it has in him. He's going to stay that way until he's stopped."

Ary's gaze went to Nick again. His rage troubled her; the ease in which killing came to him was concerning. Sure, they were jaguars at heart, they were all hunters, killers, per se. But it was different in Nick. Almost as inbred as it seemed to be with Sabar, only Ary didn't think Nick's parents were like this, either.

"And you're sure about how the drug made you feel?" Rome asked Ary.

"Positive. The rage was uncontrollable. I was not myself at all."

"This woman definitely did not look like herself,

whoever she was," Nick said. "She didn't look at all human. *Grotesque* doesn't capture it."

That was another thing: Nick hadn't told her about this woman he'd encountered in the parking garage today. Yes, he'd come into the condo angry and bewildered, looking like he'd had the shock of his life. But he hadn't confided in her. Ary didn't know how that made her feel.

No, that was a lie. She knew exactly. Pissed off.

"Can we trust this doctor to remain quiet about what he finds?" she asked to keep her mind on the situation at hand. The other, she'd deal with later.

"X says he's in the network," Kalina said.

Ary must have looked confused because Nick clarified for her. "That means he's a shadow. X has put together a network of all the stateside shifters so they can be easily located when needed."

She nodded. "Smart. I'd like to meet him."

"X?" Nick questioned and looked as confused as he sounded.

Ary sighed. "The doctor."

Rome immediately agreed. "That would be a good idea. You can share your knowledge of healing from the forest perspective and he can give you some insight into Western medicine."

"We talked about that already," Nick added. "About Ary heading up a medical center here for the shifters. She's going to medical school so she'll have knowledge from both sides."

Rome was nodding, his gaze falling to his wife. "We need a space large enough to include this medical center."

Kalina smiled. "I'm on it."

Their communication was silent, but on point. They didn't have to say everything, Ary was almost positive, but each knew what the other was thinking and could finish the thought easily. It was a deep connection, one she longed for desperately.

Nick looked at her, and her fingers tightened on her glass. Could Nick ever be that open to her? Could he ever give her everything Rome seemed to give Kalina? She doubted it. He hadn't even shared the incident in the garage with her, and that was serious. How could she expect him to share the little things like why he was so damn angry all the time? But she refused to feel sad or let down. If her life had taught her anything it was to deal with whatever came your way. She knew where she stood with Nick—sort of. Their dinner had gone wonderfully, they'd both seemed so relaxed, so comfortable. But now this— now he was as distant as if she'd just met him in the forest for the first time. One thing Ary knew for sure was that if that wasn't working for her, she had to do something about it. Only she doubted her body was going to cooperate with the move-out thoughts she was having.

"We should let X know what's going on," Nick suggested.

"He's working his connections, trying to find out where Sabar's selling his drugs," Rome said.

Kalina sat up, her elbows resting on legs that looked tanned to perfection. "Really? I can probably help him with that. I still have a ton of contacts on the street."

Ary watched as Nick and Rome exchanged a look. Then Rome cleared his throat. "We can talk about that later," he told Kalina.

"Or I can call X now and see what kind of information he needs."

Ary watched anxiously, waiting to see what would come of this exchange. It was apparent that Rome did not agree with what Kalina said but was making a valiant effort to keep from saying so.

"You can call X, but I don't want you on the streets working with any informants. Let X handle that part," Rome replied finally.

Kalina smiled at him as she stood and walked over to him. She rose up on tiptoe and kissed his lips once, then twice, a little longer that time. "Whatever you say, Roman," she said then turned to leave the room, stopping to wave at Nick and Ary on her way out.

Ary was no fool. The look in Kalina's eyes said she was going to do whatever she deemed appropriate. Ary wondered if that was the way to be in shifter unions.

"We'll get going," Nick said and looked at Ary.

She stood and tried to muster a smile but couldn't. So much was going on in her head right now, she didn't know how to act or react. "If he finds someone to cleanse the damiana first, he could create something lethal. I mean, I don't know a lot about street drugs or how much they go for, but mixing damiana with anything stronger isn't going to be good."

"That's why we need to stop him before there's more death," Rome said sadly.

Chapter 18

X turned down an alley that faced the back of Athena's Adult Club. He'd picked up a couple of hits from the police scanner indicating that there was some activity here. Located in one of the higher-end neighborhoods of DC, Athena's seemed to be a pretty decent establishment—if you liked scantily dressed woman shaking and strutting their stuff in your face while you tossed dollars at them and sat with a rock-hard dick.

X wouldn't exactly say he liked it.

Then again, judging from his own rock-hard dick as he watched some of said women file out the back door still wearing what looked like their work clothes, he figured he could temporarily like it just fine.

Stepping out of his truck X walked toward the women, his boots a muffled sound over the slightly damp pavement. The three women were talking and pulling out cigarettes to smoke. A slight turn-off for X, but he reminded himself that he was here for business, not pleasure. The tallest one held the lighter and flicked the Bic for her two friends before lighting her own stick. She had long black hair, falling in deep curls down to her waist. On her legs were some sparkling type of nylon, on her ass was a silver thong, and barely hugging her breasts were a few straps and what looked like a pasty. His dick twitched.

The second female, the one closest to the door, was a little shorter than the first, maybe around five-nine or -ten. She had a dark-chocolate complexion with gray eyes and long thin braids. X watched as she caught the cigarette between heavily glossed lips and took a puff.

Athena's beauty number three was the shortest of the trio, with ivory skin and flame-red hair. Her heels were metallic and looked like pitchforks digging into the ground. The material that covered her breasts was sheer so her nipples greeted him as he stepped up closer.

They looked at him, startled because they'd been so busy talking and puffing they hadn't heard his approach.

"Good evening, ladies," X said, mustering a smile so his height, size, and general appearance in the middle of the night in an alley behind a strip club weren't too intimidating.

"Get lost, dude," Tall Lady said, her lips curling with an unattractive frown that made her look a lot harder than X had originally thought.

"Yeah," Flame Hair said with a loud crack of the gum she chewed on the left side of her mouth. "The action's inside, not out here. No freebies," she stressed.

X's gaze zoomed in on the dark-chocolate one, who looked at him with those cool gray eyes and smiled. Bingo!

"I'm looking for a hit," he said slowly, licking his lips as he held her gaze.

"We don't sell nothing," Tall Lady said, stepping closer to him.

X pulled a small plastic bag out of his back pocket. It had been retrieved from evidence of a DEA bust. Once he'd started asking questions about the drug game in the city, he'd been inundated with information. This wasn't normally his area of expertise at the Bureau, but being a senior agent gave him leeway to ask around without anyone becoming too suspicious.

"This is what I want," he said, showing Gray Eyes the bag.

Recognition sparked. Her eyes shot to his then over to her friends before she took a step back.

"I said we don't sell nothing."

The tall one had come to stand face-to-face with X, blocking the other two in a protective stance.

"Do you know where I can find a seller?" he asked her.

She stank of cigarettes and liquor, disdain, and plain old cockiness. X didn't like her much.

"That's not our line of work. But," she cooed, reaching out a hand to touch his left bicep, "if the price is right, we might be able to work something out."

"No freebies," Flame Hair said, coming up on X's other side and massaging his other bicep.

His dick stayed hard but he didn't want either of them. These two had been used and reused until they most likely possessed nothing else of themselves. They were like robots running the same program day and night. It disgusted and saddened him. But not as much as when he looked at Gray Eyes again. Because her two flunkies had attached themselves to his side, she was left standing alone, her back against the wall, hands thrust behind her back.

X was sure she not only knew who sold the drug that came in the small plastic bag with the stamped black symbol on the front, but knew a lot more as well. Knowledge was clear in her eyes, just as clear as the fear and trepidation she felt at his proximity.

He didn't even look at the other two, simply took a

couple of steps forward and left them floundering behind him.

"What's your name?" he asked Gray Eyes.

"She's Diamond," Flame Hair said from behind him, cracking her gum loudly.

"Diamond," X said, looking at the woman, who now bit her full bottom lip. "You know where I can find more of this?"

Before one of the slutty twins could answer, X threw up a hand to silence them.

Diamond began shaking her head, fear pouring from her in heavy waves. He knew he'd never get her to say anything in front of her co-workers. They were apparently pulling her strings here. Up close she looked a lot more innocent than X would have originally presumed. Reaching into his pocket again, X pulled out a business card and extended it to Diamond. He held it just out of her reach so she'd have to step away from the wall and closer to him to take it. This was a test of sorts. If she came to get the card, she wanted help. If she blew him off, he was wrong and she was just as lost as the other two.

"If you remember who might have some of this, give me a call," he told her.

Diamond looked down at the card, then up to him.

"She don't read," Tall Lady laughed and came around to stand next to Diamond. "All she can do is dance and fuck, that's why they hired her."

Flame Hair laughed and stood beside Tall Lady. She didn't talk—just gave X a knowing glare. "If you want real action and you got real cash, you're gonna want someone with more experience than her."

"I'd like you to call me, if you need to, Diamond." X said her name with precision and looked directly at the other two so they'd know he didn't give a damn about their opinions.

He felt like his arm was going to fall off, he'd been holding it out to her for so long.

"She don't need you. There's fifty more johns like you inside with cash in hand ready to make it rain for her when she hits the pole. Why would she need to call you?" Flame Hair laughed as she talked.

Tall Lady smiled, pouted her lips, and stuck her breasts out farther, bringing up a hand and bright-red-painted nails to circle her protruding nipple. "She's right, we've got work inside."

They moved toward the door. X was about to pull his arm back and accept that he'd gotten nowhere with these women when Diamond bolted forward and grabbed the card from his fingers. She didn't say a word, just balled it into the palm of her hand and turned away before he could say anything.

When the door slammed shut and the threesome anything gone, X left the alley, knowing he'd hear from Diamond soon.

He only hoped it wouldn't be too late.

From a distance Rome watched Nick standing at the grave site of his parents. Henrique and Sophia Delgado were buried about five feet from Rome's parents. Their names were scrawled on the headstones just beneath the Topètenia tribal insignia. But that was all that was left of them here, since the bodies had been burned immediately after their death. Their kind could not afford to leave any traces of themselves to be discovered. Still, the human part of them went along with the formalities of a funeral and burial. It was all a necessary pretense.

Rome had looked for Nick at the office, then at his condo, but he wasn't either place. Ary said he'd left early that morning. It was now late afternoon. Nick didn't share his problems; he wasn't that type of shifter. He would keep whatever was bothering him personally to himself, masking it with the rage he wore like an old suit. Watching him here, in the cemetery, gave Rome a heavy feeling, one he recognized as his own.

After a while he walked toward the spot where Nick stood. He could see the lift and decline of his friend's broad shoulders. He was thinking about the past, wondering, guessing. Rome knew because not too long ago he'd stood at his father's grave doing the same thing.

"They did what they had to do," Rome said when he was close enough for Nick to hear him.

Nick didn't startle; he had probably scented Rome a while back. They were as close as brothers, knew each other's minds and actions as if they were their own. Yes, he knew Rome was there, had known the minute Rome stepped out of the car to approach. Eli and Ezra weren't far away. Too much was going on within the tribes for them to leave their leaders unprotected. But the guards would maintain their positions out of sight.

"Was lying necessary?" Nick spoke without turning to face Rome.

"Possibly. All I know for sure where they're concerned is that we can't go back and make them tell us what they did."

"Do you think they betrayed us? Did they tell a human about the tribes?" Nick asked.

Rome inhaled deeply, then let the breath rip free. "I think it's possible. X hasn't reported on the Comastaz Lab, and Bas didn't mention anything about it in a our last call. I found proof that my father was communicating with someone—I just don't know if that was someone we could trust or not."

Nick did turn then, facing Rome and recognizing the like mind of a shifter and the connection of a friend. If there was anyone he could trust with his innermost thoughts, it was Rome.

"I think my father knew about the shipment that went out of the Gungi that night. I think that's why he was so adamant about me leaving and never coming back."

Rome was quiet at first, thinking: Nick knew. Nick wanted to do something, he wanted to roar in frustration, rip something apart, rage, yell, kill. But for the last hour he'd only stood here, looking at the headstones of two people he feared he may have been totally wrong about.

"If he knew about the shipment, then he knew about Davi," Rome surmised. "Is that what you're saying?"

"We were only nineteen," Nick said, thinking back to that time.

"In college. But the Assembly had already been in contact with me. I knew I'd be a Faction Leader, just as I knew I would one day help support the tribes."

"But you weren't sending any money or supplies yet. So how were they getting by?" Talking seemed to cause Nick's mind to reel a little faster, thoughts coming in quick snapshots.

"I don't want to believe our tribe survived off drug money," Rome said solemnly.

Nick shook his head, his brow furrowed. "Not wanting to believe doesn't destroy the possibility. If someone was shipping drugs from the Gungi to the United States and using the funds to take care of the tribe, is that bad or good? Would it be called necessary or a betrayal of the *Ética*?"

Nick hated the Shifter Code of Ethics but he followed

it, for the most part. The rule that shifters should obey all human laws was a sketchy one, and one he doubted the Rogues gave a rat's ass about.

"Today, as I lead the stateside shifters, I'd call it a betrayal. Because we're both attorneys bound by the laws of the human judicial system, it's illegal." Rome sighed. "But there's nothing we can do about the past. If that's what they were doing, we can't fix that."

"And if someone decided they'd like to pick up where our parents left off?" Nick asked.

Rome looked at him. Nick held his glare. They seemed to communicate, silently. Both their cats roaring and pacing, sounding off their opinions.

"We'll find out what our parents were up to," Rome said finally.

Nick shrugged. "I don't think we have any choice. Our sanity depends on it."

Rome gave a small smile. "Your sanity depends on it. I'm resigned to whatever the outcome is. I found out who killed my parents and have a semi-concrete reason why."

"But Darel and Sabar are still alive and still working side by side to bring us down."

"They'll die trying" was Rome's quick reply.

Nick chuckled. "You've been around me way too long," he said to his old friend. He was glad Rome had come, glad they could both share what was turning out to be a mutual personal problem. Nobody else would understand what they were dealing with, not even X, because his parents hadn't been involved with the Assembly or the forest tribes. They'd lived in Atlanta and hadn't socialized more than absolutely necessary with the stateside shifters once they'd moved to DC. Only X had been drawn to Nick and Rome and the overall cause. And he never spoke of his parents. Ever.

"Find out what you can about that shipment and who it came from or went to," Rome told Nick.

"Already on it," Nick said.

"Good." Rome turned and began to walk away from the headstones.

Nick followed.

Rome continued to talk. "I'll contact Bas about the lab, see what's really going on there."

"You heard from X today?" Nick asked.

"Not yet."

"I'll give him a call."

"No." Rome shook his head. "You go home and see to your mate. I'll talk to X."

Nick didn't miss a step; nor did he miss the jab Rome had tried to slip in on him. "I already know she's my mate, Rome. You don't have to try to convince me."

"Not trying to convince you," Rome said, approaching his car and using his remote to unlock the doors. "Just trying to educate you on the mating game."

Nick's car was parked directly in front of Rome's. The guards' SUVs were a short distance down the path.

"I don't need any education where women are concerned," Nick said with a chuckle.

Rome opened his door and was just about to move inside when he said, "She's not just a woman. She's a shifter and that's totally different from the game you're used to playing with women. Trust me on this one, man. I know."

Nick only nodded. "I'll be fine," he said.

Slipping into the driver's seat and starting his car, he felt only marginally lighter about what was going on around him. The fact that Rome had brought up Ary was what tipped the scales. She would be at his place waiting for him, with that luscious body and pretty smile. He sped out down the driveway, certain that Ezra was cursing trying to keep up with him in that bulky SUV he drove.

Suddenly Nick wanted to hurry home. He wanted to get there as soon as possible, to get to Ary as soon as possible.

Chapter 19

Nick didn't hate his parents. But he'd been damn upset with them for a lot of years now. He'd say almost since they'd left the Gungi sixteen years ago. And it wasn't just because of Ary.

After they'd returned from the forest his father had become very secretive. Where he and Nick had once been very close, his father had begun shutting himself in his study after dinner, spending hours in there doing something Nick could never figure out. When Loren Reynolds, Rome's father, was killed, Henrique had pulled back from most of the secret meetings those two used to attend together. But it seemed to Nick that his father simply traded one secret for another.

Of course, asking his father what was going on wasn't productive. He'd get either a pat on his back and a bleak smile along with assurances that things were okay—or a stern look and a lecture about being true to the Topètenia no matter what. Nick knew it was the tribe and the Assembly that were taking up so much of his father's time. He also knew that whatever his father was doing, the Assembly had no idea about it, either. He'd overheard phone calls in which his father was being just as noncommittal with the Elders about what was going on as he was with Nick.

One night Nick decided it was time to find out exactly
what his father was up to. That would mark the second
time he'd seen the shield symbol.

Henrique had left the house right after dinner, telling
Sofia he was going to the office. He was an architect, and
their firm had just landed a huge contract to construct
government buildings. So the excuse hadn't come off as
an excuse at all. Not to anyone besides Nick.

He'd climbed into his car and followed his father's
through the dark streets of DC until it stopped at a house
in an area where college students were prone to live and
entertain. For a fleeting moment Nick thought his father
might be having an affair with a younger woman, but he
hurriedly thought better. If there was one thing Nick knew,
it was that his father was madly in love with his mother.
That was a grounding fact in Nick's life, one that probably
shouldn't have tainted his thoughts about mating—but did.

No, Henrique was not having an affair. But he was
meeting with someone. A man in an old grungy apartment
building that had the same shield symbol Nick had seen
on the crates in the Gungi spray-painted on the side wall.
Funny how that little detail hadn't been as concerning to
him then as it was now. Nick had gotten as far as the man's
front door when there was a shooting right outside. As a
college student, with his sights already set on becoming
an attorney, Nick knew it was only a matter of time before
the place would be swarming with cops. Cops who would
be asking questions of everyone in the vicinity—including
his father, who was behind the closed door. Reluctantly,
Nick left without Henrique, but waited for him to come
home.

"Who was the man you met with?" he'd asked the second his father walked through the front door.

It was well after midnight by that time; his mother and

Caprise were in bed. Nick sat in the dark living room waiting.

"What are you talking about?" Henrique asked, going immediately to one of the end tables where he switched on a lamp.

Nick had looked into his father's dark eyes and searched for the truth, but couldn't tell if he was going to get it or not.

"I followed you," he said candidly. "I saw you go and visit that man. I'm asking you what it was about."

"I am the father here, Dominick," Henrique said sternly.

"And it is with all due respect that I ask you again, what's going on?" Nick wasn't backing down.

Henrique took a deep breath and sat on the couch. He was a tall man, well over six and a half feet; his skin was the color of cola, his eyes even darker, his hair slicked down in heavy ebony waves.

"Nothing that concerns you. I want you to focus on school. Get your education and you can help the tribes when your time comes."

"Was this meeting about the tribes?" Nick pressed. "Because I don't see you communicating with the Assembly as much as you used to. It's almost like you've been working on your own since Mr. Reynolds passed away."

That had his father jerking back as if Nick had struck him. "Loren was my best friend."

Nick nodded. He knew how his father felt about Loren Reynolds because he felt the same way about Rome. And he wasn't questioning their friendship.

"Dad, I'm here to help if I can. Tell me what's going on."

Henrique stood quickly, his voice barely restraining his anger. "It is not your concern."

"If it involves you it is my concern." Nick jumped to his feet, trying to meet his father eye-to-eye.

"I am doing what is right for our people. That is all you need to know. Now go to bed."

He'd been dismissed, but that wasn't working for Nick. He wasn't leaving without answers. "Dad—"

"Enough!" Henrique yelled. "It is enough with these questions, Dominick. You will respect me at all times. I will not tell you this again."

And he hadn't. Henrique had walked away from Nick that night, leaving him to stare after him with no more knowledge than he'd had before his father had come home. And the rage that had begun to simmer in Nick when they'd left the Gungi was left thoroughly inflamed.

In his condo, alone, because Ary hadn't been here when he returned, Nick walked into the living room where he had a desk and his computer. He fired up the Mac and waited until the Internet was visible on the screen. As he'd walked down Memory Lane, pinpointing the second he realized his father was a liar, that symbol had appeared, proving itself an intricate part of what was going on in the here and now.

So he typed in symbols and shields and waited. Clicking on various sites, he searched for anything similar to the symbol he'd seen, any link to what he feared was going to be a huge problem for the stateside shifters.

His gaze remained focused on the computer screen even as his mind wandered to Ary and where she might be. He'd been more than concerned to find her not here waiting for him. Had even gone so far as to call Rome's house looking for Kalina. Only to have Rome laugh at him and once again reiterate that there were different rules to the mating game. That wasn't what Nick wanted to hear so he'd hung up feeling a little better that Ary was in fact with Kalina, but concerned that she hadn't left him a note.

He drummed his fingers on the desk reading websites that contained the keywords *shield, symbols, Brazil*. One in particular caught his eye. He clicked and saw an almost exact replica of the symbol staring back at him.

It was a picture of the Portuguese flag. Portugal's coat of arms consisted of a white shield on the flag's red-and-green background. Inside the shield were five smaller shields that represented the five Moorish kings who were defeated by the first king of Portugal.

Nick read the description then studied the flag once more. The five shields inside the one bigger shield looked just like the black tattoo-like symbol he'd seen on the crates in the Gungi, on the wall of that apartment building, and on X's cell phone. Only the symbol he'd seen didn't have five smaller shields. It had four.

That was significant, Nick thought. It had to be. But before he could think on it any longer the buzzer near his front door went off. He walked to the wall unit and pressed the TALK button. "Hello?"

"Hi. I'm back."

She sounded winded, happy. Nick's pulse jumped at the sound of her voice, and he pressed the buzzer to let her into the building.

He was holding the door open a few minutes later when Ary stepped off the elevator and walked toward his unit. Nick watched her move. Her muscled legs were bare beneath khaki shorts. Flat sandals with straps that wound up her calf adorned her feet, while the white tank top she wore hugged her awesome breasts. Her hair was straight, hanging over her shoulders and glittering with different tones of brown he'd never noticed before. She looked amazing. Simple and still breathtaking.

"Spa day," she said as she approached him at the door.

She held up half a dozen small bags and smiled up at him. "I have so many things in here, I don't even know what to do with them."

He caught her scent as she moved past him into the condo. Sweet and sensual, like flowers and honey. Closing the door, he watched her move into the living room, the material of her shorts fitting her ass like a glove. At his sides his own fingers clenched with the desire to grip those delectable globes just as those shorts were.

"I've had a full-body massage, which was heavenly," she said with a gushing sigh.

Nick leaned against the wall, folding his arms over his chest as he watched her. She was leaning over the sofa where she'd dumped all her bags. Digging inside, she pulled out jars and tubes of stuff, tossing them to the side as if they weren't what she was looking for. She talked as she moved, her voice sounding hurried and so happy he thought she'd bubble over with excitement.

That was what kept him quiet. The light lilt to her voice, the sound of her actually happy with something she'd done or something someone had done for her. He'd never heard her sound that way in the Gungi.

"I don't know what this does, but this one, yes!" she yelled and turn to face him, holding a black tube in her hand. "This one does something to your skin, it causes this stimulation, a sensitive-type hum that, I don't know. It just drove me crazy."

Nick pushed away from the wall and walked to her. He took the tube from her hands and felt his own smile spread wildly. It was exactly what she'd said, a lotion that caused stimulation, sexual stimulation.

"You used this at the spa?" he asked, wondering now about her full-body massage and whether it was a male or female who'd given it to her.

"Yes! And it felt fantastic!" With both her hands free she tucked her hair back behind her ears on each side and licked her lips.

Nick almost groaned.

"Alexi, that was the masseur, he said it would make me and you feel good. So I asked if I could try it first. He put it on me and I felt like . . . like I feel when I'm with you."

He didn't know what to say first. Didn't know what part of that sentence he wanted to address. "You had a full-body massage by a man?" That was probably the most important issue.

She nodded. "I was apparently very tense," she said with a shrug.

"Tense, huh." Nick's teeth clenched. "And where did he put this lotion for you to sample?"

"He rubbed it along the backs of my thighs at first—"

Nick instantly saw red. "He did what?"

Ary frowned. "He was giving me a massage as we talked about the product. I was already on my stomach so he rubbed the lotion on the backs of my thighs. When I told him I liked how it felt, he capped the tube and sold it to me."

"And what else did he do? What else did you let Alexi do to you, Ary?"

She took a step back from him. "You're an idiot!" she yelled. "No matter how many times I try to ignore that fact, you keep forcing it into my face."

Moving across the room, Ary began scooping up her items and tossing them into her bags.

"I asked you a simple question," he said.

"You're accusing me of doing something wrong. Well, I didn't. I was enjoying myself for once."

"You didn't even tell me where you were going. I came home and you weren't here. The least you could have done was left a note."

"Oh, really?" she asked, spinning around to face him. "Is that the least I could have done? Well, tell me this, Mr. Delgado, did you leave me a note this morning telling me where you were going? When Rome called here looking for you and I foolishly told him you were at work but obviously you weren't, a note would have been beneficial. Or is that just a rule I need to follow?"

"I go to work every weekday morning" was his tart reply.

"And what else? You come and go as you please and don't say a word to me about anything. But I'm supposed to sit here and wait for you or document my every step?"

"I'm supposed to be protecting you."

"But you're not supposed to be fucking me!" she yelled back. "Either you're my protector or you're my lover. Choose which one and act accordingly!"

"Stop yelling and calm down," he told her, moving over to grab her wrists, shaking them until she dropped the bags she'd slipped there to carry away. "You're twisting my words."

"No. I'm telling you how I see things."

"I just want to know where you are at all times. Is that so bad?"

"I'm not a child and I'm not some pet you need to keep on a leash. I'm a woman."

"You're my woman, Ary! My mate! Therefore, the thought of some other man rubbing your thighs is not acceptable."

She pulled away from him, stumbling back onto the chair then quickly pulling herself back up. "Don't tell me what's acceptable. I'll do what I want, when I want, and neither you nor anyone else is going to stop me."

"I'm your mate!"

"You're an ass! Just like my controlling father and the

rigid household I grew up in. You want to bark orders and dictate my every move and thought. Well, dammit, I'm sick and tired of living like that. I won't live like that again!"

When she stalked past him this time, her shoulder bumped his chest. Nick was the one to stumble back.

"Fuck you, Nick Delgado!" she yelled as she hit the steps, not with a run, but a gentle stomp that said she was spitting mad.

Nick stood for a moment, watching those same legs he'd just admired minutes ago disappear up the spiral staircase. When the door upstairs slammed, he cursed. Picking up the tube of lotion from the floor, he slung it hard across the room until it bounced off the patio glass and twirled back to the middle of the floor.

Sitting down heavily on the sofa, he put his face in his hands and sighed. Maybe Rome was right about the rules to the mating game being drastically different.

Chapter 20

"Did you give it to her?" Sabar asked Norbert.

"Yes. Yes, I did," Norbert stuttered.

Sabar wondered how this man was so great at his work. The research he conducted at George Washington would have required him to make presentations before investors to receive funding. With all the stuttering and sweating he did whenever he was asked a question, the investors should have been instantly turned off.

They were at the safe house, the brownstone where Sabar lived. He'd wanted to keep a close eye on the development of the new drug and its first test dummy. Norbert would be returned to the warehouse in Virginia, where his lab and sleeping quarters were located, along with the Rogues assigned to keep watch over him there. Darel would stay at the brownstone with Sabar and the test dummy.

"She's a looker," Gabriel said, licking his lips. His beady eyes opened wide to trace up and down the length of the half-naked female who lay on the bed.

"She's young," Darel added.

"She's a test dummy," Sabar told them both and pushed past them so that he was now standing right beside where her body lay on the bed.

The room was dark except for the small lamp on the table next to the bed. The walls had been painted a lighter shade than the thick hunter-green carpet that lined the floors. No other furniture had been put into this room, so Sabar had designated it the test room.

"You stay here and watch her," Sabar told Darel. "I want a report in the morning on her every reaction."

Norbert had already begun shaking his head. He stood at the end of the bed, wringing his ashen hands so that they made a chafing sound with each motion. "Maybe I should stay with her just in case something goes wrong."

"You're going back to the lab to mix more of the drug. If something happens, Darel will take care of it," Sabar said in no uncertain terms.

Norbert put his head down while Darel nodded his agreement. "I won't leave her."

"Yeah, I'm gonna stay, too," Gabriel said, rubbing the female's thigh, then down to her knee and calves with trembling fingers. "I'll make sure she's just fine."

Sabar slapped his hand away. "You'll keep watch and that's it. Get him out of here first!" He ordered Gabriel toward Norbert.

"We shouldn't rush the drug. I've never worked with it before. And the cocaine we used was pure. She could d-die," Norbert told Sabar nervously.

Sabar had covered the space between himself and Norbert in about two seconds, pulling the man's face up to his by yanking his collar and lifting him off the floor. "You listen to me, ass brain, I call the shots around here. So when I say produce the drug, that's what the fuck I mean! Now get back to your job before I cut off your horny little dick and feed it to you for supper."

Norbert paled, rightfully so, at Sabar's threat and his strength. The chemist fell to the floor after Sabar released him, only to be yanked up again and dragged out of the room by Gabriel.

When they were alone, Sabar clapped his hands together and looked at Darel. "This is it. This new drug is going to bring us a big steady payoff."

"What about the deal with Slakeman? His office has been calling all week. You want me to handle that?" Darel asked.

"No." Sabar shook his head. "I'll handle him for now. If he doesn't cooperate, then you can do your thing. Right now, she's your number one priority. We can't move up in the ranks without some serious pull around here. A new drug will give us that."

Darel nodded. "Cortez won't be happy."

"Cortez is the past. By the time that bastard figures it out he'll be dead." Sabar touched the female's face with blunt-tipped fingers, lifting one eyelid, then the other.

"And what about the Factions? They're hunting us now."

He wiped his hands on his pants and continued to stare down at the female. "Good, let them hunt. When I'm ready for those fuckers, they'll get exactly what's coming to them."

Darel nodded again. Something he'd been doing a lot lately. "Gabriel knows where the Faction Leader lives. You want him to sit there?"

"I want him to stay with that fool-ass chemist for now. We'll deal with the Faction Leaders and those female cats they're hiding later." He definitely had not forgotten about them. He had a personal score to settle with Kalina. And the other one, the *curandero,* well, she would die for being so stupid and to prove his point about the jungle cats.

Sabar laughed as he left the room. Darel didn't.

His mood was somber as he looked down at the still body in front of him. She didn't look that old, maybe twenty at the most. Her skin was dark, like his. Her nails were fake and long and colored a hideous black that made everything about her appear dismal. That shouldn't have been a problem for him, but Darel didn't like it for some reason.

He remembered Kalina Harper, remembered the way her scent had permeated his senses, making him need and hunger more than he ever had in all his life. Every female he'd taken since then had been a substitution for the one who'd gotten away. He didn't know the *curandero* and didn't really give a damn about her one way or the other. But if he got the opportunity again, he was fucking Kalina, no questions asked and damn the consequences. She owed him that much for embarrassing him when he'd tried capturing her for Sabar weeks ago.

There was a sound, the sheets rustling as the body moved. Darel moved closer, picking up one long braid in his hand and rubbing his fingers over the textured hair. She moved again; this time the wisp of a bra she wore slipped and one dark nipple was revealed. His mouth watered. Her eyes remained closed as he reached out to rub a finger over the puckered nipple. His hand hovered there for what seemed like endless moments, lightly touching her as his dick grew harder.

She stirred again, this time lifting a hand to clasp his wrist. Darel's eyes moved to her face, saw her eyelids flutter open to reveal smoky gray eyes. She didn't smile at him, but Darel didn't need smiles. She did, however, press his hand closer onto her breast. He obliged by squeezing the palm-size mound tighter. She made a sound that vaguely resembled a moan. And Darel lowered his head, took the nipple between his teeth, and bit down. Her back arched, and he sucked her entire breast into his mouth with force. Ripping the material from her chest, Darel gorged on the next breast, then pushed past the thin panties and cupped her mound. She moved beneath him as if she were trying to give him more.

He wasn't turning it down. Pulling her bottom half off the bed, he pressed a palm to her back and bent her over. Her body was so pliant that, whatever he did, she obliged without a word. If he'd stopped to really pay attention he would have noticed that she moved like a rag doll or that from her mouth a steady stream of white foam bubbled. But all Darel saw were plump ass cheeks that he readily separated with one hand while his other hand unzipped his pants and pulled his erection free.

In the next instant he was buried deep inside her, feeling the warmth and tightness of her core grabbing him tightly. It was a good thing shifters were immune to human diseases such as sexually transmitted afflictions and cancer. Because Darel didn't know anything about this female. He didn't know her name or where she came from, nothing. Right now it didn't matter. As he closed his eyes and slammed in and out of her wet pussy, the face he saw was of a lighter complexion, with hazel eyes that turned golden when she was in cat form. He twisted his hand in the long braids of the female he fucked, but his fingers felt the short silken strands of another.

Her name echoed in his head, her scent filtering through his nostrils. He pumped harder and harder, not giving a damn if he was hurting the female beneath him. He lifted her legs, planted her knees up on the bed, and continued to pound deep into her core until his head fell back and he roared as his release pumped deep inside her womb.

Pulling out of her once he'd finally caught his breath, Darel turned his back and pushed his still-hard cock back inside his pants. He was taking deep breaths, trying to steady his thoughts as well as his heart rate. His cat was wild, ready to break free and do some serious damage.

And apparently so was someone else.

He felt her nails on his shoulder and turned to tell her not to touch him. What he saw when he looked into her face rendered him speechless for a few seconds.

The long braids seemed frayed at the ends, giving her a wild look. Her eyes bulged like the retinas would burst right out of the sockets. Now he saw the foam, trailing down her chin. She raised her arms again and clawed his face with her nails.

Darel grabbed her wrists, pushing her back so hard her body flipped over the bed. She bounced up again and took one leap that landed her right in his face once more. This time she opened her mouth and bit him on the shoulder. His cat—already raging just beneath the surface—broke free. His clothes ripped as muscles bunched and stretched and he fell to the floor. When he stood again and looked at the woman it was through the eyes of his cat. The thick heavy scent of sex lingered in the room, along with another acidic stench the man couldn't name.

He didn't have time to examine it any further, as the female lunged for him once more. Her arms moved quickly as a war cry was wrenched from her mouth. She wanted to harm him, to kill him if she could. Her eyes looked frantic, filled with fear and defense. Without recourse the male cat came up on its hind legs swiping at the female, with one heavy paw ripping the side of her face off.

With blood spewing all over the bed and the carpet, the female continued to come at him. She seemed to feel no pain as she charged him again. He doubted she had a clue she was fighting a jaguar and not a man. The cat used its body to block her this time, ramming into her so hard she crumpled to her knees. With a deep roar, the male turned, quickly latching its massive jaws on the back of her neck and locking. She whimpered and thrashed beneath him for longer than she probably should have. His teeth sank deeper into her skin, piercing her skull. There was a series of cracks; the body beneath him seized and shivered, then finally went limp.

The cat pulled away from her, pacing back and forth in the room. It was a clean kill, and yet the animal felt a strange rising inside. Its flanks heaved with its motions, blood dripping from its sharp teeth. The door opened and the cat turned to the sound, ready to pounce again if necessary.

But it was only Sabar standing in the doorway, an eerie gleam in his cat eyes.

Chapter 21

Ary refused to cry.

He wasn't worth it.

The bastard.

Instead she paced the floor. Pulling an elastic band from her pocket, she gathered her hair into a ponytail and continued walking the length of the room she'd been using in Nick's house.

Nick's house. Nick's rules.

She should have known. Her heart pounded as her cat pressed for release. It had been a couple of days since she'd been able to shift and run free. In the forest she ran daily. In the city she didn't think that would be possible. In which case she was going to slowly lose her mind. Nervous energy bubbled inside her, coupled with the irritation of her conversation with Nick. Correction: That hadn't been a conversation. He'd made demands, puffed his chest all territorially, and barked orders just like her father used to do.

Her teeth bared in rage, claws emerging from her fingers. She wanted to scream. No, she wanted to run.

Finally unable to stand the four walls that seemed to be closing in around her, Ary opened the door quietly and slipped out. Nick was still downstairs—she could tell because his scent was like a lure to her own. Her body instinctively wanted to go wherever his was. But she resisted, moving with the customary quiet of a cat through the kitchen and to the front door. A quick glance over her shoulder revealed Nick standing out on his balcony, a cool breeze sifting through the open door, causing the curtains to billow in its wake. Ary flipped the lock and slipped through the door without another glance back.

She took two steps before being grabbed by the arm and turned around so fast her neck almost snapped.

"Where do you think you're going?" Ezra, the shifter guard assigned to Nick, said in a stern voice.

Ezra and Eli were twins, both about six feet tall with coffee-toned skin. They both had green eyes, the color of creek water, with brownish tints around the edges. Their hair was cut low and left to wave on top. With large builds and lethal stares, they could intimidate in both jaguar and human form. The only difference between the two, which Ary had noticed the first time she'd seen them at Rome's house, was that Ezra wore a diamond earring in his left ear. Eli had no earrings as far as Ary had seen.

"I'm leaving," she answered him finally, trying unsuccessfully to pull her arm from his tight grip.

"Not without Nick," Ezra told her.

"He's not my keeper!"

Ezra laughed. "No, he's your mate."

"That's a load of bull, too," she quipped.

"Say what you want, that's the way it is. I'm not letting you leave without him, or without him telling me to do so," he told her seriously, tightening his grip on her arm.

He looked like one of those men on the television who wrestled with his tight T-shirt on and jeans belted at his waist. His arms were huge. Trying to break away from him was futile.

She opened her mouth to speak then quickly closed it. The argument most likely would have continued, but the elevator doors opened and Rome, Kalina, and X stepped off. As if that weren't bad enough, another door opened behind her. Ary knew without turning around that it was Nick.

"What are you doing out here?" he asked, looking from her to Ezra.

Ary thought the guard would happily announce that she'd been trying to escape her prison, but he only smiled and nodded his head to her as if giving her permission to do the honors.

"I was going out for some air. Is that allowed or do I have to stay locked in that condo until you say so?"

Kalina walked up, placing a hand on Ary's shoulder. "Hello, are we interrupting something?"

Ary looked at Kalina, at her only friend in this new world of hers, and replied honestly. "I need to get out of here."

Kalina only nodded. "We'll go get some air."

Rome looked a little strained but didn't say a word, just took out his cell and sent a text. Ary figured it was to Eli, the other guard, to tell him they were coming down. The Faction Leader took their security very seriously. She had to hand it to him: The stateside shifters had a pretty good setup in place already. With the plans she'd heard they were currently making, there would be a democracy for the shifters in no time. Where she fit in to that, she still didn't really know. Regardless of what Nick had said, it would be her decision in the end. On that, Ary was adamant.

"Let's go inside," X said grimly to Nick. "You look like you could use a drink."

"A drink? I'm still trying to figure out what the hell's going on. One minute she's not here, the next she is and she's yelling about some guy massaging motion lotion on her thighs, then she's trying to leave. I don't know what's going on with her."

Rome and X filed in behind Nick as he entered the condo. He heard the door close but moved into the living room to drop down onto the sofa again. He'd already spent an hour there wondering what had happened with Ary, without success. Now it seemed he was back in the same spot.

"So that's why you're so tense," Rome said. "Another man touched your mate."

He took a seat on the couch, leaning forward to rest his elbows on his knees. "You want to kill him, don't you?"

X chuckled before Nick could even answer. "Who doesn't Nick want to kill? He probably has a Rolodex with an alphabetical listing of everyone on his hit roster."

Nick didn't find that funny. Nothing about this situation was funny. Jealousy was a new emotion to him, and he wasn't sure he liked it much. "How the hell am I supposed to feel?" he asked in response. Then he glared at X. "And if you came out of your cave for personal reasons once in a while you'd find some woman to drive you crazy, too."

He was talking to X, who had already hit the bar to fix himself a drink. Each of their homes seemed to have a bar in at least one of its rooms. Shifters didn't have the same reaction to liquor as humans; you'd never see a piss-drunk shifter puking in the gutter or falling off a bar stool. No, the shadows held their liquor perfectly. What the drink did was calm them a bit, taking the edge off their already volatile personalities. X almost always drank Hennessy, straight. Tonight was no exception. He poured a glass and downed it, then poured another.

"Don't need no woman claiming me," X said taking another swallow.

Nick knew that what his friend really meant was that he didn't think a woman would claim him. X was really jacked up when it came to women. That didn't mean he didn't get sex when he wanted it, but other than the physical his mind just couldn't process the concept of a woman or a mate.

Unlike Nick, who'd always known who his mate was and had accepted that he'd never have her. Until now.

"Mating makes us stronger," Rome said.

"Elder Alamar tell you that?" Nick questioned. He remembered when Rome found out Kalina was his mate. The Elder had been the one to break the news to the infamous bachelor. Rome hadn't taken it too well originally, but Nick had to admit he seemed to be settling into the concept pretty well now.

"I talked to the Elders while we were in the Gungi. It's a proven fact that the joining increases the male shifter's strength because he knows there's a female standing behind him every step of the way."

Nick nodded. "That old 'behind every good man is a good woman' bit, huh?" He didn't automatically dismiss the notion, but he wasn't totally sold on the idea, either. He was good without Ary, or at least he'd tried to be. Lately, however, he didn't like to think about the time he was without her.

"Good shifters are born," X said. "It's in their genes."

He looked sullen when he said that, and Nick and Rome shared a knowing glance as he took another swallow of his drink. Time to change the subject, they agreed silently.

"X has some information. We were coming over to see if you and Ary wanted to go out to dinner so we could talk about it." Rome shrugged. "Now I guess the three of us will discuss the new developments."

Nick decided it was better not to comment on the Ary situation right now. Especially since he still had no clue what had happened with her.

"What's up?" he asked, making an effort to keep his mind off Ary, at least for a couple of minutes.

"Sabar's circulating his drugs. I talked to some of Kalina's colleagues at the MPD and they showed me their stash from a raid in Silver Spring last month." X tossed the small plastic bag onto the table in front of where Nick sat.

Nick leaned forward and picked it up. His thumb traced over the symbol he'd been researching just a couple of hours ago.

"It's a replica of the Portuguese flag," he said.

"What is?" Rome asked. "The symbol? How do you know?"

"After we talked I thought back to each time I'd seen the symbol and figured that was the link among my father's involvement, the shipments, Davi's involvement, on up to what Sabar's doing now."

"It makes sense in the context that Portuguese is the language of the Shadow Shifters," X added. He rubbed a hand over his bald head, still thinking. "But it's kind of thin."

"There are five shields on the flag that represent all the Moorish kings who were defeated," Nick started again. "But on this symbol there are only four."

Rome was looking at the little plastic bag now, then up to Nick. "Why?"

Nick waited a beat before he said what had come to him right after the run-in with Ary. "There are four Faction Leaders," he said solemnly.

"Shit!" X exclaimed.

Rome exhaled and inhaled, over and over again, his brow furrowing more each time.

"He's sending me a message," Rome said through clenched teeth.

Nick was already shaking his head. "He's sending all of us a message."

"I know where some of his product is moving. I'm putting more guards on the inside to keep a lookout," X said. "And we're getting more protection for all the FLs."

"We should call all of them now, let them know what's going on," Nick said, standing. "We need more guards who've been trained. Everybody needs to be ready for whenever or wherever Sabar strikes again."

"Wait a minute," Rome said quietly. "I'm still the FL."

Nick and X were quiet, both watching Rome stand. He eyed them as if he still couldn't believe what had just been stated. Then his shoulders squared and his eyes shifted. No longer were his pupils the brown of the man. Now they were dark slits against bright green pupils. They were his cat's eyes—which wasn't good at all.

"I want details on each of the FLs and their families. Then I want guards on the streets tracing every tangible lead, including that bastard's scent. I want him found and I want him alive," he said with a deadly calm, his fists clenching and unclenching at his side.

X and Nick could only nod their agreement.

Nick knew what Rome wanted, knew the overall goal for the stateside shifters, but had to admit he was certainly glad they were beginning to take some real action.

It was no secret that Nick was the most resistant of the three to building this democracy that would govern all the stateside shifters. He was the one who accepted their differences a lot easier than the others.

He wasn't only a man. He wasn't human. He was a

jaguar shape shifter and he was proud of it. Had been all his life, despite the battle of his parents and friends to stay secluded and inconspicuous. Still, a part of Nick recognized the need to proceed with caution where this commingling of species was concerned. If he didn't he would have shifted in front of one of those ridiculously arrogant attorneys he'd gone up against and scared the shit out of them long ago.

Nick knew there was more at stake here than just his personal feelings. That's why he worked alongside Rome and the other FLs instead of going rogue himself.

Rome and X had gone to the bar to fix themselves another drink, so Nick paused and took a deep breath. He stilled and thought he heard something, but the sound translated to much more like a feeling. A yearning, deep and burning inside him. His dick hardened, his mouth watered, and he thought instantly of Ary.

"I know just what you need," Kalina said when they were once again at Rome's place.

She led Ary down a long hall and into a very homey-looking room decorated in dark browns and beiges. There were deep cushioned chairs and a fireplace and a pool table. It seemed very comfortable and very unlike the Faction Leader.

"It's the game room. Rome and the guys chill here a lot. Well, not lately with Sabar making his appearance. But anyway, we can go out this way." She nodded to the sliding doors just before walking over and opening them. "Let's go."

Ary followed without saying a word. They walked across plush grass. Ary slipped off her sandals and let the soft blades rub against her bare feet. Inside there was a sigh, her shoulders releasing some of the stress she held there faster than Alexi had been able to do even with his heavenly massage. Ahead of them were rows and rows of trees. Ary's heart sang out, her cat pacing impatiently.

"We have to get a little farther inside," Kalina said, unbuttoning her shirt. "Rome warns me constantly that people driving on the highway might get a glimpse of us if we're not deep enough in the trees."

Ary still didn't speak, just pulled her shirt over her head and held the material in the same hand she held her shoes. When she was finally able to slip out of her shorts, she fell to her knees, chest heaving with heavy breaths. Her cat ripped free with a long stretch, muscles that hadn't moved in days elongating and shifting. With a moist tongue the cat licked its muzzled face and sharp teeth. Looking over her shoulder, she saw another cat and leapt forward, running, finally.

Kalina's cat burst in front of Ary's after a few seconds, as Ary had never run here before. Both cats went through the land that Rome owned specifically for this purpose. They ran up small inclines and traipsed through shallow pools of water. They scored trees that weren't previously scored and roared with complete satisfaction.

Adrenaline flowed through Ary's blood, made it pump wildly, her pace increasing. There was something else she felt as she moved through the trees, an intense pull on everything inside her. She'd needed to run, there was no doubt about that, but there was another need. The more energy she exerted darting through the trees, over downed trunks and stubborn inclines, the deeper the need went, until it was a dull ache inside her.

In response to the ache Ary roared, her teeth bared to the air, her nose prickling with scents. It didn't ease the need but added to its urgency, and so she roared again.

And she didn't notice they were being watched.

He'd been on his way back from the warehouse in Alexandria, with all the windows to his truck rolled down. The air was stifling him, even with the slight breeze. Gabriel wanted to be out in the open, he wanted to run and climb and stretch, all things a human could not do to the cat's specifications.

The minute the scent hit him he'd pulled over on the side of the road. Getting out of the truck, he stood there for endless moments, speeding cars whooshing past him on the highway. It was a musky smell, the heavy scent of a female shifter—one in heat. The cat inside him stood on hind legs and roared, begging for release. It had to have this female, wanted to mate just for the physical purpose of doing so. Gabriel had no clue who the cat was, just knew it was in need and so was he.

In no time he had shifted, darting down the incline that led away from the highway. In the distance there were thick crops of trees that stretched as far as the eye could see. She was in there, he knew, and raced to find her.

Chapter 22

The roar was loud, a cry of hunger. Both female cats stopped, their large heads lifting, noses tilted toward the breeze. A glance at each other and a low chuffing was all the warning they could afford to translate before they both broke into a run.

Trees whizzed by Ary at a speed she hadn't seen in a long while. She was no longer running for fun, but running for her life. There was another cat in the trees, one that wasn't friendly. The sour scent of a Rogue filtered through the trees with the wind. In a blur of tawny fur Kalina darted past her, leading the way. Ary followed, heart hammering wildly, ears still pricked for any more sounds from the Rogue.

As if she'd summoned it, the strange cat roared into the night air. It was getting closer.

Kalina shot over two downed tree trunks and down through a small clearing. Ary remembered this spot. Just a few feet ahead they'd clear the trees totally and once again be on Rome's lawn. Unfortunately, so would the Rogue.

Looking upward, she quickly thought of going up, but was reminded that this was not the Gungi. And while the trees were tall, they would not support the weight of a full-grown female jaguar, and they weren't tall enough to take her into the canopy that would further hide her from the Rogue approaching. No, their only hope was to get to Rome's house.

Just as Kalina cleared the trees Ary heard gunshots and skittered to a stop. They'd come from the direction of Rome's property, she was almost sure. Her eyes had already switched to night vision so she could see as deftly throughout the forest as if it were broad daylight. In the distance there was nothing. Turning slowly, she noted nothing behind her.

Then there was a rustling of twigs and a roar. Not the fierce roar she'd heard before, but a low, whining one. The Rogue had been shot. Ignoring the warning bells in her mind she went in the direction of the Rogue, moving at a steady pace so that whichever human had done the shooting wouldn't get a chance to follow her. At this point she didn't know who to trust—cat or man.

She came across the cat first, a big dark brown male with black rosettes. It lay on its side, legs spread, flank bleeding profusely from the bullet holes. Its eyes found hers and she stared at them. It licked its muzzle, baring its teeth and making a lazy swiping motion with its front paw. She got as close as she could because she didn't feel like it was any threat in its present condition. She didn't recognize it, and it didn't seem to have any knowledge of who she was. But they were both shifters, there was no doubt about that.

Behind her there was more rustling. She picked up a human scent, one that was vaguely familiar.

"You should go back. Ms. Kalina is waiting at the edge with your clothes."

It was Baxter, the tall, older man with watery brown eyes and wrinkled brown skin. In one hand he held a rifle.

The other lifted and pointed in the direction he wanted her to go, back toward the house.

"I'll take care of him," he told her when Ary continued to watch him through her cat's eyes.

She hadn't said much to this man in the past, but she knew he was Rome's caretaker, or something like that. The other thing she was positive of now was that he knew about the shifters and the Rogues. He wasn't a shifter himself—a fact she'd gleaned before, but confirmed now. And yet he protected them and kept their secret.

She didn't wait to examine the situation any further but trotted off until she could see light shining through the trees. Not wanting to shift yet—then she'd be naked, and she wasn't sure who was beyond the trees—she moved at a slower pace, watching carefully what was going on ahead. There were lots of men, some with flashlights, others with guns walking around the perimeter as far as she could see. Kalina caught sight of her and stepped through the trees, offering her clothes.

Ary shifted and asked questions as she dressed. "What's going on? Who was it?"

"A Rogue. They don't know his identity yet. Guards are all over the place trying to see if there are any others out there."

"Where's Rome?"

"One of the guards called him after Baxter made the kill."

"I can't believe he killed that cat. How old is he anyway?"

Kalina smiled. "About a hundred," she said laughingly. "I don't know, but he takes care of everything around here. He knows all and sees even more. Rome trusts him with his life."

Ary shrugged and fastened the ties to her sandals. "And apparently our lives as well."

An hour later they were back in Rome's den, the tension so thick Ary felt like she could choke at any second. She and Kalina sat near the window in two leather lounge chairs. A few feet away Nick stood, his usual frown deepening as he worked a stress ball between his fingers. X was at the computer, punching the keys like he actually expected them to cough up answers. Rome faced a shelf of books, his hands thrust into his pockets, barely containing the rage simmering inside.

The threesome of shifters were beyond angry, their feeling seeping into the air like oxygen. Inside, Ary warred with feeling their same heightened fight mentality and the nagging sensations she'd felt when she ran in the trees. She could not get comfortable as she tried to sit still. It was beyond annoying to try to tamp these feelings down. They were new and intense and she wanted them gone. About as much as she wanted to be out of this room right now.

Rome's house was large; each room inside seemed like the size of her entire dwelling in the Gungi. The den was no different, with its dark-brown-carpeted floor and chocolate-brown leather furniture. It was almost a replica of the game room where she and Kalina had gone through the glass doors to seek some semblance of freedom. But instead of the pool table, there was a huge bar, and along the walls were bookshelves instead of pictures. At the door were two guards. She'd never seen them before, but they looked muscled and fierce as they stared straight ahead. And finally, putting a tray with a coffee carafe and cups on a wood table, was Baxter.

Ary had been watching the older man since she'd seen him emerge from the trees. His face looked solemn, locked. He spoke clear and concisely, giving orders as to what was to be done with the shifter body and how the search for others was to play out. It wasn't until Rome arrived that Baxter took his usual place behind the faction leader. Even then, Ary looked on with intrigue as Rome consulted with the older man even though he was the leader. It was a weird relationship these two had.

Actually, as she sat back in the chair that on any other day, to any other person, might be extremely comfortable, her gaze settled over every shifter in this room. There was a connection here, a deep one that she almost felt she were breaching somehow. It was apparent they all belonged together; they were a team. Ary had never been a part of a team, not one that worked toward the same goals, she realized now. That made her think of her father, of the man who'd raised and trained her and ultimately betrayed her. She wondered how he could have done what he did and what that really meant for her and her future.

"How the hell did he get on the property?" X said, slamming his hand against the keyboard. He was searching his database, trying to identify the shifter who'd been killed.

"I suspect he came from the highway, Mr. Xavier."

Again, Baxter was speaking in that low, even tone he had.

"But he had to know the house was here, else why even stop in this vicinity?" Rome asked.

Kalina cleared her throat and sat forward in her chair. "I have a theory on that," she said and waited until everyone's eyes fell on her. "Mel, the female shifter who was working with Sabar to capture me, picked me up here last month. She had another shifter with her, and they had a driver. That would make our location common knowledge to the Rogues now."

"Did you recognize the Rogue?" X asked her.

Kalina shook her head. "No. His scent wasn't familiar. But that doesn't mean he wasn't with Sabar that night."

Nick cursed. "We killed the cheetah that had been a part of the original threesome who stalked you. The other jaguar along with Mel, you shot. Now Baxter's killed a different one. Where's Sabar and the Rogue that escaped that night?"

"He would be the one closest to Sabar," Baxter said, standing perfectly still in the center of the room. His long arms extended in front of him, hands clasped neatly. He still wore the black suit and white shirt he'd been wearing when he shot the shifter, and managed to look as if he were heading out to a nicc dinner, instead of a debriefing about killing shifters. "It was careless to come onto this property, and to do so alone made it just stupid. He was not given an order to come here, I am sure of that."

"So he acted alone. You're right, that was stupid," Nick said. "And it got his punk ass killed!"

Baxter nodded. "You are correct, Mr. Dominick. But think about this: Why would he be so stupid? What made him stop on the highway, shift, and enter the copse of trees?"

"We did," Ary said quietly. "He scented us running."

The look Nick gave her would have burned holes through any other woman. Ary straightened her back and looked away from him quickly. She didn't like what she was feeling from his direction: Coupled with his rage was a strange heat that she swore made her even edgier as she tried to sit still.

Almost simultaneously Rome spun around, glaring

at Ary and Kalina. "You went out without telling me or Baxter."

It wasn't a question, because everyone in the room already knew the answer. And it wasn't a statement that anyone could comment on. It seemed, to Ary, that it was more like an accusation. And she didn't like it.

But if she thought the heated glare coming from Rome was disconcerting, the continuous angry vibes rolling off Nick toward her was the grand finale. She tried not to look at him, definitely did not want to catch his gaze. He was at a place she didn't think she'd ever seen him before. A place she wasn't sure she wanted to visit, despite her the gripes she had with him from earlier.

"I needed to run," Ary spoke up in their defense.

"We thought it was safe," Kalina added. "He shouldn't have known we were out there."

"Unless he was watching the house," Nick offered. "He would remember you, Kalina. And Sabar is probably still looking for you."

Nick looked at Ary then, and she moved uncomfortably in the chair. His cat's eyes held her gaze. Everyone in this room who was a cat had looked on with the eyes of their beast. That was just a hint how bad this situation really was.

Ary licked her lips, refusing to look away from him this time no matter how desperately she wanted to. "He doesn't know I'm here."

"Do not underestimate him. He would recognize Kalina's scent, but another would have been more alluring. Sabar has been working a long time to start this war. He knows more than we want him to," Baxter stated.

"What do you mean, another would have been more alluring?" Nick asked, his lips drawing into a thin line, his brow wrinkling to the point Ary thought it would never straighten again.

Baxter looked to Ary, then to Nick. "It would be wise for you to pay more attention to your mate, sir."

The sentence was a little cryptic but brought all attention suddenly to Ary. Her cheeks heated with embarrassment as she shifted in that damn chair once more.

"We need to rethink our strategy where Sabar's concerned. It's obvious he's moving fast to achieve his goal," Rome stated. "I want this place locked down tight. Guards at every entrance and walking the grounds twenty-four seven. Send someone to your homes to get your things," he added, looking to Nick and X before either of them could speak.

"And nobody," he concluded, looking pointedly at Kalina and Ary, "nobody leaves without informing me and without taking a guard with them. Are we clear?"

Kalina nodded. Ary hesitated only momentarily then nodded as well. It wasn't wise to go against the FL. She hadn't been here that long, but she could sense that.

"First thing tomorrow, Kalina and I will visit a location she found for what we're tentatively calling Havenway. If it suits my qualifications we'll have construction immediately started and move in as soon as possible. Everyone who doesn't stay there needs to make sure their homes are totally protected."

Rome had continued speaking, not leaving room for any interruptions or contributions.

"Now that this location has been breached—" He paused, sharp teeth elongated, claws detracting from his fingertips. "—Kalina and I will need to relocate. The women need more protection."

X stood. "We'll take care of it," he vowed, looking directly at Rome.

Nick dropped the stress balls to the floor and went to stand on the other side of Rome.

"I'll meet with the guards and map out new security in the morning," he said with a nod.

They looked dark and dangerous and impenetrable, the three of them, standing strong together. They'd die for one another, Ary thought in those moments they stood there. They'd die protecting the Shadow Shifters.

She was in awe of them as she watched. And dangerously close to shifting again and roaring with impatience if whatever the weird sensations inside her were decided it was time to take charge. On shaky legs she stood. She would have walked out of the room alone, but Nick quickly stepped in front of her. He extended a hand, and Ary looked down at it.

His scent was strong and like a potion to her as she swooned toward him. The war began in earnest against the part of her that wanted to fall into his arms and pray he had a cure for whatever was ailing her—and the part that screamed for freedom, for the right to come and go as she pleased, to make her own decisions. She wanted to scream, possibly to run away again, but knew neither action was the answer.

She found herself extending her hand, until her palm was warmly fit against his. Instantly his fingers wrapped around hers and he almost pulled her out of the room. It took every bit of pride Ary had to keep from falling and being dragged. Instead she moved her feet as quickly as possible to keep up with him.

Chapter 23

"Keep your fucking mouth shut!" Sabar yelled into the beet-red face of Senator-elect Ralph Kensington.

"I don't think you're the one with the control here," Kensington shot back, even though the beads of sweat rolling down his face and the tangy, citrus-like scent of fear overruled the fake bravado in his voice. "Seems to me I got a secret you want kept."

Just last month Ralph Kensington had held a fundraiser to announce his run for the Senate. The announcement came five weeks after the death of Senator Mark Baines and his daughter—two deaths that were necessary to let everyone know that Sabar was now running the show in this town. Instead of starting off his campaign, Kensington had been elected to take Baines's place for the remainder of this term. Rumors of Kensington's unprofessional and illegal connection with his former boss Bob Slakeman, a defense weapons specialist, had surfaced but apparently hadn't been strong enough to keep Kensington out of office.

Now the obese and frankly offensive man was sitting in a high-backed leather office chair that had wheels on it. After a shuffle of his feet, he was able to back away from Sabar's fierce growl.

"You don't want to play with me, old man! Believe me when I say I've got all the control," Sabar told him, his claws emerging without warning.

"Shit! I knew it. You're animals!" he spit. Then he chuckled. "This is gonna be big."

Lifting a hand, Kensington wiped his forehead and looked from Sabar to Darel, who stood guard at the door.

"Now, you want me to keep my mouth shut about your . . . your kind, I guess. And you want weapons from Slakeman. Well, well, well."

Sabar growled, using one clawed hand to toss tendrils of his dreadlocks out of his face. The Rogues didn't really need weapons. They were already killing machines. But Sabar was thinking globally; he was thinking of the future evolution of the Rogues. They would have to be more than animalistic killers to truly rule here. He recognized and wasn't afraid of that fact.

"Don't think I've forgotten how long it took your man to pay up the last time I hit him off with a supply. Now this time you're gonna give me exactly what I want or you'll have the shortest senatorial term ever."

"How much are you willing to pay for both my silence and the weapons?" Kensington asked, taking a cigar from a box to his left. Pudgy fingers grabbed the cutter and sliced the edge of the cigar off in one clean sweep. Putting it to his mouth, he talked around the stogy. "Way I see it, I've gotta get a cut. Especially since you took away my play toy."

Sabar didn't bother to address that issue. Melanie Keys was a Rogue whom he'd planted at Rome Reynolds's law firm to spy on the FL. She was also fucking Kensington's brains out in exchange for his connections to some of the lowest, but politically best-connected, scum in DC. She'd been killed when Kalina's capture had gone bust.

Unfortunately, it seemed Kensington had fallen hard for the cat.

"I'll pay for the weapons, but your silence, you're going to do that as a personal favor to me," Sabar told him.

Kensington pulled the stogy from his lips and chuckled, his rotund midsection vibrating with the effort. "And what makes you so sure about that? Huh? Why would I want to help you—an animal, a stinking-ass drug dealer?"

Sabar was on him in seconds, his knees braced on the arms of the chair Kensington sat in. His hands wrapped quickly around the man's neck, his claws digging into the sweaty flesh hanging there. His teeth had already begun to protrude, so Sabar let his lips peel back until Kensington got a full view of his capabilities.

"Because I'll rip your goddammn throat out if you don't."

Kensington coughed, dropped the stogy, and coughed again.

"Now, I'll expect to hear from you by the end of the day with delivery dates. Or the fine constituents that elected you to office after Baines's demise are gonna be looking for a replacement for your fat ass as well!"

Sabar climbed off the now rapidly sweating senator-elect, straightened his hair once more, and rubbed human fingers—bloody at the tips from the quick release and retract of claws—down the front of his shirt and walked around the desk.

"Don't make me come visit you again" were his parting words to Kensington as he strutted out of the office.

Darel had opened the door for his boss, tossing a pitiful look and smile at Kensington before leaving.

"Norbert has three cases of the drug ready to go," Darel told Sabar when they were in the back of one of the five

Hummers the Rogue owned. "We can make deliveries throughout the city tonight if you're ready."

Sabar looked out the window, pulling his hands together and cracking his knuckles. "You said that stripper bitch was hot as hell for you the other night?"

Darel nodded. "Hot and wet. She wanted to be fucked more than she wanted to breathe."

"That was obvious after what you did to her," Sabar quipped.

"I don't know what that was about. Bitch just came at me afterward. I had to take her down."

Sabar shrugged. "Do what you have to do," he said. "Start shipping tonight. We need the capital to pay Slakeman."

"You think he's going to come through?"

"Either he will or he'll die. I get the feeling both Slakeman and Kensington are partial to breathing this smog-filled air, the stupid bastards."

Both Rogues chuckled in the backseat as they rode from Capitol Hill toward the brownstone. There waited more strippers who'd received their first dosage of Sabar's savior pills, as he'd taken to calling them.

"You left the condo without telling me," Nick started the minute they walked into one of the upstairs bedrooms.

There seemed to be at least half a dozen doors on this floor and a long hallway that she'd watched Rome and Kalina walk down. That would be his side of the house, she surmised. Ary didn't have much time to look around except to notice the large bed on the far side of the room just feet away from a trio of windows. Furniture was set up on the other side of the room to duplicate a living room; there was a huge flat-screen television on the wall above. Nothing else registered but the sound of Nick's voice.

"You tried to sneak out again and ended up here, running in the open and almost getting yourself killed! What the hell is wrong with you? You're not in the Gungi anymore, Ary, you need to think about what you're doing!"

At her sides, her own fists clenched. They were a smaller version of Nick's downstairs, but that didn't mean she wasn't just as angry as he was.

"I am an adult," she began with barely restrained anger. "I can come and go as I please."

"You are a shape shifter in a world of humans. Do you have any idea what could have happened if a human had seen you running in cat form? They would have killed you without a second thought."

Ary didn't want to think of that.

"Kalina felt it was safe because we were on Rome's property. I won't live in a cage, Nick."

In no time he was right in her face, his strong hands clasping her arms and lifting until her feet were barely touching the ground. "This isn't a game, Ary."

"Let go of me, you big idiot!" Ary bared her teeth and kicked at his legs until he walked a few steps then tossed her onto the bed.

"What the hell is the matter with you?" he roared, his cat's eyes glaring down at her.

"I'm not that helpless shifter you left in the Gungi sixteen years ago. I've changed. I've grown up and I won't allow you to treat me like some child you were forced to rescue!" she yelled back at him, scrambling until she was on the other side of the bed, staring right back at him with what she was sure were her own cat's eyes.

"You're an idiot! Traipsing around a foreign land like you've been here all your life. It's dangerous out there. Sabar is dangerous! He wants to use you for your knowledge, then he'll kill you as sure as you're standing there. How the hell do you think that makes me feel?"

It was the nearest thing to her and Ary didn't think twice before picking up the lamp on the small table beside the bed and hurling it at Nick. "You're an asshole if you think I'm going to bow down to you just because I'm in your country now! I didn't ask to be brought here! You decided, now you get to deal with it!"

He ducked out of the lamp's trajectory and skirted the bed to stand beside her as she raged at him. Ary started swinging before he was close enough to actually receive any of her hits. "I hate you! I hate you!" she yelled.

Inside her body felt like it was on fire, like a volcano bubbling in preparation for eruption. Her claws emerged from her fingers with a painful stretch and as she yelled at Nick, sharp teeth pricked her lips.

He grabbed her flailing arms and pulled her tightly to his chest.

"I was so scared," he said through his own clenched teeth, lowering his forehead to hers. "I felt you reaching for me, calling to me, and . . ."

"Let me go!" She continued to struggle, pain prickling her skin at the intense sensations swirling through her. She wanted to break free, to run and to . . . what? She didn't know what she wanted to do or what she needed.

"Listen to me," Nick yelled into her face, his eyes closed, his hands tightening on her wrists. "Listen!"

"No!" she yelled back. "No! I don't have to listen to you! You cannot control me!"

"I'm not trying to control you, I'm trying to protect you" was his fierce retort. "If you'd keep still and just listen to me you'd realize that."

No, she couldn't keep still. She couldn't hear him,

couldn't say another word. Instead she crumpled to the bed, sitting and pulling Nick with her. The pain was increasing. It was tearing through her to the point Ary thought she would rip in two.

Then Nick cupped her face in his hands. He looked into her eyes, his thumbs running over her bottom lip.

"I was afraid he'd caught you, that he would kill you. Do you know how that made me feel?"

She still couldn't speak, could only stare at him as if transfixed by his eyes, his voice, his touch.

"You said another man touched you and I freaked the hell out. I wanted to kill him and anybody else that got near you. I couldn't think past protecting you. I can't do anything else but protect you, Ary. Do you understand what I'm saying?"

She didn't. She wanted to, but she didn't.

He didn't wait for her response, but came closer, his lips touching hers. And all Ary could think was, *Finally.*

Nick's tongue swiped along her lower lip, dipped inside and touched hers. His cat roared and reached out to hers as a part of him sank inside the glory that was Ary.

Her hands were wild, moving quickly over his shoulders and down his back where she raked her nails upward against his skin. His shirt ripped with the motion, and he felt the distinct sting of her claws against his skin. She pulled him with her as she lay back on the bed, her legs lifting and wrapping around his waist. To his hands her face felt feverish, her heart thumping wildly against both their chests. Nick tried to pull away, to look at her. She resisted, nipping his bottom lip between her teeth to keep him still. They kissed again, this time a hungry, fervent exchange that had Nick gasping for breath, his dick pressing painfully against the restraint of his pants.

"Baby," he whispered against her mouth. "It's all right," he added, trying to talk again.

She was holding him so tightly, thrusting her center upward to meet him. Her frisky fingers pulled at his shirt until it was ripping over his muscled frame. When it was gone Ary dipped her head, raking her teeth over his pectorals, her tongue lovingly stroking his nipples. With a mewling sound she moved lower, her tongue tracing a path down his abs, down, down . . .

His dick was free and in her hands before Nick could utter another word. She stroked his length with mild pressure, then released and rubbed her thumb over his engorged tip.

"Ary." He struggled, his eyes closing then opening again. He swallowed. Hard. Focused. Even her hands were hot.

"Ary." He said her name again, this time rolling slowly onto his side.

She followed, her fingers still moving over his length. He knew she wouldn't let go. His cat growled at the human's thought that he wanted her to. When she dipped her head, her tongue started at the base of his cock, moving upward in one slow, smooth stroke. Nick thought he was going to explode.

On a surge of strength he didn't know he possessed, he grabbed her face and pushed her back away from his erection. She didn't remove her hands, and he had to move fast to take her wrists and pull those away, too. Once he was free and before she could pounce again—the growing growl he heard from her said she was thinking of doing just that—he twisted his hips out of her reach. Reaching out, he circled his arms around her waist and turned her so that when she fell against him, it was her ass against his erection and not her waiting pussy.

She was not happy and showed it by raking her claws up and down his arms.

"Stop," he whispered sternly into her ear.

She whimpered, shaking her head. "I can't." She heaved and hissed. "I need."

At those words a thought occurred to Nick, and he felt like kicking himself for not realizing this sooner. Even Baxter had known what he'd ignored. Ary was in heat.

"Shhh," he whispered again, holding her tightly. "I'll take care of you."

"Nick." His name was a whisper—one that totally threatened Nick's sanity.

Her body was so warm and so pliant against him, Nick kissed the spot beneath her ear and felt her lie back against him. "I'll take good care of you."

He kept kissing her as his arms loosened around her. With each kiss she sighed deeper. Pulling her shirt from her shorts and over her head was simple enough. Discovering that her bountiful breasts had been virtually unbound beneath it sent a spark of fire scorching through his body and he cursed. The goal was to get her naked, get inside her, and make both of them feel better—but mostly to soothe her need. But he was swayed by thoughts of her breasts and found both his palms making their way to cover the mounds without any direction. She had the softest ass, and when she pressed back against him he wanted to sink between her cheeks once more, to drown in the tightness of her.

"I've never felt like this before."

He heard her words filtering vaguely through the thick haze of lust he was stuck inside.

"You drive me crazy" was his reply. As he continued to palm her breasts roughly, his teeth nipped her neck. "I can't think about anything but you, keeping you safe, keeping you here, keeping you . . ." He growled into her ear, pulling her body back farther against him.

When he was finally able to pull his hands away from her breasts, he let them slide down her stomach until he found the snap of her shorts. Snaps, zippers, none of it mattered. They were off her in seconds, along with her panties. She was blessedly naked, and his fingers immediately delved between the heated folds of her pussy to find her center drenched with desire.

"Please," she begged. Every part of Nick roared with pleasure.

"I can't stand this. Now, Nick. Now!"

He didn't want her to suffer, but he needed something himself. Something he'd been thinking about since he'd peeled that sinfully sexy black dress off her the other night. Shifting so that she was now lying flat on her back, Nick lifted her legs, draping them over his shoulders, and put his mouth to her sweetness. When his tongue met the smooth damp folds, his cat growled with satisfaction. Licking her became almost a ritual as he took his time making sure to taste every delectable inch of her desire.

She moaned, lifting her hips off the bed as if feeding him. Nick fed like a man dying of starvation. God, she was delicious. He could do this all night . . . and all day . . . and all night again. But his cat wanted more. It wasn't easy untwining her legs from around his shoulders, but Nick managed. And he rose over her, looking down at her glowing eyes and pouting lips. His erection moved on its own, finding her wet center and slipping easily inside her warmth.

She called his name, made it sound like a long note in a song as she lifted her hips and reached for him.

Nick didn't take her hands, but pulled her legs up to hold each ankle in a hand. Spreading her legs into a wide

V, he looked down to see their joining, watched as his length, now glistening with her arousal, slid all the way out, then sank so far in it looked as if they were born connected.

Again and again he watched the motion, loving the feeling of ownership, of complete satisfaction and protectiveness, wash over him. Her head thrashed wildly on the pillow as he pounded into her mercilessly. With each stroke Nick lost a little more of himself. Inch by inch as his length went inside her he knew he could never leave her again, could never lose this woman. His *companheiro*.

Chapter 24

"I need you with me," he said in the dark of night as they lay in the big bed side by side.

Ary had been listening to him breathe, wondering if he was awake. They didn't touch, but their bodies were close. It was quiet. She was still trying to get used to that, a night without sound.

"My father controlled everything. When the shipment would come from the States, he'd bring it into the great hall of the medical center and separate everything. Then he'd tell me what we could have and what to do with the rest. That was before he started stealing."

She paused, took a deep breath, and continued, "He told my mother what to do. From the time she woke in the morning she was his virtual slave. Cook the food this way. Heal the people that way. Say this, don't say that. There were days I swear he told her how to breathe. I hated looking at her, watching her blindly obey whatever he said. I listened to his teachings about medicine but resented everything else he said. I wanted her to yell at him, to tell him to go to hell and just do one thing for herself, one thing without getting his permission or even caring enough to ask for it."

She was shaking her head before she realized it, warm

tears streaming quietly from her eyes. Now she was grateful for the dark.

"He always said that we were the heart of the tribe, we kept the blood flowing with our talent. That they would forever need us. That's why it was so important for me to stay, for me to learn everything there was to know about healing. I was responsible for the tribe."

"You are only one person. The weight of the world should not have rested on your shoulders," Nick said.

There was some movement, and in seconds he had her hand in his. Ary didn't pull away. It was nice.

"Yuri was great. In a sense I guess he saved me. First, I mean," she said when Nick seemed to stiffen beside her.

"I stumbled upon him one day in the forest. He was performing a purification ceremony with a couple of locals. They weren't taking it seriously, snickering behind his back. But Yuri was focused, his face like some kind of god amid the smoke. He saw me and knew instantly I had the gift of healing. From the first time we talked I knew I could learn so much from him. And I did. I learned that healing goes beyond just the physical fix; that your soul has to be open to the change, to whatever medicines or procedures are meant to help. Your energy needs to be just right to receive the gift. My father hated Yuri for teaching me. But I would not stop going to see him."

"Good. You shouldn't have listened to him blindly like your mother did."

"Or like you did," she said quietly. "You left because he told you to."

It was Nick's turn to inhale deeply then sigh. "I left because I was too young to know what was good for me. I didn't want to cause trouble with my parents and your parents. They said it was your job to stay there. The *Ética* said it was your life's responsibility. I couldn't go against that. Not when I was already rebelling against so much."

She turned on her side to face him. "What else did you rebel against?"

"I didn't believe in a democracy for the shifters at first."

"Why?"

"Because we're different. Why should we beg to fit in?"

His words were said with such force that she jolted and pulled her hand out of his. He searched for it again and found it, this time holding it between both his hands.

"I know we need to govern ourselves, but I'm not for all this peace-and-be-kind stuff Rome promotes."

Ary didn't know what to say; then again she did. "Then why aren't you with the Rogues? Why stay here under the pretense of believing in the cause?"

"Because I believe in the Shadow Shifters. I believe in our tribe, our people, our lives. That makes me different from the Rogues."

He didn't sound like he really believed that.

"You seem so hostile all the time. That is not healthy."

"It's necessary."

"Why?"

There was a long silence, and Ary almost gave up on getting an answer.

"I don't like being lied to. If I act like a loose cannon all the time that makes people nervous enough to tell the truth the first go-round."

"People, not shifters," she said seriously. Rogues wouldn't be bluffed, by anyone; even Ary knew that. But Nick didn't sound like he was in the mood to debate the fact. He'd even adjusted so that she was now spooned against him.

"I want you to stay with me. When we leave Rome's I want us to live together."

"Does it matter what I want?" she asked. The fingers he'd been running through her hair paused.

"Of course it matters." He sighed again. "Look, Ary, I'm not trying to be your father. I just want to keep you safe."

"But I want a life. I have to be able to lead my own life without you dictating to me."

"I would never dictate how you run your life."

"Really? 'You'll be the head of the medical center,' 'you go shopping with Kalina,' 'you use my credit card.' Shall I go on?"

Silence again. For him to be an attorney, he had to know how to clam up when he wanted to.

"I thought you wanted to become a doctor."

"I do. On my own terms and in my own time."

"You needed things. I thought I was being considerate by telling you to go with Kalina and footing the bill. Most women would love to hear that from their man."

Was he her man? A smile tickled her lips, but she clamped that bit of happiness down for a moment.

"I don't want to owe anybody anything. I want to make it on my own here. I know I can do it."

Nick kissed her ear. "I know you can, too, but you don't have to. You are my *companheiro,* it is my duty to take care of you."

He was right, Ary knew. As her mate he was charged with the duty of protecting her and their family. That most likely included buying her things, and she probably should be happy about that. But, she admitted, she had her own rebellious streak.

"When I become a doctor, I'll make my own money," she told him.

"I'm sure you will. But for now—" he began.

"For now, I'll spend yours," she finished for him. And actually, hearing herself say it out loud made it seem like a better idea than she'd originally thought.

"Dammit!" Caprise cursed, shaking her hand as the door swung open in front of her.

She'd called Nick a dozen times and he hadn't answered. Probably asleep, or dead to the world. Nick used to be a heavy sleeper—either that or he was ignoring the hell out of her all those early mornings she'd tried to wake him. He'd been her role model during her teen years, the big, bad brother who didn't give a crap what anybody said, he was doing his own thing. That's exactly what Caprise wanted to be when she grew up—well, not the brother part, but everything else. Her life had been simple then, those days of attending private school, noticing boys, making friends with snobby girls, seeing her parents together each night at dinner. Simple. She'd naively thought it would stay that way.

And she'd been wrong.

Caprise had just broken into her brother's house and was walking in unannounced. It hadn't escaped her that this might not be a good idea, but she needed a place to stay. So if Nick had a female here, that was his business. She just wanted a nice hot shower and his empty couch to crash on.

Another mistake to add to her already growing list.

A strong arm wrapped around her waist, another around her neck to cover her mouth. She kicked out the moment she was lifted off the floor, but that was futile. Whoever carried her was big and strong, and, if she could rely on the genetics she'd fought for longer than she could remember, his scent revealed that he was a shifter.

* * *

There was a distinct antiseptic smell here. The cool temperature allowed it to stay stiff in the air, draping the entire dwelling like a blanket.

Ary's shoes were muffled on the tiled floors. They were the cutest shoes she'd ever seen, and even though they were so not Kalina's type, she'd had to agree that the Alegria paisley nursing clogs were adorable on Ary. And as Ary had followed Dr. Frank Papplin from the entrance of the hospital down to where they now entered the morgue, she'd seen several other employees with the same type of shoe. That made her feel good, like she was fitting in with her new environment.

They entered through double swinging doors to a small reception area. There was a desk that looked like someone should be there, but no one was. Another set of double doors were in front of them. Dr. Papplin, a tall, lithe man with olive-toned skin and tepid blue eyes, pulled a card from the extending wire clip at his waist and swiped it past a black control pad until the red light blinked green.

The doctor walked with a confident stride, his white coat billowing around him as he moved. Behind Ary were X and Nick, both silent but imposing forces. She could hear their footsteps along with Dr. Papplin's in the otherwise quiet section of the hospital. They came to a hall that split in opposite directions, with another set of doors directly in front of them. To the left there were rows and rows of stainless-steel drawers. One was still open, and she could see that it extended to a long empty slab. To the right, the direction Dr. Papplin guided them, was an examining room with another table and cabinets with counters full of utensils.

The smell of antiseptic was even stronger in here, the

air so chilly she almost expected to see her breath appear in smoky billows when she asked, "Is this the female?"

"It looks like her," Nick said from beside her.

He'd come around, touching her arm lightly as she moved closer to the table sitting in the middle of the floor with the dead body on top.

"This is the body Xavier brought to me. I have had a chance to examine it extensively."

"Is this safe?" Nick asked, his voice lowering only slightly.

Papplin nodded. "There are more examining rooms down another hallway. This is the main room, but all staff are out for the morning at meetings. Besides, this was not a shifter."

He retrieved a clipboard and turned a few sheets before reading. "African American female, twenty-five to thirty years of age. There's evidence of plastic surgery, extensive plastic surgery including implants in the breasts and buttocks. No signs of trauma or blunt force. Otherwise healthy."

"She didn't look healthy when I saw her," Nick grumbled.

Ary was already lifting her hands to the corpse. Her fingers were steady as she touched the lips, around the mouth, and the chin. "There's some sort of residue here. It's chalky."

Nick spoke first. "She foamed at the mouth as she collapsed."

"That's what I was going to get to next," Papplin began. "Toxicology results show a couple of different substances. Cocaine for sure—that was the easy one. There's another substance that showed remnants of some type of herb. The third is not known. It could be a poison because it's very potent. I can't readily identify it exactly, but I suspect the combination caused the unknown reaction."

"So she literally went so crazy she killed herself because of whatever she'd taken?" Nick asked.

Ary touched the arms, which were swollen and splotchy. She moved down the body, hearing Nick and Papplin talk but drawing her own conclusions.

"I believe she ingested all of these substances. I cannot tell if they were a mixture or taken separately," Papplin was saying.

"They were mixed," Ary told them as she lifted one leg that looked as if it had been injected with fluids. To the touch it was cold as ice, but the splotches here were ruby red, as if fresh blood still pulsed through the veins.

"He's mixing the damiana with the acids and solvents used to base the cocaine," she said.

"What acids and solvents? How do you know?" Nick asked.

Papplin stood on the opposite side of the table, looking down at the leg Ary held. He was a knowledgeable man, and clearly open to her comments as he watched her with interest.

"Cocaine starts with the coca leaf, but there are several chemicals needed to complete the final product. In the jungle, tons of solvents, acids, and bases are moved daily to the labs where the cocaine is manufactured. Acetone and potassium permanganate are just a couple of the chemicals they use that also have everyday uses in the jungle, like keeping bananas from ripening too fast, or serving as an agent in house paint. It's not hard to get these chemicals," she told them.

"But there's something going on when these chemicals are combined with the herb and the other mystery agent?" Papplin asked.

Ary nodded. "Something unpredictable."

"Okay, let me get this straight," Nick said as he walked around the table.

Today he wore jeans of a washed-out blue; a loose-fitting polo shirt did nothing to mask his bulging muscles and alluring build. The dark burgundy color of the shirt made his light complexion seem brighter, his dark hair and eyes, darker, his entire appearance more dominating.

"He's mixing all these chemicals together with the damiana to make some sort of synthetic drug to sell on the streets. Only there's no way to know how each person will react to this drug."

Ary nodded. "That's right. The drug in its unpurified state is going to filtrate into the system of each person who ingests it. But each reaction will be different because it's not just a physical process at work. Remember I told you about what Yuri taught me? The energy surrounding the herb must be purified. Without this process, it's a living source of negativity."

"Ingestion by a person with already negative energy would exacerbate their dark traits. One who is normally vulnerable would become utterly dependent and most likely hyperactive, overzealous," Papplin finished for her.

"So a woman who was already promiscuous would become a walking sex machine, ready to perform any and every sexual act anywhere at any time," Nick added quietly.

He was thinking of the dead woman as she'd approached him. Ary remembered him telling Rome how the woman had come on to him, pulling down his zipper and . . . she didn't like to finish that thought, but she knew the dead woman's actions were imperative to what they were unveiling.

"This must be what he gave me in the forest. It made

me angrier because at the time I was already upset about
the kidnapping and what was going on with the lack of
supplies. It didn't make me more sexual, because—" She
stopped. Papplin didn't need to know she'd been celibate
for the sixteen years Nick had been away from the forest.

Nick, however, already knew the end of that statement.
"Putting this drug on the streets in this unpurified state
could create an urban holocaust."

Her gaze met his and held, neither one of them knowing exactly what to say to that assessment. It was true,
that was clear from the silence in the room. Even Papplin
looked as if he agreed. The question now was: How would
they stop it from happening?

"Another female body was found in a Dumpster near
Georgetown," Kalina said, walking across the hardwood
floors in the building where Rome had texted Nick to
meet them.

They'd driven for more than forty-five minutes from
the hospital where they'd just seen the woman who had
confronted Nick, to this location in Virginia, just beyond
Great Falls National Park. It almost looked like a forgotten locale, as the tall white oak trees gave way to what
appeared to be a one-level dwelling that spanned a couple
of acres in a type of U shape.

"Was she mutilated?" Nick asked immediately.

Senator Baines and his daughter and two prostitutes
had been reported mutilated in the last eight weeks in DC.
His gut told them this one would be the same.

Kalina nodded. Nick swallowed. He'd always trusted
his gut no matter what.

"Part of her face was gone, mauled. The base of her
skull had been cracked; ten-inch-deep puncture wounds

penetrated her skull, causing instant death. Homicide fears they're looking at a serial killer. The mayor and the chief of police are organizing a task force. The FBI are on standby to take immediate action if need be. The war has barely started and the casualties are adding up," she finished.

Rome stood right beside her, his features hard like a mask of the deadliest jaguar ever.

"This building has enough space to be our headquarters. It's secluded enough for us to shift if need be to protect everyone here. I want this to become our base for the East Coast. I've already talked to the other FLs about finding a location similar to this for their Zones," Rome said sternly.

Nick nodded his agreement, looking around the large open room as he did. They'd come through a set of double wood doors and met Rome and Kalina in this spot, but he could see about thirty feet beyond where the room branched off to a hallway and most likely the rest of the space. This was the case to the right and the back. After seeing the dwelling from the outside, Nick was sure it had more than enough space. "Medical facilities can be down that way," he suggested, looking over to Ary.

He lifted his brow to show her he was asking and not telling, to prove that he'd heard every word she'd spoken last night. Watching her in the morgue with Dr. Papplin had given him a new sense of this woman who was his mate. She was knowledgeable and serious and focused on her craft. When she should have appeared to be an outsider in a human morgue, around human medical supplies and concepts, she wasn't. She'd known more about the death of the female than even Papplin had, proving to Nick that she was the one to run the medical facility without any doubt. But even with his positive conclusion, the decision would have to be Ary's.

"We can look at the entire place to see if anything is more suitable, but I'm inclined to trust your judgment," she said, holding his gaze.

"What about this new body? Should we try to get a look at it? I have contacts at the city morgue," Kalina interrupted. "I just think we need to take a closer look at the casualties this time. We didn't look at Baines's or his daughter's body, or those other two females. There could have been clues to let us know positively if it was the Rogues."

She was right. It was time they started looking at every angle Sabar would play. That sonofabitch thought he had the upper hand, and it was up to them to prove his ass wrong.

"If you can get Ary in to see the body, that would be good. We just came from George Washington University, where she looked at the body X took to Papplin. Tell them what you figured out." He deferred to Ary once more.

She looked a little surprised at his words, tilting her head only slightly, her eyes twinkling just a bit. She wore dark gray pants that were only a fraction thicker than pantyhose, hugging her legs and her ass like a second skin. Her sheer white buttondown shirt came to her kneecaps like an air of enticement. Through it he could openly see the white camisole that hugged her breasts and covered her torso. But it wasn't enough; he knew what she looked like naked, knew what those clothes did nothing to hide.

Clearing her throat, she began to talk. Pride moved through Nick like blood flowing through his veins.

"Sabar is mixing cocaine with the damiana. He's probably hired a chemist to help him with the process here in the States, and they've added another agent that we can't specify. The female at the morgue was in perfect health before her insides virtually exploded as a result of the high potency of the cocaine and the additional chemicals in her system. I think he's created a pill that's easily swallowed, breaks down fairly quickly, and reacts according to the genetics of the victim. In other words, if you're inclined to be high-strung and more than a little excited, taking this drug will put you right in the sights of a crazy hospital. You'll be erratic, nonsensical, in short out of control."

"Jeez," Kalina breathed, leaning into Rome, who'd wrapped his arm around her as Ary spoke.

"Yeah, my sentiments exactly," Nick said with a sigh.

Chapter 25

"What are you doing here?"

"It looks like I'm being held captive," Caprise quipped.

The minute X had walked into Rome's house Ezra had pulled him aside, whispering that the guards had caught someone breaking into Nick's house when they'd retrieved some of his and Ary's things last night.

"She's a shifter and she's mad as hell" was what Ezra had told him before walking off chuckling.

X had no idea what he was walking into when he entered the room at the far end of the hall on the third floor away from the FL and the others staying there. He'd entered knowing he might have to fight or at the very least subdue the intruder, but never, ever would he have considered it would be her.

"You were breaking into your brother's house?" he asked Caprise Delgado with all the confusion he was feeling evident in his voice.

"How else was I supposed to get in?"

X shrugged. "I don't know, call him and tell him you wanted to come over. Knock and if he's not home come back later. What the hell's the matter with you, breaking and entering?"

"Go to hell! You of all people cannot stand there and judge me," she spat.

What was she talking about? X stared at the young woman he hadn't seen for at least five years. She'd changed a hell of a lot since then. He distinctly remembered her butter-toned complexion, almost identical to Nick's. Her hair was raven black, like her older brother's as well. But that's where the physical likeness between the Delgado siblings stopped.

Caprise was shorter, possibly about five-eight or -nine, from what he could tell as she stood near the balcony doors that no doubt were padlocked as well. Her legs went on forever and ever, holding X's gaze for much longer than they probably should have. Thighs spread to curvy hips, a slim waist, and breasts that made his mouth water. The less-is-more vibe her short-ass skirt and skintight blouse gave off made it damn hard to do anything else. But it was her eyes that had done the most changing. You could tell so much from a shifter's eyes.

Hers were dark, emotionless, scary. Thick eyebrows arched above slightly slanted eyes that watched him closely, too closely.

"Nick said you were back," he said for lack of anything better. "I doubt he realized you'd be breaking into his house."

"Oh, please; give it a rest. I needed a place to crash so I went to my brother's. He wasn't home so I let myself in. No harm, no foul."

X nodded. "I believe you."

"Well, aren't I the lucky one. Can you tell your hired monkeys to let me go?"

"That's not going to happen," he said solemnly. "Not until Nick gets back."

She'd turned her back, to retrieve her bag he surmised, but at his words she spun around with a dark blur that was faster than light.

"You've got to be kidding! You cannot hold me hostage. Isn't that illegal? Aren't you some kind of cop?"

Hostility poured from her every motion, every word. She was anxious and nervous—and he wanted to say scared, but he wouldn't pin that on a woman like Caprise.

"I'm an FBI agent. Look, Caprise, there are things going on here that won't allow me to let you walk out of this house unprotected. It's a dangerous time for shifters out there."

"I'm a woman," she said, licking her lips and crossing her arms over her chest as if to punctuate that announcement.

X looked her up and down. "I can see that. Another reason I'm not letting you walk out of here."

Their meeting had begun as cordially as that of any human with another human. She'd walked into his home office, closed the door behind her, and taken a seat in the guest chair in front of his desk. He'd looked up, acknowledged her presence, and stood to greet her. After all, she was older than him by at least ten years. She'd also been his former mentor's female, and she deserved his respect.

Taking her hand in his, bringing it to his lips as he went to his knees in front of her was beyond any allegiance Sabar had bothered to pay another living soul, be it shifter or human. But Bianca was, to him, beyond any other living soul. She had forever been the one bright spot in his life. Even when he believed Kalina was his *companheiro*, he knew she'd never have his heart. That was Bianca's alone.

She'd taken his hand, rubbing hers along his cheek, and beckoned him to stand.

"You have come such a long way," she said when he was standing fully in front of her.

She was shorter by at least a foot, and she was enigmatic. Her hair was in two long braids hanging down to her bottom—which by the way was as plump and enticing as any twenty-year-old's. Her skin was not olive, not ivory, and not darker; it was simply perfect. Ice-bluc eyes blinked and changed quickly to white and back again. His heart beat faster, his cat leaping and growling inside.

"I was thrilled when you called," he admitted, because with Bianca there could be no lies.

"You have been very bad," she said, a long nail scaling along the line of his jaw.

"No. I am doing what Boden taught me."

She shook her head. "You told me once you'd never want another but me. You lied."

Fuck! She knew about Kalina. "You belong to Boden" he gave as his defense. "You said you would never leave him. He was my mentor so I couldn't kill him to take what I wanted. I had to let you go."

"And get yourself another?" She walked around him, her fingers trailing down to his pecs, his abs, around his waist to his buttocks and thighs. "Did she suck you?"

"No!" Sabar replied instantly, adamantly. "No. I did not touch her and she did not touch me."

"But not because you did not want it—because you could not take her from the shadow she is joined with."

As much as he hated hearing that truth, Sabar gritted his teeth and nodded his agreement. "That is in the past."

Bianca was once again in front of him. "I think not. You still want her."

"I want to kill that bitch for choosing him over me. I'm sick of females choosing weaker shifters over me!" And he was. As much as he respected Boden for all that he'd taught him, the fact was, that jaguar had nothing on Sabar.

"I did not choose," she said, her heart-shaped lips pouting. "The choice was made for me."

"And you're here now because?" Being in love with her didn't make Sabar a total idiot. There was a reason Bianca had contacted him, a reason that she'd traveled from the wetlands in Africa to see him. He wanted to know what it was before they went any farther.

"I missed you," she said simply, coming up on tiptoe to touch her lips to his.

Well, Sabar figured as her tongue traced a hot path around his lips, over the seam that separated them, along his tongue that he readily gave to her, he could always get the real reason later. After.

Her screams were so loud they could be classified as deafening. Her claws scraped the red velour wallpaper off his wall in angry slashes as he pumped into her with vicious strokes. When he bent her over the desk, thrusting his full length into her ass, she screamed again, this time his name. It had thrown him right over the edge. Not only was he fucking Bianca, he was making her his in every possible way. And when his release took him she'd twisted her body so that her face now lined up with his. The kiss she gave him was a scorcher and had his dick hardening once more. But she'd led him to the shower where they'd bathed and she'd fallen to her knees, taking his length into her mouth. She'd watched him with those bewitching eyes as she milked his cock, swallowing his essence then rising to kiss his mouth with the remnants of his seed on her lips.

If Sabar thought he was in love with her before, he was totally obsessed with her now.

Still, half an hour later as he stood at the end of his bed, his body wrapped in a black velvet robe, he looked down on her naked body and asked once more, "Why are you here?"

Bianca sat up, not an ounce of modesty in her entire body. She crossed her legs so that he could see her center, see the damp lips of her core and want her once more.

"I have what you need to lead the shifters."

Chapter 26

The room was completely dark, as they'd been told to have it. Only candles provided illumination, and they were placed in strategic locations throughout the space.

Sabar hadn't been thrilled with the news of Gabriel's death. Darel had knocked on his door to tell him just as he and Bianca were finishing their discussion. That discussion had led to this ayahuasca ceremony being performed in one of the back rooms of his safe house in Arlington.

"She thinks this will make us stronger," Sabar told Darel a couple of minutes after he'd left Bianca in the bedroom.

Darel had grumbled. "Can you trust her?"

A laugh rumbled in his chest. Sabar looked up to the ceiling, his bedroom was just above them. "You know I don't fully trust anybody. But just think of how much power we'll have with our new drug on the streets and an army of Rogues with no fear, no past, no inhibitions."

"Too much, too soon, isn't always the best route," Darel said with a nod. He'd been standing near the fireplace that wasn't lit, staring into the dark pit.

"I'll be the judge of how fast we move. You just focus on getting the product out on the streets and watching my money. If you're still thinking about using those strippers as dealers, they'd better be good at keeping numbers. The first time they're short, they're dead."

Darel nodded. "I know the drill."

"Good. Then let's get in here and watch what the hell's going on with this holy man Bianca brought me."

Now they were standing near the door of the room, just beyond a double row of candles and hopefully out of the line of fire, so to speak.

"So what's this all about?" Darel asked while they watched the short man engulfed in shadows moving about the room.

The male inside looked as if he was preparing, putting candles here, taking things out of a huge duffel bag, and placing them in allotted spots. Whatever he did was done in complete silence. If Darel hadn't been staring directly at him, he'd have never known the man was moving about. He was wearing a loincloth and nothing else, clothing-wise. Around his neck was a rope of what Darel thought might be bones. At his ankles were smaller bands of bones that didn't even clink when he moved. And straight through his chin was a longer, thicker bone that looked too painful and too disgusting for Darel to continue to stare. It was eerie how silent things were and yet how alive they felt.

To say he didn't like what was happening here was an understatement. But Darel knew better than to keep going against Sabar. The fact that he was the lone survivor of their original foursome meant something. And despite what Sabar said, Darel knew the Rogue had at least a minuscule amount of trust in him, or else he'd never allow him to run the drug trade almost exclusively on his own. After Gabriel's death, Darel would directly supervise

Norbert and the dealers. He was Sabar's number one Rogue, and he liked that position. So much so that he'd keep his mouth shut and his eyes open where the mysterious Bianca was concerned.

"His name is Yuri and he's a shaman. For a fee he was willing to come here to do us this favor," a female voice said, sending warning spikes up and down Darel's spine.

Speak of the devil.

"He will perform an ayahuasca ceremony, an infusion of sorts, which will alter the minds of each of the shifters we've selected," Bianca continued.

"Why do we want to alter their minds?" Darel asked.

Behind him he felt Sabar stiffen. "So they'll do exactly as I say instead of going off on their own like Gabriel and that cheetah we had before. I need total submission to take down each of the Factions; I can't be all over the world at one time. These new Rogues will be able to travel, making our new regime among the shifters a reality."

That sounded good, but Darel still had reservations. Instead of speaking them again he figured it might be best just to watch and see what happened. Maybe this little experiment wouldn't work; after all, they weren't in the jungle. They were in Sabar's house in the middle of the city. How successful could a holistic jungle ceremony be?

Six shifters were ushered into the room and lined up in the center. Around them double rows of candles were lit. Yuri and another who was dressed just like him moved in a circle around the shifters. The shorter male used a rattle, shaking it in rhythm. Yuri lit incense. Smoke filled the room, quickly creating a warm buzz throughout.

Once Yuri stood in front of the shifters, he motioned for them all to go down on their knees. It was weird to see this array of strong jaguar shifters doing as the thin, wiry human male directed. Darel stood, hands clasped in front of him, eyes focused on the center of the room.

The shorter male presented Yuri with a bowl. Steady streams of steam swirled as Yuri took it in his palms and put it to his lips. He drank, tilting his head back until it was finished. Meanwhile, as he drank, the smaller male walked to the shifters, touching each on the shoulder and motioning for them to tilt their heads back similar to Yuri.

"He is drinking the ayahuasca. This will allow him to see into the soul of each shifter," Bianca whispered.

"And see that they're all evil," Darel muttered.

"Or see their possibilities," Sabar added.

Yuri walked from one shifter to the next, touching each on the forehead with the palm of his hand. The room seemed to fill with more smoke streams, the smell of incense permeating the air. Then Yuri stopped at one shifter and touched his chin. The shifter's mouth immediately opened and Yuri bent forward, breathing smoke into the shifter's mouth.

Darel wanted to vomit at the sight. A man putting his lips on another man's lips wasn't cool with him, at all. The fact that this smoke seemed to simply be sitting inside Yuri's body was another deal he didn't want to know about.

"I'm done," he said, moving past Sabar and using his nocturnal vision to see toward the door. Out in the hallway he took a deep steadying breath.

He wasn't sure about what was going on in that room, not sure at all. But there was no talking Sabar down once he'd decided on something. Darel just hoped this was something they wouldn't all live to regret.

"We've got the truck at a garage in the city. Prints and scents are being lifted and run through X's new database as we speak," Eli said as they sat at the long table in Rome's conference room.

Nick had called this late-afternoon meeting after his visits to the morgue and the new Havenway property. As head of security for the Faction, it was his job to map out how Havenway as well as the FL's home and family would be protected. Preliminary maps had been drawn up of the Havenway location, roads in and out and the entire perimeter hundreds of feet out into Arlington. Older blueprints of Rome's estate were also spread out on the table.

In total there were twenty shifters in the room at present: Nick, Eli, Ezra, and seventeen guards who would carry out whatever plans they came up with. They were preparing for war, and Nick's adrenaline flowed like a river.

"That's good. Bring me the results as soon as you have them. And keep the truck, we might need it later," Nick told Eli.

The shifter—identical to his brother Ezra, who was older by fifteen seconds—nodded and leaned over the table, pulling one of the blueprints closer for his own scrutiny.

"We need to layer the protection here by the highway. This is where the shifter came in," Eli told everyone in the room.

"There are cameras there already. Motion lights would be a good addition. And sensors," Nick said.

"Heat sensors, since shifters naturally have a high body temperature," Ezra added.

Nick rubbed a hand down the back of his head. "Let's aim for something targeted to shifters. I don't want a sensor going off if a deer crosses into the trees."

Ezra nodded and wrote on the legal pad he had in front of him. "Okay, so we want specific body temperature, maybe scent, too. Our scent doesn't match any other animals—or humans for that matter."

"Right," Nick agreed. "What about personal patrols? Right now Jax is assigned to the First Female." That was Kalina's title now. The moment she became joined with Rome, she'd assumed it. Their human civil ceremony of marriage had happened within hours of their return to the States. Now her protection was just as high-priority as Rome's.

"And I put Leo on Ary," Eli told Nick.

Nick nodded. Leo Arrington was a good shifter. He came from a family of guards and was trained well. Nick knew; he'd trained the guy himself. Ary was in good hands.

"I'll stay with you when you go back to your apartment," Ezra told him.

"And I'll stay with the FL" was Eli's reply.

"Zach's going with X," Ezra said, nodding toward the six-foot-nine Brazilian shifter with the crew cut standing four men down at the table.

He nodded to Nick. "Wherever he goes, I'm going with him," Zach said, his heavy accent making the words almost indecipherable.

"I want a rotating detail around the premises here. We'll need at least a hundred more guards at Havenway to start. Here's the preliminary layout of the facility. FL and First Female are going to stay in this section of rooms. Construction's already been ordered to insulate these walls with steel and soundproof barriers. The locks will be programmed into a computer. X is going to take care of that. But the FL's locks will be on a separate mainframe.

We'll have the medical facility here. I want these walls insulated as well and cameras throughout."

He didn't want Ary out of his sight at all, but Nick knew that was going to be next to impossible to achieve. He had his law-firm business to attend to, and she would have her career. The thought was not to smother her, but to keep her safe. It was a hard pill for him to swallow, but he'd gotten her message loud and clear.

"We can set the medical center up on a separate mainframe as well."

That was Tobias, who worked with X sometimes on the computer stuff and was getting pretty good at it.

"Good idea," Nick complimented the young shifter.

Two hours into the meeting Nick felt like they'd mapped out good preliminary plans to keep a blanket over the high-ranking shifters until Havenway was fully operational. He wanted to talk about weaponry and different defense mechanisms but figured he'd run that by Rome and X first.

He was just about to tell everyone they could leave when the door opened. In came a draft of sweet musky scent, and the entire room of shifters turned, muscles bunched, mouths salivating.

"She's begging to be let out of this prison she thinks she's in," X said.

When Nick looked to the door he was shocked and more than a little annoyed to see X with his hand tightly around his sister's bicep. Caprise struggled against him to no avail. Her struggle raised her shirt so that half her midsection was showing; the floral swirls of a tattoo on her right hip were just barely visible.

"Meeting dismissed," Nick said tightly, already smelling the scent of arousal in half the shifters there.

Eli and Ezra stayed in the room, moving to stand behind Nick as they were probably smart enough to sense his annoyance. Lord knew they'd been around him long enough to recognize the warning signs.

"Holding me here is illegal," Caprise said with a frown as the other shifters moved past her to get out of the room.

Only one had been stupid enough to stop and openly stare at her and that damn tattoo. Before Nick could say a word, X growled.

"Keep it moving!" he yelled at the shifter, who quickly took the hint and moved a little faster to the exit.

X slammed the door and released a cursing Caprise.

"I don't have to stay here if I don't want to!" she yelled.

"What the hell are you doing here?" Nick asked, pushing aside two chairs to get to where she was standing. "You said you were looking for an apartment."

"More like breaking into yours," X replied, leaning his bulky frame against the door. That was a warning for Caprise not to even think about a getaway.

The highly volatile glare she tossed X's way said she didn't give a damn where he stood.

"What's he talking about, Caprise?" Nick asked in what he considered a very calm voice, even though his temples throbbed at what the thought of her answer might be.

Caprise sighed. "I needed a place to stay. I knocked and you didn't answer. I picked the lock. End of story."

Behind him Nick heard a snicker. He didn't turn around to see which twin had lost his battle with self-control.

"Why didn't you just call me?"

She shrugged. "Forgot the number."

Nick pinched the bridge of his nose. If this were any other shifter at any other time, it might be funny. But now was not the time for Caprise to be gallivanting around town, picking locks and whatever else she might be up to. Because now, more than ever, Nick suspected something wasn't quite right where his baby sister was concerned.

"Fine. I won't press charges. But X is right, you can't leave this house," he told her and steeled himself for the onslaught.

Nobody, and Nick meant absolutely nobody, in this entire world could throw a temper tantrum like Caprise Delgado.

Her eyes narrowed, hands going to her hips as she squared her shoulders and subsequently pushed her breasts farther out. Throats cleared throughout the room, with the exception of Nick who only glared at her, wishing he could yank down one of those thick brocade drapes and wrap it tightly around her body.

"I'm a grown woman. I will come and go as I please and neither you nor the goons who follow you and Rome around like you're some kind of gods can stop me."

"Caprise, this is not a game. There's some serious shit going on out there. You could get killed," Nick told her.

"I tried to explain that to her, but she's got one hard-ass head," X added from his perch at the door.

Her eyes shot to him. "Shut up," she snapped. "Fine, there's stuff going on in your little shifter world, I guess. So I'll just stay at your house. But I can't stay here."

"You don't have a choice," X told her. "Rogues are out there and they're hunting us."

"You!" she yelled at X. "Do not control me!"

Nick sighed, tossing a pleading look at his friend and fellow commanding officer. He knew where X was coming from and agreed with him wholeheartedly: Caprise could not go out unprotected. At the same time, he loved his sister and didn't want to even consider the fact that she might run and be gone another five years if he didn't at least act like he was on her side. The scent of fear still lingered around her, and until Nick found out what that was about, he wanted her close.

"You don't have to be on lockdown, Caprise. But you will have to travel with a guard." Before she could protest, Nick held up a hand. "All of us are walking with a shadow now so don't give me grief on this. I'm trying to keep you safe."

"I'm fine," she said, looking away from him. "I've been fine for a long time now."

Nick stepped closer, put his hands on her shoulders. "And I'd like to keep you that way. So do me a favor, let X find you a guard. You can go about your business during the day and at night come back to stay here with the other females."

"What other females?" she said, shooting him a questioning glare.

Nick couldn't have thought of a better time for Ary to knock on the door.

"It's me, Ary," she said when X didn't move to open it.

Nick nodded toward him, and he let her in.

"Hi," she said, stepping in tentatively. "Am I interrupting something?"

She was watching him closely, tension filling the air. It was then that Nick realized his hands were on Caprise, another female, and his mate was staring right at him.

"Aryiola Serino, this is my sister, Caprise," he said and hoped it was fast enough to calm Ary's rising temper.

Her smile said it was. "Hi, Caprise. It's nice to see you again." She crossed the room and extended her hand.

To Nick's shock Caprise managed her own smile, and

it looked genuine. "So you're the one who's changed my brother's scent and I daresay some of his attitude."

The females shook hands. Nick looked at X, who was already shaking his head. He got the feeling the odds against him had just shifted.

Chapter 27

Three weeks later

This seemed like as good a place as any to test the allegiance of his newest enforcers. Sabar sat in the back of his Hummer with Bianca at his side. Darel thought it was more important to stay with Norbert, who'd been a little shaky lately, and oversee the deliveries of their product to the new dealers he'd recruited than to attend this little initiation. And only because Sabar could see the logic in that did he allow the shifter to make such a decision on his own.

They'd pulled onto the busy street known as Pennsylvania Avenue and double-parked beside three cars. The truck in front of them housed two of his original shifter enforcers and four of the ones who'd attended the shaman's ceremony.

Sabar checked his watch and looked at Bianca.

"Three seconds," she said to him, a wide smile spreading across her face.

His hand rested on her bare knee, moving upward to caress her thigh since the dress she wore was so fucking short. He loved looking at her body, which she showed every chance she had. Her breasts were abundant and almost drooped right out of the low-cut blouse she wore.

His dick was getting harder by the moment. But he wanted to be here, he wanted to see the success of his new enforcers. Once they had what they'd come for he'd fuck Bianca again. Maybe right here in the backseat or on the floor in his living room, in front of the fire. It didn't matter where, as long as he could sink his length inside her again. Soon.

He'd stopped thinking about why she'd left Boden or what would happen if Boden found out where she was. Sabar knew his former captor well. He would find Bianca because nothing would be more important to him than that right now. And when he came, Sabar would be ready for him. As for Bianca, she wasn't going anywhere until Sabar was ready to let her fine ass go. Judging by his feelings for the female, that would be the day after never.

The doors opened on the truck in front of them, and out stepped four men dressed in all black. Their physical features were different, the coloring of their cats as versatile as the humans walking right past them. They didn't use masks because what people would remember about them wasn't going to appear in any police lineup. With long strides, they walked into the front rotating glass doors of the Rigory National Bank.

"Forty-two seconds," Bianca said, spreading her legs wide for him.

He decided to indulge, sending his hand on a journey upward until he touched the moist bare skin of her pussy. She licked her glossed lips as his fingers pushed past her folds, pressing hungrily into the stretched opening of her center. He'd been in and out of her so much in the weeks since she'd been with him. And he loved it. Had longed for it for years. No, he wasn't likely to let her go easily.

Three bank tellers behind the marble counter and bulletproof glass looked on in fear, each of them backing away from the counter, reaching into their cash drawers and pulling out stacks of bills.

George Fletcher had seen them coming, knew from the moment those four goons stormed into the bank there was going to be trouble. George was a relationship banker; his office was across the room from the teller windows, about forty feet or so. He didn't have a door but a walk-through and a glass wall so he could keep an eye on the happenings in the bank. Today he wished like hell he had a door and a steel wall to encase him in his office. Instead he'd been ordered to the floor, facedown—even though he looked up every few seconds to see what was happening next. He should have kept his forehead on the floor. What he was seeing could not be real.

Their faces were huge, as if the bones beneath were too large and the skin had no choice but to stretch or be ripped free. Eyes the color of gold coins surveyed the area. One goon rested his on the door to the safe. He tossed his head in that direction, and one of the others followed him, a vicious grin on his face. That grin allowed George to see sharp elongated teeth and feel his entire body shake with fear.

They walked like humans and even talked like them, but they weren't. Of that, George was positive. Sure, movie makeup could create this as some form of disguise, since they hadn't bothered to put on masks. But George had a feeling that wasn't the case, either. These weren't humans. But they were robbing the hell out of this bank.

Already they had three duffel bags full from the teller drawers and the drop safe at each teller station. Since the vault was located across the floor, there was a cash cow—the steel safe on wheels, which held even more money so tellers would not have to travel back and forth to the vault—behind a wall close to the teller line. They'd emptied that as well. Now two of them were standing in the vault, filling another set of duffels. Another of the intruders was near the door, looking at his watch then out the door. And the last was walking around scaring the hell out of everyone else in the place. He bared his teeth and actually growled. When Lenny, the security guard, made a move for his gun the robber grabbed him by the collar, lifting him until Lenny's feet dangled off the floor. Then he roared loudly, right in Lenny's face. George felt like crap as Lenny wet his pants. He used his elbows to scoot along the floor and was planning his own little heroic move about a second before he watched the robber twist Lenny's 210-pound body in his hand like he was some kind of rag doll, and planted those sharp-ass teeth into Lenny's skull.

Women screamed, men turned their faces to the floor, probably peeing in their pants as well. As for George, all pretenses were given up the second that freak's teeth broke Lenny's skin. He yelled like a sissy and covered his eyes. An act that only served to draw the attention of the freak at the door, who was in George's office faster than a blink. Next thing George knew his feet were dangling in the air, too. Then George didn't know anything.

Sabar watched his enforcers walk out of the bank as if they'd just gone in to check their safe-deposit boxes. With Bianca's orgasm still permeating the interior of the car, Sabar licked the wet fingers that brought her that mighty climax and waited for his cell to ring.

When it did, he answered quickly. "Yeah?"

"Done."

"Fucking A!" he said, sitting back with a huge grin on his face.

Chapter 28

"She wasn't supposed to leave the house," Nick said, glaring at Ezra, who in turn glared at Nivea, one of the female guards with too many piercings to count, who was assigned to watch Rome's house.

"Leo is with her. She's not alone" was Nivea's reply.

Leo Arrington was also one of the guards. He'd had a rough childhood, having been adopted by a man who despised everything Leo was. But in the years he'd been with the shifters, going on five or six now, Nick couldn't really pinpoint, he'd grown into a respectable man and valued shifter.

"Get him on the phone and find out their location," Nick directed Ezra as he climbed the stairs heading to the room now occupied by his sister.

He hadn't spoken to her alone in the weeks since she'd been at the house and had been wondering how she was holding up. If he knew Caprise, the answer would be not good. Not good at all. She'd been moved down to the second floor, where the rest of them had rooms. All the third-floor rooms were now occupied by guards. It was a bit crowded, a fact that irritated Rome just a little. He'd put the plans for Havenway into action immediately and wanted to move in by the end of the month. Since he would still own this property, Nick had talked him into letting it be transformed to a training facility for new guards. Of course Rome didn't like the idea, since there was a good chance Sabar knew the location, but he'd finally agreed noting that training facilities would also be added on to Havenway eventually.

Running scared just wasn't Nick's thing, but he'd held off telling Rome that he and Ary would soon be finding their own house to live in. Nick didn't want them to live in the condo forever, so he'd already had his secretary contact a real estate agent to see what was available. Ary could work at Havenway, but Nick wanted them to have their own space.

Arriving in front of Caprise's door he paused, scenting anxiety in rippling waves coming from the other side. He knocked quickly and turned the knob to go in. Of course, it was locked. And when Caprise came to tug it open, she glared at him with all the discomfort she was feeling.

"Oh, it's you," she said before turning and walking back into the room.

"Were you expecting someone else?" Nick asked, entering the room and closing the door behind him.

"Your melodramatic friend or those two military goofs he has following me," she tossed over her shoulder.

She fell onto the bed, flipping through magazines, not looking at him. Nick sat on a chair that had been positioned by the window.

"X is doing his job," he told her.

"Then give him a raise, why don't you?"

"What's up with you, Caprise?" Nick raised his hand when her head snapped up and she prepared to tell him nothing. "Don't lie to me anymore. I asked you before and you asked for space. I gave it to you and decided to just wait until you felt you were ready to tell me. Your time's up."

"I told you I was fine."

"And your lies are stinking up this room. So here's the deal: You can tell me what the problem is or I'll search until I find out."

Their gazes held, and for a minute Nick thought she was going to give in. Then she shrugged. "If you want to waste your time looking for nothing, go right ahead."

"Where did you go when you left?"

"I went away."

"Why?"

"Because I needed to think."

That's how the exchange went, question, answer, question, answer. But Nick didn't feel like he was getting any real information. The sense that something was really bothering his sister increased. And yet he realized in that moment that she wasn't going to tell him what had happened to her. He'd have to find out on his own. Fine. He'd get X to do some digging as soon as he left.

"Sabar's got his new drug on the streets already. It's more dangerous than any drug that's been out there before. We're worried about the human death toll this is going to take."

As he expected as well, she looked at him with concern. It was blanketed by a smirk, but Nick knew she wanted to know more. Maybe, just maybe, if he kept her in the loop about everything going on, she'd reciprocate.

"There're always going to be drugs on the street. You're never going to win that war."

Folding his hands and resting his chin on them, he nodded his agreement. "You've got a point. But we can stop Sabar, if we kill him."

"Then that makes you no better than him," she said sadly.

"That's not true. We're fighting for peace."

"Uh-huh." She nodded. "By killing?"

Nick sighed. "You're starting to sound like Ary."

"Yes, let's talk about Aryiola Serino, the sexy little shifter doctor you rescued." Caprise unfolded her legs and let them fall off the side of the bed. She leaned forward on her knees and watched him carefully. "Are you in love with her?"

The question was quick, succinct, no-nonsense, just like Caprise. And Nick thought he had an answer, but realized with a start that he didn't.

"She's my mate," he said instead.

Caprise shook her head. "You don't believe in those jungle laws."

"I do, and you should, too. They're our heritage. Mom and Dad would want us to uphold their beliefs."

"Mom and Dad were doing something behind our backs and you know it. They lied to us on a daily basis and now you want us to put them on some type of pedestal. Give me a break." She'd waved her hand and stood from the bed. On the dresser a couple of feet away Caprise picked up a pair of earrings and put them on. She lifted her hair and pulled it into a quick ponytail.

"You knew they were lying about something, too?"

She turned, her hair swinging with the motion. "I'm not an idiot, Nick. I could hear the arguments you and Dad had. I overheard conversations he had with his friends. I heard him and Mom arguing one night. See, if you keep quiet people tend to overlook you. They never even knew I was there half the time."

Nick didn't argue that fact. Caprise had just entered high school when they'd returned from the Gungi. He remembered she'd been very involved in activities at school and tended to spend more time there than at home—or at least that's what he'd thought. Their parents had died five years ago, killed in a car accident on Interstate 95, and Caprise had disappeared two days after they'd buried them.

"What did you hear?" he asked her seriously.

She eyed him for a few seconds like she was considering whether or not to tell him. Then she folded her arms and stood with one hip leaning against the dresser. "He set up a lot of meetings. Mentioned Loren Reynolds's name a lot and continuing what he'd started. Mom didn't always like whatever he was doing. She told him it was dangerous, he told her it was necessary." Her shoulders hunched. "That was about it."

That was about what Nick already knew.

"I think he was doing something illegal, or at the very least a betrayal of the tribes. But I can't prove it."

"You want to prove it? You want to prove to the world that our parents were no good? I mean, if nothing else, they loved us and they loved each other. Sort of like I believe you're in love with Ary."

She was making him dizzy. On the one hand she wanted him to know that she thought their parents were liars. On the other she questioned his quest to prove them as just that. "Caprise, you don't know everything that's going on."

"And I don't want to know. I just asked you about the woman in your life. She's really pretty."

He nodded. "She is."

"And she's going to be a doctor."

"Right."

"And she's in love with you," she said as if she were telling a secret that Nick should have already known.

Nick ran his hands down his face. "Why am I talking to you about this? You're my sister, for God's sake."

"Because I know you better than any of those females

you've messed with before. You're in love with her. I can tell."

"How can you tell?" He wanted to know, especially since he wasn't 100 percent sure of that fact himself.

"The fact that you're still dealing with her after the rescue is the biggest clue. You've never had a long attention span when it came to women. And you're keeping her locked up in this fortress Rome calls a house just like you are with me."

"It's for your safety," Nick said, exasperated. This conversation was not going the way he'd planned. "It's for everyone's safety right now. I told you Sabar is—"

Caprise held up a hand. "Yeah, yeah, Sabar's dangerous and all that. I get it."

The door to her room opened unexpectedly and Ezra walked in.

"Leo's in trouble. Rogues at the museum. He needs backup," he said, his brow furrowed, lips twisted in rage.

"Fuck!" Nick cursed, standing from the chair.

The phone call had been weird and suspicious. Ary knew that right away. Just as she'd known there was no way she could resist following up. She had to know for sure.

Walking into the museum Ary tried not to be too enthralled by the exhibits—she'd never been to a place like this and made a mental note to come back and check out all the buildings of the Smithsonian. He said he'd meet her near an exhibit titled *Communities in a Changing Nation*. And wasn't that highly appropriate.

The Shadow Shifters had come here and built their own community. Now that union had evolved to the point that a democracy was being created and security was becoming an issue. Their kind was on the brink of change, and if not for everything being more than a little scary, Ary might say she was excited.

Until she saw him.

He walked with a limp. Wearing human clothes for the first time she knew of, Davi Serino moved around a particularly large statue of some sort of beast, lifting his head slightly so he could look at her. He'd been hurt badly in that fight in the village. Actually, Ary thought he'd been killed. That's what Rome had reported, that all the shifters—Rogues and the ones the Rogues were looking for that night—had been killed. Yet here he stood, her father. And right behind him was another she'd trusted.

"Yuri." She whispered the shaman's name even before she was close enough for him to hear her.

With movements much slower than they used to be, Davi motioned for her to join them in the corner where they stood. She looked around, placed Leo about ten feet from where she was standing. He was watching her intently as he had been since Ezra assigned him to her. She lifted a hand to let him know she was okay and to show him where she was going. His look remained dour, and Ary figured he'd come closer no matter what she said. So she'd be quick with this meeting.

"What the hell are you doing here?" she asked Davi the moment she was near him.

"I'm finishing what I started," he said, grabbing her by the elbow.

"Get off me!" Ary said through gritted teeth. "You're supposed to be dead."

"That's what your friends wanted you to believe. They think they're in control. They are not, Aryiola. Sabar is, and you need to understand that."

"I understand you're a spineless coward. Doing the

bidding of another coward. And you," she said to Yuri. "You were my friend."

"There is much you need to learn about the world, dear *curandero*," he said in that whispery soft voice of his. He'd put on human clothes, too. The loincloth he usually wore would definitely draw too much attention in a place like this. As for the tribal bone through his chin, that was covered with a thick wool scarf that looked totally out of place for early September in Washington, DC.

Yuri reached out, and Ary knew he meant to grab her other arm. She twisted away from him and yanked her arm from Davi. "Both of you can go to hell! That's what you get for working with the devil," she spat and turned to walk away.

When she did she slammed right into two men she knew were shifters. Each of them stared down at her with gleaming cat's eyes, and Ary swore she wouldn't scream. She would run, but only after she let them know she wasn't afraid of them. With quick self-defense motions she'd learned from Lucas back in the Gungi, Ary performed a one–two punching combo that landed right in the first Rogue's groin. She spun in a circle, dodging shifter number two, and when he reached for her landed a kick to the side of his jaw. That was all of her training she was able to show before Leo appeared, gun drawn.

He pulled Ary behind him, extending his arm with the gun to Davi and Yuri, who were still dumbfounded by Ary's moves, and the two groaning Rogues that were quickly recovering.

"Don't even think about it," Leo barked when the Rogues looked ready to pounce.

They stopped but bared their teeth and growled so loudly that a few passersby stopped to see what was going on. If it weren't so serious it would be funny the way they looked at the replica of a prehistoric elephant with tusks as long as Ary was tall.

Then they saw the gun and all hell broke loose. There was screaming and running and Leo turned, pushing Ary ahead of him. "Go!" he shouted.

She had no idea where she was going and eventually he must have figured that out because he ran up beside her and grabbed her arm, taking the lead and pulling her behind him. Before Ary could turn and see if Davi, Yuri, and/or the Rogues were following them she was pushed through a door and would have fallen down the steps if Leo hadn't caught her by the legs, throwing her over his shoulder. Later she'd tell him she didn't like the Neanderthal treatment, but for right now she kept her mouth shut.

Pandemonium did not accurately describe the scene outside. People seemed to be running frantically everywhere. When they finally made it to Leo's car, two trucks pulled up right beside it. Doors opened and shifters poured out from all directions. The one her gaze locked on was Nick.

Leo was putting her down as Nick skirted the car, coming to her and grabbing her to him. "When we get home I'm beating that pretty little ass of yours for not listening to me."

Ary opened her mouth to speak then closed it as his lips crashed down on hers. "Don't say a word," he told her, pulling back and staring into her face. "Just get in the car."

"Where are you going?" she asked when she was being pushed toward the back passenger-side door.

"I'm going to do what I should have done in the fucking forest!" he told her without looking back.

Ary did not like the sound of that.

Chapter 29

They tracked the Rogues to an underground parking lot across the street from the museum. Ezra had locked on their scent and was leading the pack toward them.

Four shifters stood near a white Hummer. All Rogues. They'd just closed the back passenger door so Nick knew someone was inside. And that someone was Davi Serino. When Ezra reported that Leo swore one of the men Ary was talking to was Serino, Nick had cursed until his eyes almost crossed. Something about that too-neat battle in the forest had been nagging at him since they'd returned, but knowing everyone was growing tired of his battle-armor attitude he had kept it to himself. Besides, the last thing he'd wanted to do was upset Ary with talk of her parents still being alive. Now he felt like an ass because he should have acted on his instinct, as usual.

Now he wasn't going to be dissuaded. Serino and whoever else was with him were going to die. That was all there was to it.

Nick charged forward, passing Ezra and the other shifters, growling as he approached the Hummer. The Rogues turned and bared teeth and claws, ready to fight back. He didn't give a shit. Beneath him he felt his shirt ripping, his body shifting, the cat taking charge.

The six-foot-long, 250-pound jaguar that lived inside Nick lunged through the air, landing with its underbody smacking against a Rogue smaller than him by maybe 50 pounds and darker than him in color. Dispatch was quick and lethal as Nick's teeth sank deep into the Rogue's neck.

When the body fell to the cement floor the cat, now irritated and pushed closer to the brink, charged the Hummer, jumping up on its roof and dropping down to break the entire front windshield. Shattered glass spread everywhere as heavy paws hit the driver's and passenger seats, plowing past them to get to the back. Both passengers cowered, hands reaching for the door handles, eyes wide with fear.

Nick moved to Davi first, giving the man a vicious growl that probably should have ripped his head off. Instead it only startled, then pricked the cat inside Davi until his claws bared and reached to swipe at Nick's cat. Big mistake. Nick swiped back with such fierceness Davi's body fell right out of the back door and hit the ground with a sickening *thump*. Nick jumped down on top of him. He roared once more, then let his teeth sink into the back of Davi's neck, lifting the body slightly off the ground and holding on until all movement stopped.

Before Nick could enjoy the kill, there was noise coming from behind him. It was chanting. He let the dead body drop to the ground and remained still, trying to place the sound. Some weird smoke drifted through his nostrils. It permeated his senses, making his cat growl and roar louder. Turning to look over its shoulder, his cat spotted Yuri, the shaman, arms lifted, smoke emanating from his mouth. The cat shrank back and the man reached out a long arm, grabbing Yuri by the throat squeezing so hard he began to wheeze.

"What the fuck are you doing here? Who brought you here?" Nick yelled in the shaman's face.

Ezra had just shifted back himself, running over to where Nick stood with Yuri. "Dead or alive?" he asked Nick, glaring down at Davi's dead body and looking back to the shaman.

Yuri didn't speak; he couldn't, since Nick was probably crushing his larynx. The smoke had stopped dripping from his mouth and his eyes were watery, probably with the effort. Nick wanted to kill him, too, the healer Ary had called a friend. But that wouldn't get the answers they needed.

"Take him with us. Bind him, and don't let him out of your sight. And put a muzzle on this one, he has a tendency to leak," he added, tossing Yuri's slim body onto the ground. Another guard quickly stepped up, grabbing the shaman.

Out of the trunk of Ezra's SUV, Nick and his guard slipped into extra jeans and T-shirts. Even though shifting in public was against their laws, one of Rome's obsessions was to always be prepared. As they climbed in the front seats, Nick's blood pulsed.

"Why was he still alive?" he asked the minute Ezra started the truck. "He was supposed to have died, yet he's here in DC trying to get at Ary. And that shaman, he's a fucking liar."

"You know money rules here," Ezra said as they pulled out of the garage. "Maybe it's starting to rule the jungle as well."

Nick pulled out his cell, growling as he punched each number. "What's your location?" he asked Leo the minute the guard answered. "Good. I'll meet you there. She's not to move a muscle until I get there."

Tossing the phone to the floor, he let his head fall into his hands. And for the first time since Ezra had come into the room to tell him about the Rogues at the museum,

Nick breathed a sigh of relief that Ary was safe. Then he vowed to get to the bottom of this mess with her father and Sabar before it got her killed.

Ary wanted to scream. Then she wanted to cry. Her heart beat so fast she thought it would burst from her chest and then she'd die. Clenching her fists at her sides she cursed the rapidly changing emotions and the tears welling up in her eyes. She absolutely hated crying!

But the moment Nick walked through the door of the bedroom they shared and closed it behind him, she'd done just that. Turning to face him, she saw his furrowed brow and angry cat's eyes. She scented the anger and frustration pouring from him. And she noticed the scratches on his arms and neck, which indicated he'd been in a fight.

"I didn't know," she began. "I thought he was dead." The damning tears fell the minute she spoke, lining her cheek with moisture and making her feel a few millimeters shy of a weakling.

He didn't speak, just walked to her. When he pulled her into his arms and hugged her so tight, she thought he'd break her ribs, Ary's tears turned into full-out sobs.

"He's dead now," he whispered into her ear, still holding her safely in his arms.

Ary's crying increased, her chest throbbing with the effort. She cried for so much in those few minutes—for the betrayal she thought her father had committed, for the shifters in the Gungi who'd also trusted him, for her mother, for the future of the *curanderos* and the shifters as a whole, and lastly for being a total fool about Yuri.

"You killed him," she said through quivering lips.

She felt him stiffen against her but did not release her hold.

"I won't say I'm sorry for killing him, because I'm not.

I am sorry for how this situation continues to hurt you," he told her.

"Everybody I trusted was lying to me," she said when Nick finally pulled back a bit and she wiped her face with the back of her hand. "I thought we were doing good for the tribes. I thought he was teaching me because he believed in me."

"And they lied. But that's not your fault," Nick told her. "They're the assholes here, not you. And believe me, all of them will pay for their treachery."

"Davi already did," she said brokenly.

"It had to be done," he said with a sigh then sat down on the bed.

He reached out to grab her hand, pulling her down beside him. "I know you think I have a kill-now, think-later mentality. I won't deny that. But I also will not allow anyone to hurt you, not ever again," he said adamantly.

She didn't respond. Couldn't really, because there was a part of her that had already accepted Davi's death. Another part was still processing that the man she was in love with had been the one to kill her father. It should cause her more pain, that hideous fact, but it didn't. She couldn't allow it to. Davi betrayed the tribe; Nick was a protector of the tribe. He was also her mate. That was all she needed to know.

"Ezra took Yuri out to the guest house to lock him down while Rome figured out what to do with him."

"Do you think he'll kill him?" If so, that would be another death she'd have to come to terms with. Another person she'd allowed into her life whom she shouldn't have trusted.

Nick kept her hand tightly in his. "There might not be any other choice. If he's determined to help Sabar, we can't let him live."

She nodded, sniffling. "I don't understand how Yuri's involved," she told Nick.

"I don't, either, but he was spitting some foul-smelling smoke into the air until I started choking his ass."

Ary looked up quickly. "A foul-smelling smoke? Coming from his mouth?"

Nick nodded. "Yeah, I could smell it, but then I was so pissed off I just grabbed him. I wanted to strangle him right there."

She was nodding her head, too, everything making perfect sense to her now. "It's ayahuasca. That's the other element in the drug Sabar's making. Ayahuasca."

"What are you talking about?"

Ary turned on the bed, still keeping her hand in Nick's and looking him directly in the eye. "Ayahuasca is an infusion. It's a psychoactive infusion from the banisteriopsis, a vine found in the jungle. They call it the Spirit Vine because it's said to give shamans the ability to speak to a person's spirit directly."

He looked like he was concentrating deeply on every word she spoke. "And that's what was coming from Yuri's mouth?"

She nodded. "And that's what I think Sabar is adding to that drug. Without the ayahuasca ceremony, which can only be performed by a shaman, the vine can be used in a tea form. It opens up the soul, but doesn't give it any direction. The unpurified damiana adds its negative energy, and that's why anyone who takes the drug goes crazy."

"Damn, I don't know why but that makes sense. So Yuri was giving him the ayahuasca?" Nick asked, his cat's eyes subsiding as Ary continued to rub her fingers over the back of his hand.

He'd been so wound up when he came in. For that matter, so had she. They'd had a tumultuous last couple of hours. But now he seemed to be coming down; his brow wasn't as furrowed, either. She liked him so much better this way.

"Why else would he be with Davi and Sabar?"

Nick shook his head. "I can't think of another reason. I guess money is starting to rule even in the jungle. Ezra said that earlier but I was having a hard time believing a shaman would be attracted to money. Guess I was wrong."

There was a knock at the door and Ary jumped. Nick dropped her hand and wrapped his arm around her, pulling her closer.

"Come in," he said when she looked up at him with relief.

"Hey man, you okay?" X said entering the room.

Nick nodded. "Yeah. I'm cool."

"How about you, Ary? You didn't get injured, did you?"

Ary almost smiled. She really was starting to feel like a part of this family. "I'm cool, too," she said, trying to keep her voice steady like Nick's.

"Heard you had some impressive moves in the museum," X said to her.

She shrugged. "I can defend myself."

Folding his beefy arms over his chest, X nodded. "That's good to know. Because I've got some bad news."

Nick sighed. "What now?"

"Rogues, what else?" X began. "Local news is broadcasting a robbery at Rigory National."

"So they're through selling drugs, now they're robbing banks?" Ary asked, not sure she believed the connection.

X frowned. "Looks like it. Every human in the bank is dead, necks snapped, blood all over. Close to two million gone."

Nick cursed. "Dammit! He's doing whatever he wants and we're just sitting back with our heads up our ass."

"I wouldn't say that," X started. "It was definitely a setup, though. How did you know to go to the museum, Ary?"

She inhaled and sighed shakily. Nick wasn't going to like what she was getting ready to say. "I got a call on my cell phone."

"The one I just gave you that nobody besides us should have the number to?" Nick questioned.

She shook her head. "I don't know how he got the number. All I know is the call came through. I answered and he asked me to meet him. I couldn't believe it at first because I thought Davi was dead. But I'd know his voice anywhere. So I had to go and see for myself. Leo was with me the entire time."

"It's a good thing," X said. "I think they had Davi call you because they knew we'd all come to rescue you again. They were diverting our attention."

"Sonofabitch," Nick murmured, standing to pace the floor.

It was starting again, Ary noted. He was keeping a tight rein on his temper, and for Nick, she knew that was an effort. For that she was proud. For the fact that he was going through this at all—she hated that it was because of her.

"That's not all," X continued. "There was a witness at the bank. In her car parked out front. She told the police about two black Hummers that pulled up. Four got out of the first one and went into the bank. Minutes later they were out again."

"Okay, at least that's something to go on, right?" Ary asked.

"That's not all she said. She told them they didn't look like men. She thought maybe they were wearing Halloween masks on their face and gloves with claws on their hands."

"Can this get any worse?" Ary asked.

"Shit yeah! If we don't get a handle on these Rogues, it's going to get much worse" was Nick's retort.

X didn't look happy about the assessment, but he couldn't argue it, either. "I think this time you might be right. Rome's talking with the Assembly tonight. Get some rest, we're meeting with him at the club first thing in the morning."

Nick nodded as X left the room. Closing the door, he let his forehead tap against the door. Thoughts of Ary being captured, tortured, killed, of all those innocent people in the bank, of the shifter he'd killed and the shaman he had locked away on this property, all bounced around in his head. He wanted to scream with rage, to rake his nails down the door, splintering the wood until he felt some sort of relief. Instead he could only remain still.

Her touch was like a salve, small hands moving up his back, spreading warmth that wasn't so much arousing as it was comforting. When she wrapped her arms around his waist and pressed her front against his back, Nick wanted to sigh with relief, he wanted to lose himself in the simple feeling of her holding him. But he couldn't.

There was too much going on, too much at stake. And for all the years he'd lived with the rage against his parents and the anger against the shifters who refused to accept that they were different, Nick felt fury that made him shake. He wanted to kill again. Pure and simple he wanted to kill the next person who walked up to him, or who looked at Ary wrong. It didn't really matter who it was. And that was what scared him most.

"We'll come up with a way to fight them," Ary said from behind him. "We won't let them win."

He heard her words, wanted to swallow them up like two Tylenols and a glass of water, in hopes they'd cure this fury rippling through him. But he didn't think that was going to happen.

"I want him dead." He spoke slowly, quietly. "I want the shaman as dead as your father. Is that normal?"

He asked the question and turned, pressing his back against the door and watching her take a half step away from him. "Is it normal to believe that killing is the answer?"

She hesitated a moment, then licked her lips nervously. "If you're asking me if you're normal, Nick, the answer is yes. You are what you have been bred to be, a man and a cat. Reactions of both will come to you all your life, and that's normal."

"How could I kill your father? How can I hurt you like that?" Even though he knew he'd do it again in a heart-beat, a small part of him wondered what kind of man that made him.

Ary touched her palms to his cheeks. "How could he hurt me the way he did? I don't have that deep desire to kill, Nick, but I don't have any love lost for him, either."

He closed his eyes, tried like hell to rein in what he was feeling because at this moment Nick didn't really know what it was. Anger and rage he recognized and embraced eagerly. This foreign entity was new, surfacing only with the sound of Ary's voice, the touch of her hands.

There was something swirling around inside him, something that almost—but not quite—conquered all the dark and evil. It was soft and light and just hovered over the surface of his being. With a lift of his arms he was touch-ing her, squeezing her shoulders, and whispering her name.

"I need you, Ary. I need you so bad."

She touched a finger to his lips to quiet him. "Let me take care of you," she said, her hands slipping down his torso, pushing the T-shirt he wore up and over his head.

Light kisses peppered his chest and Nick let his head fall back, rapping against the door. Her touch was so soft and yet so damn hot. When her tongue circled one of his nipples, Nick's fingers clenched at his sides. Teeth raked over the skin she'd just kissed as she bit down on the nipple lightly at first, then hard enough that he sucked in a deep breath. Her tongue licked the area once more and his cock strained against the zipper of his pants.

As if she'd read his mind, her nimble fingers moved over the button of his jeans and slid the zipper down. Pressing her breasts close to his chest, she breathed heavily as she used both her hands to push his boxers and his jeans down at once. They were at his ankles and Nick wanted to curse because his boots wouldn't let him simply kick them off. He felt trapped here, but the moment Ary's warm hand wrapped around his turgid length, he thought here wasn't such a bad place to be.

Every touch was soft, with the gentlest of care, as if she were worshiping him even as he basked in the feel of her. He couldn't resist touching a hand to the top of her head, smoothing down her silky hair. She sighed with his action and he continued, moving so that both his hands were in her hair, his fingers wrapping the long strands around and around. She'd lowered herself to her knees, her hand still wrapped around his erection as she rubbed her cheek along his length, touching the tip to her skin then whispering her warm breath over it.

"Dammit! Dammit! I need you," he heard himself say and felt empty. He knew there was more he wanted to say, probably needed to say, but he didn't.

"You've got me" was her reply, and everything inside him tightened. "I'm right here with you, Nick. I won't leave you," she stated clearly.

Nick opened his eyes and looked down at her to find

she was staring right back up at him. "I won't leave you, Ary. Ever again," he told her with everything he had inside. He would not leave her and he would not let anything happen to her.

"You're my *companheiro*," she told him just before opening her mouth over his dick and taking the bulbous head between her lips.

It was hot there, moist, and so fucking fantastic he almost came instantly. "Ary, you are my *companheiro*. You are fucking mine!"

She took his entire length into her mouth then, letting his tip sit at the back of her throat and holding him there. Nick tensed all over, his fingers pulling at her hair as he struggled not to pull back and pump full force into her mouth. She was so his, so definitely his. No other female, even the most promiscuous of the lot he'd been with, had ever turned him on the way Ary did, had ever done things to him the way Ary did. So yes, she was definitely his until either or both of them drew their dying breath.

Nick couldn't stand it a second longer. He pulled her up to him, loving the way his length slid so slippery from her pouting lips. "I need you now!" he told her.

She grabbed his cheeks and rose to her tiptoes. "Take me, then," she told him before running her tongue over his lower lip then dipping it inside his mouth.

In no time Nick was ripping her clothes off, popping buttons, tearing fabric. He didn't give a shit. All he could think about was her, all he could smell, see, feel was Ary. When she was naked he pushed her down on the bed, had her palms flat on the mattress, her arms fully extended but her back bent over.

Nick kissed down the line of her spine, spreading her cheeks as he neared them, licking over the pretty globes before pressing a finger inside her anus.

"Take me!" she yelled.

"I will!" he told her, inserting yet another finger, stretching the pretty entrance.

"Now!"

"So bossy," he told her before pulling his fingers out and positioning his tip at the opening. "I'm going to take you."

"Yes!" she moaned, wiggling her ass at him as if an invitation were really needed.

He pressed forward slightly. She wiggled again. He slapped a hand to one cheek, watched it blush, and slapped the other one.

"Nick!"

"Oh yeah, baby, that's my name. Say it again." He pressed in deeper. She wiggled again, gasping his name over and over.

Through with the theatrics, Nick sank his entire length inside her, palmed her ass cheeks, and pulled out. When he pushed back inside she came, thighs shaking, his name rolling off her lips like a litany. Nick pumped until he felt like his legs would falter or his back would break. Instead his essence poured from him in thick streams, shooting inside of her, taking all that he had, all that he was. He closed his eyes and saw her face. He inhaled and smelled her scent, their combined *calor*. In his ears was her voice saying his name, saying he was her *companheiro,* saying she loved him.

Chapter 30

"Felipe Hernandez, one of the Cortez Cartel's lieutenants, was captured in New Mexico last night. I made a few calls and had him transferred to Bas's resort for safekeeping," X said.

"That's great. Commit a couple hundred murders, ship millions in drugs to American soil, killing thousands of humans, and get rewarded with a night's stay at a four-star resort in beautifully scenic Sedona," Nick quipped.

Rome shook his head at Nick. "You sound like a commercial for a fun-filled vacation."

"Well, that's what this crook is on, a vacation."

"He's locked down tight in one of the wine cellars. Bas isn't giving him any VIP treatment, I can guarantee you that." X motioned for the bartender to bring him another drink. "I want to head down there sometime this week to talk to him."

"That's a good idea," Rome said.

They'd left Rome's mansion right after breakfast, making sure the females were in the house and safely guarded—especially after yesterday's events. Now they were at the country club where Rome was an upstanding member, even after he'd married a local police officer instead of some high-powered female on the political scene, having drinks.

After the botched attack at the museum and the bank robbery, messages had gone out to all the shifters in X's database to be on alert for the Rogue scent and suspicious shifter activity. Every trained guard they had was at Rome's mansion ready to roll out at a moment's notice.

"I also found out that Julio Cortez is living in a luxurious nursing home in Colombia. Word is dementia keeps him pretty busy these days."

Rome drummed his fingers on the table. "There goes any information we could expect to get out of him. My father's notes said he talked with Julio on a regular basis. That would have been more than twenty-five years ago."

Nick nodded. "Julio would have been in control of the cartel at that time when running cocaine was the biggest part of their business. Under Raul's auspicious leadership, they've moved into ecstasy and human trafficking. I hear he specializes in teenage girls."

"Bastards," X said with a growl.

Both Rome and Nick looked at him.

"You okay, man?" Nick asked. "You've been a little tense."

X cut his eye at Nick then looked back down to his drink. "This is a tense situation. We've got a few things going on at one time and all of them are damn volatile. It's going to be hell trying to keep control of each situation."

"Then we don't control them, we just counteract," Rome replied. "I want to know what our parents' connection was to Cortez and that symbol that's now displayed on drug packages being sold on the streets. But our safety comes first. Sabar remains the priority."

Nick nodded his head. "Any more news on the bags?"

"They're being sold out of a club called Athena's. I've got a couple of shadows down there keeping watch."

"People are dying because of what he's putting in those bags." Nick took a deep breath and decided it was time to spill. "Ary thinks he's mixing the cocaine with damiana and another jungle root called ayahuasca. She says that's probably what's adding the crazy factor in all the overdoses. That woman I saw was freakin' out of her mind."

"So who's manufacturing it? The shaman we caught last night?" X asked

"I'm betting he has someone here, too. A human, probably," Rome added.

"Yeah, you might be right. The shaman's costing him some money. Once he figures out how to duplicate whatever he's giving him, Sabar will probably kill him. The human, however, he can intimidate to accept the fact that he's letting him live as payment." Nick dragged his hands down his face, sitting back in his chair. "What a mess. I don't think even our parents could have predicted this."

"But they knew something would happen. You've got to wonder how they knew," Rome said quietly.

"Probably because they were orchestrating the beginnings of the war before we even knew what we were," Nick added glibly.

"So what are we going to do about it?" X asked.

All eyes rested on Rome, who looked almost as evil and animalistic as Sabar at this moment.

"We're going to bring the war to their backyard. Make that shaman tell you where Sabar is," Rome told Nick.

"We finally get to kick some Rogue ass?" Nick asked.

Rome nodded. "And then some."

Rome's guest house had probably been lavish at one point; now it was simply a neat dwelling that nobody bothered to use. Well, it was currently being put to good use. Nick had suggested facilities be built at Havenway for captives such as Yuri, and Rome readily agreed.

For now Yuri's thin body had been shackled to a pipe that ran down one of the back walls of the kitchen. He was gagged, his hands chained behind him, his ankles linked together with the same chain that led to the pipe. And around his neck was a brace that beeped with a red light. This was the prisoner collar Nick and Ezra had suggested to Rome a couple of years back. Rome thought they'd never need it, but Nick had wanted to be ready. It was a good thing.

The thought was that if they had to hold a shifter, they'd fit him with this collar. If he shifted while wearing the collar, the instantaneous growth of the neck would trigger electromagnetic waves from the collar; the cat would die as its paws hit the ground. They hadn't used this on the cheetah shifter they'd held because he was never meant to live long.

Yuri wasn't a shifter, but Ezra probably figured it was wisest to slip on the collar anyway, just for the hell of it.

"When I first came to see you, I wanted your help," Nick said, moving until he was standing completely in the small kitchen.

The shaman gazed at him with bleak eyes. The man looked like he starved for a living instead of milking people for their money or personal belongings to give them fake-ass remedies.

In the center of the beige-tiled floor was a round table with two wooden chairs. Nick pulled one out and took a seat. He leaned forward, resting his elbows on his knees, and glared at Yuri.

"This time I'm not asking for your help. I'm telling

you what I want to know and you're going to supply the information. It's that simple."

Yuri didn't even blink.

"Nod if you understand."

Yuri didn't nod.

Nick shrugged, got to his feet, and walked over to were Yuri was propped against the wall. He punched the shaman in the gut and watched his eyes bulge a millisecond before he doubled over.

"I told you to nod if you understand."

Yuri kind of dangled there, his head held low, the lower half of his body now crumpled on the floor.

Undeterred by the continued lack of cooperation, Nick grabbed his hair, pulling his head back until he almost snapped a neck that looked thin enough to slip right out of the collar.

"Nod if you understand."

The shaman blinked rapidly, and Nick felt the slight pull against the hold he had on his head. He smiled. "Good.

"Now, where did you meet up with Sabar? I want to know his exact location."

Yuri shook his head.

"Oh, you know. I'd suggest you not lie to me," Nick warned, his claws emerging on the hand that didn't hold Yuri's head.

He watched as the man's eyes closed and he heard some sort of moaning coming from him. Nick pulled on his head again then dragged four of his fingers down the side of his face. "Don't fuck with me, old man! I want answers!"

There was a muffled scream as Nick's claws penetrated the skin of Yuri's face. He remembered the gag and used his claws to pull it out of his mouth. "Start talking."

Yuri gasped and blinked, probably trying to get himself together since now he was bleeding like crazy, as well as being tied to a pipe. He coughed when Nick shook his head again.

"A house, I went to a house when I get off the plane," he said in a hoarse tone.

"Where was the house?" Nick asked as if he were talking to a toddler.

Yuri's eyes glassed over and his lips pursed, and Nick thought he was going to start with the smoke again. He punched Yuri in the mouth just as a warning. "All you're going to do is answer my questions. Nothing else, just answers," he told him.

"I do not know. I do not live here."

Nick didn't know if that was meant to be sarcastic or not, but it had some semblance of truth. If Yuri wasn't from here, without an exact address he might find it a little hard to describe where Sabar lived.

"How many shifters are with him?"

Yuri's eyes lit up then. His thin lips spread into an awkward smile considering the huge bone going through his lip. And yes, that was some disgusting shit to look at, and it would have hurt his human knuckles like a bitch if his skin and bones hadn't thickened when his claws came out.

"New shifters are good. Souls are obedient," Yuri said with a hiss. His tongue moved over the bone, touching lightly against his lower lip, then his top one. "It worked."

"What worked? What did you do to his shifters?"

"He now owns the souls."

Nick hit him again just because he didn't like what the hell the shaman was saying. Had he blown that smoke onto shifters? Now there were some brainwashed shifters running around town? Fuck!

"I'm sick of the bull, tell me where he is. Where were you supposed to meet him again?"

"You will not defeat him," Yuri said.

"And you will not live to see another sunset. Tell me where the fuck he is!" He pulled Yuri up so that his feet dangled off the floor. Nick held him by his hair, and the shaman yelled in pain as he was hoisted up higher.

"Talk!"

"D," he hissed. "It is on a road called D."

Nick released him immediately, not giving a rat's ass about his body slumping to the ground. "If you're lying I'm coming back here to rip your guts out."

He grabbed the rag off the floor and stuffed it back into Yuri's mouth. "Sit tight, I'll be back."

Chapter 31

"You've got ten minutes," the short, pudgy man told Kalina. "I could lose my job doing this."

Kalina smiled and rubbed the guy's arm. "Thanks a lot, Pete. I really appreciate your getting us in. We'll only need five of those minutes. Right?" she asked Ary and X, who stood behind her waiting to get through the double swinging doors.

Ary was anxious, had been since last night when Kalina had announced they'd be able to get in to see the latest corpse today. Weeks had passed since this female had died. According to Pete, no one had claimed the body and the police were still investigating. The truly astonishing fact was how well the body had held up. Decomposition should have already started, but it seemed as if the body had been frozen in death. If Sabar's drug was capable of what Ary thought, it was going to be a catastrophe once it went global. X had that same fear; that's why he was here with them. The fact that Rome had doubled both their security was another reason X was tagging along. Jax and Leo were both standing right outside the front doors of the city morgue just in case anyone tried to come in while they were there.

"I'll wait right out here," Pete told Kalina, his chubby cheeks flushed red at her touch. "Ten minutes."

Kalina smiled and gave Ary and X a nod as she moved through the double doors. From behind, Ary heard X growl at the man who was no doubt still watching Kalina with his big blue eyes.

"You're an agitator," she told him once they were walking down a short hallway that lead to a second set of double doors.

"What? He was looking at her like he wanted her for his breakfast, lunch, and dinner. She is the First Female, you know," he said in his defense.

"Whatever," Ary said with a chuckle. "Bully."

"It should be this one," Kalina said once they were through the doors and near a wall full of handles and tags with dates on them.

Ary came up beside her as she reached for the handle.

"I'll get it," X said, motioning for both of them to move out of the way.

Ary immediately unzipped the black body bag, pushing it to both sides.

"Goddammit!" X yelled.

Both Kalina's and Ary's eyes shot up, wondering what had happened to make him explode like that.

"You okay with seeing a dead body?" Kalina asked.

X was rubbing his eyes, the veins in his neck bulging, his bald head glistening with tiny beads of sweat.

"I know this girl," he said before taking a deep breath. "I just spoke to her a few weeks ago. She's a stripper from that club Athena's."

"Oh," Ary said for lack of anything better.

"Was she the one you thought had information on Sabar's drug?" Kalina asked.

X nodded, looking down again at the girl, reaching out to close the one gray eye that was still open. The other eye wasn't exactly in a position to be closed since it barely hung in the socket while the rest of her face had been ripped off.

"Her name's Diamond," he said, clearing his throat. "The drug didn't do this to her," X finished adamantly.

"I agree," Ary told him, wanting to touch him, to console him in some way but refraining. X did not look like the type of man you consoled. Cussed out or punched, maybe, but not hugged and consoled. "There are scratches over here on her arm as well."

"So a Rogue did this? Why?" Kalina asked.

X cursed. "They don't need a reason, the filthy bastards!" He looked like he wanted to say more but squeezed his lips until they were in a tight line as he kept staring down at Diamond.

"Maybe the Rogue is infected," Ary suggested.

"You mean the Rogue took the drug, too?" Kalina asked Ary.

"No. I mean, maybe Yuri was able to perform the aya-huasca ceremony and opened the Rogue's soul. He could be controlled and made to do anything for any reason, without a second thought."

"Rogues don't second-guess anything. They decide and they act. Period. And they don't hesitate to kill. The other females were mauled, too," X said.

"Not in the face like this," Kalina said.

"And look here." Ary parted the legs of the female; thick, deep scratches had ripped her skin there as well. "Give me a hand," she said to Kalina.

Together they pushed the body—already in rigor—until they could see more scratches up and down her back, deeper and longer ones on her buttocks.

"You think he raped her?" Ary asked.

Kalina shrugged. "If she's a stripper, he might not have had to."

"She was a good girl," X said, his voice sounding more than a little agitated.

"In a very bad place and at a very bad time," Kalina told him as they lowered the body again. "Maybe she did know about the new drug. Maybe she knew Sabar and this is what she got from having that knowledge."

Ary was shaking her head even as X reached down and began zipping the body bag closed.

"Sabar wouldn't infect himself. He has to remain in control at all times," she said.

They took a step back as X closed the drawer with a solid click. He hadn't told them to watch out or even that he was putting the body away. But both of them were wise enough not to question him.

"He has to rule," Kalina began. "So he would want everyone who worked with him to be under his complete control."

"Owning their soul would be equivalent to having complete control," Ary said.

Kalina shrugged as she followed behind X, who was already moving toward the doors. "You're right."

Ary followed, walking besides Kalina. "I wish I wasn't."

"Why aren't you eating?" Nick asked Caprise when they were all seated around Rome's mahogany dining room table.

Custom-made blinds were closed tight at each window, drapes closed. The FL didn't want to risk anyone seeing what went on in his house. Especially since it was now filled with shifters.

"I don't eat meat," Caprise said, her facial expression conveying her discomfort at being here.

"That's why you're so bitchy all the time," X grumbled.

Nick shot him a warning glance to which he only shrugged.

"You," Carpise said, using her fork to point at X. "Are a pain in the ass!"

He dropped his fork and glared at her. "Let me tell you—"

Rome cleared his throat loudly. "Children, please. We're having dinner."

Kalina chuckled. Ary simply shook her head. It did feel like they were having a family dinner, and at such siblings did usually bicker. Younger siblings, that is; X and Caprise were too damn old for this. But anytime the two were near each other they were ready to bare claws and go at it.

"I'm not hungry," she said, pushing her plate away.

"You're too skinny," X replied.

Caprise's gaze shot straight at him again, glowing with the tawny glow of her cat's eyes.

"So we went to the morgue today," Ary put in.

Nick smiled at her in thanks.

Kalina joined right in. "The latest body wasn't killed by the drug."

"What happened to her?" Rome asked.

"A cat killed her," Ary said. "Half her face was ripped off, and there are scratches all over her body. He just tore her to shreds."

"Like he was super pissed off," Kalina said before taking a sip of her wine.

"So you think he took the drug first?" Nick asked Ary.

She shook her head. "No. I think he was infected with the ayahuasca."

"Why do you keep saying that?" X asked. "Shifters don't need a reason to kill."

"Let her talk," Rome interjected.

Nick looked at X, who didn't look like himself at all. Yes, his friend was usually a mean SOB, even more so than Nick most days, but when he was with them—meaning him and Rome—X was usually a little more laid back. Tonight he was edgy. And that had Nick concerned, because dealing with an edgy X was like walking into the middle of the jungle with blinders on. There was no telling what would happen next.

"There's a distinct difference between the drug and the ayahuasca itself. If it's mixed with the damiana and the cocaine, its effects are out of control. Alone, the ayahuasca takes a more dominant role. A shifter with his soul altered and controlled by someone else—it's like having a terrorist for a neighbor. You know something bad's going to happen, you just don't know when, where, or why."

"Sabar could build one hell of an army with shifters like that," Nick said.

"Exactly what I'm thinking," Ary added.

"So the drug is what? A distraction?" X asked.

At the far end of the table where it had been quiet for the last few minutes came a loud sigh. "It secures him a spot in the human world as a dominator. He has to lead from both sides, remember? Baxter told you this already. If he controls shifters, that makes him a leader among the cat people. Cornering the drug market gives him street cred to rival any power that politicians or cops could ever garner," Carpise said shooting an evil glare at X.

Before X could reply, Rome spoke up. "She's right."

"So playing both sides, he figures he's a winner either way," Ary said.

"He's counting on us not interfering at all," Nick said. "Evil bastard."

"But when I find him I'm sticking both my feet up his ass then snapping his punk-ass neck!" X said with vehemence.

"Bad kitty," Caprise cooed.

Nick sighed. These two were going to give him a fucking headache.

"Let's head to Havenway. There's something I want to show you two," Rome said, standing and dropping his napkin onto his cleaned plate. Bending over, he kissed Kalina and whispered something to her that had the female smiling broadly.

Nick pushed his chair back from the table and looked to Ary, who was already staring up at him. Expectantly, he thought. He mimicked Rome's actions, only his kiss was longer, deeper, as he couldn't seem to touch Ary's lips in a quick motion. He had to taste and enjoy every time. "I want you naked when I get back," he whispered to her and was rewarded with a pretty blush on her cheeks and a nod of her head. Who said this mating game had different rules?

"They're alone," the muffled voice said into the cell phone.

In the background Darel could hear cars and other outside noise. He figured the shifter had to come out of the mansion to make the call. "You're sure?" he asked. If they walked into an ambush Sabar was going to be royally pissed off—and the little shifter friend who'd happily delivered the information was as good as dead.

"Positive. FL and his two shadows just rolled out in the Tahoe with four other shifters. Three females are in the mansion with only the old man in there watching them."

"Three? We're only looking for two," Darel said, now a little more hesitant.

"Then you're getting a prize. She's fucking hot as hell

with her long legs and big boobs. I'd like to lick her all over," he said with a sigh and a hand to his growing erection.

"Don't blow your cover, idiot! Keep your dick in your pants, we'll be there soon."

"Sure. Right," he said, clicking off the phone then heading back into the house to get another look at the one they called Caprise. If he couldn't touch her, he could certainly get his look on while she showered and got ready for bed. He'd been doing that the last few nights and felt like he was falling in love.

Chapter 32

"I hate them all!" Caprise said with vehemence, dropping with a plop onto the chocolate-brown leather couch in Rome's den.

Across the room Kalina sat in one of those chairs that Ary refused to ever park her behind in again. She prayed that whatever she'd been experiencing the first night she'd been in this den that kept her from getting comfortable was over and done with, but didn't want to chance it. She sat on the love seat folding her legs up beneath and cuddling a pillow.

The scene was contented—a normal evening among friends. But there was a buzz in the air, a little sizzle of something she couldn't name. It wasn't grief, because she only grieved for people she loved. Davi was not one of them. And it wasn't fear. They were protected here, and as soon as Nick returned she'd feel even safer. No, something was in the air, Ary just couldn't figure out what it was.

"Who do you hate now, Caprise?" Kalina asked as if she were already bored with the conversation.

Caprise slapped a palm on the arm of the chair. "Men! They're all a bunch of high-handed bastards with nothing better to do than boss females around. I'm sick of it!"

Ary nodded. "I can relate to that sometimes," she

agreed, remembering how much Nick had ticked her off when she'd first arrived here.

Kalina looked at Caprise in shock. "They're just trying to protect you."

"Protect me from what? I'm not the one who pissed off this Sabar character. Hell, I don't even know who he is," Caprise argued.

"He's a bad-ass shifter who grew up in the Gungi, then was taken away to some godforsaken place by an evil bastard and royally messed up. Now he's set his sights on the stateside shifters. He wants us all dead. Me especially, because I wouldn't help him create a new drug to sell on the streets," Ary reported.

Kalina was shaking her head and drinking from a cup of piping-hot coffee that Baxter had delivered to them minutes ago. "No. I think I'm probably tops on his list since I've thwarted him and his goons three times now."

"See," Caprise said, lifting a hand in the air to flail it around then drop into her lap. "This has nothing to do with me. I haven't pissed this guy off."

"But you're one of us, Caprise. Whether you like it or not," Ary told her. She'd gotten the impression that Caprise did not want to be a shifter at all. Not that Nick had told her anything about his sister.

When she'd asked about Caprise, he'd told her they used to be close; then their parents were killed and Caprise took off. He wanted to protect his sister, that was clear, but he certainly wasn't being up front about what he was trying to protect her from. Spending time with Caprise today gave Ary a sense that his sister wasn't telling Nick what was really going on with her. Ary wondered why.

Ary leaned forward to pick up her cup of coffee but was baffled to see a glass of orange juice instead. She looked around to the other ladies; they had coffee. It wasn't like

Baxter to make such a mistake, she thought. Before she could think to call for him, Caprise was talking again.

"I don't know about you, but I'm a woman. This shape-shifting thing is not for me. I've never liked it and can't think of a reason why I'd start now," she was saying.

Kalina looked startled. "It's your heritage," she said.

Ary felt sorry for Kalina at this moment. Since they'd been spending a lot of time together, Ary had learned of Kalina's lonesome upbringing with human parents. She'd only learned she was a shifter a couple of months ago. So to her, this was the chance to be a part of a family. On some level, it was the same for Ary. Even though she'd lived with the tribe all her life, this family—the stateside shifters she'd met so far—had proved much more caring and loving than the ones she'd had before. For that reason, Caprise's words perplexed her, too.

"How could you not want to be what you are?" she asked her.

"Because it's not normal," Caprise said, pulling her black hair back and lifting it off her neck. "There are two groups on this earth, human and animals. Being part of each is an abomination."

"Talking like that is a slap in the face!" Kalina yelled, rising from her chair.

Caprise rolled her eyes. "You asked a question and I answered." Then she sighed and sat up, letting her elbows rest on her knees. "Look, I'm not here to make anyone uncomfortable. In fact, I don't even want to be here. I have my reasons for feeling the way I do. So I don't expect you to understand."

But Ary thought she might understand, just a little.

"Sometimes I wish I were one or the other, too. I used to think my life would be better if I weren't two halves of a whole."

"Exactly," Caprise said, swallowing from her cup of coffee.

Ary ran her finger around the rim of her glass of juice. Still not sure why she'd received something different, she picked it up and took a sip.

"We are what we are," Kalina said glibly.

She'd settled back in her chair and cradled her mug in her hand. "I'm happy I met Rome and happy to have found out where I came from."

"Then I'm happy for you." Caprise gave Kalina a salute. "For me, I'll stick to my guard."

And Ary figured she would. There was something Caprise was hiding, something that made her change her mind about the way she was born. The Delgado siblings were a pair of mysteries.

"It is getting late," Baxter said, coming into the room on quiet feet again.

"I'd like some coffee," Ary said quickly before he'd even come near the end table where she'd set her glass.

Baxter stopped, looked at her long and hard, then moved closer to her. He put his palm to her forehead, then traced a finger down her neck. Ary jerked at his touch and settled when he didn't move but smiled down at her instead.

"Just as I thought. Drink the juice, Ms. Aryiola," he said in his totally neutral, all-knowing voice. "Here, I'll take it up to your room for you."

Ary opened her mouth to argue, then thought better of it. She'd just go to her room, wait, then come back down and get her own damn coffee.

"You take care of everyone around here, don't you?" Caprise asked Baxter when she stood and stretched.

"That is my duty. We all have a duty we must live up to."

Caprise was shaking her head. Kalina had already

stood, giving her a look that said, *Let it go*. Ary only hoped Caprise took the hint. She did. And the three of them took to the stairs.

When she was alone in the room she and Nick were sharing, Ary looked out the window to the night sky. She thought about Nick, wanting him here with her desperately. While she wasn't feeling that suffocating heat anymore and her body had ceased its twitching and whatever else it had been doing, she still felt anxious.

After a warm shower, she slipped between the satin sheets, her naked body loving the cool softness against her skin. Her eyes closed and thoughts of dead bodies and bad drugs ran rapid through her mind. She saw flashes of the cat in the trees, lying on the ground, dying. His blood still smelled fresh; her chest heaved with the exertion of running that day. In a blink her thoughts shifted to days in the forest, studying with Yuri, the scent of incense replacing the acrid stench of blood and death.

A chill ran down her spine and she shivered as she slipped out of bed and grabbed her robe. Wrapping her arms around herself, she sat back down on the edge of the bed, her gaze instantly falling on the doors that opened to the balcony. And in that moment everything changed. All thoughts fled from her mind but one.

Rogues.

The window broke and sirens blared, stinging Ary's eardrum with the sound. But she was immediately on her feet bracing herself for unwelcome guests.

Two of them came through the glass, tall, dressed in all black, teeth bared. As if they followed her scent, their heads turned and they headed straight for the bed. After a moment's hesitation Ary jumped up on the bed, reaching overhead for the canopy pole on the side and swinging on it as if she were on a tree branch in the forest. Her feet caught the first Rogue square in the chest, and he tumbled backward. The second reached over his head for her as she sailed through the air, landing on her feet just behind him.

When he turned she was ready, punching him in the gut and when he bent over landing a duo of punches to his face. A face that by the way was not human. She'd noticed that when the two headed for her, their faces were in cat form, eerie green eyes, flat noses, muzzled mouths, whiskers—totally cat, but with human bodies.

During her assessment the Rogue swiped an arm out, catching Ary's shoulder, and she screamed with the pain of its claws ripping her flesh. Locking her legs, she watched it charge her again then jumped off the floor, extended one leg, and let her foot connect with its face. It roared and stumbled back.

The other Rogue was coming at her again when Leo broke through the door, his cat big and vicious as it charged past her and jumped on the Rogue's chest. In a flash there was another cat taking down the second Rogue.

"Let's go." Kalina came in, grabbing Ary by the arm. She held a gun in her other hand and was limping as they headed for the door.

"Wait, you're hurt," Ary said, stopping so Kalina would have no choice but to stop with her.

"It's fine. We have to get downstairs to the tunnel," Kalina said, trying to remain steady and breathe.

"Here, lean on me," Ary told her. She wrapped her arm around Kalina's waist to support her weight. "That leg looks bad."

"We just need to go."

"Yeah, we're going. Where's Caprise?"

There was a scream from the direction of her room and they both headed down that way. Kalina pushed Ary out of the way and extended her arm. Aiming right at the doorknob, she shot it off. Ary pushed through the door to see one of the Rogues with a hand wrapped around Caprise's neck. As Ary charged him Caprise raised her knee, slamming it into the human groin. The Rogue roared, released her, and bent forward. Ary extended her arm for a chop across his back and watched as he fell to his knees. Then Kalina came up from behind and shot him in the back of his head.

"Go!" they heard a male shout and turned to see Jax coming through the broken window, a Rogue on his tail. "Get downstairs now!"

Seeing that Kalina was injured, Caprise mimicked Ary's movements and they both supported the First Female as they headed out of the room. Baxter was in the hallway, where it seemed chaos had entered and made itself at home.

"This way!" he yelled to them.

Ary was only minutely surprised to see a flap in the wall open. Kalina wasn't surprised at all and went through first. Caprise followed, and Ary went next. She thought Baxter would be right behind them but he wasn't; the panel closed and they were in the dark.

It only took a second for their nocturnal vision to kick in. Kalina limped through what felt like the longest tunnel in the world. There was a decline and Ary figured it was a hill in place of the steps they would have traveled down in the house. Then there was a burst of light as Kalina's shoulder rammed a door. She fell through, Caprise and Ary right behind her.

Ary's wounded shoulder connected with the concrete and she hissed. Caprise helped her up, and they both got Kalina to her feet.

"There's a truck right around this corner. The keys are

in the glove compartment. We need to get to Havenway," Kalina told them.

Clearly this was a getaway plan she and Rome had discussed. Nick probably knew, and Ary bristled only slightly at the fact he hadn't told her. It didn't matter; they were away from those weird-ass Rogues. No, she corrected after they'd shoved Kalina into the backseat and she'd climbed into the passenger side, while Caprise got behind the wheel, they were infected Rogues.

"Where to?" Caprise yelled.

On the backseat Kalina was stretched out, but her words were clear. "Hit 95 south and go until I give you the exit to turn off."

"Right," Caprise said, starting the engine and driving down a path that could just about fit the width of the vehicle. They went up an incline to a wide door.

"Hit the button under the dash," Kalina said.

Ary reached under the dashboard, running her hand along until she hit a button and pressed it. The door rose upward and they were introduced to the night. Caprise pressed on the gas and they shot out onto the road.

Kalina continued to give directions. "There should be a cell in the glove compartment, too. Get it out and push pound-one." Then she moaned and Ary, cell phone in hand, turned back to see how she was doing. There was a huge gash in her leg; blood was trickling out of it in a steady stream.

"Shit! She's loosing a lot of blood," she said.

"Make the call then get back there to help her," Caprise said, turning them onto what looked like a busy highway.

She nodded and dragged her finger along the base of the phone to turn it on. She'd been in the States for almost a month, where learning how to work a cell phone was almost as important as knowing how to read and write.

A male answered. It sounded like Rome but Ary wasn't 100 percent sure. But since this was a private phone she figured it had to be someone who at least worked for the FL.

"Where are you?" he asked.

"Going to Havenway. Caprise is driving. Kalina's hurt," she said.

The string of curses that followed assured her it was Rome she was speaking to. "I'll meet you there," he said. Then hung up.

Ary dropped the phone and leapt over the seat to get to Kalina.

"Okay, this is going to hurt," she told her as she ripped the bottom side of her robe. Wrapping the material around Kalina's leg, she tied it as tight as she could.

Kalina's scream echoed throughout the car. Ary tried to ignore it as she pressed down on the wound, praying she could at least slow down the bleeding. At the rate it was going, Kalina might bleed out before they could get to Havenway.

Chapter 33

"Where the fuck are they?" Rome roared as he paced the floor of Havenway's foyer.

"It's an hour-and-a-half drive to get here, Rome. Caprise probably doesn't even know where she's going," X said, his voice gruff with the rage he was trying to hold back.

"She knows these roads like the back of her hand. She'll get them here safely," Nick said. He was worried about Ary but somewhat relieved that she'd been the one to make the call.

"Kalina's hurt. Did I tell you she said that?" Rome asked, running a hand over his head as he paced.

"You did," Nick said, understanding exactly how his friend was feeling. "But Ary's there. I know she's helping her."

Rome nodded. "You're right. I know you're right. Still."

"Yeah," Nick said. "Still."

It didn't matter that a healer was with her. His mate was hurt and he was here, helpless for the most part. That was a bitch of a situation, and Nick didn't want to relive it for anything in the world.

When they'd gotten word there was a break-in at Rome's, their first instinct had been to return, to get their females and fight off the bastards attacking them. But Baxter, the voice of reason, had warned against it. They were the government for the shifters at the moment, at least for the East Coast. Rome was the FL and Nick and X were his seconds-in-command. If all of them were killed in battle, where would that leave the rest of the shifters? Funny how it had taken an attack to have Nick agreeing with this type of logic.

The safety of all shifters was a priority. Not over his mate, never over her, but it was still a priority. One that took consideration over his rash thinking.

The latest call had news of eight Rogues dead. Baxter was safe and so were Jax and Leo. Nivea had been wounded, but was still fighting. And two guards were dead.

Lights flashed outside and Rome tore through the door, running at the truck even before it stopped. Nick and X followed him out. Rome yanked open the back door and had Kalina in his arms. Nick smelled the blood. His heart pumped wildly as he looked at Ary, who wore a lot of that blood on her torn robe. She'd climbed out of the door on the opposite side. Nick was immediately on her, rubbing his hand down her front and back.

"I'm okay, I'm okay," she said. "I have to go help Kalina."

"Right," Nick said, breathing a sigh of relief.

He turned and saw Caprise getting out of the truck.

"You good?" X asked, standing about a foot away from her.

"Just peachy," she said with a smirk. Then she looked over at Nick. "It was an ambush. They came from every-where all at once, like they knew we were there and you guys weren't."

The last was said pointedly. X looked at her with slight disbelief but Nick simply nodded. Caprise was like that—

not at all what she appeared. He figured X was getting his first glimpse of that.

"Another setup? Is that what you're saying?" he asked.

She rolled her eyes and started walking toward the door. "He's a genius. You should definitely keep him around."

X growled, and Nick couldn't help but grin.

An hour later Ary had stitched up Kalina's leg and given her some antibiotics and pain medicine. It was a good thing Rome had insisted on the medical facility being one of the first priorities at Havenway. Not all the supplies and equipment were in, but she'd had enough to do what was necessary.

The room Nick had led her to so she could shower and get some rest wasn't as lavish as the one at Rome's place—or the one at Nick's apartment, for that matter. But it was clean and she was dead tired. She came out of the shower and he was right there wrapping her in a heavy terry-cloth robe.

"Baxter's going to bring some tea," he told her.

She sighed. "Oh, good. He's all right. I was worried that we'd had to leave him."

"Baxter's going to live forever," Nick told her as he helped her to sit on the bed. It didn't look big enough to hold both of them, but Ary figured they would worry about that later.

Except Nick was still dressed.

"Aren't you going to shower and change?" she asked him.

He looked at her—and that's when she saw it. The furrow in his brow, the tinge to his eyes that said he was on the brink. "We're heading out."

"Out where?" she asked, knowing damn well what he was about to say.

"One of the Rogues talked after some manipulation. We've got an exact locale for Sabar."

"No!" she said, standing abruptly. "You are not going to fight him."

"He's the top dog—or cat, I guess. We've got to dispatch him for this madness to stop. Or humans and shifters are going to keep dying."

Ary heard his words but couldn't really decipher them because she was adamantly shaking her head. "No. You cannot go. They weren't normal. Nothing about them was right. They were both halves and they were focused on killing and, and . . ."

He touched her shoulders, but Ary pulled away. "No! Nick! No! All you think about is killing, all the time! I'm sick of it!" she screamed. "I won't live like this! I can't! You said you wouldn't leave me again. You said it and I heard you!"

Tears streamed down her face and she didn't care. He came at her again and she instantly started swinging, pain searing through her wounded shoulder. "You said you wouldn't leave! They're killers! If you leave . . . if you go they'll—"

"Stop," he said, holding her wrists and pulling them together with her body flush against his front. "Just stop. I know what I'm doing."

"You don't. You don't know what they are, what they're capable of," she said, her voice sounding more shaky by the minute. "You don't know."

She pulled away from him, staring at him through tear-blurred eyes. But this was Nick so he didn't back down; he only followed her until her back was to the wall, his stare firm as he pressed his hard body against hers.

His palms came to her cheeks, holding her face as

gently as if she were a child. "Ary, I would do almost anything for you. I hope you know that," he whispered.

She nodded, heart hammering wildly, love overflowing for this man, her mate. She didn't want him to go, had just about begged him to stay. But she knew he wouldn't listen. He bent forward and dropped the sweetest kiss on her lips. Ary savored that kiss, let the warmth filter through her body, soothing the ache in her arm and the pain in her chest.

When he pulled back, his dark brown human eyes had shifted to the yellow-gold eyes of his cat. "Please don't ask me to be a coward."

Ary was shaking her head, her body warm from his touch. "You're not a coward," she told him and meant it. With everything that Nick was, everything that he wanted to be—coward was not on the list. "You just need to think before acting this time."

He looked for a long minute. "I know that now."

"No. You don't know. I need you to really think . . . about . . . about everything you have here. About us, about what we can be. About Rome because he needs you, and Caprise because she does, too, even thought she'll never admit it. About X because he's going to kill Caprise if you're not here to stop him. And . . . and . . . about our family."

"Caprise has a guard—she's safe. X knows the boundaries. And you're staying at Havenway until we find a house. This place is loaded with guards."

She shook her head again and moved his hand from her check down to rest over her abdomen. "Your new family."

Baxter's insistence on giving her orange juice while the other females drank coffee had started her wondering. Lying in the bed just before the attack, she'd thought like the *curandero* and not the woman. She could've smacked herself for being so stupid. Of course that incessant pain and craving she'd been going through the night that shifter had chased them in the trees was because she was in heat. Most likely that was why the shifter had been chasing them in the first place.

"What are you saying?" Nick asked, looking back up at her.

"I think I might be pregnant," she said, lifting a hand to wipe away her tears. "I haven't had a chance to officially test myself, but Baxter seems to think I am, so . . ." She shrugged.

"Baxter," Nick said with a sigh, looking back down at his hand resting on her stomach. "Baxter knows everything."

She couldn't tell if the possibility made him happy or sad. But it didn't stop his resolve.

"I'm coming back to you," he told her. "To us. I promise."

The plan was to go to the address on D Street that X had found using the FBI's database. Rome, Nick, and X were going, despite Baxter's arguments. This may have been the first time Rome blatantly went against Baxter's advice, but Baxter had to understand how personal this was. Not only was one of his father's killers in league with Sabar, but they'd hurt his mate. He was gunning for blood.

Nick was in the same boat, needing to put an end to this threat before he lost his sanity. He had so much to lose now. He thought of Caprise being back and somewhat with them, then of Ary and the possibility that she was carrying his child. All were reasons for him to return from this operation. Not that he thought he wouldn't. His plan was, as always, kill first, ask questions later. Because in his mind the answers weren't as important as sending Sabar's black soul directly to hell with no pit stops.

As for X, Nick watched his usual dour demeanor deteriorate until he looked more like a soldier at war than an FBI special agent. He was going to do some real damage, and Nick figured, *Good for him.* Whatever ailed his friend might be healed after tonight. They all might have a little healing after the bloodshed they planned.

There was a truckload of shifters riding behind them — two truckloads, actually. They probably looked like they were moving something in the dead of night with the black truck leading the entourage. The possibility of human exposure was a big consideration.

"If we don't protect the humans, they're going to die without knowledge. I feel like this is a part of our job even though we might be breaking one of the rules of the *Ètica*," Rome had told them before leaving the house.

"Fuck the *Ètica!*" X had shouted, and Nick had agreed with a nod.

And so they'd left, like soldiers heading off to war. Only they didn't have a government and a country behind them, just the cats that lurked beneath the surface.

"The house is in the next block," X said as they rode down a dark street.

It was a warm night so the air-conditioning was going in the truck. Two guards were up front, with Nick, Rome, and X in the back. There wasn't a lot of talking going on, just waiting, tension thick. Outside it was still, almost like a movie just before the scene turned to utter chaos.

That thought should have been warning enough.

In a blink cars were turned over skidding into the street in front of the truck they rode in. The guard up front pressed the brake almost to the floor and still hit one of the tumbling cars. Behind them brakes screeched as the other trucks tried to stop as well. Small trees lined the residential street. Nick watched as what looked like humans in the dark stood and uprooted the trees, throwing them at their vehicles.

"Infected Rogues, just like Ary said," Rome whispered.

X growled so loud the truck shook.

Nick nodded at him. "Right, let's kick some ass and talk about this bullshit later!"

He was first out of the truck, leaving the door swinging open. X and Rome were right behind him, Rome yelling something to the others in the back. They all had semi-automatic guns they could use to take the Rogues down, instead of shifting. But Nick didn't care: He was killing these bastards any way he could. And right now, his cat was pacing, roaring, ready to go.

A tree barreled at him and Nick reached up a hand to catch it midair, feeling the adrenaline rush through his blood like a drug. He opened his mouth and roared as he threw it back at the Rogue and watched the idiot fucker let it slam right into its burly chest. When it stumbled back, Nick pounced, landing on its chest and flipping it over, letting his sharp teeth sink into the back of its neck.

His claws had elongated and he almost felt like the beasts they fought with his human and cat halves joining together to get the job done. They seemed to be everywhere, like some sort of infestation, and Nick wondered how many had been infected before he captured Yuri. Baxter had informed him that the shaman had still been in the guest house when his creations had attacked, and because they were simple soulless shifters, they'd killed him without thought. It didn't matter to them who he was or what he'd done for them, he was a commodity and they'd been directed to take everyone at the mansion out. Nick couldn't find any pity for the man, it served his ass right.

Another one came at him and he grabbed it at the neck, letting his claws sink in deep. It roared, its mouth opening wide to reveal sharp teeth. When it reached for Nick with its own claws, Nick shook the big body until the feet were off the ground. With his other hand he sank his claws into its stomach then tossed it about a block away.

Nick was moving toward the house they suspected Sabar was living in, at least part-time. There was no way the shifter would have only one location; that would be dangerous, and Sabar seemed to be a little smarter than that. So they knew there was a chance he wouldn't be there. But the plan was to do as much damage to his operation as they possibly could, both in retaliation for the attack on Rome's house and to send a message that they were no longer playing with his sadistic ass.

In the distance he saw Rome plowing through Rogues making his way to the house while shadows from behind took on more of the renegades. Nick was just about to catch up with Rome when he was knocked to the ground, something heavy bearing down on his back. He heard the deadly roar and realized the position he was in. Every muscle in his human body tensed. As the hot breath of the Rogue that had downed him rippled across the skin of his neck, in preparation for the kill, visions flashed before his eyes.

Caprise as a little girl, running with a frilly pink dress on and two long ponytails. She loved to dress up so Sundays were extra special for her. A more adorable little girl Nick had never seen.

Ary's eyes appeared next, amber orbs holding his gaze as if he were hypnotized. She smiled and her plump lips called to him. She turned to run, her brown-streaked hair following behind her in a swirling stream.

Then there was a cradle, white with lace all around it. As he approached the cradle to see who was inside, his parents appeared. Dressed in the dark colors they'd worn as they lay in their caskets at the funeral. Henrique and Sofia smiled as if welcoming him home. He was out of breath as he ran toward the cradle, his clawed hands grabbing the sides as he looked inside. It was filled with blood. He looked up at Henrique and Sofia and their faces were mauled, but their arms were extending, again beckoning him to come with them.

In that instant Nick shifted, his cat tearing through the human flesh with a deafening roar. The quickness of the shift threw the Rogue to the side but it came back at the cat once more. Balancing on its hind legs, the cat came up to its full length of six feet, extending one of its paws so that it connected with the Rogue's face with a sickening smack, blood spewing as it retracted. The Rogue stumbled back against a car, shattering the side windows with its weight. The cat jumped at it, attacking again, roaring deep guttural sounds that echoed up and down the residential street. When it was tired of playing with the Rogue—which was no match for its strength and fighting skills no matter who controlled its mind—the cat simply bit into its neck, going so deep its head dangled to the side as the body finally fell dead to the ground.

Flanks heaving, blood tickling the back of its throat, the cat headed up the street where it had seen Rome and X enter a house. It pushed through the half-open door following the scent of the shadows up the stairs.

"He's not here, fucking coward!" Rome yelled as the cat entered the room.

X turned to see the cat enter and opened his mouth in

a low roar that said he knew who it was. The cat returned the growl, tongue licking its muzzle as it moved throughout the room.

"He was here. And he had Diamond here, too. I want his ass, Rome. I want to kill that motherfucker in his sleep!"

Rome nodded. "My sentiments exactly. Take his computer and anything else you think is important. And you." He pointed at the cat. "Get the hell out of sight before a human reports a fucking jaguar on the streets."

They were on their way back to Havenway, had just crossed the boundary into Virginia when their truck swerved off the road. Nick had changed into jeans with a shirt, and Rome and X were in the back with him like before. The collision had them tumbling around the backseat, cursing. As the truck flipped over they struggled to get the door open and roll their bodies out before the vehicle slammed down an embankment and exploded.

One truckload of shifters had stayed behind in the city to clean up the mess they'd made there, while the other traveled about ten minutes behind Rome's truck. So they were nowhere in sight at the moment. The three shadows rolled in the dry grass, coughing with the smoke now filling the air.

"What the fuck?" Nick yelled. "Rome, you okay?"

More coughing. "Cool. You, X?"

More cursing. "I'm here."

When the three of them met up, they looked down the embankment to where the truck they'd been riding in was in flames.

"What the hell hit us?" X said about a second before what hit them came running quickly out of a thin line of trees on the other side of the highway.

It was a cat, its dark rosettes visible in the headlights

of the car it almost plowed right into as it headed for the shadows. The car swerved a bit then sped up—getting the hell out of Dodge, which was probably a smart thing to do. The cat approached them in a slow, predatory manner.

"I recognize the scent," Rome said his claws emerging.

Just as he spoke another cat appeared, a bigger, darker one, green eyes gleaming in the night.

"Fuck this!" Nick yelled a second before shifting. His cat emerged with a majestic roar that translated into English meant, "Bring it!"

The first cat charged directly at him. Nick took its hit and the battle was on, both cats swiping and growling, skidding down the embankment in a cloud of dust. The cat was as big as Nick, trained in hunting and battle just as Nick's cat was, so the fight was on equal ground. Teeth and claws made their marks on each.

When Nick's cat could feel the heat from the crash, it stopped and edged away from the fire. The other cat didn't move, but growled again in challenge. It said it didn't give a damn about the fire. Nick did. He had a lot to live for. *Think first,* his human roared inside the head of the cat.

Nick swiped at the air and the other cat followed suit, rising up on its hind legs, mouth wide open. It was calling Nick out. The bastard! Nick moved to the side slightly, watching the cat's eyes follow him. He made a chuffing sound, his heaving flanks vibrating with the sound. It was the equivalent of talking shit, a come-and-get-me-motherfucker noise. The other cat took a step toward Nick. He made the sound again and it charged him. Nick was ready, coming up on his hind legs and swinging his paws in rapid succession. His teeth nipped the cat and Nick tasted blood. He pushed back with all the force he had; the other cat stumbled and rolled. Nick jumped on it, sank his teeth into its side again.

Bright lights lit the scene, the sound of cars and sirens echoing in the distance. Nick scented other shadows coming, heard their footsteps, and the cat beneath him wriggled free. It ran down past the burning vehicle and kept going. Nick shifted instead, walking up the embankment toward where he saw Rome already standing.

"The fucker took off as soon as it heard the sirens," Rome told him.

X came up behind them. "We should do the same. Last thing I want is to be questioned by some pigeon-head cops while I'm in the buff."

All three of them were naked after their shifts. The truck with the other shadows had pulled close to the guardrail just a few feet away. They jogged down and climbed into the back.

"A couple of you stay here to answer questions. The truck just swerved and flipped off the road. You thought maybe you saw a deer shoot out in front of it. That's all," Rome said adamantly.

Nivea, who had been driving the truck, shook her head, her right arm still bandaged.

"Not you, Nivea. You, you, and you two, stay. Nivea, you drive."

The shadow gave Nick a scathing look he knew he'd have to deal with later, but it didn't matter. He wasn't in the mood to have another one of their females in danger tonight, so she was going back to Havenway with him.

They were all heading back to Havenway, alive. Just as he'd promised Ary.

Chapter 34

Even though the rooms weren't completely furnished, the private bathrooms were just about done. Nick sighed as hot water lapped over his battered and scarred skin. The sunken tub in this minimalistic stone-tiled bathroom was just what he needed after the night he'd had.

The sun was just rising. Slim rays slashed through the room from a narrow window that completed the decor as well as boasting a new security design. No way a shifter was fitting through that window, or anyone else for that matter. But it gave just enough of the outside to whoever was inside that they didn't feel jailed.

This tub was more than long enough and wide enough for Nick's body, which was another plus. In fact, he could fit at least two more people in here with him. But today the silence added to his comfort. He let his head fall back against the edge of the tub and closed his eyes. So much had happened tonight; his emotions had turned from rage, to a pure adrenaline rush, to anxiety that almost choked him, to a fear he'd never thought he'd experience, and then back to a simmering rage that felt like coming back home. And let's not forget the mixed feelings about Ary's announcement.

She was pregnant.

Or at least she thought she was.

How did he feel about that?

Lifting a wet hand, he rubbed it down his face and let the droplets of water roll over his skin there as he inhaled deeply. He would be a father. And Ary would be the mother of his child. He would once again be part of a family, one that belonged solely to him. Pride swelled inside and memories of all the things his parents used to do with him resurfaced. Christmas mornings and endless hours of training, family dinners, vacations—all made Nick feel warm inside. The betrayal came later, but he was beginning to think there was an explanation for that as well. One he and Rome still had yet to discover. But it was entirely possible that their parents were acting in the best interest of the tribes, even though that may have meant they broke some laws—both human and shifter.

Suddenly those thoughts vanished, replaced by the memory of a bubbling waterfall, the damp scent of the forest, and the softness of her skin. He opened his eyes and she stood right beside him, her naked body alight with the golden rays of the sun. Without a word he extended a hand to her. She accepted it and stepped down into the tub beside him.

"Kalina finally settled," she began when he was lifting his arm to pull her comfortably beside him. "Even with the pain meds she was a wreck with Rome out fighting. Now that he's back and all patched up beside her, she's doing a lot better."

"That's good to hear. We heal pretty fast, so she should be all right soon."

She gave him a playful slap on the chest that sent water splashing over both of them. "I'm the medical expert here, I'll give the diagnosis."

He chuckled. "Excuse me."

"Okay. So, she'll heal pretty fast and be back to normal in no time." She gave him a side smile. "Rome's injuries were minor, and X simply refused to let me look at him."

"Yeah, he's not big on doctors."

"And neither are you, since you bypassed the medical facility and headed straight here."

"I'm fine," he told her.

"I'll be the judge of that," she said, moving in the water, her hands touching his skin.

She lifted his foot, pulled it up out of the water, and felt his leg all the way up to his thigh. Her touch alone had him going crazy, but Nick struggled to keep his thoughts in check. She was just doing her job, not trying to arouse him. When she repeated the motion with the other leg, he hoped her impromptu exam was over. He was wrong.

She straddled him then, lifting his arms and tracing her fingers along the scratches he had there. "Superficial, should be healed in a day or two," she told him.

"I told you—"

"Hush," she said cutting him off.

When she let his arms fall to his sides, her hands flattened against him just beneath the pit of his arm, running down his torso in slow motion. Her fingers flared feeling against him, then pressed into his ribs. He didn't budge. She leaned back, looking down at his chest and stomach as her nimble fingers checked there as well. By this time his dick was hard and poking into the wet crevice of her buttocks. There was definitely no hiding his arousal now.

Ary wrapped her arms around him, her hands searching his back. She sucked in a breath when she felt a gash and tried to pull back so she could shift behind him to get a better look. But Nick put his arms around her, pulling her close, loving the feel of her naked breasts against his chest.

"It's fine, Doc. But I've got something else that needs

fixing," he whispered in her ear seconds before his tongue stroked her lobe.

She sucked in a breath. "Really? Where's the injury?"

He lifted her slightly until the tip of his length rested against her core. "Right here. It needs some attention, badly. Battling Rogues makes it a little anxious."

She smiled down at him, her eyes alight with arousal. "I think I have just what it needs."

With his hands moving to her hips, he felt her pushing herself down, his dick slipping effortlessly into her depth.

"How's that?" she asked when he was buried deep. Her plump folds rubbed against his groin as his balls scraped against her anus.

He moaned, a growl rumbling deep in his chest. "Just what the doctor ordered."

"When will you know if you're pregnant?" Nick asked when they were lying in the bed that was, in his estimation, too small to comfortably accommodate his stature and his mate with him. He'd have to buy new furniture even if they only planned to live here a short time. He was sure there would be occasions where they stayed here, and he wanted them both to be comfortable.

"I already know," she said, rolling to her side, resting her head on her hand as she looked down at him.

"And?"

"I'm pregnant," she announced, her lips trembling in what he knew could easily turn into a smile.

"Wow" was the only word he could manage.

Her expression turned serious.

"Female shifters are in heat four times a year—you could say quarterly depending on their own individual schedule. During their heat they can become impregnated. Normal incubation for a shifter is twelve to eighteen weeks. I'm about three and a half weeks along." She took a deep steadying breath and continued. "While full jaguars are known to birth anywhere from two to four cubs, shifters usually average a birth of one or two."

The entire time she'd been talking, Nick had been looking at her body. Loving the curve of her hips, the natural hang of her heavy breasts, the curl-covered juncture of her sex. And now his gaze rested on her stomach, the tiny slit of her navel, the beginning of a small bump at her stomach. He put his palm there and closed his eyes.

"Baxter's ordering ultrasound equipment along with other radiographic tools we may need. For right now we've decided that besides myself, Dr. Papplin will be my doctor. It wouldn't be smart to go into a human hospital and tell them I'm giving birth after eighteen weeks."

Nick heard her words but was still focused on her stomach and what was at this very moment growing there.

"I love you," he said without a second thought.

"What?"

She grabbed him by the chin, lifting his face so she could see him. "What did you just say?"

He sat up then, keeping one hand on her stomach, touching the other to her cheek, tracing a line around to her eyebrows, over her eyes, down her nose, over her lips. "I love you, Aryiola Serino."

Her eyes had already started to water, her bottom lip quivering before a laugh bubbled from inside her and she wrapped her arms around his neck, pulling him down to her. "I didn't think you were ever going to say it. I hoped and prayed. And Caprise and Kalina said not to worry because it was so obvious that you did. But you wouldn't say it. Acted like it was going to kill you actually. But I'm so happy. So very, very happy!"

Her voice was music to his ears, her words raining

down on him like a downpour when all he wanted to hear from her were three words in return. Reaching behind him he unlaced her arms from his neck, holding her hands in his, bringing her fingers to his lips to kiss.

With their gazes locked he said once more, "I love you, *companheiro.*"

Tears rolled down her cheeks, but she smiled. Oh, she smiled so prettily, it was like a fist clenching Nick's heart.

"I love you, *companheiro.*"

Hundreds of miles away, in a room with two long stainless-steel tables, blood splattered onto cement floors.

"This is not what I do. I'm a chemist. A researcher," Norbert cried frantically. His sweaty hands shook as he pushed his glasses up on his nose.

"Shut up!" Bianca yelled. "You're the only doctor here, so you're up. Now get over there and fix them. Him first." She pointed to Sabar, who had a jagged gash on his neck.

His body was riddled with scratches and lacerations that all bled like a flowing spring. Darel was on the second table, part of his side hanging open, blood and a multitude of other things hanging out.

But Sabar was their leader, he was the important one. He needed to live through this. If he didn't, everything Bianca had worked for would be for nothing. When Boden came looking for her she'd be alone and vulnerable once more. She'd come to Sabar for protection because she'd seen something in the boy that Boden had brought to them years ago. There was a spark in his eyes that said he was going to be something one day, something big. And as the shifter had gotten older, his body and mind maturing, Bianca had watched, mouth watering, waiting for the exact moment she could stand beside him and claim the power and respect that Boden couldn't give to anyone.

So when Norbert continued to stand there and stare at Sabar's bleeding body, Bianca's claws emerged and went to the stupid human's throat. "You can do what I tell you or die where you stand."

Norbert stepped toward the table where Sabar lay gasping for breath. He pulled on latex gloves and moved closer. "I'll need some of that gauze over there and a bucket of warm water. I can't do anything if I can't see what I'm working with."

Used to being a slave for another, Bianca moved around the room getting the chemist whatever he said he needed, watching with bated breath as he tried to save her new lover, her savior's life.

Chapter 35

One week later

It was breakfast time at Havenway. They'd all moved in, except for X, whom they hadn't seen much of in the last week. The dining hall was complete with high vaulted ceilings and six-foot tables lined in rows four wide and seven long. There were two head tables in the front of the room, turned to face the remaining tables. Those were for the FLs, commanders and their families.

There was a large pitted fireplace on one side of the room that reminded Kalina of the pictures she'd seen of medieval times. In the kitchen, which had connecting doors that opened on one side to the dining hall and on the other to a back hallway, there was another pited fireplace, gas grills, and a professional stove. Three Sub-Zero refrigerators, deep freezers, and more pots and pans than Kalina had ever seen in her life had also been added to the kitchen.

Baxter supervised everything at Havenway, just as he had at Rome's house. He hired staff using X's database—which by this time had become an invaluable tool for the stateside shifters. And even with those added duties he still found time to see to Kalina's and Rome's needs personally.

Not to mention the way he doted on Ary as she carried Nick's child.

Next week Rome was flying three of the Elders and a handful of females from the Gungi to the States to assist in Nick and Ary's official joining. After that they'd have a civil ceremony at the local courthouse just as Kalina and Rome had done to seal their union in both the worlds they lived in.

It was an honor and a privilege to be a part of this shifter family, Kalina thought as she looked up and down the table at them. Even Caprise had mellowed a bit. Okay, that might be taking it a bit far. Kalina agreed with Rome and Nick: There was something eating at Caprise, something that was tearing her up on the inside so that she was a living, breathing bitch on a daily basis. To Kalina and Ary she seemed to be relaxing a little more, not snapping at everything they said, and even offering her opinions during their conversations. Kalina thought that if she'd ever had a genetic sister, this is how they would act. Not always agreeing with or even liking each other, but caring deeply what was going on in each other's lives and being loyal enough to keep whatever secrets were necessary. While Caprise hadn't opened up to them yet, Kalina felt a confession might be coming soon. At least she prayed so.

"Another stripper was found dead last night," Kalina said when it looked like everyone was finished eating and sipping on coffee or orange juice, as she glanced at Ary.

"I'm not surprised," Rome said.

"The drug is already out there. It's going to do its damage until it's gone," Nick chimed in.

Rome shook his head. "He's not dead," he said solemnly.

Nick sighed heavily. "I don't think either one of them is. That would have been too easy."

"Then they would have had to have gone to a hospital. You both said you wounded them. Even shadows don't heal that fast on their own," Ary told them.

"They couldn't have gone to a regular hospital," Kalina said. "So how would they have gotten treatment?"

Caprise put her mug down with a loud clanking sound against the marble table. "The same way he got your shaman here and your father to turn against you and the tribes. Money. It rules here in the States. All he has to do is flash some green and he'll get whatever he wants."

"Yeah, but at an even higher price." Nick grimaced. "Money doesn't buy silence, not for long anyway. So if he's pulling in human doctors to help him out, he's risking exposure."

"You mean more exposure than you guys have already risked?" Caprise asked. "Have you seen the news lately? You'd think a spaceship landed in the middle of DC. They're speculating about the sounds that were heard that night near Sabar's house and on the highway. I read in the paper the other day that people are reporting sightings of weird-looking cat-like people. I'd say the exposure element is already out there."

Kalina sighed. "Unfortunately, she's right. How are we going to deal with that?"

"It might die down, just like the alien thing did years ago," Nick said without much hope to his tone.

"Or it's going to spiral out of control," Rome added dourly.

"So where do we go from here?" Ary asked.

"Get Sabar and deal with the rest afterward." Rome spoke with finality as he pushed his chair back and stood from the table. "And continue to make money so we can help the tribes."

That was Nick's cue to leave as well. They'd go into the city to work, leading their human lives as if they had no other care in the world. Kalina accepted her husband's kiss and watched him walk out of the dining hall in his custom-made suit and shiny tie-up shoes. He looked as good as he had the day she'd first met him in his office. Only now, her heart swelled with more love and respect than she'd ever thought it possible to feel.

Ary walked with Nick as he stopped in their bedroom to get his suit jacket. It was charcoal gray today, with a crisp white shirt and gunmetal-gray tie that she'd finally gotten the hang of tying for him. In the morning they'd made love and lingered in bed for as long as possible before they knew Baxter would be knocking at their door. Then they had breakfast with friends who were more like family and she walked him to the door, watching as he drove off in his car for work.

Later in the morning she'd leave to attend her first classes at the university. She had a long way to go to achieve her goal of becoming a doctor, but loved that at least she was on her way. Late afternoon she'd return to Havenway and to the medical center where she checked supplies and studied some more, this time using the herbs Rome had shipped in for her. Already she'd begun taking care of the minor scrapes and bruises the guards-in-training received. And she was getting to know everyone at Havenway, the same way she'd known all the tribesman in the Gungi.

She didn't miss Davi, didn't think about him or his betrayals anymore. It was done. As for her mother, there were tinges of regret there, and a slight bit of longing, as Ary sometimes sat alone staring out a window, her hand on her quickly growing belly. It would have been nice to have her mother here with her during this time. But that was a useless thought.

"Be careful today," Nick said, turning to her and pulling her into his arms.

"You say that every day," she told him, wrapping her arms around his neck.

He laughed. "I mean it every day, too. Make sure Leo sticks close, and come right back when you're finished."

"Yes sir," she said, twisting her lips because this diatribe was getting old. She always told Leo where she was going, which didn't matter because now that he knew she was pregnant Leo was as big a shadow to her as Nick. Like right now: He wasn't in sight, but Ary knew that just around the corner he stood, ready and able to do whatever was necessary to save her and the baby's lives. It was comforting and not as stifling as she'd thought when she originally came to the States.

"I'll miss you," Nick said, bringing his lips down to brush over hers.

"I'll miss you more" was her soft reply.

When he pulled away he knelt down to kiss her stomach, another thing he did now on a daily basis.

Nick wanted a boy. Ary wanted a girl. Kalina said that was natural. Rome wished them a happy, healthy baby. Caprise jokingly prayed it wouldn't look and act like Nick. X broodingly watched Ary like a hawk when he was around. He'd be the overprotective uncle, she knew instinctively.

And when Ary shut the door that day she leaned against it, closing her eyes and thinking of how happy she was at this very moment. How perfectly normal and quaint her life seemed to be.

The question of whether that would last didn't dare creep into her mind.

* * *

Agent Dorian Wilson sat in his closet-size office, pictures spread out over his desk. His fingers moved in a pecking motion over the keys on the keyboard as he searched the hard drive for other photos he'd saved there. It was an old file he'd stumbled upon, just like the link connecting Roman Reynolds and his law firm to the accounts in Brazil. There seemed to be so many loose ends, all dangling in the air in front of him. Like they were teasing him, daring him to put the puzzle pieces together.

When the pictures flashed on the screen Dorian sat back in his chair staring, still in disbelief. The images were of a man—body, face, legs, arms of a man—with claws of an animal. Dorian wasn't naive; he knew all about Photoshopping pictures and airbrushing images. But something told him this image wasn't a fake. Or at the very least, if the claws were fake, they'd still been used in the commission of a crime.

Senator Baines and his daughter had been mauled to death. So had those two prostitutes they'd found a couple of months ago. The MPD was supposed to be working on the cases, forming some sort of task force to get to the bottom of the murders. But Dorian's superiors had already called him in for a briefing. They thought all of this was connected somehow to Reynolds and his still-unproven cartel connections.

Dorian believed them.

So what he had in front of him now were more pictures, more connections, but nothing concrete. Except the business card that had been found on one of the bodies recovered.

Diamond Lauray Turner was twenty-one years old. She lived in a dingy hotel two blocks from Athena's where she worked as a dancer. She'd graduated from high school and was taking online college courses working toward a degree in business administration. On paper she looked like a good girl.

Dorian picked up one of the photos from the MPD's homicide file. Half her face had been ripped off. On this paper, Diamond looked like a statistic. And Dorian didn't like it.

In one hand he held a photo, in the other the business card. He'd read the name over and over again, feeling his adrenaline kick up a notch each time.

Xavier Santos-Markland was the name on the card. Special agent at the Federal Bureau of Investigations.

Statements from one of Diamond's co-workers said a man approached them in the alley behind Athena's the last night Diamond was seen alive. She said the guy took a special liking to Diamond and wanted her to do some special favors for him; he'd told her to call him whenever she needed something. The other girls claimed they warned Diamond to stay away from the guy, but she was young and stupid and probably hooked up with him anyway.

Dorian prayed she hadn't. Then again, praying for Diamond was too little, too late. Now all he could do was seek justice for her. And that's precisely what he planned to do, even if it meant arresting one of his own. He picked up the phone and dialed the personal cell phone number of Special Agent Xavier Santos-Markland.

Read on for an excerpt from
the next book by A.C. Arthur

PASSION'S PREY

Coming soon from St. Martin's Paperbacks

X had the perfect view.

T&A (tits and ass) were bountiful in Athena's, one of Washington, D.C.'s premiere adult nightclubs. When he'd walked in, the two bouncers standing on either side of the doorway looked him up and down. They'd even frisked him to make sure he wasn't carrying a weapon. Little did they know he didn't need one—*he* was a weapon. A hostess, which X thought was a nice touch to the establishment, walked him to his seat. Five feet, ten inches tall, tiny waist, thick thighs, rounded ass, and breasts that made his mouth water—just what the doctor ordered for his state of mind.

Which he'd rank close to being fucked completely up.

He'd consumed an entire bottle of Hennessey while sitting alone in his apartment. But because he was a Shadow Shifter, he wasn't falling-on-his-face drunk. Instead, he was mellow to the point of wanting to pull this physically perfect female onto his lap and give her every pent-up stroke his dick had stored for the last few months. He was in that place that he lingered in sometimes after the dream. The lonely dark space that threatened to suck him in if he didn't get a hold on something tangible, something that could handle all that was pent-up inside him.

X slid into the booth directly to the right side of the stage and watched as the hostess placed a slim drink list and a napkin in front of him, leaning forward so her ample breasts jiggled in his face.

She had a ready smile, thin lips, and eyes that looked like she was used to having sex—*normal* sex. That definitely was not what X had in mind. Not tonight.

No, after the day he'd had, he wanted—was at the point now where he desperately needed—something more.

So he ordered another Hennessey, straight, and sat back in the booth, waiting for the next act to hit the stage. He watched with one hand on his thigh, close to his semi-erect dick, all the T&A on display, because as far as appetizers went, Athena's was doing a pretty damn good job.

The lights dimmed, and members of the audience began cheering. The next act was about to begin. There was a flurry of lights dancing around the room in slow motion as the first notes of a sultry tune began to play. The spotlight stopped on the pole, shined to perfection. The crowd went wild, jumping up out of their seats already. X remained perfectly still.

He'd picked up a scent.

Her leg appeared first, wearing a strappy silver number with heels that looked too high to be legal. X's gaze followed her calves to her toned thighs as she'd kicked her leg out to line up with the pole. He shifted in his seat, adjusting his growing length.

The spotlight spread wider, the music's sexy slow rhythm pulsing throughout the room. Her thighs were killer, the plump globe of her ass only slightly covered in the silver sparkling boy shorts as she jumped onto the pole and did a twisting move that put her entire body upside down, her legs splitting in mid-air. The crowd roared, but X tuned out their sounds. Dollar bills were already flying through the air, but X didn't reach into his pocket to retrieve any of his own. Instead, his eyes stayed trained on the body. Her skin was a milky, heavily creamed coffee complexion, the hoop ring threading through her navel sparkling as if in response to the crowd. He had no idea what the material was that was able to hold her heavy breasts inside the bra that matched her shorts, but the plump mounds gyrated with her movement, giving everyone a view of what could possibly be her most prized possessions.

His breath froze, his gut clenching when his gaze fixed on her face. She'd just turned so that she was upright, long, ebony hair sliding down her back like a cloak. And even though her make-up was plentiful, making her look like an exotic temptation, there was no mistaking who she was.

Caprise.

His fists clenched on his thighs as his dick threatened to break free of the zipper that held it back. Questions filled his mind, but Caprise alone filled his sight. He couldn't look away, couldn't move to grab her ass off that stage, and couldn't open his mouth—now salivating with lust—to yell at her.

Once again she bounced on the pole, this time extending her legs forward, then opening them so her crotch was displayed. Lucky for the covering of the shorts, he thought with only minor relief. That was short-lived. In the next second she was off the pole, ripping the shorts from her ass to reveal a tiny string with more sparkles disappearing into the curvy cheeks of her ass.

A man tried to jump onto the stage, money in hand. His mouth was hanging open, eyes all but bulging out. X felt his cat roar and slapped a hand on the table in front of him. A bouncer grabbed the man by the collar and yanked

him back, dropping him into his seat. X let out a quick
sigh. When his gaze returned to the stage, her bra had
been removed to reveal pasties on her nipples, more sparkling, as if that were what he was supposed to look at.
She was basically naked, he thought, swallowing hard in
an effort to regain his senses. When her hands grabbed her
breasts and she leaned over, shaking them to the crowd,
X's sharp teeth pricked his lower lip. He wanted her. The
thought hit him like a punch to the gut. She licked her
finger, traced it along the small patch of material at her
juncture, and X had to drag a hand down his face.

The rest of the show was lost on him as he'd stood and
made his way to the side of the stage. There was a bouncer
there giving him the don't-even-try-it look. On impulse,
X flashed his FBI badge, and the bouncer, intelligent
character he was, took a step back. Vaguely he realized
her music had ended. He was more focused on the fact
that she was sashaying her naked ass off the stage. Because the bouncer had taken a hike, X was able to slip
through the STAFF ONLY door and was right there the moment Caprise stepped those sex-on-stilts shoes of hers on
the floor.

He grabbed her by the arm. "Don't say a word," he
warned when she looked up at him in surprise. "Not one
word!"